Praise for M

'Diving into this book is like di

in story form – I absolutely lov

Milly Johnson, *Sunday Times* bestselling author

'A sizzling seasonal read from the Queen of Hot Heroes!'

Heidi Swain, *Sunday Times* bestselling author

'Great characters and a sunny setting make this the perfect beach read'

Bella Osborne

'A lush summery read, guaranteed to satisfy all the sense. Her exquisite descriptions of food won't be the only thing you salivate over. Scrumptious sun-kissed romance at its best!'

Samantha Tonge

'Sizzling, summery and totally delightful, this book is everything a holiday read should be! Mandy Baggot effortlessly transported me to the clear blue skies, sparkling azure sea and the perfect beaches of Corfu. A gorgeous hug-of-a-book and the ultimate summer romance'

Zara Stoneley

'A perfect beach read, this one had me hooked. Mandy creates characters that are full of life and absolutely delightful. I thoroughly enjoyed this book!'

Jenny Hale

'It made me want to pack my flip-flops and head straight to Corfu – laugh-out-loud funny, full of heart and melting with h⋯⋯⋯⋯⋯⋯⋯⋯⋯⋯⋯⋯⋯⋯⋯⋯ is fun,

flirty ⋯⋯⋯⋯⋯⋯⋯⋯⋯⋯⋯⋯⋯⋯⋯⋯⋯⋯⋯⋯ Lyons

Mandy Baggot is an award-winning romance writer. She loves the Greek island of Corfu, white wine, country music and handbags. Also a singer, she has taken part in ITV1's *Who Dares Sings* and *The X Factor*.

Mandy is a member of the Romantic Novelists' Association and the Society of Authors and lives near Salisbury, Wiltshire, UK with her husband and two daughters.

Also by Mandy Baggot:

Single for the Summer
One Christmas Kiss in Notting Hill

Desperately Seeking Summer

Mandy Baggot

EBURY
PRESS

1 3 5 7 9 10 8 6 4 2

Ebury Press, an imprint of Ebury Publishing
20 Vauxhall Bridge Road,
London SW1V 2SA

Penguin
Random House
UK

Ebury Press is part of the Penguin Random House group of companies
whose addresses can be found at global.penguinrandomhouse.com

First published in the UK in 2018 by Ebury Press

www.penguin.co.uk

A CIP catalogue record for this book is available
from the British Library

ISBN 9781785039249

Typeset in 10/13.75 pt Adobe Caslon Pro
by Integra Software Services Pvt. Ltd, Pondicherry

Printed and bound in Great Britain by Clays Ltd, St Ives PLC

MIX
Paper from
responsible sources
FSC
www.fsc.org   FSC® C018179

Penguin Random House is committed to a
sustainable future for our business, our readers
and our planet. This book is made from Forest
Stewardship Council® certified paper.

To Mr Megalos, you are my rock, my soul–mate,
my everything …

One

The Travellers' Rest, Romsey, Hampshire, England

8 June

To-Do List

- Re-jig Ladies Who Lunch meeting.
- Speak to Stanley about the smell in Room 26 … *and* his own individual fragrance.
- ~~Email Mr Kimber about the iPhone charger left in Room 10~~ DONE!!!
- More flowers in the lobby? Summer scents. Not too expensive.
- Book tickets to the new play coming to the Orb. Maybe Bistro Côte before?
- Buy some luxury cat food to stop Poldark straying to Mr Clements' house. Is Sheba still the best?
- Remind Darrell it's Amber's birthday next week. Suggest the new Beyoncé perfume … or the latest weepy book about a dog who must fend for itself … or maybe an Oxfam goat gift.

Abby Dolan sipped her frothy coffee. Cold again. Still, cold meant she had been totally focused on setting up her day with lists. Shaking back her long, brunette hair, she took comfort in the blissful contentment of having scheduled her day. She had focus. She had order. And her superb organisational skill-set was exactly why she had been successfully managing The Travellers' Rest, Romsey for the past eighteen months. Well, she wasn't *officially* the *actual* manager, that was Kathy. But Kathy was more an *overseer* rather than a *do-er*. And Abby was pretty sure Kathy had her sights set on the Birmingham Maypole branch. It was just a matter of time until Abby got promoted. And along with the new job title would come a bigger salary, perhaps even enough for her and Darrell to finally move out of the compact flat above M&Co. Maybe even into a house with a garden. Nothing worthy of needing help from Monty Don, but just big enough for some planters – lavender, jasmine, perhaps some herbs. She'd been secretly dying to try and infuse a little spice into Darrell's eating repertoire for a while now. There were only so many Mug Shots you could eat in a week.

Her eyes went back to her list. If she tackled Stanley – not literally, that would be too close for comfort while he was eau-de-sewer – perhaps she could reward herself with calling the Orb. The rumour was Benedict Cumberbatch was going to play the lead in this six-week run. Who didn't love a bit of the Cumberbatch?

'Abby.'

Kathy's voice at close quarters had Abby dropping her pen to the counter-top. She spun around, a smile on her lips and a mind like Facebook analytics good to go.

'Morning, Kathy,' Abby began. 'Now I know you said we had to rein things in a little, but I was thinking, how about some lavender on a plinth, next to the leaflets about Stonehenge and Avebury?'

'Lavender,' Kathy breathed out.

Was it Abby's imagination or did her manager look a little out of sorts? Those were very tired, stressed eyes staring back at her. Perhaps Birmingham Maypole had spurned her professional advances already ...

'Yes,' Abby continued. 'They're cheap to buy, with a lovely colour and a sweet, clean fragrance. They also need hardly any water – you know how forgetful Stanley can be sometimes ...' she forged on. 'Not that I'm having a dig at Stanley or anything ...' She pushed her to-do list under the morning's newspaper. The raising-the-body-odour issue was her pet project.

'Shall we go into my office?' Kathy said.

Abby swallowed. Her boss's tone was straight-to-the-point and, frankly, a little brusque. Brusque was usually reserved for the salesmen who always insisted they could save them a fortune on Post-it notes. Everyone knew that cheap Post-it notes were a false economy. A few pence saved could be the difference between actually sticking or falling into the gourmet cannon of lamb you had placed on the reception desk for *one second* while you multi-tasked.

'Shall I get us some of Chef's limeade?' Abby suggested. 'It's going down so well now the weather's turned more South of France than South Shields.'

'No,' Kathy replied. 'Thank you.' She paused. 'This won't take long and ... well, let's just ... have a chat, shall we?'

Seven minutes. That's what her eighteen months at The Travellers' Rest had boiled down to: *seven* minutes. Tears were falling from Abby's eyes as she staggered down the high street, not knowing where she was going or what she was doing. How could you possibly know what to do when you had just been told you no longer had a job! Just thinking the words made a little bile lurch into her mouth. Pretty Romsey with its cobbled market square, its shoppers' arms laden with produce under multi-coloured summer bunting, budding hanging baskets swaying from pale-painted buildings and iron lamp-posts; the gorgeous scenery barely registered with Abby as she half walked, half stumbled towards her flat. It couldn't be real. It had to be a mistake. That was what she had first uttered to Kathy when Kathy had said head office had 'forced her hand'. Her boss had said that no one had worked harder for the company than Abby, but times were tight and they no longer had the budget for an assistant manager. Even now, when it shouldn't matter to her anymore, Abby began to wonder who exactly would ever get up the nerve to tackle Stanley about his body odour issues. Not Kathy. Kathy had been side-stepping it for months. Perhaps Abby had jinxed her own luck by putting it on today's to-do list! How could this be happening?! Who was going to make sure Mrs Gerald had her favourite table in the restaurant on Wednesdays? Who would coach the boy from the bakery in all things *Home and Away*, so he could woo the Australian girl at college? Who would remember to pay the window cleaner? She had never been reimbursed from the last time. She sniffed hard. She was not going to go back for the sake of twenty pounds. *And* head office didn't want notice worked. They were going to pay her an extra month straight into her bank account because they wanted her gone. Now. Well, gone she would be. A little sob escaped as she thought about never standing behind the reception desk again. Never again would she be looking at the Constable painting of Salisbury Cathedral, or running a duster over the bust of Sir Terry Pratchett ... and now her dreams of a house with a garden were dead in the water too. Her job! Her lovely, lovely job was gone! She needed a hug. She needed Darrell.

Two

The Oven Door, Romsey

Abby guessed she had to look at it as an opportunity. She hadn't *really* been happy, had she? Except she had. Predominately. Apart from the fact that a pay rise wouldn't have gone amiss if her dreams of whole-house ownership were to be realised. *Pastry*. She needed pastry. Gazing into the bakery window her eyes fell on the extra-large flaky delights of the world famous in Romsey sausage roll. She loved everything about sausage rolls. From the slightly salty, hot seasoned pork in its centre, to the glistening, warm, melt-in-your-mouth outside … Darrell loved them too and despite trying to get him to be more fava beans than Heinz beans lately, treats were allowed. And God, did she need a treat right now.

Ping! A text message! Yes! This was going to be from Kathy. This was going to be the I've-made-an-awful-mistake-I-should-have-fired-useless-receptionist-Miranda-who-doesn't-know-the-difference-between-a-paper-clip-and-a-staple-instead text. Eagerly unzipping the front pocket of her bag, Abby pulled out her phone. She looked at the screen. It wasn't Kathy. It was Melody. Her slightly younger, bouncier, blonder sister.

There was no message, just a photograph. A perfectly calm, azure sea, a picture-postcard blue sky and … what was that? Abby had to squint at the screen to ascertain which male anatomy part was set just to the right of frame. Knowing her sister like she did, it could literally be anything. Bicep ... she was going for bicep.

And then another message arrived.

Whoops! Soz! Sent pic too soon. Out on a boat today with Igor #GreekLife

Igor? That wasn't a Greek name. Abby sighed. What did that matter? All that mattered was she had lost her precious job, the career independence she had wanted so much, and her sister was flaunting a sea scene that *she* had turned down eighteen months ago. Turned down for The Travellers' Rest and Darrell. At least she still had Darrell ... and fluffy, slightly flea-ridden Poldark, her cat ... and a proper English sausage roll coming her way ... She pushed open the bakery door.

That delicious waft of warming bread, grain and a sweet undertone of icing-topped buns hit Abby's senses and suddenly she was plunged back to being eight years old, holding her mum's hand tight, she and Melody being allowed to choose a sticky treat. Was it really a sausage roll she craved right now or something sweeter?

Before her eyes could meet the glass-fronted counter, a laugh permeated the bakery air. A laugh she recognised. Darrell's secretary, Amber. Model-thin, glossy red-haired Amber surely wouldn't hang out at a bakery? She was all David Lloyd Clubs and saving the snow leopards. Abby turned her head towards the section of chairs and tables where customers could sit down for a quick bite ... and there Amber was ... with Darrell.

In a microsecond, the time it took for Abby's brain to engage, the scene went from perfectly-innocent-boss-having-lunch-with-his-assistant to why-was-Darrell-holding-Amber's-hand, then quickly why-was-Darrell-brushing-a-crumb-from-Amber's-mouth-with-his-little-finger, to finally why-was-Darrell-edging-forward-in-his-seat-over-a-plate-of-macaroons ...

Abby wanted the world to stop. Just cease. Just long enough for her to walk over to the table, move the macaroons, move Darrell and deposit him down a wormhole, back to a time when Amber wasn't his secretary, when his secretary was church-organ-playing, Mavis. Mavis may have fed him home-made scones which hadn't helped his waistline, but she would never have allowed the corner of her mouth to be wiped with a pinkie ...

Eyes brimming with tears for the second time that day, Abby watched as the inevitable happened right in front of her. Darrell and Amber, lips meeting, hands clasped together like they wanted to be entwined forever, a kiss that said this literal tête-à-tête was not *just* business.

Ping ping!

Abby was brought to by her phone again and the noise rose above the gentle hum of the coffee machines and slushy maker. Enough to make Darrell draw his eyes away from his date to her.

Through her tear-glazed vision she saw him mouth the word 'shit' and then immediately get to his feet. And that action, happening ultra-fast, her world spinning like the National Lottery big money balls, made Abby react. She didn't want to hear a word that would spill from his mouth. Flashbacks of snippets of conversation fell like summer blossom through her mind. *I've got to work late tonight on the Crosby account. It's the bowling work event, no partners and ... you're not keen on the shoes anyway, are you?*

Just how long had this been going on? Just how long had she been played for a fool?

'Abby,' Darrell called.

Well, no more. Not even for a second. With the once welcoming hug of a smell from the Eccles cakes now making her feel queasy, Abby about-faced, head high, blurry eyes focused on her escape route. A few hurried, desperate steps and she was out of there.

Three

Abby Dolan's flat, Romsey

The text that had landed in the bakery some three hours and forty-eight minutes ago had been another one from Melody. This time a selfie, presumably with the owner of the bicep, Igor. There was her sister, long, tightly curled blonde hair mostly wrapped in a Greek blue-and-white headscarf, her deep-brown tanned body taut and slender, pearly white smile spelling out joy, perfect contentment, utter bliss ...

Abby took a hefty swig of the copper-coloured liquid in the glass she was holding and gathered her knees up into her chest as she sunk into the sofa she and Darrell had chosen just a few months ago. They hadn't been able to decide between upholstery or leather so had plumped for a mix of the two. It seemed a ridiculous dilemma now. Swallowing back the Greek Metaxa brandy, Abby looked back to her phone and the text accompanying Melody's last message.

Not my Mr Right but my Mr Right Now. Rich, sexy and ... did I mention rich? He has a brother ...

There were emojis of a flamenco dancer, the Greek flag, two beers, a martini and a bottle of champagne. Abby's thumb sat poised above the keypad. She hadn't replied to Melody's texts earlier in the week either. Those times it had been photos of their mum trying to do a bottle flip with a Bikos – the Greek equivalent of Buxton. But what to say? Not the truth, obviously. How could she possibly tell her sister she was sat drinking brandy on a Wednesday afternoon having lost her job and her boyfriend?

Her phone vibrated in her hand. She had switched it to silent as soon as she had got back to the flat. It had pinged and beeped and rang all the way down the high street and she hadn't needed to look to know all the contact had come from Darrell. Her heart in her throat, beating like a frightened deer and an angry cat at the same time, she had rushed along, blinded to anything but her own grief. Only when she was inside her apartment, greeted by the calming sand-coloured walls and palm tree feature paper of the open-plan lounge-diner, did she take a breath, and then, finally, sob.

Abby it's not what you think. Please call me. D x

God! Did he really think she was stupid? What excuse was he going to give for suckering up to Amber? Perhaps they had both joined the local amateur dramatic society and were rehearsing, or perhaps it was National Snog Your Secretary Day – in 2018 there did seem to be a national day for everything.

No, she was not going to reply. He didn't deserve her attention. He hadn't been there for her when she needed him, she had lost her job and he was lunching with Little Miss Just Giving. Perhaps that was her attraction. Abby had always been taught that charity began at home. She never really had the financial stability to set up direct debits for worthy causes. But could it really be a reason Darrell decided to opt for Amber? Was it not more likely his head had been turned by her gym-bunny body and tinkling laugh?

Come out here! You must be due a holiday! Mum would love to see you. I would love to see you! Pretty sure Igor's brother would love to see you too …

Melody again. And her words hit hard. Corfu, Greece, visiting her sister and her mum or staying here, lonely, contemplating where she went wrong on the hotel ladder and with the man she'd seen a future with. They may not have discussed marriage, but they had rented the flat, bought the sofa and had planned on checking out the Sky Q options if she got her pay rise. Abby took another sip of the brandy then put the glass on the coffee table, sniffing sorrow and regret right up her Eustachian tubes. Thumb working over the icons she made her reply.

Won't you be busy with the estate agency? I don't want to be in the way.

It was a hesitant response. A test of the water. From the fortnightly or so phone calls with her mum, their business, Desperately Seeking, was full-on. There were always gorgeous bougainvillea-clad villas being described on their website, ruins in idyllic rural locations, compact beachfront apartments … and it was a whole world away to Abby. To her, when the move was suggested, heading to Greece had felt a spontaneous step too far.

Cum on Abs I'm never 2 busy 4 u. Cum out. It will b so much fun!!!!!!!

Melody had resorted to numbers where letters should be. That usually meant she was busy or drunk. Neither thought appealed. And it was crazy to even consider packing a bag and heading off to the airport, wasn't it?

And then a shadow cast itself across her back window, momentarily blocking the shaft of sunlight that had been flooding the space. Abby blinked, narrowing her eyes against it. Getting up, she crept across the room, careful not to make a sound. What she saw behind the glass brought another lump to her throat. Behind the net, slowly tip-toeing across the window ledge like he was on a high-wire, was Poldark, tail up in the air, posture set to swagger. And, as the cat reached the next sill along, Abby saw a gnarled hand appear, beckoning with fingers full of corned beef. Mr Clements was just about to complete the triple whammy. No job. No boyfriend. And now, no cat. There was only one thing left to do …

Four

Villa Pappas, San Stefanos, Corfu, Greece

Three weeks later ...

To Theo, it felt like his skull had been cracked open and someone other than a neurosurgeon was having a go at operating on his brain ... with a screwdriver. Were his eyes even capable of opening? And, if his eyes were truly closed right now, why was it so light in the bedroom? He opened and closed his mouth. Arid like the sand on the nearby beach. His black shoulder-length hair was all over his face and he was hot. What had happened to the air-conditioning?

Then, all of a sudden, he was choking. A sweet yet completely nauseating scent was growing thicker and fuller with every inhalation. He coughed and the screwdriver in his head stabbed harder.

'Good,' said a female voice. 'You are still alive.'

There was a woman in his bedroom. Another one. And she sounded older. Just what had Leon got him drinking last night after the multitude of beers? His senses became more aware. He couldn't feel the bed sheet. *He was naked*. He reached out a hand, but nothing seemed willing to move too rapidly.

'You will get up now. Half the day is gone already,' the woman continued.

Then the room got lighter still, and Theo's sticky eyes began to ease themselves apart. The voice echoing around the bedroom sounded familiar. Had he revisited the first one-night stand of this break already? He knew the village was small but there should be enough holidaymakers to avoid making a repeat so soon. Maybe Leon needed to be a better wingman.

'Theo!' the voice barked. 'I said it is the middle of the day!'

Now the tone had kicked up a notch he knew exactly who was in his bedroom and she was not a conquest from the night before. It was his aunt, Spyridoula. His nakedness needed immediate attention no matter how much his head hurt. Snapping his eyes open, retinas pierced by the blinding sun flooding through the bi-fold doors, he grabbed at the white sheet, dragging it up his body.

'Spyri,' he greeted, lips barely able to form the words, eyes back to squinting.

'Ah!' she exclaimed. 'Not only does he live, but it appears his mental faculties are still in working order!'

Theo laid his temple against the headboard of the bed as his aunt's figure span around his vision. This wasn't good. He cleared his throat and attempted to look compos mentis. 'Where is Leon?'

'Working,' Spyridoula snapped. 'You remember? That thing most people do between the hours of eight until eight on this island.'

It didn't matter what he said. He was not going to win this conversation when he was hungover, utterly vulnerable and without excuses. Had Leon let his aunt into the villa as well as got him blind drunk last night? He was going to kill him when he came back.

'Up!' Spyridoula ordered. She stalked towards the bed, high heels clacking on the marble floor, bracelets and necklaces of all colours and materials jingling together in a cacophony of noise that sounded like someone running a fork up and down glass. Theo clung onto the bed sheet as his aunt's face came into focus. Long dark hair twisted up into a chignon, dark eyes outlined with thick kohl and vibrant red lipstick on her mouth. He had forgotten how formidable his aunt was and, he guessed, she was no doubt unimpressed he had been in San Stefanos for three nights now and not been to visit her.

'Up!' Spyridoula repeated. This time her hands grabbed for the sheet.

'Please!' he exclaimed, gripping tighter to the fabric like it was a tug of war. 'I am wearing nothing.'

'And I have seen it all before,' she replied. 'Do you want me to list the times?'

He really didn't and went to open his mouth to protest until—

'The very day you were born. It was legs first and more screaming than your mother … then there was the pool incident when you were three. You said the bathing suit was too restrictive. Next was when you were sixteen and the older boys stole your clothes for a joke—'

'All right!' Theo interrupted. 'You have made your point. I am moving.' Wrapping the sheet tightly around his body he eased himself off the bed a lot more quickly than was probably safe in his condition.

'Good!' Spyridoula clapped her hands together.

He didn't feel well. He was doing his very best to stand still without swaying.

'You will shower.' Spyridoula threw two items she had plucked from somewhere onto the bed. 'Then you will put on these clothes.'

Theo looked at them. It seemed to be a polo shirt and trousers.

'I have clothes here,' Theo stated. 'I did bring some luggage.'

Spyridoula sniffed. '*This* is your uniform.'

Uniform? What did that mean? A shiver ran over him.

'Your father called me last night.'

Immediately his hackles were up. He knew coming here was never going to be a permanent solution, but he thought he might just be able to buy himself some time. More than three nights before confrontation perhaps? It seemed not.

'He is worried about you,' Spyridoula continued when Theo failed to answer.

Already Theo was shaking his head. It was his natural reaction to most things these days ... except alcohol. Alcohol he seemed only capable of nodding at.

'He has asked me to keep an eye on you.'

Theo exhaled loudly, all his feelings expelling into the humid air. Why *was* the air humid? Perhaps his aunt had switched off the air-conditioning in a bid to use heat as a form of interrogation torture. That was exactly the sort of thing she would do.

'I am surprised he cares,' he answered. 'And I do not need an eye kept on me.'

'No?' Her eyes went from his bare feet on the tiled floor and slowly upwards seeming to linger on every sheet-covered inch of him. He held onto the material and tried to match her gaze. It was difficult, his aunt had eyes like the hypnotising Kaa from *The Jungle Book*.

'No,' he replied.

'Humph. That is not what your father thinks ... and it is also not what Hera at The Blue Vine thinks either.' Spyridoula sucked in a breath, the buttons of her pink silk blouse tightening over her bosom. 'Ten bottles, Theo! Ten bottles of Mythos, then shots!'

Her voice had risen in volume and each one of those bottles of beer began to dance, Zorba the Greek-like, across his cerebellum. He shifted his neck in an attempt to ease the tension.

'Right! Outside!' Spyridoula gathered up the items of clothing on the bed.

'What?' he exclaimed.

'Out onto the veranda! Right now! Come!' She clapped her hands loudly and made steps toward him. He wasn't having her stripping him bare, so he hurried toward the bi-fold doors. Folding them apart quickly, he stepped out onto the wide balcony, the heat from the sun more intense than any warmth inside the villa. It licked his exposed skin and he automatically closed his eyes, letting the light feeling seep into him.

'What are you doing?' Spyridoula's presence at his shoulder, bracelets clinking, made his head hurt.

'Nothing,' he replied, eyelids gradually lifting up.

'Exactly!' she snapped. 'And that is what your father thinks too.'

How was it he couldn't manage to say anything without it containing a double meaning? He really needed to remember his auntie was just as cunning as his father, if slightly more well meaning.

'I mean what is going on, Theo?'

He moved up to the brick façade, white marble pillars creating the boundary between air and ground. And there was San Stefanos in all its glory, laid out before him. The horseshoe-shaped bay of glistening blue water shimmered and sparkled like it always had, set in the midst of green hills. There were thickets of lush emerald-coloured bush, barer patches of dusty land leading down to waving eucalyptus trees. A small array of shops, tavernas and businesses sat at the sand-and-shingle waterfront where boats were tethered to various pontoons. Still, here it was all about the water.

'Nothing,' he answered softly.

'You have spent the past few months roaming,' Spyridoula stated.

He wasn't sure what he was supposed to say. It was true. Since leaving the mainland, his father, the business, he had been drifting and finding that, for the time being, drifting was suiting him just fine. When you drifted no one asked too much of you and he liked that 'here today, maybe gone tomorrow' vibe. It avoided him having to think too much. And drinking too much seemed to stop the nightmares invading his sleep …

'You need a focus.' His aunt pushed the clothes towards him. 'Here!'

He took the items, being careful not to drop his hold on the sheet. What were these? He turned them over in his hand, hoping to come to some sort of realisation.

'You start work tonight at The Blue Vine.'

'What?!' he exclaimed. 'No.'

'You say no to me?' Spyridoula narrowed her eyes, looking more foreboding than ever. 'After your display last night with the Mythos and the blazing sambucas or whatever it is you drink? You are lucky Hera even agreed to let you into the building again, let alone to give you a job.'

'I do not need a job, Spyri.'

'Humph! So, what do you plan to do? Because your father says you cannot stay here for free.' She held out her hand as if displaying the merits of the Corfiot resort in front of them. 'Do you know how much rent your father could get from this place for the summer?'

'He never rents out the family villa,' Theo pointed out. That was one of the reasons why he knew he could come here. He had a key and it had always been for the family to come whenever they needed to get away. Knowing his brother and sister were at home had sealed the deal. It had been time to move on from Lefkada anyway.

'Your father is a businessman,' Spyridoula reminded him. 'For a long time, this property sits with no one in it. If you will not pay the rent he could get this summer, then he is thinking of selling it.'

His heart actually lurched. Whether it was fear at having to move on again when he had hoped he was set for a summer in Corfu or whether it was a lance into the memories of his childhood holidays here he wasn't quite sure. All he knew was he didn't want that to happen. But he also didn't want to work. He was having time off. Working required thought and consideration and involving himself with people. He wasn't ready to involve himself with people. Only those looking for a good time and not asking questions.

'There is no choice, Theo,' Spyridoula urged. 'Be clear on that. No job, no staying at the villa.'

He didn't know what to say. What could he say? He was backed into a corner.

'Good,' Spyridoula said, taking his silence as agreement. 'Get showered, get dressed. There is bread and home-made tapenade in the fridge.' She clip-clopped towards the door of the bedroom.

'You made tapenade?' he queried, still holding the uniform.

She turned back to face him then. 'I said it was home-made. I did not say it was made in *my* home.' She smiled then. 'Your shift starts at six.'

Five

San Stefanos Bay, Corfu

'Here we are! San Stefanos! The most beautiful place on the entire island of Corfu!'

Abby looked out of the taxi window towards the cerulean water and something stirred inside her. It was still just like it had been all those years ago when she had first visited. She had been twelve and it had been a holiday booked for their dad to recover from a heart operation. A whole long summer in the Corfu sunshine doing nothing more than swimming in the turquoise water, dipping nets to catch fish, eating hunks of fresh bread dipped in *tirokafteri* and licking ice creams of all different flavours. Their dad had recovered, but only for a while, just two years later he'd passed. Abby hadn't thought about Corfu again until her mum's announcement at that fateful Jamie At Home party. *I'm moving to Corfu. I've bought an estate agency.*

And now she was here again. The rent on the flat was paid up for the month, she'd felt the need to tell Mr Clements she was heading to Greece – Poldark was tush-licking on his sofa seemingly oblivious to it not being his actual home – and she hadn't felt the need to tell Darrell anything. If he wanted his stuff he would have to ask for it. As it had been three weeks since the bakery break-up and she had ignored the first week of 'wanting to talk' texts, she could only assume he had bought a new razor and toothbrush and was leaving the white goods for her.

'You would like me to drive you around the village? Show you all the best places?'

The taxi driver snapped her out of her reverie and she plucked her purse from her carry-on bag, taking out some euros. They had agreed a price at the airport. It was the new her. Determined not to be taken advantage of by anyone. Not men. Not hotel managers who really didn't know how to manage …

'No,' Abby answered, sitting forward a little and passing over the cash. 'I've actually been here before. Several times, actually.'

'You have?' the taxi driver inquired, turning a little in his seat and seeming to pay proper attention.

She nodded, passing over the money. He was in his twenties with dark hair spiked into a rather regimented position that didn't look like it would move at all, even if a category 4 storm rolled into the bay. 'It's been a year or so.'

'Oh, well, everything has changed,' the driver told her. 'There is a Nandos just around the corner and a roundabout at Avlaki.'

Just as the confusion and horror about both of those things near this sleepy resort took hold in Abby's psyche, the driver let out a high-pitched squeal of a laugh.

'I jest! I jest!'

Abby swallowed and wondered who had taught him the word 'jest'. 'Thank you for bringing me here.'

'Wait,' the taxi driver said, unfastening his seatbelt. 'I will get your luggage.'

Abby opened the door before he could get out and do it for her. Who needed a man faking it at being someone you could count on? Newly purchased gladiator sandals touching the rough concrete she breathed in the wave of heat that greeted her, together with all those delicious summer scents she still recalled – clematis, a gentle brine coupled with sand and fresh coffee. Her eyes went from the gorgeous hoop of shimmering bay to an old stone building with a rather modern sign in Greek blue declaring The Blue Vine. She didn't remember that bar from her last visit. There had been a more traditional-looking taverna with white tablecloths embroidered with Kalamata olives.

She continued to look along the row of properties. There was the small supermarket, set a little way back, two trees part-covering the exterior, budding white blooms and a well-clipped hedge either side of a paved ramp leading up to the entrance. But it was the property a little further along that took her breath away. It was the ugliest thing she had ever seen. Two large neon pink parasols were shading rattan tables and chairs and, flashing above the bright fuchsia-painted doorway, was a sign that would have looked more at home in Las Vegas. *Desperately Seeking* … Since when had her mother's estate agency been pinker than the pinkest flamingo?

'You have sunglasses?' the taxi driver asked as he put Abby's case down next to her.

'Sorry?'

'The colour of that shop! It is so bright, no?'

'Yes,' Abby answered. 'Yes, it really is.'

'I do not think it will stay this way for long,' the driver continued.

'No?' Abby queried, looking at him.

He made a sucking noise through his teeth and shook his head. 'The elders in the village do not like it at all.'

Great! Her mother was upsetting the locals. There had been a distinct lack of information about that in Melody's texts.

'Where do you stay?' the driver asked her.

'Oh,' Abby began. 'It's not too far to walk from here, thank you.' She was not about to divulge her location to the first man she had spoken to on the island. She was a no-go zone and ready to windpipe-chop anyone who meant her a disservice, thanks to a recap on self-defence at Romsey Sports Centre.

The driver stuck out his hand. 'My name is Leon. If you need a taxi or to hire a bicycle or a moped or a quad bike, my family run Revolution.' He pointed. 'It is just behind, around one hundred metres.'

Abby took his hand and gave it a professional shake. 'I'm Abby.'

'It is nice to meet you.'

'Well, thank you again,' Abby said. '*Efxharisto*.'

'*Parakalo*.'

As she watched Leon get back into his rather seen-better-days SEAT Ibiza, Abby felt her phone rumble in her bag. She took a deep breath. She knew it could only be one of two people. She was hopefully just about to see one and the other she had no further interest in.

Six

Desperately Seeking, San Stefanos

The pink only got more vibrant the closer Abby got to the building. Comparing the colour to that of a particularly garish flamingo had been spot on as there were two of the plastic birds stuck in blossoming pots of bougainvillea outside the entrance. The gorgeous buds didn't need any synthetic enhancements. What was her mother thinking? And why wasn't Melody being the voice of reason about the look of the business? If there was one thing Melody excelled at it was appearance.

Abby stopped just outside, finally able to see past the salmon glow to the property listings in both the front windows. All those laminates were topped with a pink header too. It stood out, but not necessarily in a good way, and it was also distracting. Still, it must be working. She guessed that pink paraphernalia didn't come cheap.

As she stepped up to the windows and paid closer attention to a two-bedroomed townhouse in Corfu Town she heard her mother's voice coming from inside.

'Well, I would have to agree to disagree. It does have a sea view … no, Mrs Morris, I don't believe you have to stand on one leg in the kitchen cranking your neck a hundred and eighty degrees to see it because I visited that property personally and … yes, it does have a garden, it has a *lovely* garden … well, I'm sorry if you personally consider it no bigger than an

A4 envelope with inadequate provision for a donkey but the measurements are all accurate I can assure you ... yes, believe me, Mrs Morris, there is no one more aware that you have been on our books for some considerable time ... no, Mrs Morris, of course I wasn't being rude, your custom is highly regarded of course ... yes, I do realise Aleko at Ionian Dreams is offering a free spa day when you sign up with him, you're only the third person to mention that to me today ... no, of course you're not boring me, Mrs Morris ...'

Abby couldn't bear to hear any more. Pulling her wheelie case hard she stepped on to the thankfully cream tiles of Desperately Seeking and saw her mother for the first time in twelve months.

Jackie let out a loud gasp somewhere in the middle between shocked and excited. 'Oh! Oh, Mrs Morris, I am going to have to love you and leave you. I will email you later this afternoon with something else I am certain you are going to adore.'

Abby smiled as her mum put down the phone and leapt to her feet, bustling around the desk in a frantic bid to get to her. She swallowed back emotion. Her mum's usual dyed-black bob was speckled with grey at the roots and she had put on quite a bit of weight. She was wearing a shapeless ethnic-printed kaftan – pyramids and gazelle heads – and was without her trademark high-heels. She also had on large dark-rimmed glasses she hadn't ever needed before. Worn bright green Havaianas hugged her feet, her toenails unpainted.

'Don't look at me!' Jackie ordered straightaway as she hurried to the entrance. 'But let me look at you! Look at you!' She reached Abby and caught her up in a tight embrace. 'You look lovely, Abby. So lovely.'

Lovely had always been one of her mum's favourite words. She would be very surprised if it wasn't in all the descriptions of properties on Desperately Seeking's books. It was a piece of welcome familiarity and Abby had to do her best not to let emotion flood all her senses. This was a break. A holiday. Nothing more. She was holding everything together and her mum didn't need to know the ins and outs. But she knew she really didn't look lovely. Because there was only so much magic the No. 7 counter could work when you were the owner of a broken heart.

'What time did you get in? I thought you were going to phone me when you arrived?' Jackie asked, stepping back but holding onto Abby's arms like she might disappear. 'How was the flight? Did they run out of focaccia? They always run out of focaccia … and chicken Caesar come to that. Or did you have a two-for-one wine? I do think—'

'Mum, slow down.' She shook her head but smiled at the same time. 'I thought one of the attractions of Greece was the easy pace of life.'

Jackie quietened down as if absorbing Abby's comment. And then she nodded, uncertainly at first, but then with slightly more conviction. 'Yes. Yes, it is. It's all lovely here. You'll see. Shall I put the kettle on? Or do you fancy an ouzo?'

Abby instinctively checked her watch. What was she doing? She was on holiday. She could have ouzo no matter what the time. Although she hadn't had a cup of tea since Gatwick …

'Or frappé,' Jackie continued, moving back towards her paper-littered desk. 'Yes, we'll have frappés at Damianos. It will be nice. They'll give us crisps and you can feed the fish like you did when you were little.'

Her mum's enthusiasm was evident, and Abby didn't have the heart to admit she had been up since the very early hours and was tired. She smiled. 'Frappé sounds good.'

*

Jackie let out a long, loaded sigh of deep contentment and Abby relaxed into the cream-cushioned chairs set around tables at the water's edge. Her legs and half of her body were in sunlight that was warming her every inch, the rest was in cooling shade. Here, looking out over the floating speedboats to people splashing about in the water, then beyond to the open sea where larger vessels were anchored, Abby was getting all the feels of her last holiday in San Stefanos.

'We had Bruce Willis here last week,' Jackie announced, sucking at her frappé. 'And Jude Law actually ate next door, in Galini. Melody got a photo. She'll probably show you later.'

Abby sat forward, reaching for her glass of mocha-coloured liquid frothing with cream. 'She's sent me three pictures of someone called Igor.'

'Ah!' Jackie said. 'He's lovely.'

'Is he?' Abby asked. 'Because I'm sure you said that about Panos and Ricardo and … what was the other one called? The one with the beard jewellery?'

Jackie almost spat. 'Oh, Zeke. He definitely *wasn't* lovely. Although I do now know several different ways to cook mung beans. Not that we're overrun with mung beans on Corfu, not that I've started cooking, but …'

'Tell me about Igor,' Abby urged. 'I want to know that Melody isn't going to fall hard for someone unsuitable and get hurt.' There was no way she was going to let what had happened to her happen to her sister. Despite Melody's happy-go-lucky-the-Kardashians-are-my-role-models exterior, Abby knew there was a fragile heart beneath. And, for the time she was in Greece, she was going to keep an eye on her younger sister. And her mum. And she was going to casually stalk The Travellers' Rest Facebook page. It was a heartbreak to-do list to keep her mind off Darrell and Amber, who she was not going to stalk at all.

'He's Russian. The son of a property developer. And the gold bracelet he wears on his arm is heavier than any of my handbags. You can remember how heavy my handbags can be, can't you?'

Abby shivered. She had wanted to know a little of his personality not whether he could rival Bill Gates in wealth. 'Mum ...'

'His father, Valentin, is dripping with it ... gold, that is, not handbags. Melody's been trying to get me a date so I can get him interested in my high-end places but ...' Jackie sniffed. 'He seems more interested in *Diana*.'

The name Diana had been uttered like a jalapeño had just burnt her mum's tongue. It wasn't a name that was familiar from their phone conversations.

'You're looking to date?' Abby inquired.

'Well, I ... maybe ... I mean, I have been ... a little bit, I suppose.' Jackie sucked at her frappé.

'Oh,' Abby replied. Her mum hadn't said she'd started dating. Not that she shouldn't. It was just, after so many years of being widowed, Abby had drawn the conclusion that Jackie was happy being single. 'You didn't say anything.'

'I told you I went to the sardine festival in Benitses last year,' Jackie answered. 'Well, I went there with Derek.'

Last year! She had kept this dating lark quiet for almost a year! 'Who's Derek?'

'He was quite lovely but he had a bunion. Meant he couldn't walk too far and you've seen the hills around here, even I struggle.'

'I'm guessing he wasn't Russian,' Abby commented.

'No, he was from Grimsby. Like that Kevin from *Strictly*. Couldn't dance, though, not even a very tame *sirtaki* with one of the dancers calling out the moves.' She pulled in a breath, gaze going out to the ocean. 'That was probably down to the bunion too, or the gout ... he did like a brandy.'

Abby swallowed. There hadn't been any of her brandy left when she'd departed the flat. Despite being on holiday, she didn't want to start falling into a I've-been-dumped-I'm-going-to-drink-myself-into-a-tearful-coma-every-night position. She was strong, and her new mindfulness app was keeping her on an even keel.

'Then there was Robert,' Jackie continued her. 'He was fun while he was here and we keep in touch on email.' She sighed. 'But he had a lot of hats.'

'You have a lot of shoes,' Abby reminded her. She couldn't see how having a hat collection was a heinous crime. It wasn't exactly up there with a collection of severed heads ... although if you had that many hats ... Abby shook her head. 'But, if this ... Igor's dad ... if he isn't that interested then—'

'He might be,' Jackie said. 'If *Diana* wasn't sticking her collagen in the way every five minutes.'

'Who *is* this Diana?' Abby inquired.

Jackie gasped. 'Don't let her hear you say that!'

'What? Is she famous or something?' She was now racking her brain to think of every celebrity Diana she knew that wasn't sadly deceased. She was struggling.

'She's a novelist,' Jackie whispered. 'Writes sweeping romances about billionaires.' She sniffed. 'Valentin is just research to her.'

'And why is it you don't like her?' Abby inquired. Her mum did have a habit of being a little judgemental. 'Because she's had enhancements?'

'Ssh!' Jackie hissed, looking over both her shoulders in turn like she was a turncoat on the run from the Mob. 'I don't *know* she's had enhancements, but Melody said if it wasn't Botox keeping her worry lines non-existent she'd eat an octopus.'

Octopus. The memory of that delicious texture embellished with just a little salt, pepper and a squeeze of fresh lemon licked across Abby's mind. Her sister, on the other hand, wasn't a lover of seafood. All this Greek fresh-off-the-boat sea fare was definitely wasted on Melody.

Jackie continued. 'She runs the English part of the village.'

'What?' Abby exclaimed. 'The English part? Since when has there been an English part?'

'They like their home comforts – English tea bags and sausages. And the latest thing is Avon products. Diana found a girl from Sidari who does it.'

Abby's brain was officially hurting now, and as she sucked at her frappé she really wished it was a cocktail. It seemed a lot had happened on Corfu in the past year.

'Anyway, we're letting Diana dominate our catch-up like she dominates everything else,' Jackie stated, sitting forward in her chair and adjusting her glasses. They'd turned dark in the sunshine. 'I want to hear all about what's been going on with you.' Jackie smiled. 'And how's that gorgeous Darrell?'

Abby's heart sunk and right then she wished a giant squid would land itself on the nearest pontoon, so she could stuff it into her mouth.

Seven

The Dolan House, San Stefanos

Her mother's house hadn't changed at all. Abby remembered, when she had first visited, being underwhelmed by this supposed dream home in the sun her mum had purchased with almost everything she had.

It was old. No one seemed to know just how old, although there was an archway that led to the small patio of garden with 1829 written into the plaster. Apparently that couldn't be relied upon, and Abby had always wondered if ancient builders used to finger-draw made up dates just for fun while chuckling into their tsipouro.

The shutters that were, at one time, originally dark green, were still very much in the half-faded green olive and bare wood state they had been when Jackie took ownership and, as her mum struggled with the key in the door lock, Abby realised that the very first item on the renovation agenda – security – hadn't been addressed either.

Abby turned away from Jackie's sighing and twisting at the door handle and took in the view. It wasn't a frontline property but, over the shelving tiled roofs of the one-level houses across the small road, you could see the lush headland on one side and a glimpse of that aquamarine sea. It *was* tranquil and beautiful here.

Suddenly the door was yanked open and a scream had Abby snapping her head back to the house.

'Wanging hell! You're here! You're here!'

Before Abby could even take in anything about her sister's appearance – except the hair straighteners in one of her hands – she was grabbed and woman-handled into a vice-like hold she was sure she'd seen in an Olympic taekwondo bout.

'Can't breathe,' Abby rasped, then 'Ow!' She recoiled, escaping Melody's hug and putting a hand to the back of her neck.

'Shite! Soz! The straighteners are still on,' Melody said as if suddenly realising she was holding them. 'Don't know why I'm bothering really. They don't work so well when you've got hair as frizzy as Sarah Jessica Parker's.'

'Are you all right, Abby?' Jackie asked.

'Fine,' Abby answered, squinting away tears.

'I'll get some ice,' Melody said, grinning. 'And then I'll get out the vodka.' The grin widened. 'Proper Russian stuff. One bottle costs more than the iPhone X apparently.'

Abby smiled. Just like the ramshackle house, her sister hadn't changed either. As effervescent as Lambrini, half of her blonde hair trying to pass for straight, the other half buffed out like corn-coloured candyfloss. She was beautiful, would be completely enviable, if she wasn't just as beautiful on the inside. Abby felt a warmness grow as she realised, for the first time in a long time, just how much she loved and missed her sister.

'Come on in.' Jackie grabbed Abby's arm and pulled her into the house. 'We'll have a drink and then I'll get your room finished.'

Melody nudged Abby. 'She's been poking about in it all week. You've even got cushions.'

'Oh, well, you didn't need to go to any trouble,' Abby said.

'You're joking, aren't you?' Melody stated. 'It's you, Abs, here in Corfu again! Not even Bryan Adams would get this treatment and you know how much Mum loves a bit of Bryan Adams ... shite, did she tell you about Jude Law?!'

'Melody, will you let your sister relax?' Jackie called.

Melody grinned. 'It's wanging ace that you're here!'

Abby smiled at her sister. 'Well, in your last text you told me Igor's brother would die if he didn't meet me.'

'He'll be all over you when you tell him you've got a boyfriend at home. He's a bastard for a challenge.'

Abby swallowed. She knew the first stage of recovery was acceptance, but she just wasn't ready to accept in the public arena yet, not even a family arena. And that meant a few white lies that had started with telling her mum that Darrell was 'fine, just very busy at work'. The second the words were out, the memory of him suckering up to no-wider-than-a-strip-of-wheatgrass Amber had hit her right in the feels. But each day it was just slightly easier to hold in the tears. As long as she kept busy.

'Melody! Let your sister come in!'

Eight

'See! We've got rugs now and throws!' Melody bounced Tigger-like into the open-plan space. It wasn't a new, spacious, designed-to-make-the-most-of-the-space area, just a relic from when the previous owner had kept six sheep, two goats and a donkey in it. Rustic was Abby's first thought when they had done the first viewing. Rustic sounded a lot better than 'shit'.

'You've painted,' Abby remarked. The walls were now a pale lemon instead of the original colour, which could only be described as bogey green. And it was cool, the thick walls seeming to make up for the lack of air-conditioning.

Melody laughed as she threw herself down onto the Grecian-patterned throw-covered sofa. Dust from the parts of the bare boards not covered by rugs speckled the air. 'We didn't paint it. George did.'

'Do you want a cup of tea?' Jackie asked, bustling over to the kitchen area. Abby's eyes followed her. Still the same old cooker, one of the knobs cracked, the odd mismatched tiles with heads of various farmyard animals in no particular pattern above the wooden worktop.

'Who's George?' She seemed to be asking who people were a lot since she got here. It made her wonder just what her mum and sister had been sharing with her in their telephone conversations. It didn't feel as if she really knew anything about their lives here any more.

'No one,' Jackie said a little too quickly.

'George is mum's *friend*,' Melody made quotation marks in the air before setting back to work on straightening her hair.

'But ...' Abby started. 'You told me about Derek and ... someone with a lot of hats and—'

'He just did the painting last year,' Jackie said. 'It needs doing again. I'm not sure I like the yellow.'

'I like it,' Melody said. 'It's better than that snot green.' She grinned at Abby. 'Do you remember the snot green?'

Abby nodded. 'Yes.'

'Shall I make something to eat?' Jackie asked, beginning to take crockery from the draining board and putting it away in the cupboards.

'Not for me,' Melody stated. 'I'm working, then I'm going out with Igor.' She turned to Abby. 'You should come out with us later. We're meeting up for drinks at The Blue Vine about eleven.'

Abby swallowed. *Meeting up* at eleven. She had taken to being in bed at ten catching up on *Orange is the New Black*. But that was home. And this was her holiday. She could do something different. She could stop herself reminiscing about holidays gone before – sharing *mezes* for two and a large carafe of sweet white wine ...

'Did you say you were working?' Abby asked, turning her attention to Melody. 'Are you doing a viewing?'

'I—'

'Yes,' Jackie stated. 'She is. It's this beautiful villa in the hills. Only small but with a lovely established garden. Fruit trees and beautiful flowering borders—'

Melody broke in. 'One massive double bedroom with a walk-in wardrobe, then a smaller room you could just about fit twin beds in. Gorgeous tiling throughout, modern yet traditional at the same time, you know, like grey and swirls and Greek keys and the neighbours are nice. They have a dog called Malcolm.'

'Malcolm?' Abby queried. 'They're not Greek then?'

'No, Scottish ... at least I think so,' Melody continued. 'I've never really been very good at deciding if someone is Scottish or Irish ... or from Newcastle, if I'm honest.'

Abby's brain hurt. Was this how life was here in Corfu? Despite the picturesque surroundings, her mum and sister were like bundles of frenetic energy. It was making her feel the opposite of relaxed. Business must be good, though. Evening viewings surely meant more properties on the books.

'I could come with you,' Abby suggested. Although she had chosen to stay in England and not form part of the family business, the estate agency idea hadn't been unappealing. She had quite liked the idea of visiting holiday homes like Laura Hamilton in *A Place in the Sun,* noting down distance from the beach and en-suite assets. It would be good to know more about what her family had devoted their last almost two years to and see them in action.

'You can't,' Jackie exclaimed somewhat hurriedly.

'It's not that I don't want you to, Abs,' Melody waded in. 'It's just the owners are a bit picky. It's taken me about thirty emails and phone calls to build up a rapport with them. They weren't sure about selling at first and then I said how much they could get for it and what a prime property it was and ... it won't be interesting ... and ... there's snakes in the garden.'

Abby laughed. 'Snakes have never bothered me. It's you who hates them.'

'I do hate them,' Melody admitted. 'Last time I went there I wore wellies and long socks.'

'We'll go out for dinner,' Jackie said, clapping her hands together. 'The two of us.'

'Mum ...' Melody said a little oddly.

'No,' Jackie continued. 'That's what we'll do. I'll take Abby to dinner at The Blue Vine. Diana is always raving about the divine *loukanika* wraps and I haven't tried one yet.'

'Sausage,' Melody stated with a snigger. 'Haven't I been texting you all week about getting some of that?'

'Ignore her, Abby,' Jackie said, pouring water into three mismatched mugs. 'She's just teasing. We all know Darrell's the only man for you.'

And there it was. The karma-pinch for someone who was hoodwinking her family. She begged herself to hold it together.

'Dinner out sounds nice,' Abby said quickly. 'And I'll pay.' She may not have a job and would need some of her house-with-a-garden savings to live on soon, but she could afford a few treats. And when your self-esteem was as low as the belly of a native snake and you had been avoiding heartbreak splurges on Next.com, half a dozen small plates of food seemed like a well-deserved alternative.

Nine

Villa Pappas

Theo looked at his reflection in the mirror on the wall of the living area. He had swept his hair up into a man bun but he just hadn't had the energy to shave. It had been just over a week since razor had met skin and his roughness was definitely getting towards more beard than stubble. He hardly recognised the man he was from the man he had looked like just a few months ago. His hair had been shorter, his face clean, the epitome of business.

As if sensing his reverie, a spasm invaded his right arm and he shook it out hard, the cool blue material of the polo shirt wafting against his body. A uniform. A warning from his father. He stared at himself almost critically. He wasn't sure his father had ever understood exactly how the boat accident had affected him. He wasn't sure anyone had.

Theo sighed, closing his eyes as the memory threatened to come back. He had been driving the boat. He had been showing off its speed and prowess for the customer just like he had so many times before. It had been a perfect day for the sea. Hyacinth-blue sky, calm waters, but suddenly there was a swell. He was starting to feel anxious now, just thinking about it. It had been too late for him to drop the speed. He had tried to make a turn, pulling on the wheel with all the strength he could muster, desperately willing the sea to stop its surge. The next thing he knew he was being swallowed up by the water and the rest of his passengers were nowhere to be seen ... The breath caught in his chest.

'Hello! Oh! Wow!'

Leon let out a laugh as he threw his taxi keys into the glass dish on the sideboard below the mirror and stood back, regarding Theo. 'What is going on? There is a dressing up party and you are going as a waiter?'

'If only that were the case,' Theo answered, blowing out a breath and tucking the polo shirt into the black trousers he was wearing.

'Wait,' Leon said, studying him closer. 'You are really doing something at The Blue Vine? Like working?'

'It seems that way,' Theo answered. 'If we both want to carry on staying here for the summer.'

'What?!'

'Well, what did you think Spyridoula wanted when you let her in earlier?' His tone was a little accusing, but he knew it wasn't really Leon's fault. His aunt never took no for an answer.

'Theo, she had a bucket and a mop in one hand and a plastic box of tapenade.' He sighed. 'She said she was coming to clean and to make you lunch.'

Theo shook his head. 'Leon, when have you ever seen my auntie make anything to eat? Or clean, for that matter.'

His friend seemed to stare through the bi-fold doors of the living area to the infinity pool, then beyond to the sparkling Ionian before he even thought about attempting to make good on an answer.

'Spyridoula is not like a typical Greek woman in the usual way, except when it comes to getting her own way, particularly when it concerns family.' Theo did up the top button of the shirt, then, thinking better of it, unfastened it again. 'My father is thinking of selling the villa.'

'He is!' Leon exclaimed.

'No,' Theo replied. 'Not really. This is what Spyridoula has suggested he says to make me get a job and pay my way.'

'Oh,' Leon said. 'I'm not sure I understand.'

'He wants me back home. *Not* in Corfu. Back in the boat business.' He looked at his friend. 'He will think I cannot cut it as a barman. That I will fail. That I will have no choice but to return to the mainland.'

'Oh,' Leon said again. 'So, do I need to move back to my mother's?'

'No,' Theo said quickly. 'Not unless you want to.'

'Are you crazy? I have three sisters and five cats who could eat me in the night – and I'm not talking about the cats.'

Theo smiled and went back to checking his appearance. 'This is a temporary thing,' he insisted. 'I will do as Spyridoula has asked for a while. And then it will all blow over.' He knew his father. His father would be too busy focusing on the business, orchestrating press releases a-plenty to restore vital confidence.

'So, you are really to work at The Blue Vine?' Leon checked again.

'My shift starts at six,' he informed. 'How do I look?'

'Like you spent way too much time on the other side of The Blue Vine bar last night,' Leon admitted.

'I will clean my teeth again,' Theo said, running a finger over his lips. 'How was the taxi business today?'

'Lucrative,' Leon answered, throwing himself down onto the cream sofa that dominated this room. 'Three airport runs from here and then I picked up a cute girl from the airport and brought her right back here to San Stefanos. And she speaks a little Greek. Said she had been here before.'

'Did you give her your number?' Theo asked.

He shook his head. 'I am not as good as you at that kind of stuff. Although I did tell her my family run the bike-hire shop.'

'Well, the village is small, my friend. You are bound to see her again.' Theo checked his watch. 'Almost six. I am sure Spyridoula will be in a booth making sure I arrive.' He sighed. 'If I am doubly unlucky she will have brought all her friends with her.'

'Stay strong, Theo. Once I have endured tonight's family dinner to celebrate Spiros doing well at a test at school I will come down.' He smiled. 'You can take the lid off my bottle of Fix.'

'Of course, there is an alternative to biding my time,' Theo said, tightening the band at the back of his hair.

'There is?' Leon asked.

'I could always turn into the worst employee the bar has ever had.'

'Oh, Theo, do you think that is wise?'

Theo moved towards the door, heading for the bathroom. 'I think, if it's bad enough, then Spyridoula might have no choice but to retreat.'

Leon furrowed his brow and looked at Theo questioningly. 'She really does not cook?'

Ten

The Dolan House

'Right, better buzz or I'll be late.'

Abby's mouth fell open as Melody skitted into the lounge. She was wearing a pair of scarlet-coloured hot pants with tassels dangling from the hem and a cropped top that was barely bigger than a bandana. In fact, Abby squinted, *was* it a bandana? The one from the last photo on iMessage? The one that had been wrapped around Melody's head instead of now making a desperate attempt to cover her boobs? Her sister was also wobbling on the highest pair of heels Abby had ever seen. They were … *stripper* heels. Platform bases, PVC, completely clear. Abby wasn't stupid. She had seen *Lap Dance* on Netflix. Something was going on here.

'Melody,' Abby said. 'Where is it you're going?'

'What?' Melody picked keys off the large wooden plinth on the wall at the edge of the kitchen area containing what looked like hundreds of identical sets.

'She's going to show the house,' Jackie said, pouring ouzo into two glasses.

'The one with Malcolm the dog next door. The Geordies,' Melody said, slowly edging towards the front door.

'You mean the Scots,' Abby reminded.

Melody laughed. 'See, I told you I get mixed up with accents.' She grabbed a silver sequin handbag from the back of the armchair.

'But you don't show houses dressed like … like … someone from Stringfellows!'

Melody let out a gasp, both hands going to her mouth, the silver clutch bag hiding her lips but not the look in her eyes.

'Sorry,' Abby said quickly. 'I just mean … if Desperately Seeking is a professional estate agency then you need to look a little more professional.' Or was this how things were done on Corfu? 'Don't you think?'

Melody's hands came down. 'Well, that's where you are short-sighted.' She pointed a finger. 'You see, me and Mum cater for everyone on a very *individual* basis. That's why we take so long to get to know people. That's why rapport means everything. You have to make clients feel special.'

Abby swallowed. Her sister was right, of course, but in the outfit she had on she was severely concerned about the brand of special Melody was pedalling.

'Donald's somewhere between seventy and death,' Melody informed her. 'He likes looking at my legs. Said I remind him of a girl he used to know.'

Abby closed her eyes. It was all kinds of wrong, wasn't it? And why wasn't their mother saying anything about it? Or did she dress up the same on occasion?

'You should get going,' Jackie said. She put a glass out towards Abby. 'Here you go, Abby. Have a pre-dinner ouzo.'

'Oh, I don't know if I should—' Abby stopped herself. Had she really been going to say 'this early'? She took the glass.

'*Yammas*,' Melody encouraged, eyes bright and friendly again.

Abby downed the shot and straightaway coughed, the aniseed and alcohol working like an evil duo set to flail her throat and seep into her liver. '*Yammas*,' she croaked out.

'Don't get her too drunk, Mum, I want her to try Igor's vodka later.' Melody opened the front door then waved a hand, tassels on her legs vibrating. 'Bye!'

It was a perfect evening, the sun making the temperature a subdued early twenties and, as Abby left the house with her mum, she breathed in the mix of heat, dust and fragrant bougainvillea.

'Best time of the day, this is,' Jackie announced with a soft sigh.

Abby looked to her mother and noticed that, although she had had changed into another shapeless chiffon number in leopard print, she hadn't changed out of her flip-flops, nor had she refreshed her make-up. Back in England, Jackie Dolan had never been seen without show-stopping eyeliner and a fresh slick of Burgundy Blush on her lips. Not to mention the heels she still hadn't seen any hint of in the hours she'd been on the island. Perhaps Melody had pinched them all to go with her nightclub outfits.

Abby adjusted her handbag strap to settle on the cotton of her navy-blue dress, rather than bare skin, then looked ahead. The small winding road leading to the water's edge was lined by old stone houses, their terraces shaded by grape vines, large pots spilling growing fruit and vegetables as well as flowers. Further ahead she could easily see the neon of Desperately Seeking together with the waving shop banners advertising ice creams and the edge of rainbow displays of lilos and rubber rings.

'Quick,' Jackie said suddenly, eyes open, grabbing Abby by the arm.

'What is it?' Abby asked.

'Ssh! Just keep walking and put your head down.'

Jackie's grasp was firm and Abby was glad her mother's nails were short and untended. Falsies would be piercing her skin right now.

Abby stooped a little but felt ridiculous. Who were they hiding from? 'Mum, what's going on?'

'Ssh! Keep moving.'

'Mum, whatever it is—'

'Bugger, he's seen us,' Jackie rushed out. 'Stand up, Abby. Don't look like we were hiding. And smile ... like you're Michelle Obama.'

Abby couldn't help herself, she was definitely showing more teeth like her mum had asked, and she then noticed a man was approaching them, two expensive-looking boutique bags swinging from his hands. He was in his fifties, definitely Greek, with dark hair that just touched the collar of his pale-lemon short-sleeved shirt.

'*Kalispera*, Jackie,' the man greeted, coming to a halt as he reached them.

'*Kalispera*, Aleko,' Jackie replied.

Abby racked her brains trying to remember from all the frenzied conversations she'd had since she got here who Aleko was. She was sure he wasn't one of her mum's failed dating experiences.

'*Yassou, omorfi koritsi*,' Aleko said, greeting Abby.

Before she could do anything, the man had taken hold of her hand and was lifting it to his lips.

'Abby is my daughter,' Jackie said. 'She's engaged to be married. And she speaks a bit of Greek so you can keep your "beautiful girl" comments to yourself.'

Aleko laughed. 'It is nice to meet you, Abby.' He shook the bags he was carrying in Jackie's direction. 'I have been to Corfu Town today. Extra-special gifts for all the customers taking advantage of the free spa day when they sign up with Ionian Dreams.'

Now Abby remembered where she had heard the name Aleko before. During her mother's phone conversation when she'd arrived. It sounded like he was the main competition for Desperately Seeking's business.

'I'm sure they will all have a lovely time,' Jackie said, taking hold of Abby's arm again. 'But if you'll excuse us, we have a client meeting to get to.'

'What's Ionian Dreams?' Abby asked, paying Aleko her full attention.

'What is Ionian Dreams?' Aleko asked, taking a deep-breathing-in-yoga kind of inhale. 'Well, beautiful lady, it is an experience everyone is craving, even if they do not know it yet.'

'Is it one of those places men go to experience a release like no other?' Abby queried in her most innocent of tones.

Aleko looked horrified and one of the bags fell out of his hands. A 'no' came out a little strangled, then, 'It is an estate agency selling the dream of home ownership on Corfu.'

'Oh,' Abby said, clapping her hands together. 'Just like Desperately Seeking!'

'No,' Aleko stated firmly. 'Nothing about my business is like that ... that ... pink mess over there.'

'I beg your pardon!' Jackie exclaimed. 'Did you just call my business a mess? I'll have you know that I was nominated for an award last year.'

'Tsk!' Aleko sneered. 'It can't have been for customer service. So many people they come to me after they have been blinded by your colour and say you are late to appointments and you take them up into the mountains with a car that makes more noises than the aeroplane they arrive in.'

'I've never had any complaints about my car, and anyway, if they don't like it, they can get to the properties under their own steam.'

Abby watched the verbal battle going on and saw her mother's usual confident stance begin to fold. Just what was going on here?

'And that is where you are going wrong. *Everything*, Miss Jackie must be about the customer. With you it is all about the sale and never mind the rest.' He put on a smug face. 'And that is why everyone comes to me in the end.'

'None of that is true!' Jackie exclaimed. She was definitely close to tears, and Abby wasn't going to stand by and let that happen. She had, after all, first-hand and very recent experience of street-sobbing and she wasn't about to have it turned into a thing for their family.

'It was so nice to meet you, Mr Ionian Dreams,' Abby said, holding her hand out to Aleko. 'But, as my mum just said, we're meeting a very important client in just a few minutes and we want to make that very special first impression.' She shook his hand then took hold of Jackie's arm.

'What important client?' Aleko asked as Abby led the way down to the waterfront.

'I'm not at liberty to say,' Abby called from over her shoulder. 'We had to sign a non-disclosure agreement.'

She could feel her mother's tension as she held onto her arm and she waited, until she was sure Aleko was out of range, before she said anything.

'You OK, Mum?'

'Yes, of course.' Jackie sniffed. 'He's nothing I can't handle.'

'Where is this Ionian Dreams? Here in San Stefanos?'

Jackie nodded. 'He hasn't got the beachfront like me, he's back there.' She hitched her head. 'Around the corner near the quad bike place. But he likes his freebies and so do the customers.'

'Well,' Abby began. 'In my experience giving out things for free usually means the real product is substandard. And people aren't fooled by cheap gimmicks these days.' She swallowed. Although the time she gave a complimentary teacake with every pot of coffee between three and five on Friday afternoons had increased bums on seats during the restaurant's quiet time at The Travellers' Rest.

'Diana would do anything for a free spa day and she has a lot of friends.'

Abby stopped walking and eyed her mum. 'But business is going well, isn't it? I mean, Melody is out doing this viewing tonight and you've got things booked in every day and more houses to value, yes?'

Jackie beamed. 'Of course we have. There's no stopping us. And the pink branding has certainly attracted a lot of attention.'

She didn't dare say anything about the taxi driver's comment about the villagers' opinion on it. She scrutinised her mum's expression. Jackie seemed genuine. She would tell her if there was a problem. She wasn't the type to keep things to herself. Apart from the testing the water with the dating ...

'Come on,' Jackie said, bright demeanour restored. 'Let's go and fill ourselves with Greek sausage.'

'OK.' Abby's stomach growling indicated it was time to have something to eat.

'So, who shall we pretend our fabulous new client is?' Jackie asked, grinning. 'Tom Hanks? He's a lover of Greece.'

'Mum, we don't have to pretend it's anyone,' Abby reminded her. And then she sighed. 'And you didn't have to pretend I'm engaged to Darrell either.' Was this it? The moment she told her mum the hard truth that actually they weren't attached at all any more? She opened her mouth ...

'Well, it's only a matter of time, isn't it?' Jackie remarked, waving a hand in the air. 'And I like to daydream about it sometimes. Have you thought about having the wedding here? In Corfu? It doesn't have to be a big, fat, Greek *Mamma Mia*-style thing with coordinated dance routines. It can just be very simple and very stylish and ...'

'Not pink?' Abby suggested as the moment disappeared.

Jackie laughed. 'I don't know what everyone seems to have against pink! It's the colour of love and ... lobster and taramasalata and ...'

'Sunburn,' Abby offered.

'Now you're just being mean. And it will cost you. You know the rules. Be nice or it's something to eat you haven't tried before, just like with your veggies when you were babies.'

Abby smiled. Believe it or not, it had been how she had fallen in love with pastry.

'I'm absolutely unafraid of trying new things these days,' Abby said as they began to walk again. 'And we'll start with a carafe of wine.'

Eleven

The Blue Vine

Theo tried desperately to stifle the yawn that was creeping up from the back of his jaw ready to invade his whole face. He hadn't had nearly enough sleep today and now Hera, the owner and manager of The Blue Vine, was running through every drink they offered on the menu. He wasn't even sure why. They were all engraved on an olive wood board behind the bar – beers, wines and a whole range of cocktails. He liked the bar. It was a mix of traditional and new with its beamed ceiling and stone walls alongside bright white walls, up-lights and candles in jam jars providing the ambient glow. Subtle, cool mood music was playing over the sound system.

'I am sorry, Theo, am I boring you in some way?'

He clamped his teeth together, praying the yawn didn't override the strength of his commitment to containing it. He shook his head before he trusted himself to open his mouth. 'No, of course not.'

'Then you can tell me how you would make an Old Fashioned.'

He swallowed. He had worked a bar before. His uncle had a bar. He had even made cocktails before – been good at it – but right now his brain was still in a terribly low gear.

'Old Fashioned,' he repeated. Quickly he scanned the bar for anything that looked familiar, trying to recall the recipe.

He had worked a few bars in Lefkada but there hadn't been a call for cocktails where he had been staying. It was bourbon, definitely, and orange, but what else …

He picked up a bottle of bourbon with as much confidence as he could muster and then let his eyes wander to the entrance. Yes! Two new customers were arriving, about to sit at a table by the bay. He put down the bottle, and grabbed a pad and pen.

'Hera, we have customers,' he said, hastening out from behind the bar. 'I will serve them.'

'Theo, no, that is what I do … Theo!'

He pretended he couldn't hear and raced from the building before she could do anything to stop him. When he got back behind the bar he would google the top one hundred cocktail recipes … except Hera had everyone's devices locked in the safe for the duration of the shift. He swallowed as he approached the tables across the road. It was probably a good thing. Googling and researching sounded like he cared about this job, cared about pleasing his aunt and his father. He *didn't* care.

'Hello,' he said. 'Good evening. Welcome to The Blue Vine.'

The two women had settled at the only vacant table for two close to the water. Around them, diners were already tucking into meals and carafes of wine, other Blue Vine employees bringing out meals and refreshing drinks.

'Good evening,' the older of the two women greeted. 'You must be new.'

'No,' Theo answered. 'My name is Theo.'

The woman laughed. 'Well then, it's lovely to meet you, Theo. I'm Jackie and this is my daughter, Abby.'

He turned his attention to the older woman's companion as she looked up from perusing the menu. She had dark brown hair and a blue dress with a V-shaped neckline. It was subtly captivating, and he found his eyes wandering to her bare legs.

'We'll have a carafe of white wine, please,' the younger woman ordered. 'The local wine.'

'Very good,' Theo said, noting this down. 'Anything else?'

'We're going to have a look at the menus,' the older woman said.

'No problem,' Theo answered.

Theo was about to leave when he watched the girl remove her mobile from her bag. This was his chance.

'Excuse me, I know this is a little rude, but may I use your phone?'

She looked up, studying him as if he might be someone who would snatch, grab and sell the item to the nearest highest bidder.

'Use my phone?' she repeated.

He nodded. 'Yes, not to make a call. You see, this is my first evening here and ...' What to say? Be honest? For the first time in months? 'I really need to know how to make an Old Fashioned or I might not have this job tomorrow.'

Abby smiled at him, then slipped her phone back into her handbag. He shouldn't have asked. Now there would probably be a customer complaint to go with his lack of knowledge in the cocktail area. Not that he cared about this job! What was wrong with him?

'Bourbon,' Abby answered. 'Angoustura bitters, orange bitters and sugar, poured over ice.'

He stared at her. Each word had trickled from her full lips like they were ingredients to the sweetest, most alluring cocktail. And now her hazelnut eyes were fixed on him he couldn't look away.

'Abby Dolan! How come you know how to make cocktails?' Jackie exclaimed excitedly.

The spell was broken as Abby turned her attention back to her mother. 'I worked, I mean, I *work* at the bar sometimes at The Travellers' Rest. We had ... *have* very discerning clients.'

'Thank you,' Theo said. 'You have saved my life.'

Abby replied and waved a hand. 'It's just a cocktail.'

'Maybe,' he said. 'But you have not met my new boss.'

His eyes connected with hers again and it was causing a rather inappropriate colouring of her cheeks despite her best attempts at quelling the action with thoughts of icebergs, walk-in freezers and Slush Puppies. He was a gorgeous, archetypal Adonis, all olive complexion and dark hair swept back off his face, rolled into a tiny knot at the base of his head. She'd never been keen on the 'man bun' but this waiter could be the poster boy for the style. But then something else happened, as her gaze drifted to his strong nose and thick, brooding lips, *guilt* threatened to submerge her as if she was somehow still one half of the her-and-Darrell whole. Ridiculous but, in this moment, real.

'One carafe of white wine,' Theo stated. 'I will be back.'

Despite herself she watched him leave, dark trousers hugging lean thighs and a rather muscular butt. Melody would definitely have approved.

'Well, he was rather lovely,' Jackie remarked, a light sigh leaving her lips, fingers going to the small arrangement of daisies in the centre of the table.

'I don't remember Corfu having much call for Old Fashioned cocktails last time I was here,' Abby said.

'Oh, you'd be surprised,' Jackie answered. 'There's more English here than ever now. So.' She plucked up a menu. 'What shall we have to eat?'

Abby knew exactly what she was going to have because she had been craving it from the moment she had booked the flight to Corfu. A starter of lemon-infused octopus followed by spanakopita. Spinach, feta cheese, onions, garlic and herbs, all wrapped up in fine filo pastry. She could almost taste it now, being washed down by that local wine.

'I think I need to do a Diana and have the sausage,' Jackie breathed. 'See if they really are as divine as she makes out.'

'Why don't you have what you actually want?' Abby asked. 'I'm worried this Diana is turning into some sort of anti-role model.'

'She's nothing of the sort,' Jackie pounced. She sniffed. 'She just has good clothes and ... a great figure for her age. Like Debbie McGee. And ... everyone likes her.'

Abby looked a little more closely at her mother. She was looking every one of her fifty-five years right now and her hair needed colouring. But it was nothing that couldn't be fixed. Perhaps that was the reason Fate had stepped in and planted this almost-enforced holiday on Abby, to help her mum pick herself up out of the middle-aged doldrums.

'Since when did everyone not like you?' Abby asked.

'I'm not interesting like Diana,' Jackie continued. 'I don't have tales of "the time I spent in Malaysia" or "the night I went dancing with Anthony Hopkins".'

'I'm not sure dancing with Hannibal Lecter is something to brag about,' Abby attempted to joke. 'Good job it wasn't dinner, or she might not have survived to tell the story.'

'The first eligible bachelor that sails into the village and she's there like a praying mantis before anyone else gets a look in.'

'And is that what you really want, Mum?' Abby asked. 'A look-in with eligible bachelors?'

'I don't know,' Jackie sighed. 'Maybe. Not that I've had much luck so far.'

'Well, stories about Singapore and Welsh actors will only win favour for so long,' Abby reassured her. 'Maybe I should sign up with Ionian Dreams, get us a free spa day and a bit of pampering.' She really couldn't just tell her mum her hair, nails and skin needed a desperate refresh. It wasn't like working up to telling Stanley about his odour issues. This was her mum. Someone who usually took such pride in her appearance ...

'Why would you sign up with Ionian Dreams?' Jackie snapped.

'To get a free spa day,' Abby replied.

'And there's the proof that it's enough to tempt people away from Desperately Seeking!' Jackie looked positively panicked. 'No matter what I do!'

'Mum, I'm obviously not going to look at properties I just thought ...' Abby started.

'I need to do something more, don't I?' Jackie rushed out. 'I need to do more than I'm doing. Something bigger.'

'Well ...'

'I need to ... put on a party. Yes! That's what I'll do! I'll put on a party for all my existing clients and invite potentials.'

Abby watched her mum come alive, eyes brightening, shoulders loosening.

'I'll get out the fliers and sign-up sheets. We can have it outside the offices, get a gazebo to keep the heat off, and do the food ourselves to keep costs down. Oh, Abby, thank you!'

She wasn't sure quite what she had done, but flashes of her mum looking more excited than she had since she had arrived on Corfu could only be a good thing.

'Here we are ... one carafe of white wine.'

The waiter was back, depositing a carafe and two large glasses on the table. Abby gazed out over the shoreline and drank in the exquisite view. Softly the sea caressed the fine stones and sand, easing its way forward and back in a motion so delicate it would be easy to just drift off and forget everything.

'Abby.'

Her name being spoken in that heavy, sultry Greek accent had her turning her head.

'*Ya sena* … for you,' the waiter said. He held out a thick ornate glass tumbler, its rim speckled with sugar and orange, a short black straw inside. The liquid was orange too and cubes of ice floated. 'An Old Fashioned.'

'Oh,' Abby said. 'You didn't need to do that.'

'*Parakalo* … please. It is my pleasure.'

She reached out, taking the glass, and their fingers connected for the briefest of seconds. Just long enough for it to cause a tornado-style whirling in her stomach. It was uninvited and unwelcome and totally down to a distinct lack of pastry in her life. Hopefully this would be remedied soon. Quickly she steadied the glass with her other hand and put the drink to the table. 'Thank you.'

'*Parakalo*,' he responded. 'Now, what can I get you to eat?'

Twelve

Theo wasn't sure he had ever worked this hard before. The Blue Vine was busy and manual labour wasn't ordinarily his remit. He had made cocktails, served food, cleared tables, swept floors and now, while balancing plates up his entire forearm, his aunt had arrived with half a dozen other women from the village.

'Look!' Spyridoula announced, hands in the air like she was praising Greek gods, beaded bracelets knocking together. 'My nephew is working!'

There were enraptured noises from the other women as if they hadn't picked up on any of Spyridoula's sarcasm. Theo smiled. 'Good evening, ladies. Would you like a table for dinner or just some drinks?'

'We can find our own way,' Spyridoula replied. 'You go to the kitchen with your dirty dishes then come back to take our order.'

Theo smiled then rushed towards the main building to dispose of the crockery. There, he was thankful to see a friendly face.

'I told you, didn't I?' Theo said, greeting Leon as he came past the bar. 'Spyridoula is here with her friends. Checking up on me.'

'Perhaps she is just here for drinks,' Leon suggested, sipping at his beer.

58 · *Mandy Baggot*

'You do not believe that any more than I do,' Theo stated.

'What time does your shift end?'

'When the place closes,' he answered, placing plates on a tray destined for the kitchen. 'I suspect Spyridoula will get out her pack of cards and begin a game of bridge that will last the whole night just so she can keep me here.' He still wasn't entirely sure why he was being punished. Didn't everyone deserve a time out? Space to self-reflect?

Leon laughed. 'Perhaps I will stay for the cards. The scenery is good tonight.' He hitched his head towards the outside tables as if indicating something of interest.

Theo looked to the seating by the water, then a little further to the boats moored close to the cove. Anchored in deeper water were the large, uber-expensive superyachts. He could tell a potential buyer everything there was to know about those boats and convince someone to buy with minimal effort. That was the business he was more familiar with, not mixology. But it felt like a lifetime ago. He looked back to Leon. 'There is no way, even with my heaviest discount, that you are going to be able to afford a boat like that.'

Leon laughed hard. 'I was not talking about the boat. I was talking about the English girl. I cannot remember her name.' He moved his head, as if trying to remember. 'From my taxi today.'

Theo regarded the guests he had been serving all evening. There were family groups, two men in business suits, a party celebrating a sixtieth birthday ... that only left Abby and her mother.

'Wearing the blue dress?' Theo breathed.

'Yes!' Leon exclaimed. 'She is cute, no?'

'Her name is Abby,' he stated. He watched her take a spoonful of honey ice cream and slip it into her mouth. He had been watching her all night and he had no idea why. She was pretty, without any of the heavy make-up and tight, figure-skimming dresses of his previous conquests. Nothing like the women he had actively pursued since he had left the mainland. Maybe it was time for a change. And there was definitely something different about her. The way she looked at everything so intently as if sucking in its very deepest fibre – the blue of the sea, the ruggedness of the mountains – the way she had slowly eaten her spanakopita as if every morsel were the finest caviar …

'Yes, that is it,' Leon said. 'Now I remember.' He took a swig of his beer. 'Do you think I should invite her to the *panegyri* maybe?'

Theo shrugged. 'I do not know.' He hated that idea. What was wrong with him? A blonde-haired tourist at a table just behind them had already made it very clear she would enjoy hooking up with him later.

'Who are *you* going to take to the village festival?' Leon asked.

'I have not thought about it.' Given the situation with his father and his father's spy, he didn't even know if he was going to be hanging around for any of the summer festivities.

'We are here! We need vodka!'

The loud, Russian accents boomed over the sound of the bar's subtle chill-out vibe and a handful of men burst through the entrance, beginning a roaring chant, then moving to the bar and drumming their hands on the wooden top. Straightaway Theo prickled, putting down the last of his plates and standing tall.

'Ugh,' Leon stated with a shake of his head. 'The tsars are back.'

'Who are they?' Theo asked.

'The owners of that boat you were just looking at,' Leon said.

'Waiter! We need drinks!' one of the men bellowed, directing the request at Theo.

'*Tora!*' another man ordered.

And then began a chant of the Greek word for 'now'. '*Tora! Tora! Tora!*'

'What's that dreadful noise?' Jackie asked, looking towards the building.

'I'm not sure,' Abby replied. She sat back in her seat, stomach over-content now it was filled with seafood, pastry and the sweetest ice cream. The food had been heavenly. All she had remembered about Greek cuisine and so much more.

'Well,' Jackie sighed. 'Diana was right about the divine sausage. I wonder where they get them from? I've not found anything like it in the butchers in Acharavi. Maybe I could ask Hera and we can do some for the Desperately Seeking party!'

The party-to-end-all-parties was all Jackie had spoken about over dinner and Abby was glad. Her mum was back to seeming her jovial self and there had been no awkward pauses or asking about The Travellers' Rest ... or Darrell. She just hoped that everything Jackie was planning – table magicians, gourmet food, a Tom Hanks look-a-like – wasn't going to be beyond them.

'We need more chairs! Mum! Quick! More chairs! Igor, Andrei, Boris and Kevlar are here. Valentin's coming and Diana's on her way so we need to make sure the men sit down with us!'

It was Melody, still wearing the cabaret outfit but the pizzazz not quite reaching her eyes. And had she said there was someone called Kevlar? Who named their child after body armour?

'Abs! Come on! Help me!' Melody screeched. 'We'll pull two tables together.'

Abby watched her mum leap into action, backing away from their own table, picking vacant chairs up and rearranging. What *was* this frenzied almost-circus behaviour?

'Abby! Come on!' Melody hissed, beginning to haul a large table towards the one they had been sitting at in seashore tranquillity a few moments before.

'What's the rush?' Abby asked, as she finally moved to help her sister. 'I mean, if Igor's your boyfriend he's going to be sitting here with you, not with anyone else, isn't he?'

'It doesn't work like that here,' Melody answered almost under her breath.

'What do you mean?' Abby inquired.

'Igor isn't my boyfriend – not yet.'

'Well, what is he then?'

'You don't understand. Things aren't the same here as they are in Romsey. It's not all holding hands and trips to the New Forest show. It's more organised than that.' Melody finally stood tall, hands on her hips as the table was set in place. 'It's tactical.'

Abby shook her head, wanting to replace the conversation with something much more normal. Was she mistaken or had her sister just described relationships like they were planned out in a battle-room bunker?

'Tactical?' Abby hadn't meant to say the word aloud but out it had come.

'Things aren't all feta cheese and bouzoukis like they were here when we were kids,' Melody stated a little wistfully.

They weren't? But she was sure the traditional Greek charm was what their mum had moved here for. To try and recreate some of that positive peace and relaxation they had all felt on that family holiday with their dad. Or perhaps she hadn't listened hard enough when the move had been in the works. Maybe she had been too caught up with Darrell when he'd asked her why she was even thinking of Greece when their whole lives were in the UK ...

'Mel-o-dy!'

The voice was super-loud and eastern European. Abby turned around and saw four men moving across the road towards them in a way that could only be described as a swagger-cum-stagger. Dressed almost identically in cream-coloured trousers, brown shoes and slim-fit short-sleeved shirts in various colours, they moved towards the two tables pushed together as confidently as their alcohol-saturated bodies seemed to allow.

'Igor!' Melody exclaimed in obsequious tones, rushing to meet him.

'That's Igor?' Abby remarked to Jackie, who seemed to have her hands down the front of her kaftan adjusting her boobs in her bra.

'He is lovely,' Jackie replied. She picked up her wine glass and checked her reflection in it.

'He's drunk,' Abby stated.

'Oh, Abby, they're on holiday, just like you.'

But, so far, she had managed to have half a carafe of wine and an Old Fashioned and still keep her voice a normal level. *And* was able to walk without looking like she was doing a Korean pop routine.

'Jac-kie!' Igor greeted, swaying up to the table. He had a cigar tucked into the pocket of his shirt and a large bottle of vodka in his hand. He was attractive in a rather hard, surly, solid way but Abby thought his eyes were a little beady. She had never been fond of eyes that looked like they could be set inside the head of a creepy doll.

'*Kalispera*, Igor,' Jackie greeted, blowing him a kiss and smiling like a contestant on *Take Me Out*.

'No *kalispera*!' Igor roared. 'You must learn Russian!' He waved his hands until his comrades all grunted their agreement. He said a word that sounded like 'Dobby'.

Jackie attempted to repeat it and all the men fell about laughing. Abby was intensely annoyed.

'Igor,' Melody interrupted the laughter. 'This is my sister, Abby.' Her attention then went to the man next to him. 'The one I told you about, Andrei.' He was a little shorter than Igor and had fairer hair.

'Ab-by!' Igor announced.

'Hello,' Abby said. All at once she felt like the fish out of water she was. So much for thinking earlier that flying here had been the right thing to do. In this moment, all she wished she was doing was huddling up to Poldark – even if he had taken to sneering at the Tesco cat treats lately – and watching an episode of *Narcos*.

'Hello, beautiful lady,' Andrei said. He was moving towards her, swaying past his brother and Boris or Kevlar – she wasn't sure who was who – until he was next to her. He too had beady eyes, and halitosis. He reached out a hand and Abby backed up fast.

'I must go to the loo,' Abby said, rising to go towards the building across the road.

'Not now,' Melody hissed, taking hold of her arm. 'We need to get them settled.'

'Settled?'

'In place.'

'In place for what?' Abby asked in the same hushed tones her sister was using.

'You don't understand,' Melody said with an annoyed shake of her head.

'No, I really don't. So why don't you tell me what's going on.' Abby swallowed. 'Are you in debt to them somehow? Like Liam-Neeson-needed-to-kick-arse kind of debt?'

Melody didn't even smile, let alone laugh. Now Abby was worried.

'This isn't a film, Abby,' her sister replied.

'I know, I think, but I can't do the right things if you don't tell me the whole story.' Abby sighed and looked to her sister's tiny shorts. 'And I know there's more to that outfit than giving a seventy-year-old man sweet dreams.'

'Mel-o-dy! Come sit on me!' Igor called.

'Please tell me he meant "with" not "on",' Abby begged.

Immediately Melody's bubbly exterior began to overflow again, and she let go of Abby as soon as she saw Igor sit down in one of the chairs at their tables and pat his lap. 'Don't be long,' Melody said. 'You need to meet Andrei properly.'

Abby looked to Igor's brother, who was currently trying to get a slice of bread to stick to his forehead. She really didn't want to spend any time with him at all, but she needed to find out who these people were and just why they were so important to her family. But to do that she definitely needed another drink.

Thirteen

'I will be glad when they all leave,' Spyridoula announced. Theo watched his aunt's eyes go to the group of Russian men outside, and she tutted, shaking her head as he prepared her table some more drinks.

'Hera tells me they come here every night for the past two weeks.'

'Did she also tell you they spend hardly any money? Come in here and order bottles of water then drink their own vodka.'

'What?' Theo queried.

'We all know they have money,' Spyridoula continued. 'They show it off with their gold jewellery and their boats the size of the Parthenon. So why they think they can disrespect our island by taking over our bars and restaurants and not paying for that privilege I do not know.'

Theo looked to the men again. He knew all about this sort of person. He had sold boats to scores of them over the past five years. He had turned on the charm to persuade them into parting with their millions of roubles. Here they were irritating and seemingly taking advantage of his new employer.

Spyridoula let out a sigh, hands toying with the bracelets on her arm. 'I expect Jackie is getting involved with them so they can donate towards more of her ugly pink painting!' She shook her head. 'It cannot stay. We are having a meeting about it this week.'

'A meeting?' a woman's voice gasped. 'About my mother's business?'

The bottle of retsina almost slipped out of Theo's hands as he looked up to see Abby at the bar, next to his aunt.

'*Kalispera*,' Spyridoula said quickly. 'I do not think we have met before. I am Spyridoula Pappas.' She held out her hand to Abby and Theo watched the two exchange a somewhat awkward handshake.

'I'm really sorry that my mother's new rather garish shop-front is upsetting the villagers,' Abby said softly. 'I can see, well, it's rather obvious, that it isn't in keeping with the surroundings.'

Spyridoula patted her on the shoulder. 'If it were up to me there would be a place for everything.'

Theo laughed internally. His aunt was skilled at saying everything and nothing all at once.

'But,' Spyridoula continued, 'San Stefanos is a traditional place. We already have the Russians with their demand for borscht instead of avgolemono. And I fear the council will make orders against your mother if she does not change this of her own will.'

Theo watched Abby, distracted from his fixing of the drinks. She looked suddenly despondent, those big, doe eyes reacting to the news, her expression one of heavy burden. Well, she couldn't possibly be as worry-laden as he was.

Then Abby nodded, somewhat more confidently, as if she had taken note of his aunt's words and her mind was working on a plan. 'I will speak to her,' she said. 'Could you give me a few days? Perhaps hold off the meeting?' She sighed. 'I can't promise anything ... but I will try my best.'

Spyridoula smiled then and picked up her glass of ouzo and water, raising it slightly. 'Of course,' she said. 'What is a few days between friends?'

'Thank you,' Abby replied, a long, slow breath leaving her body.

Theo finished pouring the wine and looked to his aunt. 'I will bring the drinks out to your table.'

'You will not,' Spyridoula snapped back. 'I am capable of carrying a tray. You will serve the daughter-of-Jackie.'

With that said, Spyridoula picked up the collection of drinks and began to meander through the bar towards her card-playing friends outside.

'What can I get for you?' Theo asked.

'An escape would be good right now,' Abby answered, another sigh slipping through her lips.

'You wish to escape?' Theo asked. 'But you have only just arrived on Corfu, no?'

His question seemed to wake her out of her thoughts. 'Yes, I'm being dramatic. It's still paradise despite the slightly odd company.' She swallowed. 'I didn't mean you, sorry, I meant … the loud people.'

He laughed. 'I understand.'

She took a breath. '*Ti protinete?*'

He smiled. 'What would I recommend?' He looked to the vast array of bottles on the counter just below the sparkly granite countertop, liquid of varying colours inside them. He grinned, holding one up. 'Something pink perhaps?'

'That isn't funny,' Abby responded, but a smile was easing onto her lips.

'*Kalispera*, Abby.' It was Leon, climbing up onto the bar stool next to her. 'You remember me?' He smiled. 'If not for me you would not be in San Stefanos.'

Theo shook his head. His friend really needed to work on his lines.

'Leon,' Abby answered.

'You do remember!'

Theo ignored the curling of his gut and focused on preparing a knock-out cocktail.

'So, you have had a good evening?' Leon continued.

'Yes,' Abby replied. 'The food was delicious and the sunset was to die for.' She sighed, eyes going to the sea scene still visible from inside. The water was gently rippling now a soft, warm breeze had arrived. 'I'd forgotten just how wonderful the sunsets are.'

'One of the best places to see the sunset is 7th Heaven.'

'I haven't been there.'

'It is at Logas Beach, on the west coast. I can take you.'

Theo began to shake his chosen ingredients together as loudly as possible. He had not seen Leon act quite so forward before … and he wasn't enjoying it.

'Thank you, but I'm going to be busy helping my mum and my sister with their business,' Abby answered. 'Actually, Desperately Seeking is going to be having a party soon. You should come.'

Leon slapped his hand to his forehead as if in sudden realisation. 'The pink business!'

'I'm hoping it isn't going to be quite so pink for long … you should come too.'

Theo realised that Abby had addressed him.

'Theo is not sure how long he will be staying on Corfu,' Leon said quickly.

'Oh,' Abby said. 'I assumed you both lived here. My mistake.'

'When is the party?' Theo asked her.

'Next week,' Abby replied. 'Probably. If my mum can find someone who looks like Tom Hanks.'

Theo put a glass down in front of Abby, uncapped the cocktail shaker and began to pour. Watching her, not the glass, he caught her expression of delight as the turquoise liquid slowly slipped into the vessel. When he was finished pouring he added a lime wedge to the edge.

'It looks beautiful,' Abby breathed.

'It will taste even better,' Theo assured.

'What is it?' she asked him.

'An escape,' he replied, offering her a hint of a smile.

She laughed. '*Efxharisto.*'

'*Parakalo.*'

'You should come to the *panegyri*,' Leon jumped in, lightly touching Abby's arm. 'We have wine, of course, but there is food and dancing and good times.'

'I'm not sure how long I will be staying on Corfu either,' Abby responded.

'You have to stay for the festival,' Leon encouraged. 'I will not let you leave before, and I am the only taxi in San Stefanos.'

Abby smiled. 'I should get back to the table.'

'I will come to clear your plates in one moment,' Theo said as Abby left.

'Wow. She is pretty *and* funny and ...' Leon began, his eyes following Abby all the way back to the table where a woman in short shorts began to grapple her into a seat.

'She was quite clear she was not looking for a date,' Theo told him.

Leon laughed. 'You are jealous, my friend. Because she looks at me and not at you.' He shook his head as he swigged at his bottle of beer. 'Maybe you are losing your touch.'

Theo smiled as he deposited the cocktail shaker into the dishwasher, but the words meant in jest burned. Because they were true. He was losing his touch, *had* lost it already, and not just when it came to bar chat. He seemed to have lost his grip on everything and it wasn't getting any easier.

Fourteen

Abby had spent the past hour listening to Igor talk about his nation like it was its own separate planet, its people stronger, more intelligent, good at all things. And she had alternately watched Melody, soaking all this bravado up like she was an ardent Catholic at an audience with the Pope, and Andrei, who seemed to like balancing all things on his forehead – cutlery, flowers, a passing cat.

The journey was beginning to catch up with her and all she wanted was her bed at her mum's house. The lovely patch-work bedspread in blues and teal with the inch of sea view to look out upon. And quiet. Peace and quiet to enable her to slip into a delicious semi-consciousness that would either allow her to regroup or be filled with the same re-run of Darrell and Amber's passionate peck by the pastries. As harrowing as the dream was, it did seem to strengthen her resolve.

'Air, hair lair.'

Brought right back into the present that was rowdy Russians ruining the gentle shushing of the water and the Greek music emanating from the bar next door, Abby looked to the newcomer. Straightaway she knew who this woman was. With her hair the colour of corn, her make-up immaculate, and wearing a lilac sleeveless dress straight out of Phase Eight, it had to be the much talked about Diana. And then, all at once, she realised that the words she'd uttered weren't 'air, hair lair' but in fact 'oh, hello' in her rather upmarket British accent.

'Di-an-a!' Igor bellowed, leaping to his feet and roughly grabbing a chair.

'Sit down, you silly boy,' Diana ordered. 'Have you not learned any of those manners or correct English diction I have been trying to teach you?'

At once, Igor dropped back to his chair, appearing suitably admonished.

'Hello, Diana.' Jackie got to her feet. 'Would you like my chair?'

'Oh, Jackie darling, you are a love,' Diana said, slipping into the vacated seat no sooner than Jackie's kaftan-covered behind had left it. Abby immediately bristled and looked to Melody, instinctively waiting for her sister to say something testy. Melody, however, was stroking Igor's hand, her fingers gently circling over his gold-bracelet-embellished wrist.

'And who have we here?' Diana directed the question to no one in particular, but her eyes were on Abby like she was channelling Prue Leith and Abby was a nervous *GBBO* contestant.

'Diana, this is my daughter, Abby. She's visiting from England where she runs a luxury hotel.'

Abby felt her blood turn colder than the ice cubes in her daiquiri. She hugged the glass like it was a buoyancy aid and she was a non-swimmer. *Runs a luxury hotel.* As much as she adored The Travellers' Rest it was only a three-star, and there had been some rather picky reviews on TripAdvisor recently. And she hadn't really been the one to call the shots – as she'd found out to her detriment.

'A luxury hotel.' Diana sniffed like Abby was halloumi well past its eat-by date; her disdain was obvious and subtle all at the same time. 'Which chain? Warner? De Vere?'

'It's a boutique establishment, actually,' Abby responded. 'High standards. Wall-to-wall *de riguer.*' She so hoped '*de riguer*' meant fabulous.

'*Fantastique,*' Diana replied, nailing pure soft sarcasm. 'Well, I am Diana Le Carré. Accent over the "e" like the *other* author.' She rolled her eyes. 'No relation. And it's a *dreadful* bore having to explain that all the time.'

Abby went to reply but was interrupted.

'I always say, when people ask, "I'm the Le Carré who will give you more high than spy".' She laughed then. Like a cage full of monkeys.

Abby had truly had enough, and she reached out, tapping Melody's arm. It took three attempts for her sister to acknowledge her.

'How's your *little* business going, Jackie? Have you managed to sell any properties this month?' Diana asked.

Melody frowned at Abby and practically bit out. 'What is it?'

'I'm tired after the trip. I really want to go now.'

'Well, you can't,' Melody retorted, turning immediately back to Igor.

What?! She *couldn't* go? It was her holiday! Not a hostage situation. She poked Melody's arm hard causing a yelp and a furious expression when her sister turned again.

'I'm going back to the house,' Abby stated, picking her handbag off the floor and preparing to get up.

'No,' Melody said, taking a firm grip of her. 'Please, Abby. Not quite yet.' She made head-jerking motions towards their mum and Diana.

'Six properties this month!' Diana exclaimed, hands flying to her mouth, a diamond as big as Donald Trump's ego on one of her fingers. 'Really, Jackie? Because news like that would surely have filtered down to my Pow Wow and Pikilia group.' Diana sucked a breath in. 'Six sales in a month in a village this size is practically an evacuation.'

Abby watched Melody round on the author. 'We don't only deal with properties in San Stefanos, Diana. We have a much wider reach than that.'

'I believe Ionian Dreams have clients as far as Kavos.'

'And,' Melody continued. 'If you know the property market as well as my mum and I do, you will know that properties in the south are a third of the price of properties in the north. We cherry-pick at Desperately Seeking, Diana. We're not interested in wasting our time on cheap, seen-better-days, in-need-of-extreme-renovation trash.' Melody sent Diana a sugary smile then looked to Jackie. 'Are we, Mum?'

'We've just taken on a beautiful villa in the mountains,' Jackie stated quickly.

'Is that so?' Diana asked. 'Because as I was saying to Valentin over dinner earlier, I wasn't sure there was anything suitable for his budget on the market here at the moment. You know.' She took a breath. 'Over two million euros.'

'And where is Valentin?' Jackie inquired. 'Recovering from after-dinner tinnitus?'

'Actually, darling, he had to take an important business call.' Diana swirled her finger around the rim of a wineglass. 'And then he's meeting me here for a nightcap.'

Abby got to her feet then and grabbed her sister's hand.

'Ow!' Melody exclaimed.

'Excuse us, everyone,' Abby stated. 'Just for a moment.' She turned to Melody. 'We need to talk. Right now.'

Abby made her tone just like the one she had used on the slacking temporary sous chef who hadn't known his *a la carte* from his *table d'hote*.

Her sister nodded, almost meekly and let Abby steer her away from the table of mismatches towards the pontoon. She just needed to get Melody on her own, away from this self-obsessed bully of a writer and the rather obnoxious Slavs. Far enough away to get to the bottom of the business and to learn where the red hot pants fitted into things.

It was a stunning night. The dark sky laden with stars, the water a subtle, waving ink, boats dipping softly up then down. A warm breeze tickled Abby's shoulders but all she felt was tension, the knowledge that something here was amiss. That her family's odd companions were telling a tale and she didn't understand the plot.

'Right,' Abby said, stopping in the middle of the wooden platform. Its ill-fitting planks were gappy and a little tired, making the scent of salt and surf fizz up her nose. Then she rocked on her sandals slightly, half-forgetting that jetties moved. Quickly she re-established her footing. 'What's going on, Melody? And don't try to fob me off with talk about *fantastic* villas and superyacht owners, because this is Corfu, it isn't the set of *Riveria*.' She really did need to stop referencing TV shows as if they were her only hobby.

It was right at that moment that Abby noticed her sister hadn't stopped walking, but had continued to the very edge of the platform and was facing the sea, looking a lot less assured than the confident table-organiser of earlier.

'Melody,' Abby said, her tone softer. 'What's going on?'

Her sister didn't reply and as Abby stepped a little closer to her she could hear what sounded like the beginnings of a cold, only no one got a cold that quickly …

'We're in trouble,' Melody breathed before a heart-wrenching sob left her petite frame. '*So* in trouble. And I've tried … I've tried so hard, Abs, but I'm running out of ideas faster than we're running out of money.'

Running out of money. This did not sound good. Particularly now she had met her mother's business rival and he seemed keen to chase them out of the village completely with his free hot stones and *shiatsu*.

'The business isn't thriving, is it?' Abby stated.

'The business is dying. Has virtually … died,' Melody spilled out. 'We haven't sold six properties in a month. We haven't sold *one* property this month. We only sold one and a half last month.'

'One and a half?' Abby queried.

'It was a three-bed with an *apotheke*.' Melody sighed. 'In the end they almost paid more for the shed than they did for the house.'

'And the villa with the views to die for? And the dog? And the Geordies-cum-Scots?'

'You really believed that?' Melody asked sadly.

'Well …' It was, in fact, more that she had *wanted* to believe it.

Melody looked down at her attire then back to Abby as tears snaked across her cheeks. 'I dance,' she said. 'In a bar in Acharavi. Twice a week. As a warm-up routine for the pole dancers.'

Abby closed her eyes, the full fall out becoming clearer as each sentence was spoken. 'Why didn't either of you say anything to me? When you called or text? It was all blue skies and "I'm just off on a crest of a wave".'

'I wanted to tell you,' Melody breathed. 'I really did. But Mum was so certain we were going to get out of the situation.

Once she had sold her designer shoes and got paid for the villa cooking we had a little capital, so we reinvested it in the branding to shake things up again but ... well, business is no better.'

Abby didn't know what to say. She wasn't sure what she was more shocked about: the fact that her family had kept all these difficulties from her, or that her mum had been paid to cook for people. When they were children, it had always been Super Noodles, frozen mixed veg for the five-a-day fix and Al's kebabs on the weekend.

'She didn't want you to worry and she knew you would. And it's not like you're right round the wanging corner, is it? You can't just drop work and drop Darrell and come over here.'

It hurt that her mum had held back from divulging this issue because she didn't want *Abby's* world to be rocked. It proved just how much time, energy and life force she had devoted to Darrell and her job. Time she could have, *should have*, redirected towards her family.

'And the Russians?' Abby asked. 'Where do they fit into all this?'

Right on cue a rowdy shout pierced the night and the sound of breaking crockery followed.

Melody shrugged. 'Igor's nice ... nicer when he's on his own. And ... he's rich. I thought it wouldn't hurt to get a few meals paid for, maybe a present or two. Mum was going to try and get Valentin to buy a couple of her more pricey properties ... but I'm not sure she's trying that hard.' She let out a shaky breath. 'And we really need to be trying hard.'

Abby shivered, the warm breeze making way for a shot of cold as the reality that things were so tough her mum and her sister were almost pimping themselves out to make ends meet hit home.

'OK,' Abby said confidently.

'It's not OK,' Melody replied, wiping her nose with the back of her hand. 'We're down to our last thousand euros. You didn't have three courses tonight, did you? Or fillet steak?'

'No,' Abby shook her head. 'And I'm paying.' She took hold of her sister's hand and squeezed it, suddenly realising how young Melody looked, how vulnerable. 'And it's going to be OK.'

'I don't see how. I can't take on any more extra jobs. I'm already working for the boat hire company delivering fliers as well as Desperately Seeking and the dancing and I've been making time for Igor this week in case he decides to leave early.' Melody sighed. 'If I could just get him to take me to Corfu Town for the day I know I could get him to buy me a designer handbag or maybe a diamond bracelet, just enough for a couple of supermarket visits would do.'

'I don't want you to keep doing that,' Abby interrupted. 'I'm going to help now I'm here.'

'You're going to hook up with Andrei?' Melody asked. 'I know he isn't quite as hot as Igor but—'

'I'm not going to hook up with anyone.'

Melody shook her head, smiling. 'Still hopelessly devoted to Darrell.'

Abby swallowed and quickly forced a nod and a smile she didn't feel. 'I'm going to help with the business.'

'But you can't tell Mum I've told you things are bad. She'll kill me. And you haven't been to visit for ages. You're supposed to be having a holiday, not working.'

'Well I'm not going to sit on the beach soaking up the sun while you two go bankrupt, am I?' Abby said. 'And we'll tell Mum I know together if you like. Then she can kill us both.'

'Oh, Abs, I'm really glad you're here,' Melody said, squeezing her hand tight and looking like she might descend into more tears.

'Come on,' Abby said. 'Let's go home now. It's late. We'll get a good night's sleep and tomorrow we can start revitalising the business.' She took a deep breath, her eyes going from her sister to the road, the edge of the facade of Desperately Seeking visible behind a palm. 'Starting with a tin of white paint.'

Fifteen

San Stefanos Village

Seven am. Theo was awake and, for the first time in weeks, he was completely sober. Spyridoula, as predicted, had patronised The Blue Vine until almost 2am with her bridge-playing friends, ensuring he had to stay working until the end *and* help Hera clear up. It had been surprisingly hard work. Lifting barrels, taking orders – making sure to get everything just right – mixing cocktails and trying to stop himself from ejecting the table of Eastern Europeans. He had told Hera they were drinking their own vodka but she hadn't wanted to make a fuss. He, on the other hand, was going to ensure they did not make themselves so comfortable the next time they appeared at the bar. And there *would be* a next shift for him, he'd decided – just to keep the peace, until he found himself something more suitable or the need to move on returned. There was no denying he could do with a new focus, but he was going to make sure it was one of his choosing. He was also going to make sure his father was given no excuse to sell the family holiday villa.

Standing on the terrace, he gazed out over the view. Tiny clusters of houses nestled in abundant greenery that shelved gently towards the harbour. The sea ahead like a static sheet of blue glass – calm, restful, yet also enigmatic, its shape capable of change at any given moment. It was, he considered, just like life.

He took a long, slow breath inwards. There *was* something about San Stefanos that always seemed to settle him. Perhaps it was the perfect mix of countryside and seascape, the laid-back village life, or maybe it was just the distance from his old life. Miles away from the rush and tear of a multi-million-euro business, life felt quieter, days here almost restorative. But, the moment he even *thought* about going back, his body's reaction still wasn't a healthy one.

'Ow!'

The squeal drew Theo's attention to the road below. There was Abby, a few hundred metres ahead. It appeared she had just dropped a large wooden easel on her foot and now two plastic pink flamingos were falling to the road.

'Ugh!' Abby squealed again, reaching down to rub her bare toes. 'Bloody flamingos.'

Theo laughed, then very quickly realised, the sleepy village being so quiet at this time of the morning, every sound was audible. Abby looked up and he didn't wait for their eyes to connect, he ducked down, taking shelter behind the pillared wall. Still looking, he held his breath. What was he doing? Why was he hiding? And why was he compelled to watch in the first place?

'*Kalimera*, Abby, daughter-of-Jackie.'

Theo focused through the gaps between the pillars at the sound of his aunt's voice, a resting yellow butterfly taking flight as his breath caught its wings. And then Spyridoula came into sight, walking towards Abby from the harbour. His aunt would spot him at once. He scooted for the sanctuary of the villa.

'*Kalimera* … it was Spyridoula, wasn't it?' Abby answered with a grimace. Her foot was still throbbing.

'Yes, that's right,' the woman answered, stopping and stooping to pick up one of the pink plastic birds. 'What are you doing?'

'Oh,' Abby began. 'Well, I'm just helping my mum and sister with the business, and you said the whole village wants the pink gone so ...'

'I also say you have a few days. It is very early in the morning,' Spyridoula remarked. 'There was no hurry for this. The sun is barely awake.'

'No,' Abby said. 'And neither is my mother.'

That was why she was doing this now. Getting rid of as much pink tat as she could manage before her mum opened her eyelids. She might not even confess to begin with. She could blame a strong Corfiot wind ... She just needed to remove enough bubble-gum colour so that Jackie wouldn't be able to able to protest when she appeared with a tin of white emulsion later. A lick of neutral, yet fresh, colour and a more traditional sign. Something in olive wood.

'Business is a little slow, huh?' Spyridoula stated, bracelets jangling as she reached into her designer leather handbag for her sunglasses, the sunshine becoming brighter.

'No, no they are busy,' Abby reacted immediately. 'Super-busy. Completely sooo busy.'

'Humph,' Spyridoula sighed. 'That is a shame.' She touched her chignon. 'Because I know of a very nice villa that needs to be valued. I think, being not an expert in these things, it would be close to two million euros.'

'It would?' Abby asked, her heart beginning to thump.

'But I will go to see Aleko at Ionian Dreams. I hear he is offering special treatments—'

'No!' Abby gasped. 'No, there's no need for you to do that. We will ... I can ... if you let me know the address, sorry.' She had temporarily forgotten that not much on Corfu *had* an actual address. 'Let me know where it is and I will get my mum or my sister to visit straightaway, or whenever is convenient to you, of course.'

Spyridoula smiled. 'Any time before twelve today would be convenient.' She pointed, across the road and upwards to a rather attractive looking, two-storey villa painted peach. 'Villa Pappas.'

Even to Abby's untrained eye, just from its well-kept exterior, it looked worthy of a place in the pages of a luxury home magazine. Getting rid of the pink was one thing, but if she could head back to the house before breakfast with a two million euro property to value, Melody and her mum were going to be thrilled.

'Desperately Seeking will be there today,' Abby stated confidently. 'Before twelve.'

'*Poli kalo*,' Spyridoula said with a smile.

'Thank you.' Abby picked up the second flamingo as the woman moved past her.

'Daughter-of-Jackie,' Spyridoula called, turning back to face her.

'Yes?'

'Dispose of the pink away from the main street, yes?' She made circles in the air with her fingers. 'Behind.'

'Yes.' Abby nodded. 'Yes, of course.'

The sun scorching her shoulders she leant on the easel, catching her breath, eyes going to the wonderful view. No matter the hard financial situation her mum and sister were in, Corfu, beautiful green, luscious Corfu, was both their workplace and home. The scent of honey and fresh bread wafting from the nearby tavernas hit Abby's senses and she was suddenly struck with a feeling of loss. Her dad had loved this place. He had left so suddenly and dramatically and then her mum and Melody had left too. And now she didn't have Darrell – or Poldark – she was truly, completely on her own. Tears building in her eyes, she felt her body curl into that default position of the-world-is-against-me slouch that really required a bag of Kettle Chips. *Get a grip, Abby.*

'*Kalimera*,' the soft, low tone of a male Greek spoke.

Abby straightened up, banging her elbow on the easel, securely gripping a flamingo. '*Kalimera*,' she answered.

The man was possibly in his fifties with thick dark hair, a little speckled with grey. Wearing dark trousers and a loose white linen shirt, shiny black shoes on his feet, he looked like he was ready to attend a special occasion. He looked a little familiar. He smiled at her and pointed.

'You have Jackie's flamingos.'

'Yes,' Abby answered. 'I'm taking them … to … be cleaned.' Why had she had lied? If they ended up in the village skip then everyone was going to know about it.

'To be clean?' the man repeated.

No going back now. Abby nodded. 'My mum, well, we are … sprucing up the business, you know, making smarter … good. *Poli kalo.*'

The man nodded. 'You are Abby.' He extended his hand. 'I remember,' he said. 'And I see photograph of you dressed like a kangaroo.'

Shaking his hand, Abby blushed. That damn photograph from the dress-up day at school! Melody had been dressed up like some sort of Australian Ray Mears while she had got the short straw – literally – when Jackie had bought a supposedly one-size-fits-all kangaroo costume from the fancy dress shop. It was on display back at the house along with several other gawky shots.

'I am George,' the man told her. 'From George's Taverna, just at the end of the road.'

'Hello,' Abby said. 'It's lovely to meet you. *Xero poli.*'

'*Ki ego.*'

Then she gasped. 'I remember you, and I remember your restaurant. I went there once when I was little. It has blue-and-white tablecloths and bright blue chairs with ... wind chimes made of shells.' She felt her cheeks redden as she spoke. She remembered the restaurant hadn't been there the last times she had visited because she had looked.

He smiled widely then. 'Yes, it does. But I have moved a little, down the road. It is a little smaller than it used to be.' He took a breath in. 'There have been hard times here, as I am sure you know. I have had to ... what does Jackie say?' He looked to the sky, as if the heavens would help him find the word then looked back to Abby. 'Downsize.'

'I'm sorry to hear that.'

He waved away her concern like it was of no importance at all. 'It is no matter. And this season I am busy again, almost like old times.'

'Do you still do the fish with lemon?' As she said the words, Abby could almost taste it. Beautifully cooked light-as-air fish in natural juices enhanced only slightly with lemon and pepper.

'Of course,' George answered. 'My mother's recipe.' He smiled. 'You must come. Try this again.'

'I would love to.'

'Tonight,' George stated.

'Well ...'

'Seven thirty. I will reserve the best table.'

'Oh ...'

He put one hand on the easel and looked at it. 'How you clean this?'

'Well, I was going to ...' Suddenly her eyes found the shoreline, small white-tipped waves caressing the sand. 'Wash it in the sea.'

She wanted to kick herself. *Wash it in the sea?!* She smiled, hoping that George would just nod and move along from her craziness.

'I take this,' he said instead, swiftly picking up the easel.

'Take it?' Abby queried.

'I will paint,' he said. 'I make it white instead of pink. This will be good.'

Was this the George who had painted her mother's house? George from the taverna all those years ago? Abby opened her mouth to reply, unsure what she was going to say, but George was turning back the way he had come, the easel tucked under his arm. She had to say something.

'But,' Abby called out. 'We can't afford to pay you.'

George was a good few Greek strides ahead now and appeared not to have heard. She looked to the flamingos in her hands and sighed. 'And then there were two.'

Sixteen

Desperately Seeking

'Do you think English food or Greek?' Jackie asked, glittery pen in her hand, poised over a pad of paper.

'For dinner?' Melody asked. 'Well, I was hoping that Igor might take us to that gorgeous restaurant in Kassiopi called Tavernaki. You know, the one that does the most to-die-for steaks.'

'I meant the food for the Desperately Seeking party,' Jackie replied. 'Most of our clients are English, aren't they so ...'

'But they're coming here because they want the Greek dream,' Abby piped up. And she had inadvertently booked a table for dinner at George's tonight.

They were sat on the small oblong of terrace outside the business, at one of the quite tasteful rattan-and-glass tables, a palm providing a little shade. Abby was trying to navigate her mum's rather ancient laptop to get a good grounding of what sort of properties they had on the books, how long they had been for sale, prices etc., before she announced her big news about Villa Pappas.

The sun was already centre stage, lighting up the sand and shingle beach and sprinkling the sea with flecks of bright white, then warm amber. Having whisked her arms, face, chest and legs with factor thirty, Abby was enjoying the chance to sit outside without the need to have an anorak in her handbag. And, if her mum and sister weren't in such dire straits *and* if she hadn't had another text from Darrell this morning, she could almost be relishing this sunshine break.

'How about a mix,' Jackie said, turning her attention to Abby. 'Proper English sausages from that place in Sidari with some feta cheese on sticks.'

'Bleurgh!' Melody said. 'That sounds disgusting.'

Abby looked to her sister. She was doing exactly what Abby had asked her to do while their mum was getting ready this morning. She was subtly and quickly de-pinking the display in the window. Abby's vision was for them to re-brand Desperately Seeking with a sleeker, cleaner, more professional style and Melody had concurred. It wouldn't take much to knock up a logo and print off new details for the properties. A banner for the window display might cost a little bit. She would maybe go to Acharavi later and find out how much. Maybe it would have to be a banner *or* the olive wood sign.

'What are you doing, Melody?'

Jackie had looked up from her notepad and Abby stopped tapping the laptop.

'Nothing,' Melody said quickly, standing stock still like a mannequin, one salmon-coloured sheet of paper in her hands.

Melody hadn't sounded at all convincing for someone who had been so adept at insisting she was showing a house, not dancing at a bar last night.

Jackie gasped and got to her flip-flop-clad feet. 'Where are all the details gone?! And my easel! And ... where are my flamingos?!'

'Abby ...' Melody said as Jackie began padding towards her, a furious look on her face.

'I bet it was Aleko! Or that Spyridoula Pappas! She walks along with her rich nose in the air saying "good morning" but really meaning "clear off". She's very close to Hera at The Blue Vine and she's practically best friends with the head of the council.'

Abby swallowed. Her mum didn't like Spyridoula? But the Greek woman was giving them the opportunity to value her villa. Unless it was somehow a poisoned chalice ... Abby shook her head. No, this was ridiculous. Her mum was just down-on-her-luck and thinking everyone was out to sabotage her. It was time to come clean.

'Mum, sit down,' Abby said softly.

'Why would I want to sit down? I've got a party to plan, you two are destroying my new branding ...' Jackie plucked the details of a one-bedroom wreck in Agios Gordios from Melody's fingers. 'And someone has stolen my flamingos!'

'They haven't been stolen,' Abby said quickly. 'I've ... relocated them.' She swallowed, an image of the skip coming to mind. The plastic birds nestled with lemon rind, plastic bags full of used toilet paper and a child's trike.

'Relocated them?' Jackie asked. 'Where?'

'Mum,' Abby begged. 'Please. Sit down for a minute.'

'She knows,' Melody said boldly, hands going to her hips.

Jackie looked from Melody to Abby and back again. 'Knows what?' The voice was faint and tentative.

'I told her,' Melody continued. 'About how we ... haven't got very many euros to rub together.'

Jackie suddenly inhaled like she had been deprived of oxygen for hours. Waving a hand dismissively she picked up her notepad and, eyes down, began to write. 'Things aren't that bad.'

'Oh, Mum!' Melody exclaimed, flapping her arms up in frustration. 'They *are* that bad!'

'Well,' Abby cut in, 'they have to be pretty bad to be spending time with awful men just to get given expensive gifts you can sell.'

Jackie sent a furious look Melody's way but her sister folded her arms across her chest and stood her ground.

'Mum, I don't know why you didn't tell me about it before, but right now that isn't the most important thing,' Abby continued. 'I'm here. And I'm here to help.'

'You're *here* on holiday, to spend time relaxing, enjoying the Corfiot sun, sea and *saganaki*.' Jackie forced a smile a second before she plumped back down into her seat as if all the wind had been taken from her sails.

'No,' Abby said. 'I came to see you. You and Melody. To spend time with you both.' She drew her mum's notebook away from her, taking hostage of the sparkly pen. 'And we are going to spend time rejuvenating Desperately Seeking.'

Jackie sighed heavily. Melody sat down next to her and gently pushed her cup of Greek coffee towards her. 'We've tried everything.'

'I don't believe that,' Abby replied quickly.

'We've dropped our commission rates,' Jackie pointed out. 'We gave away car bumper stickers ...'

'They were awful,' Melody remarked. 'Most of them fell off because of the heat. Stathis does still have one stuck to his bicycle though.'

'We did an email mailshot offering a free no-strings-attached valuation ...' Jackie carried on.

'People got that and then went and signed up with Ionian Dreams to get what he was offering at the time – a free lunch at the Eucalyptus Taverna.'

'I've done everything I can think of,' Jackie rephrased.

'And disregarded most things I thought of,' Melody added.

'For good reason,' Jackie snapped. 'And don't think I like the dancing now any more than I did when you started it.'

'It's kept us in bread and feta!'

'OK,' Abby interjected, hands out, palms towards the table in a bid to de-escalate the issue. 'There's no point in going over old ground. What we need to do is prioritise, then refocus and move forward. Together.'

Jackie nodded but the expression wasn't quite mirrored in her eyes. 'But, apart from throwing a party, we really have tried everything. I don't see how—'

'Well, I've made a list.' Abby swallowed, knowing some items were not going to be easily accepted. 'It's just a few things that I've implemented at The Travellers' Rest.' She turned the laptop towards her mum and Melody, then desperately tried to reposition it so the sun's reflection wasn't interfering with the visual.

Despite the reaction lenses of her glasses starting to kick in, Jackie was squinting. 'What does that say?' she asked. 'White paint?'

Melody began to shake her head, red nails going to her lips.

'Yes,' Abby said confidently. 'I'm sorry, Mum, but the pink really has to go.'

'Go?' Jackie queried. 'What d'you mean by "go"?'

There was only one way to handle this. Bravely. Quickly. With a lot more confidence than she actually felt.

'We're going to paint the outside white,' Abby said, getting to her feet and rushing to the entrance of the shopfront. 'Get rid of all the pink.' She splayed her hands across the doorframe as if to highlight the point. 'It's too … fuchsia. It's not selling "Greece" or "the sunshine dream". It needs to look more … relaxing. Tranquil.'

As the last word was out of Abby's mouth, a giant carpenter bee flew past her nose with the drone of a light aircraft. She shrugged quickly, not letting it break her stride. 'We can get it done in a morning and then, this afternoon I'll pop into Acharavi and see if we can get a new sign made. I was thinking olive wood.'

'Olive wood,' Jackie said as if it were a rare species.

'I thought it would look nice,' Abby said. 'Desperately Seeking ... ingrained in a lovely piece of traditional material.'

'Olive wood's pricey,' Melody remarked. 'There's a fruit bowl in the window of a shop there for over two hundred euro.'

Was there? That seemed a bit steep. Did it have to be olive wood? Was there something else they already had they could recycle maybe? No, not recycle, *upcycle*. That was the word she used when she wanted Kathy to take on board an idea or three back in Romsey.

'Well, driftwood then, something that gives a real flavour of everything that's around us.' Abby looked to the sea, breathing in and letting the delicious sun, salt and countryside do its thing. 'The life we're trying to sell to the customers. Carefree, permanent peace and summer days.'

'I think white would look nice,' Melody joined in. 'We could accent it with some plants. Lavender's cheap and easy to look after and the smell always makes me feel relaxed.'

Abby had said the same herself only a few weeks ago about UK lavender, which had nothing on the fragrance of Greek lavender. Abby looked at her mum who was staring out at the sea view as if her mind was lost out there in the wide blue yonder.

'Mum,' Abby said softly, waiting for the turn of head that quickly came. 'It *is* going to be all right.'

Jackie swallowed and nodded, pushing her glasses a little further up her nose. 'I know,' she sighed. 'We have the house. I mean, I've avoided remortgaging, but if we have to, then—'

'What?!' Melody exclaimed. 'Mum! You can't do that! It's our home! The only thing we have that no one can take from us.'

'Let's not get ahead of ourselves,' Abby said quickly. 'Let's see what we can come up with before any drastic action is taken.' Now was her moment. Now was the perfect time to tell them about the villa valuation ...

'Are you sure you've got time for this, Abby?' Jackie asked. 'I wanted you to come here and have a lovely time.'

'I will be having a lovely time,' she reassured her mum.

'Can't Darrell come out for a bit?' Jackie said. 'If we need to paint he could paint. I remember him being a dab hand with it when you moved into your lovely flat.'

'Don't forget that gorgeous feature wallpaper too,' Melody added.

Abby swallowed, maintaining an expression only ever mirrored on a passport photograph. 'He would be here if he could, but you know how it is with his work.' She did an eye roll worthy of being immortalised in a gif. 'It's all, you know, power meetings and ... intense negotiations.'

'Poor Darrell,' Jackie remarked, picking up her pen. 'It sounds awful.'

'It sounds like he's making a lot more money than us,' Melody quipped.

'Well,' Abby jumped in. 'Not for long.' She smiled. 'Let's talk through this list I've made before I have to go out.'

'Go out?' Melody queried. 'Oh, I see, talk a good talk and then you're off down the beach while I get hot and heavy with emulsion!'

Abby shook her head. 'No, I'm going to help you with that. I just have something to …' Where was she planning on going with this? 'Pick up from the bike-hire shop.'

'What?' Melody asked.

'A … bike.'

'You're hiring a bike?' Jackie queried.

Abby nodded. 'Yes. It's cheaper than hiring a car and it will keep me fit. It's a win–win.'

Melody snorted and threw herself down into a chair. 'You're not wrong. Have you looked at the terrain? You're going to at least need an electric one if you want a chance of getting anywhere.'

Abby's eyes went to the green hillside above them and she wondered, firstly, just how many fibs were going to spill from her mouth before lunch and secondly, if the valuation didn't go well, whether she really would have to hire a bike.

Seventeen

Villa Pappas

Abby was walking up the incline to the villa Spyridoula had pointed out to her earlier. Houses weren't in any kind of ordered streets up here, it was more like someone had rolled the buildings like dice, uncaring of where they settled. Apart from the view. She was sure that all of the properties here benefitted from a spectacular scene from their windows and outside spaces.

It was balmy, the air thick, the sunshine warm on her bare shoulders as she fanned her face with her hands and tried to stop herself from perspiring before she got to the house. She needed to look professional and sweat stains were not professional. She wanted to go into this meeting representing Desperately Seeking as well as she could. But she was starting to panic, and wished that she had told her mum and sister where she was going.

There were multiple reasons she hadn't mentioned it. One, was her mother's dislike of Spyridoula and the idea that somehow Abby had been duped and nothing was going to come of it. Two, she couldn't bear the thought of her mum or Melody pitching for this job and not getting it when they were both fragile. And three, she needed to prove to her new and improved, confident, single-and-loving-it-even-though-she-was-lying-about-it self that she could do this. She could win this property for the DS books. She was not on the business scrapheap just yet.

She stopped walking when she saw the sign. Villa Pappas. Engraved in olive wood. Gah! But it made sense. What would a sign costing a few hundred euros be to someone who owned somewhere like this? There was blooming clematis and striking red and purple bougainvillea trailing over the outside walls, together with corn marigolds and purple bellflowers visible just inside the garden. For a second Abby closed her eyes. It was like being in the middle of a fragrant field, surrounded by every summer scent you could imagine. It brought back every beautiful memory she had ever had. Sliding down riverbanks with Melody, getting grass stains on their shorts before rolling into the deliciously cold stream. Lying on their stomachs on the grass with egg sandwiches and mini pork pies, watching their dad play cricket. Cuddling up with Darrell in the sand dunes at Shell Bay ...

Abby snapped herself out of that particular memory and breathed in, the heat of the air almost scalding her lungs. It was time to get serious. It was time to get her mother's business and her own entrepreneurism back on track. And that started with nailing this property. She put her hand to the gate and pushed.

Ear buds playing a playlist titled Happy Pop Hits on Spotify, Theo was almost blissfully relaxed. Here, in this holiday bubble he could be anyone and no one. There was no demand on his time, his mind, or any other part of him. And that was one reason why he did his sunbathing this way. Naked. Every time he lay here he tried to shut off completely from the conformity he had spent the majority of his life living under. It wasn't that his father was an ogre, but he *was* the head of the family and, as such, he acted in the traditional way. He made the rules. The family followed them. And no one seemed to have bucked against that hierachy ever. Until now. He had left, turned his back and all manner of guilt was crushing him. He wasn't sure how he was going to get over that.

He shook his head as dark thoughts began to take over the upbeat music and the feeling of weightlessness and ownership of himself. He needed to tune into the space again, not let his mind work overtime.

And then a sound rang out far louder than the Rita Ora track he was listening to and he jumped, wrenching the ear buds from his ears and leaping from the lounger.

'God! I am so sorry! So sorry! I'm not looking! I am not looking, see, hand over my eyes, *completely* over my eyes.'

'Abby?' He couldn't be sure because the sun was now in his eyes and, having had his lids completely closed before, it was disorientating. Plus half of her face was covered with her hands as if she took in his image she would turn to stone.

'Yes,' she answered, feet swivelling on the spot until she was facing towards the pool. 'I ... that is ... Spyridoula Pappas asked me to come here to value the villa – for my mother's business, you remember – the one that was, but won't be for much longer, too ... pink.'

He was caught between looking for something to cover himself with – there was a tea-towel he had covered the jug of water with on the table a few strides away – and looking at her rather amusing display of embarrassment. But both of those things came second to the words 'value the villa'.

'I thought she would be here ... Spyridoula. I didn't realise anyone was staying here. That you were staying here,' Abby continued, head still bowed.

'I'm not.' The words were out before he had thought through the consequences. 'Well, I am. I mean, I am the gardener and the man who fixes things, just for the summer.' What was he doing? Why was he lying about who he was?

'Do you have any clothes on yet?' Abby asked, her voice a little tight. 'It's just smothering my face like this is making me rather hot.'

OK, now he really did need to find something to cover himself with because the thought of her being hot in any way at all was causing a rather speedy and obvious reaction in parts of him it would be inappropriate to share in this situation. And the tea towel was definitely not going to be big enough. His eyes went to the other side of the pool and an awful bright green inflatable lilo Leon had brought up to the villa. 'Give me one moment.'

One moment! She needed him dressed now. Before the image of his naked body was ingrained on her mind for all eternity. If it wasn't too late already. And what a naked body it was. The scream had been an immediate reaction to the desperate situation she had found herself in, completely unprepared for nudity. She had not been repelled by what she'd seen – the opposite of repelled, if she was honest with herself – but also taken aback and unprepared. Eyes still closed, her brain continued to show her a replay of the lean, muscular, sculpted, olive-skinned torso displayed like the most beautiful artwork. While she was screaming, just before he had heard and jumped to attention, her eyes had roved as if desperate to roll over every bronzed inch of him. No soft lines here, it was all deep angles, strong curves and ... the complete opposite to Darrell. She swallowed, a bead of perspiration forming on her brow. She stuck out one finger, three and a thumb still covering her eyes, and removed it. Darrell had been her Mr Right. She had been so sure of that. And perfection came in lots of different forms. Except some people were just *everyone's* idea of perfection and she had a feeling that was Theo. And what handyman-cum-gardener sunbathed naked in someone else's garden anyway?

'You can look now,' Theo spoke. 'Stop being so hot.'

Abby swallowed again, tentatively removing her fingers and wondering just what she was going to find. The answer was the naked man was still there, just with an inflatable held over his intimate parts. It only meant the toned pecs and ab-tastic stomach were more obvious. *Professionalism*. She was here representing Desperately Seeking.

'I was not expecting anyone,' Theo stated.

'I think that was quite obvious.' Abby concentrated on getting a rather nice checklist she had redesigned and printed off out of her handbag.

'This morning I did some gardening,' he continued, waving a hand towards the bordering bushes. 'This afternoon I will be chopping wood and ... sweeping.'

She was no Alan Titchmarsh but, in her opinion, looking at the overflowing borders, he could have gone a little further with the secateurs. And who chopped wood in the middle of the summer?

'Well, that's very good. To be busy.' She didn't know what else to say to a man wearing a floating bed. 'I will just be looking around, noting things down and then I will be out of your way.' She sniffed, making a tick at the top of her list for no apparent reason other than deflection.

'Please,' Theo stated. 'Let me put on some clothes and I will give you a tour.'

'Really,' Abby said. 'There's no need. I can—'

'I insist,' he answered. 'Give me one moment.'

He moved then, backing away across the terrace, the inflatable bed still held firm over everything she had already seen. Until he reached the bi-fold doors and seemed to realise fitting through with something so wide attached to him wasn't going to happen. He turned, flinging the lilo down to the flagstones and giving her an excellent view of his rather peachy backside as he disappeared inside.

Abby closed her eyes, then turned back to the equally beautiful view of the harbour below. San Stefanos really was so much different to Romsey.

Eighteen

'It's so beautiful.' Abby stood at the pillared wall overlooking the whole of the bay of San Stefanos. Theo, now dressed in black jeans and a grey vest, stood alongside her. It really was the whole tranquil-yet-buzzy-Greek-village package from up here. You could see everything, even pick out some individuals. Stathis on his bicycle, moving a lot more sedately than anyone walking. Maris from the supermarket, arms full of special-offer cans. Some of the guys from San Stefanos Boats throwing ropes and guiding tourists safely from the pontoon.

'How old is the property?' Abby asked, pen in hand and poised over her working sheet.

'It was built in 1990, or thereabouts. I think that is what Mrs Pappas said.'

He was an idiot. Why had he claimed to be a worker here and not the son of the owner? What was that going to achieve apart from making Abby think he was deceitful and dishonest? However, knowing that his father really did seem to intend to put the property on the market was eating at him. Maybe it was better Abby didn't know he had any sort of vested interest for now. The appearance of impartiality was safer all round.

'And Spyridoula is the owner.' Abby made to write again. 'Do you spell that with an "i" or a "y"?'

'The house belongs to her brother.' He swallowed.

'Oh,' Abby said. 'Usually we would take instructions from the owner.'

'Well,' Theo stated. 'I am certain the instructions will have come from him.'

'What's his name?' Abby asked. 'Do you happen to know?'

He nodded. A snapshot of his father appeared front and centre in his mind's eye. 'It is Dinis.'

'Right, D-e-n ...'

'D-i-n-i-s.'

'Great. Thank you.' She turned away from the view and took the steps towards the infinity pool that formed the rest of the boundary on this side of the property.

It was a superb villa. He had never truly appreciated the luxury when he was growing up, but, seeing the reaction from a fresh set of eyes always made him think he should have been more grateful for the opulence back then, even if, to some extent, he was turning his back on it now.

'This pool and the view. I think it will sell this property all on its own.' She looked at him, smiling. 'And I haven't seen inside yet.'

He knew she would think the inside was just as outstanding as the rest of it, or would be, had he made any effort to tidy up. But he didn't really want to sell its merits when he didn't want it sold at all.

'There are only three bedrooms,' he said quickly. 'And the lounge area is compact.'

'Can I see?' Abby asked him. She had her phone out now and was busy snapping photographs. 'I'm just taking these for now but, if Mr Pappas decides to go with Desperately Seeking, we will get some professional shots done to really show off the villa.'

He didn't want that. He knew a house in this area would be snapped up as soon as the details were loaded on the website. North-east Corfu was a property hot-spot. 'It's this way.'

The house was just as *lovely* – as her mum would say – internally as it was outside. Marble floors throughout with beamed ceilings in light wood, a modern kitchen with every convenience, three en-suites, a family bathroom and a lounge/diner that could easily host a dinner party for ten. To Abby, that wasn't compact but, she supposed, if you compared it to the vast terrace and outside entertaining space it was significantly smaller.

'Mains water and electric I'm assuming,' Abby said, her eyes still drawn to the vistas from every window. The views to the side and rear were of the mountain, its ruggedness swathed in green – cypress, carob and olive.

'Yes,' Theo replied.

'Any gas?' She turned then to look at him. He still looked a picture of hotness in those jeans and a vest that had slits up both sides, exposing almost as much torso as when he'd been topless. She had got decidedly flushed when he'd taken her into the master bedroom. His clothes, including Calvin Klein underwear, had been on the floor and he had hastily gathered them up, while she had looked at the bright white, yet crumpled bedsheets his gorgeous form had no doubt been lying in earlier. She cleared her throat and felt the need to prompt. 'My mum has those gas bottles.'

'Yes,' he answered. 'Here on Corfu we have many power cuts. We cannot always rely on electricity for cooking.'

'I didn't see a barbecue,' Abby commented.

'There is one,' Theo answered. 'You would like to see?'

'It's just for this list. My mum likes to have all bases covered.' Abby smiled. 'She's very professional.'

'You say this already.'

'Have I?' Abby asked. 'Well, she is. *We* are.' She cleared her throat for a second time.

'You work here now?' Theo asked, leading the way back towards the patio doors. 'I thought you were here for a holiday.'

'It's a combo, you know, like … KFC.' She swallowed, realising immediately how stupid she sounded but somehow unable to stop. 'A little bit of everything.'

'So, what is next for you today?' Theo asked as they stepped back out onto the terrace.

Immediately the fragrance of the blooms in those well-stocked traditional brick planters skirting the tiles filled Abby's nose. What she wouldn't give to have a place like this at her disposal. The sea almost within touching distance, a divine pool to dip into when the temperature hit sizzling and air-conditioned luxury only a few steps away … She shook herself. Corfu had been her mum's dream. *Her* dream had been keeping a steady job and feathering her nest with Darrell. Reality bit hard.

'I will be going back to the office, typing up my notes and preparing a valuation for Mrs Pappas …'

'Spyridoula,' Theo interrupted. 'She is not married.'

'She's not? Sorry. I do keep assuming things, don't I?' Abby said. 'Has she ever been married?'

'No,' Theo began. 'I mean … perhaps. I do not know. I do not think so.'

'Sorry, that was very nosy of me,' Abby said.

Theo smiled. 'It was very San Stefanos of you.'

She laughed then. 'My mum always says you can't suck the honey out of a baklava without everyone in the village knowing about it.'

Why had she used the word 'suck'? Her mother's stupid saying was to blame! And now she was stuck thinking about sucking delicious, sweet, sticky, honey while looking into the dark mocha eyes of a handsome Greek.

'Your mother is right,' Theo replied.

Now she was looking at his full lips, imagining he was sucking the baklava ...

'And then,' Abby powered on, mouth moving as quick as she could make it. 'I'm going to head into Acharavi to arrange some fliers for the business, coupling about fifty of them with an invitation to our party.' There was no stopping her now. 'You should come. There's going to be food and wine and ... a chance to win a fabulous prize.' Where had that come from? They had vaguely discussed a raffle but on Desperately Seeking's limited budget she really should limit the use of the word 'fabulous' when they might only have enough money for a bottle of supermarket own-brand champagne.

'When is the party?' Theo asked, appearing to be finding some amusement in her verbal diarrhoea.

When was the party? They hadn't actually firmed up a date. And she really did need a date if she was going to add the invitation section to the fliers she had planned.

'Saturday.' It was out of her mouth before her brain had processed 'stop'.

'*This* Saturday?' Theo queried.

She nodded, trying very much to keep her expression at 'jubilation' and not 'holy shit'. 'Yes, my mum is really keen to give everyone in the village a real taste of her plans for the rest of 2018 and beyond.'

'What time is the party?' Theo asked.

'The afternoon. One o'clock.' Well, that was settled.

'I will come,' Theo answered. 'As long as I do not have to work.'

'Good,' Abby said. 'That's ... lovely.' She really must not turn into her mum, although perhaps developing some familiar traits might win her favour when she announced they were holding the party on Saturday. She would be lucky if Melody didn't kill her. Or at the very least pull all her hair out.

'And the valuation?' Theo asked. 'How much do you think this property is worth?'

She paused before answering. She had had a figure in her mind from the moment they had finished the tour of the inside. Now, gazing out over the cove, drinking in the total beauty of the surroundings, there was absolutely no doubt in her mind. This was a property not unlike a villa Ionian Dreams was marketing for 2.5 million euro.

'I'm afraid that's something I can only share with Spyridoula and Dinis Pappas,' she answered. 'But, if Desperately Seeking gets the instruction I'll be setting up details on our website.' She smiled. 'And the whole village will know before the first bite of baklava.'

'Very good,' he replied.

'So, I think I have everything I need for now.' She slipped her sheet of jottings into her handbag and adjusted the strap on her arm. 'I'll head back to the office and prepare the valuation and you can get back to your sun lounger.' The flush was rising up her neck within milliseconds.

'I have ... wood to chop,' he reminded her.

'Of course,' she answered, taking steps towards the path that led to the gate as a vision of him, naked, wielding a chopper came to the fore. 'Wood.'

'*Yassas*, Abby,' Theo said, waving a hand.

'*Yassas*,' she called back, breaking into a jog.

Nineteen

Desperately Seeking

'Saturday!' Melody exclaimed. 'This Saturday?! Are you out of your wanging mind?'

Abby smiled confidently as she plucked an olive from the small dish on the table outside the agency. It was a smile just like the one she had the time she had convinced Kathy to bring forward a tea dance at The Travellers' Rest to coincide with Remembrance Day. It had been a stroke of genius that had seen bar takings doubled and their almost out-of-date jam for the scones all used up. She was hitting her sister and their mum with the slightly nerve-racking news first and then she was going to tell them about the opportunity at Villa Pappas and turn those frowns upside down.

'Oh, Abby.' Jackie whipped off her glasses. 'But there's so much to do. The food and the drinks and the lookalike and—'

'Well, I think the sooner we re-launch the business—' Abby took a breath, '—brighter, whiter, fresher, the more quickly you can stop clients heading to Ionian Dreams for free spas.' She smiled. 'Plus, we need to get invitations out before Alex, or whatever his name is, can come up with a similar plan.'

'Aleko,' Jackie said. 'His name's Aleko.'

'Yeah but, Abs, Saturday?!'

'It's settled,' Abby said. 'I've already invited someone so we can't change the date.' A memory of Theo and that honed physique – *all of it* – came back to mind.

'Who have you invited?' Melody asked. 'You've only been here five minutes.'

'Well,' Abby said, whipping her checklist out of her handbag with flourish. 'That's my other bit of news.' Did she want to sit down? Or keep standing? She was buzzing with nervous, excited energy she hadn't felt for a while. Not since the redundancy and the dumping anyway.

'You *are* getting married!' Jackie exclaimed, hands going in the air, raising up from her chair like someone had put a firework underneath it. 'You've been to Corfu Town to arrange the paperwork and Darrell's on his way and—'

'No,' Abby said quickly. 'Goodness, sorry, I … it *is* exciting but not a wedding.' Now she felt like the real news wasn't going to be anywhere good enough, such was her mum's thrill that there still might be nuptials in the mix.

'God, Mum, weddings aren't the life blood of everything,' Melody replied with a tut. 'She's been like this since Prince Harry said he was tying the knot. And she watches way too much *Say Yes to the Dress*.'

Abby placed her checklist onto the table, smoothing the creases and letting the satisfaction move through her like a sweet wave of euphoria.

'What's this?' Jackie asked, glasses back on, eyes on the paperwork.

'It's a client. Well, a potential client, a property,' Abby said. 'That I went to see this morning.'

'You went to see a property?' Melody leant over the table. 'You're going to live on Corfu?! Well, it had better have been one on our books … Wait. Who showed it to you?'

It was time to stop the confusion and spell things out.

'Villa Pappas,' Jackie read from the sheet.

'Yes,' Abby said. 'I went to see it today. I took photos, filled out the list, added all the details and I'm hoping you're going to be able to do a formal proposal for it.'

'What's this here?' Jackie asked, pointing at the very top of the page. 'These numbers.'

'That's what I've valued it at,' Abby said proudly.

'Wanging hell! Does that say two point five million euro?' Melody exclaimed.

'I might not have drawn the euro sign quite right,' Abby answered.

'Mum! Two point five million euro! Is this for real?' Melody asked. 'Two per cent commission of that is like … a lot.'

'Oh, Abby,' Jackie gasped, mouth so wide a flying beetle could have dropped in, landed and built a nest.

This was it. This was her moment. The moment when her mum was going to express excitement, delight, unabashed pride at what she had achieved. It was going to be the start of an upturn for Desperately Seeking. So she couldn't stop Darrell from falling for the charms of a protein-shake enhanced younger model or hold on to her almost-management position, but she had done this. And it was two point five million euros' worth of opportunity.

'You can't have valued it right,' Jackie reached out and patted Abby's arm.

What? She didn't know what to say.

'Did you do the Light and Airy Test?' Melody asked.

'The what?' Abby inquired.

'Stand in the middle of every room and assess the natural light.'

'It's a beautiful, contemporary yet traditional villa,' Abby stated.

'Ah,' Melody said nodding. 'You see, can things really be contemporary *and* traditional?'

'Darling, I know you're trying to help but—' Jackie began.

'No!' Abby exclaimed. 'Stop! Please, just stop!'

She hadn't meant to shout so loudly. Her eyes went to the road. A group of tourists had stopped still, a little blond-haired boy, mid-ice cream-lick, staring at her. Cicadas stopped chirping. She swallowed, turning back to her mum and sister.

'Sorry. I know I don't know as much as you do about properties overseas – or properties at all, really – but I have done some research and I know, well, I am almost confident, that this house is *really* worth two point five million euro.' She took a breath, trying to re-install her earlier confidence. 'At least.'

There suddenly seemed to be a lull, like someone had pressed pause on the conversation and Abby's gaze went from her mum to her sister and back again in quick succession, waiting for something to happen.

Melody moved first. Snatching up the checklist from the table, eyes roving over Abby's notes, she began reading aloud.

'Three bedrooms, all with built-in wardrobes and sea views. Marble floors. Kitchen with fridge freezer, dishwasher, instant boiling water tap … Mum! An instant boiling water tap!'

'Let me see!'

Abby smiled, watching her family finally getting as excited as they should be.

'Did you take photos?' Jackie asked, managing to prise the notes from Melody's fingers.

'Almost fifty,' Abby admitted.

'Let me see them first!' Melody exclaimed, almost vaulting the table to reach her.

Twenty

Acharavi Beachfront

Spyridoula had texted Theo. A little too late.

> Someone is coming to value the house. Be nice. Be
> dressed. Spyri x

He had been nice. One out of two wasn't bad. But the fact
that his father was doing this still wasn't sitting well. Was
Dinis really going to go through with it? Or was it all bravado?
A case of playing chicken, seeing which one of them would
give in first? Did Theo need this familiar sanctuary in Corfu
enough to save it by returning to the business he had run away
from? And would Dinis sell the property and their memories
just to prove a point?

His shift at The Blue Vine had started an hour ago but
when he had arrived Hera had been flapping around declaring
the world was going to end. Three pallets of Fanta Lemon
had been wrongly delivered and Theo had been sent to retrieve
them from one of the tavernas on the beach front of the main
town in the north of the island. And, as was customary and
polite, he had accepted a coffee before heading back.

Sitting on a green-painted wooden chair at the edge of
the white pebble beach, Theo took in the view ahead of him.
Turquoise waves rolled in and out, shushing onto the stones

and creating a fresh, crunch of sound. It really did soothe even *his* troubled soul, which was ironic, given that the sea was partially responsible for the way he was feeling this summer.

And then something came into his vision: a car, but not one moving at a normal pace, this one was creeping along the beach road. It was small and silver and he couldn't see that it had a driver. He got to his feet, taking off his sunglasses and tentatively stepping towards it.

Abby's calves were on fire. This was probably why Darrell had chosen Amber over her. She was betting if Amber's car broke down she would be able to break into a jog while pushing it, not be sweating like a jungle celebrity about to be shoved into a space helmet contraption and have spiders put in their hair. She felt like she had spiders in her hair now, but she knew it was just perspiration from the raging orb in the sky that was being particularly unhelpful in her latest dilemma.

She pushed harder, letting out a groan akin to a strongman attempting to pull a truck and then collapsed onto the door she was holding, her body folding through the open window as she gasped for air. What was she doing? How far did she think she could push this vehicle? How long before someone came to her aid?

'You have a problem?' a male voice asked.

Multiple problems were the answer. Armpits that were practically dripping, a core wound tighter than a particularly awkward jar lid, and stones in her sandals. She was beginning to wish she had hired that bike!

'The car,' she panted. 'It won't start.' As she lifted her face up she saw who had asked her the question and as the realisation dawned she bumped her head on the top of the door window. Quickly moving her body out of the space she coughed, brushing dust from her dress and standing straight.

'Abby,' he said, shaking his head.

'Theo,' she replied. 'What are you doing here?'

'It seems like I am about to try to fix a car,' he answered, striding towards her.

Abby swallowed, watching him confidently move up to the vehicle in his beautiful jeans and uniform polo shirt. Yes, he had clothes on this time ...

'What happened to it?' Theo asked, standing by the bonnet.

'I parked outside the printers on the main street, ordered my flyers, came back out, turned the key and it started fine.' She let out a sigh. 'Then I turned down Beach Road Three because I wanted to see if the little olive wood carving shop was still there, and halfway down the engine cut out.' She swallowed. 'What do you think is wrong with it?'

'I do not know,' Theo answered. 'You will have to pull the lever inside the car for me to open it up and look.'

'Oh!' Abby exclaimed. 'Sorry.' She ducked her head back into the vehicle and ferreted around beneath the glove box. Locating the lever, she pulled and there was the sound of a light metallic release. Theo pulled up the bonnet and disappeared behind the sheet of steel.

'Do you know about cars?' Abby asked, moving to stand next to him.

'I know a little about mechanics,' he admitted. 'More boats than cars.'

'So,' Abby said. 'Boats, bars and ... trimming bushes.'

She wanted the ground to open up and for her to be sucked into the Upside Down and devoured quickly by the Demogorgon. Her cheeks began to flame like she had a fever. Why had she said that? Trimming bushes!

'I can see nothing obvious,' Theo remarked. 'It has fuel, yes?'

'Well,' Abby began. 'I did ask Mum about that and she said the gauge is faulty. She said it's been saying it's empty for the last month so ...' As she said the words her awareness began to kick in. 'There's no fuel, is there. Why didn't I just put some in it?' She wanted to kick out at something. She levelled a sandal at the front tyre, her toes taking the whole of the impact.

'Ow!' she exclaimed.

'Are you OK?' Theo asked, standing up straight and sweeping some stray strands of his hair back from his face. She'd decided the man bun was hot. It wasn't quite Jason Momoa, more Tyler from *Neighbours*, but it was a pleasing style she had never really thought about before. And she didn't know why she was thinking it now. Men were off the page for her. Men let you down. Men kissed assistants they shouldn't be kissing over baked goods.

She nodded, toes throbbing. 'Yes.'

'Well, my car is just there,' Theo stated, pointing to a large flatbed truck bearing The Blue Vine company logo. 'I can take you to the petrol station then bring you back and fill up the car.'

'Can you?' Abby asked. 'Are you sure it won't be any trouble? I can always call a taxi.'

'Leon will be working in his family's shop this afternoon,' Theo said.

'Is he really the only taxi driver in San Stefanos?'

Theo smiled. 'You do not remember how Greece is?'

'I do.' Abby blew out a still-flustered breath, fanning her flaming face with her hand. 'In that case, a lift to the petrol station would be great.'

'No problem,' Theo replied, slamming the bonnet back down and brushing the dust from his hands as he came over to her. 'And the olive wood shop you were looking for. It is no longer there on Beach Road Three.' He wet his lips. 'But there is another not far from here. I can show you if you like.'

'Thanks,' Abby said. 'That would be great.' She crossed her fingers behind her back and prayed olive wood signage wasn't going to be as expensive as her sister had made out.

Twenty-one

The Olive Way Workshop,
Near Pelekito

After a visit to the petrol station the car had taken a good few turns of the ignition to restart and it was obvious that Abby was feeling nervous about its ability to continue to run. She was following while Theo drove in the direction of the workshop in the woods he had once spent a whole summer in.

Pulling off the main road he followed an earth and gravel track as it wound around groves of olives. Bent and withered old trees sat alongside new growth, the black 'catching' nets at the base of each trunk. Goats grazed at the side of the road, an old lady dressed all in black, head covered, waved her stick in greeting as he passed. And then the building came into sight. It hadn't changed a bit.

The outside looked as rustic as the trees surrounding it. A mishmash of strips of wood and corrugated iron all layered up like a collection of scrap someone had abandoned. He smiled as he parked on the scrub outside and wondered just what Abby was going to make of it.

The scent of woodland in the searing heat hit him and he was transported back to being a teenager, always looking for trouble. That's how he had ended up here, at Stamatis's workshop. A dare to break-in, to steal something, had ended with Theo being caught between a lathe and a rather long, slim and slightly pointed spindle. The owner's fury had been more than obvious. Theo had pathetically begged for leniency back then, so his father didn't find out, and Stamatis had given him a job. Those first few days hand-sanding the wood had been so hot and so hard he had almost wanted to risk the wrath of his father rather than continue enduring it. But then he'd watched Stamatis make a bread board, a relatively simple, rectangular block of wood, yet planed and waxed and cared for so delicately, the older Greek man could have been handling a newborn baby. Stamatis had caught him studying his technique and he'd nodded and smiled, seeming to know just what Theo was thinking. Tuition had followed, and Theo had spent the whole summer ankle-deep in wood shavings every afternoon, enjoying the freedom of expression, suffering the old man's terrible coffee and learning that rebelling wasn't constructive to anyone, especially himself.

Getting out of the car, he walked up to the property, drinking it in in more detail. Were there any changes other than dilapidation? Or was it like time had stopped from the moment he had last left? Perhaps the fence towards the back was different ...

He turned as he heard a car door slam and there was Abby on the rough grassland, looking a little overheated. Her hair was tousled and she was shooing away mosquitos with her hands as she walked towards him.

'This doesn't look like a shop,' she remarked as she reached him and surveyed the higgledy-piggledy mess.

Theo smiled. 'It is the best olive wood shop in this part of the island.' He reached out and touched her shoulder. 'Come.'

*

The contact – his fingertips on her bare shoulder – made Abby catch her breath. It was like someone had opened a jar of strong pickled onions and made her inhale. She was flooded by an overwhelming urge to indulge but, all at the same time, run away from the intoxicating suggestion of male contact. No matter how minute the touch had been.

'How do you know about this place?' Abby asked, words forcing recovery as she stepped behind him. 'You said you don't live here.'

'I ... have spent a number of summers on Corfu,' he replied.

'Working as a gardener or a barman?'

'For some of the time,' he answered, pushing at the door. 'Come, please, I know the owner. He will be able to give you a good price on whatever it is you would like to buy.'

The large door in a patchwork of wood creaked open and the sight inside made Abby unable to decide where to look. It was like Aladdin's cave, except there were no rich jewels or royal treasures. Instead there was sawdust, fine sand and wood-chips on the ground and, suspended from the roof of beams and girders, were pieces of olive wood in varying states – raw chunks complete with bark, cleaned and honed sections and others that looked like they had been planed into shape and waxed. All were hanging like floating wooden panpipes, as beautiful as the finest adornments, strings of lights wound around the roof casting every piece in a warm glow that made the olive wood almost sparkle.

'This is ...' Abby breathed. 'Amazing.'

'Yes,' Theo answered. 'It is.'

'I've not seen anywhere like this before.' She stepped forwards, wanting to reach up and touch the thick timber. The smell was extraordinary. It was like being in the very depths of a forest, which, she supposed, they were. She stepped further in, ducking her head a little under a low-hanging striped chunk.

'Can I help you?'

The loud, low, Greek gravelly voice made Abby stop and she bumped her arm against a shelving unit. She reached out quickly, steadying an ornate ceramic pot. A tiny man had appeared, wearing a dirty brown leather apron over his trousers and a short-sleeved shirt. The booming voice didn't seem to match his appearance.

'Hello, Stamatis,' Theo said, stepping forwards.

The man's face lit up like there had been a power surge and he rushed towards Theo, arms wide, his impish frame clapping the taller man in a hug that was both firm and emotion-filled.

'Theo! Where have you been? When did you arrive in Corfu? How long do you stay? Are you here to work?'

Abby watched Theo take hold of the old man's hands, squeezing them with affection as the two regarded each other like long-lost, life-long friends.

'I am here for the summer,' Theo answered. 'I hope.'

'And you have brought someone,' Stamatis said, looking to Abby.

'Stamatis, this is Abby, she is a … someone I know from San Stefanos.'

'*Kalispera*,' Abby said.

'*Kalispera*,' Stamatis answered, leaning in quickly to kiss Abby on both cheeks. He then looked back to Theo and shook his head. 'Your hair is too long. You begin to look like a girl.'

Abby couldn't help but smile as Theo's hands went to the bun tied at his nape. The older man's opinion was obviously important to him.

'Abby would like to buy something in olive wood.'

Stamatis laughed then. 'Something?' he queried. 'You do not know what it is she would like to buy?'

'A sign,' Abby answered. 'I just need to know how much it would be first.' She swallowed, a little embarrassed by her lack of funds. 'We have a number of things we need to get so we're prioritising a little.'

'A sign,' Stamatis said. 'For a house? With a name?' He turned away, beginning to walk into the bowels of the workshop.

'It's for my mother's business,' Abby said, following quickly and fearing she may lose him. 'It's called Desperately Seeking … you know … if you charge by the letter …' She really hoped he didn't.

'A Sea King?' Stamatis queried, turning as he walked, his dark eyes observing her. 'You talk of Theo?'

She had no idea what he meant. 'Seeking,' Abby repeated. 'To look for … I don't know the Greek for that.'

'Always on the boats,' Stamatis chuntered. 'The King of the Sea like his father.'

Theo's heart was thudding in his chest. He needed to turn this conversation into something else and quickly. 'The place is full, Stamatis. Is business not so good?'

'What?!' Stamatis exclaimed, continuing his walk through the myriad of offcuts into a zone of metal and scrap akin to a breakers yard. 'The place is full because business *is* good.' He huffed and puffed. 'When has business not been good?'

The old man's idea of good business was very different to his father's. Stamatis thought business was good if he could afford to eat at the end of the day. Anything over and above that was a bonus. But at least it had directed his attention away from talk about boats …

Finally, they came out of the souk-style passageways into an open space filled with machinery, but mainly the traditional kind. There was still nothing more hi-tech here than a couple of electric saws.

'What shape?' Stamatis asked, picking up dust-covered spectacles from a bench. 'What size?'

'Oh,' Abby began. 'I hadn't really thought about it.'

'You want this to be round? Square? Rectangle?'

'I'm not sure ... rectangle I suppose, to fit the name on ... unless we have the two words one on top of each other.'

'Stamatis,' Theo said. 'Show Abby some of the signs you have made.'

'Come, come,' Stamatis said, beckoning them on.

Theo watched Abby's eyes taking in all the somewhat crazy adornments on the walls of the workshop – buttons, doorknobs, clips and moulds – some used in decoration, other items used as tools. She had the same wide-eyed combination of fascination and bewilderment that he had had on his first visit. But now, to him, it didn't feel odd, it's quirkiness felt warm and familiar.

'One like this, I make for the hotel in St Spyridon,' Stamatis said, picking up what Theo could see was a very heavy, long sign and passing it to Abby. He watched her steady her footing as she grappled with it. 'Modern. With sharp, staccato lettering,' Stamatis explained, reaching for something else. 'This one I have just finished for a garage. With metal pieces.' He went to pass that to Abby too but Theo stepped in, taking it from the old man.

'They are so lovely,' Abby stated. She looked like she was struggling to hold the hotel sign up.

'This one is for a garden centre,' Stamatis continued. Theo watched as he trailed his wrinkled fingers over the notches in the wood. There were delicate engravings of a butterfly, a ladybird and three-dimensional flowers.

'This one is beautiful,' Abby admitted, finally shifting the sign, putting it down and propping it up against a shelving unit.

'You would like creatures?' Stamatis inquired.

'No ... I don't think so,' Abby replied. 'But I like the way the characters stand out. How much would it be for something like this?'

'This size? With things that stand out?' Stamatis queried.

Theo watched Abby nod. If he was to guess it would be in the region of three to four hundred euro. It wasn't just about the materials, it was about the skill involved.

'For you, a special price. Three hundred euro,' Stamatis said.

Theo watched Abby's expression and knew she was holding back on revealing her thoughts about the proposed figure. Obviously, *her* finances, or her mother's, were not going to be able to stretch to olive wood extravagance. He made a show of checking his watch. 'I'm sorry, Stamatis, we have to go. I have to get back to The Blue Vine.'

'You work at a bar?' the man queried.

'Yes, and we should head back now.'

'I make the sign for you?' Stamatis queried, looking at Abby. 'With Despair Sea King?'

Theo went to respond but Abby beat him to it.

'Can I think about it?' she asked. 'Come back?'

'Yes, yes, yes, this is no problem,' Stamatis stated, putting the creature-embellished sign back on one of his work benches.

'It was nice to see you, Stamatis,' Theo said, watching the old man get back behind his favourite work bench and ready himself for carving.

'I am always here, Theo,' the old Greek answered. 'If you want to *not* work in a bar.'

Stamatis's words fell heavily on Theo's conscience. He hadn't been here for quite some time, even when he had visited Corfu. It wasn't good form, to neglect someone who had been such a steadying influence when he had needed it. He swallowed, wanting to say something, say he would come and see him again …

'Thank you for showing me your lovely work,' Abby said. 'It really is beautiful.'

Stamatis waved a hand and then the cavernous workshop was filled with the heavy sound of a circular saw.

Twenty-two

San Stefanos Harbour

Three hundred euro was a lot of money, Abby thought as she drove back into the village. But Stamatis's signage was classy, stylish and traditional – perfect for her vision of the new, improved Desperately Seeking office. *Her* vision. Was it really OK to make such important decisions for a business that wasn't hers? Suddenly, slowly, it was seeping into her that whether this was a holiday or not, her life had changed substantially, completely and when she went back to the UK nothing was going to be the same. She needed to make sure that Corfu didn't become a necessary prop that, once removed, would see her directionless.

But there was that gorgeous cerulean sea to her left, a soft wake rolling into the harbour from a passing ferry, small speedboats tethered to the pontoon, some tourists disembarking from their day on the water. It was another gorgeously hot day, the kind of day where you could almost smell the word 'perfect'. A lightness filled Abby then, along with the knowledge that being in this beautiful, sunshine bubble was better than OK, even if it was temporary.

Suddenly ahead, Theo's car was braking – fast – and Abby had to thump her foot down hard to emergency stop. Thrown forwards, she inhaled a sharp breath, relieved there was no crunch or bang, then, looking out she began to see the cause of the abrupt halt. Cows. Lots of them. And at the centre of the chaos was Melody.

Putting the handbrake on, then cutting the engine, Abby got out, the heat wrapping itself over her bare shoulders.

'Wang off! Shoo! No! Not that way! Back up here! Towards your field, you know, *home*!'

'Melody! What's going on?' Abby walked forwards, stopping at Theo's car as he too got out.

'That was a joke, right?' Melody asked. Her face was crimson, hair all over the place and she was holding a rather spectacular diamante high-heeled shoe in one of her hands. 'There's bloody cows in the road! Traffic's at a standstill, they're eating the special-offer figs from the supermarket and they've pulled one of Mum's flamingos out of the skip! You can imagine how well that's gone down!'

'How many are there?' Theo asked, slipping on his sunglasses and surveying the scene ahead.

'I haven't had time to count them,' Melody answered. 'More than too many!'

'Do we need to call the farmer?' Abby asked. A rather large brown-speckled cow was striding toward them, a handful of serviettes hanging out of its mouth.

'He will not be there,' Theo answered. 'He will be at his mother's house in Episkepsi.'

'What do we do then?' Abby queried. The nearest she had got to cow-wrangling was pinning a rosette to a prize-winning one when The Travellers' Rest had sponsored an event at the New Forest Show.

'We need to get—' Theo began.

'*Ela! Ela!*'

It was Spyridoula, immaculately dressed as she was earlier, but carrying a plastic bucket she was shaking, bracelets vibrating. Calling out in Greek, she meandered down the road, waving to people like she was leading a carnival. The cows were rushing towards her, all other mischief abandoned.

'*Mila.*' Theo finished his sentence. 'Apples.'

'Cows like apples?' Abby queried, watching with curiosity.

'Like tourists like Greek dancing,' Theo answered with a smile. He walked towards the Greek woman who was appearing to revel in being the cow whisperer.

Theo plucked two apples from the bucket his aunt was holding. 'Is this the first time this year the cows have escaped?'

'Honestly, Theo, you really think this is the first time?! Panos is a *malaka*. He does not fix the fence well enough. He always disappears when there is trouble. And no one else in this village remembers how to cure this problem! They stand around with their hands clapped to the side of their faces, mouths open like they are going to swallow whole families of mosquitoes. I do the same thing every time this happens. Get the apples! What they are all going to do when I go I do not know!'

'Go?' Theo queried. 'Go where?'

'We all will die one day.'

'Not that speech again.'

'It is true.'

'It is premature.'

'No one knows when there day will come, Theo.'

Spyridoula looked a little wistful as Theo poked an apple under the nose of a dark-brown cow who was currently enjoying nibbling one of the flags of San Stefanos Boats. She seemed to compose herself. 'Do you remember when one of them ended up on the roof of George's Taverna?'

128 • *Mandy Baggot*

He nodded, a smile forming. He did remember because he had spotted the cow himself. On the beach, aged ten, chasing his brother and sister with fuzzy algal balls, he had been distracted by something large and oddly placed in his line of vision. A big black-and-white cow was making its way across the flat roof of the taverna, completely unperturbed. Theo had raised the alarm, his father rushing into action to prevent the cow from causing damage and to stop it falling off the top of the building and harming itself. It had taken almost the whole village, some ropes and the lure of apples to get the cow safely back down again.

'I still have no idea how it managed to squeeze its body up the iron stairs,' Spyridoula said, shaking her head.

'Can I help?' Abby asked, approaching the pair.

'Maybe behind us?' Spyridoula suggested. 'Make certain we have all of them on the move.' She offered her bucket. 'Take some apples.'

Abby dipped her hands into the bucket and removed three. 'Apparently a cow ate one of Diana's shoes.'

'Oh,' Spyridoula stated. 'That is something we will never hear the end of.' She reached out to the closest cow who looked like it was losing interest in her offerings and smacked it on the rump. 'And, daughter-of-Jackie, Abby, please tell your mother that her valuation and quotation has been accepted by my brother. Please begin to market the villa. He will email signed copies of the documentation.'

'Really!' Abby exclaimed. 'I didn't know she had, that is … I mean, that's brilliant. Thank you.'

Theo's heart sank. This was not what he wanted to hear. His father was obviously determined to set in motion the sale of the family holiday home. Another reminder that his leaving home and the business was still not accepted by Dinis Pappas.

He held his tongue, waiting for Abby to disappear, jogging down the street to ensure the cattle were following the apple trail.

'*Ela!* This way!' Spyridoula called to the cows.

'I'm doing what he wanted,' Theo said, dropping an apple to the ground.

'What?' Spyridoula queried.

'My father,' he continued. 'I have a job at The Blue Vine, like he wanted, I am paying my way.'

'I know,' Spyridoula answered softly.

'Then why is he still selling the house?' He had tried to keep his voice even. To not let out the depth of emotion he was feeling.

'Perhaps you should be the one to talk to him,' Spyridoula suggested.

All at once, goose bumps broke out on his skin like the hot and humid air had suddenly turned cold. Talking hadn't worked before. In fact, he hadn't been allowed to talk. His father had issued the orders, he had reacted unfavourably and ... here they were.

'And maybe, instead, I will not bother to waste my breath.'

'Theo—'

'What?' he snapped back. 'He is going to sell the house because he wants to punish me? For an expert businessman, he makes some very stupid decisions.' He threw an apple to the ground.

'Theo—' Spyridoula began again.

'I have to get to work,' Theo rushed out. 'And Dinis, we all know that he will do whatever he wants, just like always.'

Seething, anger pulsing through him, he left his aunt and the cows and headed towards the bar where at least he could take his frustrations out on the kegs in the store room.

'Theo!' Spyridoula called. 'You cannot leave the car in the middle of the street!'

Twenty-three

The Dolan House

'I can't believe it.'

Jackie had said this sentence at least five times during the rest of the afternoon. The smile also hadn't left her face, even when they were all coating the outside of the property in white emulsion that had almost blinded them because of the glare from the sun. Now they were at home, getting ready to go out to celebrate the new house on their books.

'We know,' Melody stated. 'You said so. At least a hundred times. Anyone would think that we'd never had a customer before.' She leaned over the sofa to look into the large mirror on the wall behind and apply some thickening mascara she had been crowing about since the lady had delivered her Avon products. Abby was still wondering why Avon products were a necessity when they were strapped for cash.

'Well we haven't had one for quite some time,' Jackie reminded her. 'And not one with a property valued in the millions.' She sighed, contentedly. 'And it was accepted so quickly.' She slipped some earrings into her lobes and fought Melody for some space in the mirror. 'I dropped the paperwork through Spyridoula's door and almost within a couple of hours, just after that cow debacle, there was the email acceptance.' She sighed. 'I half-thought she would have got Aleko to quote too.'

'Maybe she did,' Melody responded. 'Maybe we actually beat him to the prize.'

'That would be lovely, wouldn't it?' Jackie said, smiling.

'It would be a kick in the day spa,' Melody replied.

Abby smiled from her seat near the window that overlooked the village road outside. She was enjoying watching her family getting ready. They had had a productive day working on Desperately Seeking's external décor and the flyers-cum-invitations for the party were going to be ready to pick up the next day. Everything felt a little more stable than when she had first arrived. A pinch more control was back in her life.

A knock at the door had Melody drawing the mascara wand away from her eye. 'That will be Leon with the taxi.'

'What?' Abby asked, sitting forward.

'To take us to Kassiopi,' Melody stated with a shake of her head, wild hair unmoving thanks to being anchored down by a liberal spraying of something from a purple can.

'But, we're going to George's Taverna.' Abby got to her feet. 'I told you that earlier. I booked a table for seven thirty.'

'But Tavernaki is so much classier,' Melody replied. 'And the patitisio is so good and … Igor said he might be going there.'

'Melody!' Abby exclaimed. 'We talked about this.'

'No, *you* said you didn't think I should be hanging out with them. *I* didn't reply.'

'But they're so rude and loud and you said you were mainly doing it for the money and I'm trying to ease the money situation so—'

'Well, Mum said she'd rather go to Tavernaki too,' Melody interrupted as there was another knock on the door.

'Mum,' Abby said. 'You don't really want to chase after Valentin, do you?'

'God, he is so rich,' Melody put in. 'Like richer than ... who's rich at the moment? Still Mr Ikea?'

'It's fine,' Jackie responded a little wistfully. 'We can go to George's if you've already booked.'

'Why wouldn't you want to go to George's? You loved George's when we came here with Dad.'

It was one of Abby's most vivid memories of that long-ago holiday. That beautiful night in the cosy, homely, authentic taverna, candles on the tables, the soft lilt of the mandolin and accordion-playing from a wizened Greek in the corner of the room, her parents both smiling for the first time since her father's health scare, holding hands, drinking plum-coloured wine, Melody covering her eyes in an over-the-top fashion every time a fish dish was brought to the table.

'It's not the same place you know. He's moved,' Melody interrupted. 'You saw that, right? Basically only ten tables. You can hear everyone's conversation, if there's anybody else actually there.'

'*Yassou!*' It was Leon, calling from outside. 'The taxi is ready for you.'

'And we're going to be letting Leon down now,' Melody continued.

'Well, I booked for George's and I don't want to let *him* down,' Abby said. She was also itching to be back in that quaint setting surrounded by feel-good memories, smaller or not. 'I'll go and speak to Leon.'

'I may as well change my shoes,' Melody sulked. 'These heels will be wasted hidden under a rustic tablecloth.'

Abby left her grumbling sister and now-turned-quiet mother to answer the door. Pushing down the handle she opened the door to the bright sunlight and a smiling, high-haired taxi driver whose eyes immediately appraised the whole of her knee-length peacock-coloured summer dress and beyond.

'Abby,' he greeted. '*Mia xara fenese! Poli omorfi.*'

She blushed immediately. *Very beautiful.* What was it with Greek men? They all seemed to have that ability to make you feel special just with the tone of their voice. For some it was probably a practised technique, for others it seemed like it was written through their DNA. She shuddered, suddenly remembering the naked form of Theo. From. Every. Single. Angle …

'I take you out,' Leon continued, leaning a little closer to her. 'To the best restaurant in Kassiopi with your family. And then, later, I will take you dancing.'

'I … can't,' Abby began. 'We can't.' She straightened up, coming back into the moment and not giving head space to the type of fantasy they used to sell Müller Whipped Greek-Style Corners. She swallowed. 'I'm really sorry, Leon, but we've double-booked.'

'You jest with me?' Leon asked.

'No,' Abby said. 'Sorry. There were crossed wires, I mean, I booked a table somewhere and Melody arranged something else and—'

'You do not need me,' he replied, sounding the epitome of disappointment.

'I'm really sorry,' Abby said. 'Shall I pay for your time?' She didn't want to be paying out anything she wasn't getting the benefit from, but she was also very British and that meant she couldn't let someone be put out because of her mistake.

He shook his head. 'No euro. Instead …' He smiled, as if an idea was forming. 'You will now be ready to come to the *panegyri* with me.'

Why hadn't she sent Melody to the door to deal with Leon? Why did she feel so beholden to George and that booking *he* had really made while he was taking the easel from her? Perhaps she should have just given in and agreed to go to Kassiopi.

'I ... still don't know if I'm going to be staying until the end of the month,' Abby reminded. It wasn't a lie. She really wasn't sure how long she intended this 'holiday' to be.

'But if you are here,' Leon said, 'you will come with me?'

What to say? He was nice, friendly and wasn't about to charge her a taxi fare she could ill-afford. What harm would it do to agree? She probably wouldn't even be here.

'OK,' she answered.

'OK?' he queried. '*Endaksi?*'

'*Ne,*' Abby said. '*Endaksi.*'

He practically lit up like Blackpool Tower. Then he reached out, taking her hand in his, bringing it to his mouth and softly pressing his lips to her skin.

'Don't mind us!' Melody said loudly, brushing past Abby and stepping out of the house and onto the street.

'Sorry again,' Abby said, releasing her hand.

Leon waved her apology away. 'It is nothing. I will look forward to a night of dancing very soon.' He backed away towards his slightly beaten-up car.

'Night of dancing?' Jackie asked, making her appearance at the threshold.

'It's nothing,' Abby dismissed with a sigh. 'I felt I had to make amends for not taking the taxi and he asked me to go to the *panegyri* with him.'

Leon's car started up, smoke billowing from the exhaust and the engine making sounds akin to a washing machine on full spin with a caught-up bra strap and a load full of loose change.

'You know how Greek men dance, right?' This came from Melody who then began coughing as the carbon monoxide mixed with the humid evening air and infiltrated her lungs.

Abby didn't really remember. The last time she'd been here was with Darrell and he hadn't been into the folklore of the island.

'It's practically like having sex on a dance floor with everyone watching,' Melody continued, waving her hand in front of her face to dissipate the fumes. 'Don't Facebook it if you want to keep Darrell.'

Abby ignored her sister's comment and turned to her mum who was still surprisingly quiet. This time though there was that hundred-watt smile, eyes shining.

'You're staying for the *panegyri*,' Jackie stated, breathy and excited.

'Well, I …' What could she say now?

'Oh, Abby, this is so lovely!' Jackie exclaimed, grabbing her by the shoulders and enveloping her tight. And there was that true, pure affection Abby missed so much, the kind she thought she had had with Darrell. Her mum's light, fruity, perfume swirled up her nose, reminding her of simpler times … She suddenly wanted to cry. And out came a squeak like a baby sloth waking from an intense nap.

'Are you all right?' Jackie asked, holding her away from her body, a concerned look on her face.

'Yes,' Abby said quickly, urging her emotions to group-hug and get on with things. 'It's just … Leon's car.' She coughed.

Jackie linked their arms together, smiling. 'And you thought *my* car had problems.'

'Are we going now?' Melody called, pouting into the wing mirror of a parked car. 'Because I'm wanging starving.'

Twenty-four

The Blue Vine

He could call his siblings. As Theo mixed up a cocktail shaker's worth of Singapore Sling his mind was still on overdrive, working out how best to tackle this latest problem. Maybe his attitude had already been discussed over a family dinner. His brother would have sat there stuffing as many *loukoumades* into his mouth as he could while agreeing with Dinis. Meanwhile, his sister ... she would be quiet, saying nothing, wanting peace, preferring to waive her opinion for the sake of harmony. Or maybe neither of them knew everything. Perhaps their father had painted a different picture for them. Just that their foolish, wayward brother would amount to nothing now he had decided to leave the family business.

'Theo!' Hera called. 'Are the cocktails ready?'

The bar was busy. Every table outside was full and inside there were a number of groups taking shelter from the intense heat, ordering cooling drinks and light bites of pitta and dips as chill-out vibes filtered from the speakers.

He shook the metal container a little harder, taking his frustrations out on the mix of alcohol. Perhaps a little anger would create the perfect blend. 'One minute,' he replied to Hera.

He popped the lid and expertly poured the mixture into six glasses. His bar-work experience was coming back to him the more time he spent here. He topped each high-ball glass with a cherry and added a straw. Then, in his peripheral vision he noticed Abby, with her family, making her way past.

She was wearing a simple yet striking dress that made the most of her hourglass figure, hair gently lifting with the slight sea breeze as she walked, completely unaware of her own attractiveness. He couldn't help but think back to earlier, him naked at the villa ... then later, her reaction, not to his body, but to one of the places he loved so much – Stamatis's studio. Swallowing, he wet his lips, the other, slightly bitter feelings overriding attraction. Their estate agency was going to sell his family's Corfu home and he absolutely loathed that.

'Hey! Wake up!'

It was Leon, leaping up onto a bar stool and clicking thumb and forefinger in front of Theo's face.

He came back into the moment, beginning to carefully pick up the glasses and position them on a tray. 'You would like a drink?' he asked his friend. 'Singapore Sling?'

Leon went to take one of the high-balls and Theo speedily shifted them out of the way. 'Not these.'

Leon laughed. 'Look at you! Such a professional barman now!'

'You are having a drink?' Theo asked again.

'I will have a beer,' Leon replied. 'I am celebrating.'

'You finally have told your *yiayia* that you do not like her galaktoboureko?'

'Are you out of your mind? I can never tell her that!' Leon exclaimed. 'And neither can you! You promised, Theo!'

He smiled. 'Calm down. Your secret is safe with me.' He pulled the top off a bottle of Mythos and handed it to Leon.

'Ask me then!' Leon said, still animated. 'Ask me what I am celebrating.'

Theo gave a good-natured sigh. 'What are you celebrating?'

'I have a date,' Leon said, grin wide, eyes alive.

'Really!' Theo exclaimed. 'You have finally given in to the charms of Maris from the supermarket?'

'No!' Leon exclaimed. He leaned across the bar a little, lowering his voice. 'No, this is a real date.'

'I'm intrigued.'

'I asked Abby to be my partner for the *panegyri*,' Leon informed. 'And she said yes.'

His gut straightaway reacted to this news and he found he had to steady his hand a little on the glasses. Why did he care about this? It was just a village party, hardly high stakes in the scheme of things. And by the time *panegyri* day arrived he could be ... anywhere he wanted. The world was literally his for the taking, he just needed to find his direction, make it more about moving on than running away.

'That sounds good,' Theo replied, coming out from behind the bar and picking up the tray of drinks.

'That is all you have to say?' Leon asked, cradling his beer bottle.

'Congratulations,' Theo added. 'We should have a *panegyri* before the *panegyri* in honour of this occasion.' He hadn't meant to sound quite so cutting. He didn't mean it, not really. He took a breath. 'Sorry, Leon. I'm just busy here. Hera will fire me if I do not get these cocktails to the customers.'

Leon laughed then. 'Who would have thought it? You concerned about a job.'

He smiled at his friend, but the comment made his skin bristle. He never used to be flippant and unprofessional, concerned only for himself. The self-enforced break from employment had altered only his current outlook, not his whole person. He wasn't unreliable or untrustworthy.

He took a breath, stepping out of the door, checking for traffic, then made his way to the table of customers by the water waiting for Singapore Slings.

'Your cocktails,' he said, smiling as he began to put the glasses down in front of the customers.

'Hey! Bring us drinks!'

The loud Russian voices were unmistakable. Theo continued to deposit the cocktail glasses down, concentrating on not disturbing the liquid which would ruin the cherry display on top.

'Hey! You cannot hear?' the voice called again. 'We want drinks!'

Finishing with the cocktail glasses, Theo shoved the tray under his arm and turned, noticing the group of men now occupying a table at the back of The Blue Vine's outside seating nearest the sea. His first thought, as he moved towards them, was at least they seemed keen to actually make a purchase. His second thought was they really did need to learn some manners ...

'Please.' It was Hera, stepping in front of him before he could reach the Russians. 'Theo, I need your experience with cocktails behind the bar. They are my most expensive drink on the menu apart from champagne.' She smiled. 'There is the table of ten and three other tables drinking them tonight.'

He looked over at the men, one of them now trying to stick peanuts to his forehead, then reverted back to Hera. 'They give you any trouble and—'

She placed a hand on his arm, smiling. 'I know,' she answered. 'I will call Spyridoula.'

Her humour made him return the smile. 'I am not sure a bucket of apples will help in this situation.'

'No,' Hera agreed. 'But I have seen her deal with bigger bullies than these ones.'

Theo nodded, taking a step back. Yes, it was true, his aunt was a force of nature. Except now that force was empathising with her brother and it felt like the tornado was heading permanently in his direction.

Twenty-five

George's Taverna

The scent of roasting garlic, simmering tomatoes and a pinch of oregano invaded Abby's nose the second they arrived outside the cute little taverna at the end of the road. It was a scent that immediately made her realise how hungry she was and brought back all those long-ago feelings of joy, relaxation and total youthful contentment. It was almost as if Greece had been running through her veins in the background, just waiting for this moment of reignition. Why had she waited a whole year to come back?

'Oh, Melody, look!' Abby exclaimed, stopping before the step up into the restaurant and pointing into the room. 'It may be tinier, but he still has the dancing lady on a shelf.' There were rustic wooden shelves covering the wall behind the bar area, filled with an eclectic mix of items.

'An ugly thing covered in dust and spiders,' Melody remarked. 'New place but with all the same décor that's older than Lionel Richie.'

'Lionel Richie's still my favourite,' Jackie sighed. 'Next to Bryan Adams.'

'Don't you remember the doll?' Abby asked, disgruntled by her sister's dismissal.

'I remember why I wanted to go to Tavernaki tonight instead.'

'But you asked for her,' Abby said. 'You kept screwing your face up at the fish we were all eating and said you wanted to play with the "pretty dancing lady".'

'Was I drunk?'

'I remember it,' Jackie answered. 'And no, you weren't. You were only ten.'

'George got her down for you and you made her do Greek dancing around the salt and pepper pots ...'

A male voice interrupted. 'Then we try to put a small flower in her hair.'

It was the taverna owner they were talking about, dressed immaculately in black trousers, a pristine white shirt, tucked in, with a red cummerbund around his middle.

'Good evening, Family Dolan,' he said with a bow.

'Hello, George,' Abby greeted enthusiastically.

'Hi, George,' Melody said, sighing.

'Hello,' Jackie said, barely louder than a mouse squeak.

Abby looked to her mum. She had dropped her head slightly, and seemed to be looking at her rather sensible strapped sandals.

'Welcome,' George continued. 'For you, my best table.'

He held out his hand, directing them to a lovely round table in the corner, at the very edge of the taverna, each of its three chairs facing the sea view and the orange-turning-pink sun. It was covered with the blue-and-white checked tablecloth of Abby's memories.

The owner hurried to pull out a chair for Jackie, waiting for her to drop down into it before plucking up the white linen napkin and gently laying it across her lap.

'There's no need to fuss, George,' Jackie said brusquely. 'Not for us.'

'Have you got any watermelon gin?' Melody asked.

'What is this?' George inquired.

'Since when have you drunk gin?' Abby queried. 'Can we have a carafe of white wine please?'

'I don't want wine,' Melody stated. 'I want watermelon gin.'

'Mum,' Abby said. 'What would you like to drink?'

'Oh, I don't really mind.'

She had no idea what was wrong with either of them, but they were supposed to be celebrating the fantastic new property they had on her books and nothing was going to spoil that tonight, not if Abby had her way.

'George,' Abby said, sitting upright in her chair. 'Could we have a bottle of ... sparkling wine.' She had so wanted to say champagne, but she wasn't exactly flush and with the whole 'no-job-no-Darrell' situation she did need to be a little bit careful. But this moment needed recognition. This was her, helping her family get back on their feet, and with the plans they were putting in place, hopefully it wouldn't be too long. She caught Melody's expression, saw an immediate uplift at the words 'sparkling wine'.

'Very good,' George nodded, laying a napkin over Abby's lap.

She smiled and waited for him to depart before looking at her mum and sister. 'What's the matter? You were both a bit rude to George. I thought tonight was a celebration.'

'We wanted to go to Tavernaki,' Melody reminded her.

'I know, but—'

'We haven't been here since he re-opened,' Melody interjected.

'Melody!' Jackie hissed.

Abby didn't understand. She looked at her mum who had picked the napkin from her lap and was toying with it in her hands.

'Why don't you come here?' She swallowed. 'Has the food gone downhill since George moved premises?'

'We don't know,' Melody said in reply. 'Because we don't come here.'

'But why not?' Abby asked, this time fixing her gaze on Jackie.

'Mum doesn't really get on with George,' Melody informed.

'Ssh! Melody! Keep your voice down!'

Abby watched her mum react like a villain keeping a murderous secret from the police. Wide eyes, glancing over her shoulder, demeanour pitched at uncomfortable.

'What do you mean?' Abby asked tentatively. 'You said he did some painting at the house for you.'

'That was ages ago,' Jackie stated. 'When we first moved here.'

'Then what's happened since?' What else had the two of them been keeping from her?

'Nothing's happened,' Jackie said defensively. 'We've just been busy with the business and focusing our attention in a different direction.' She sighed, sounding a little frustrated. 'We haven't had the money to eat out all the time so he helped me and I couldn't help him, and coming here just ...'

Abby swallowed. She knew exactly what her mum was about to say, and she felt it too, so keenly already, just by being back in the ambience of George's Taverna. 'It reminds you of Dad.'

Jackie quickly nodded, then whipped the napkin off her lap and dabbed at her eyes.

'Sorry, Mum,' Abby said. 'I didn't think. I only thought about the good times and the great memories. I know things were hard for you when he was ill.'

'I thought this was meant to be a celebration meal?' Melody chipped in. 'Where's that prosecco?'

'Sorry,' Jackie said, sniffing hard. 'Melody's right. We need to celebrate. Your dad loved a celebration.' She smiled. 'It was any excuse if you remember.'

Abby smiled. 'He was Friyay-ing before it was even a thing.'

Jackie laughed. 'What about when he celebrated the car getting through the car wash without losing a wiper blade.'

'We had Chinese that night,' Abby stated.

'And a box of Maltesers,' Melody added. 'Each.'

Abby swallowed a knot that had arrived in her throat that felt about the size of one of Spyridoula's cow-luring apples. It was so nice to reminisce. Perhaps they hadn't done it enough.

'Listen to us!' Jackie said, her voice just a touch high-pitched, fingers still curled around the napkin. 'Talking about celebrating and not actually doing it isn't going to get us very far is it?' She cleared her throat. 'George, *psomi ke taramasalata, parakalo.*'

In her head Abby translated, dredging up the Greek she had tried to learn. Her mum had ordered bread and *taramasalata* – that gorgeous, pink, creamy fish roe dip.

Melody stuck her hand in the air like she was a schoolgirl trying to get the attention of a teacher. '*Saganaki ke tzatziki, parakalo* ... Abs, what are you going to have for starters?'

Saganaki was deep-fried Greek cheese and tzatziki, the famous yoghurt, mint, cucumber and garlic dip they did fantastically well on a Lidl's Greek Week, but it was nothing compared to the fresh Greek experience. Seeing her mum and sister getting happily animated over Greek food was giving her a warm feeling all over. Here, next to the gently swaying boats tied up in the harbour, the sunlight making the water glimmer, her own problems seemed a whole world away.

The beginnings of 'Summer of 69' rang out and Jackie let out a squeal as if she had no idea what the noise represented.

'It's your phone, Mum,' Melody said with an eye roll. 'That's your email sound. "Run to You" is a text. And Lionel's "All Night Long" is your ring tone.' She looked to Abby. 'She never remembers.'

George arrived at the table with a bottle of champagne. Abby checked out the label. She had definitely asked for sparkling wine. Perhaps she should have made sure that had translated to Greek as 'the cheap stuff not the expensive stuff'.

Jackie pulled her mobile from her handbag and began tapping at the screen. 'I know I shouldn't be on my phone at dinner. I know there's nothing worse … so Diana says if anyone dares pull one out at Pow Wow and Pikilia … but it might be business.'

'It won't be,' Melody answered. 'She says this a lot. It will be some Sparks card offer from M&S.'

'Do they still have M&S in Corfu Town?' Abby inquired, still half-observing George and the champagne.

'Why?' Melody asked. 'Does Darrell need some more socks to wear with his sandals?'

Abby shook her head. 'I told you that was a dress-up day for his work.'

Jackie let out a shriek at the same time George popped the cork from the bottle of whatever-it-was. There would be no stopping him from filling their glasses now.

'What is it?' Melody asked. 'I'm guessing not bonus Sparks points … unless it's an offer on essentials. They do do nice camis.'

'We've got a request for a viewing!' Jackie inhaled so hard, Abby wondered if she might actually suck in the condiments on the table. 'On Villa Pappas!'

'Wanging hell!' Melody exclaimed. 'Already! It only went on the website an hour ago!'

'That's good, right?' Abby said. 'Something else worth celebrating!'

'It's not just good,' Jackie said. 'It's fantastic. And it's nine o'clock tomorrow, which is fine – oh.' The thrill went from the end of her sentence.

'What's wrong?' Melody asked. 'I knew there would be a catch. Nothing ever goes perfectly for us, does it?'

'What's the issue?' Abby wanted to know. 'I'm sure it's nothing we can't work around.'

'They need picking up from Peroulades. They don't have a car.'

'That's OK,' Melody said. 'I can pick them up in the morning.'

'Not in *that* car,' Abby said. 'It's unreliable. And Leon's taxi – that's seen better days too. We need something that looks classier. These are people looking to spend two point five million euro on a house.'

'So why don't they have a car?' Melody offered with sarcasm.

'They're English,' Jackie said, eyes still scanning her mobile phone. 'Over here visiting relatives.'

'You can take my car.'

It was George who had spoken, in between filling their flutes.

'Can we, George?' Abby asked. 'What sort is it?' She didn't want to appear materialistic, but she was hoping for five doors and no rust.

'It is a Mercedes,' he replied.

'Benz,' Jackie said wistfully. 'W123 1978.'

Abby looked at her mum, saw the sadness creeping over her features again. George was holding the bottle of champagne over Jackie's glass but no pouring was taking place.

'That's settled then,' Melody loudly interrupted. 'I'll drive George's Benz over to Peroulades and pick them up and you two will get up to the villa at eight-thirty to dress it before they arrive.'

'Dress it?' Abby queried.

Melody laughed. 'Abs, you have a lot to learn about selling houses.'

Twenty-six

The Blue Vine

'Theo, come here!'

Spyridoula had taken up residence at a table for six under the boughs of an olive tree in the seated section closest to the main building. She and her friends had ordered a meze of dips and breads with anchovies and olives. Theo suspected that, at any moment, the playing cards would be brought out. Friends were his aunt's entire life and she had many of them. After a long period living and working in Athens she had retired to Corfu. Theo remembered one holiday, when he was a very hormonal teen, Spyridoula had arrived at their villa, dressed in every piece of finery she owned and invited them all out to lunch. They had eaten at Eucalyptus Taverna, seven courses with wine, then brandy and ouzo and finally, long after the sun had set, they had washed it all down with strong Greek coffee. His aunt was as strong as she was stubborn – family traits – but she was also someone he had great affection for and she had been good to him. He needed to remember that before he continued labelling her the enemy.

'You would like more drinks?' Theo inquired, all his aunt's friends looking him up and down appreciatively.

'You have grown so much, Theo.' He shirked a little under the intense scrutiny of Mrs Karakis. 'Such a strong boy now.'

There was general concurrence and lip-smacking broken up only by Spyridoula's laugh.

'Ladies, please, I know you are missing Roberto but remember this is my nephew.'

'Roberto was special,' Mrs Dimitria said, sighing deeply.

'Who was Roberto?' Theo inquired.

There was a collective, audible out-breath that almost told a thousand stories.

'He worked here last summer,' Spyridoula filled in. 'He was Italian.'

'He had amazing eyes,' Mrs Karakis continued, putting two fingers to each of her eyes and widening them.

'He looked like a ghoul?' Theo teased.

'He looked like a god,' Mrs Dimitria answered.

Theo laughed, shaking his head. 'Well, I may not be Roberto, but I can make good cocktails. What can I get for you?'

'We do not need anything more yet,' Spyridoula stated.

'Speak for yourself,' Mrs Dimitria said, sucking on her straw and draining her glass.

'Someone is coming to the villa,' Spyridoula stated. 'Tomorrow morning.'

'Coming?' Theo asked. 'With a delivery?'

'No,' Spyridoula said. 'With Jackie and the daughters-of-Jackie, to view for buying.'

It was quick. Too quick. He wanted to say that. But he needed to not make this about Spyridoula. She was just doing what his father was telling her to. A situation he knew everything about.

'What time?' he asked somewhat stiffly.

'Nine o'clock,' his aunt replied. 'They are picking the English people up from Peroulades.'

'I wish I had the money to buy Villa Pappas,' Mrs Karakis commented.

'I wish I had Roberto,' Mrs Dimitria responded.

Theo was about to retreat from the table when a familiar sound, growing in volume and coming from the harbour side, distracted his attention. He looked across to the water and immediately saw the group of Russians boarding a San Stefanos hire boat, engine kicking into life. His heart stepped up a notch while his brain seemed to be stalling on processing the scene.

'What are they doing?' Spyridoula questioned aloud, rising to her feet. 'They are drunk. They cannot drive a boat.' She clapped her hands to the side of her face. 'There are children swimming near the shore!'

Now Theo's brain engaged, and pure fear began to flow through every inch of him. He dropped his order book to the floor and took off, sprinting for the pontoon.

He felt sick and super-charged all at once, somewhere between terrified and determined, desperate to not let this disaster-in-the-making happen.

'Hey!' he called. 'Stop!'

They were all aboard now, jumping up and down as the engine was revved to maximum, smoke billowing into the humid air. One of the party was on the pontoon, unhitching the rope. Theo dug hard for more speed to his sprint, thighs tight, but no matter what he did, he was never going to reach them in time. He had to instead head to the swimmers. Give them a warning.

Bypassing the pontoon, he tracked to the beach, shouting and waving at the group innocently splashing around.

'Come out of the water! *Ela!* Out! Out!'

The children were looking at him like he was crazy, responding with shrieks of carefree abandon, staying in the sea, and looking unworried at the boat setting off from the wooden dock.

'Get out of the water!' Theo screamed. 'Out!'

The children were waving now and making faces at him. It was useless and that same sickening feeling he'd had seconds before the accident reared up just like the awful, unexpected wake had that day. There was only one thing he could do. He eyed the family boat, swaying gently in the water.

Twenty-seven

San Stefanos Harbour

'What's going on out there?' Jackie asked, eyes on the water-front, sipping her second glass of champagne.

'It's Igor,' Melody remarked, leaning forward to get a better look. 'In one of the hire boats! What's he thinking? Those plastic padded cushions have been sat on by allsorts.'

Abby was holding her breath. She had seen Theo sprinting down from The Blue Vine like the place was on fire. Now he was calling to somebody and waving his hands, frantic. She stood up, rocking the table.

'Are you going to ask George where the main course is?' Melody asked. 'I'm starving.'

'You can't be starving,' Jackie stated. 'Those starters were humungous, not to mention delicious too.'

Abby continued to watch. Theo was back up onto the dock now, as Igor and his friends began to power around the bay, creating white waves that were churning up the tranquil water, spray flying into the air.

'Abs, go and ask George how long the main course will be,' Melody said, swigging back her champagne.

She couldn't see Theo at all now. But she could hear the Russians on the water, jeering, fists in the air, singing what sounded like a fight song. Then there was another roar, a bigger, more powerful engine noise and suddenly a blue-and-white motorboat started to move. It was fast, but controlled, turning away from the pontoon and making room to manoeuvre. Theo was at the wheel.

'Isn't that the barman from The Blue Vine?' Melody asked, eyes back on the waterfront.

'Theo,' Abby said. 'He's also the gardener at Villa Pappas.'

'Well, no barman or gardener I've ever met has a boat like that,' Melody remarked. 'It's not *quite* the same stature as Valentin's but—'

Abby put a hand to her mouth in shock, suddenly understanding exactly what was going on. 'There are children in the water down there!' She stood, shifting herself out from behind the table.

'There's always people swimming. It's called "the sea". That's where people go when they don't live near Romsey Rapids,' Melody joked.

'But,' Abby said, finally getting herself out and into space. 'In Romsey Rapids you don't have inebriated Russians driving speedboats at you.' She swallowed and looked to her mum. 'I'll be back. Tell George to keep my dinner warm.'

'Abby,' Jackie said. 'What are you doing?'

The truth was she didn't know what she was doing but she had to do something. She ran towards the beach, her mother's voice ringing in her ears.

'Abby! Where are you going?!'

'Stop the boat!'

Theo had blasted the horn and tracked the Russians around the harbour in a bid to get them to kill their speed and listen to his warning but to no avail.

'Stop the boat!' He pulled his vehicle up alongside, as close as he could get without putting anyone in danger, or so he hoped. Everything had gone way beyond attention to detail now. He was thinking only of how quickly this joy-sail could turn into tragedy.

'You want to race with us?' came a reply.

'No!' Theo barked angrily. 'I want you to stop! There are—'

His next words, about the children nearer to shore were lost in the noise of acceleration as the Russians powered out to sea. Relief flooded him. Out to sea was where he wanted them to go. If he drove them out further, into open water, where they could do a lot less harm, the children would be safe. He turned up the power.

'You need to come out of the sea,' Abby said as strictly but also as calmly as possible. She was waist-deep in salt water, trying to make all eight children pay attention to her. Where were their parents? If this was England the parents would be right there. She supposed, living around the water, they could all swim so the parents might not worry quite so much …

'Do you speak English?' she tried again. '*Anglika?*'

'*Ochi,*' a little girl with dark plaits responded before splashing Abby in the face.

What words of Greek were going to help her here? She couldn't make a whole, grammatically correct sentence but she had got considerably through that first CD a few years ago. Surely, she could manage simple words with actions and … a roar. She took a breath.

'*Exo! Thalassa! Tora!*' She said 'out', 'sea' and 'now' with the most badass voice she could muster – something akin to the vicious grunting of The Mountain in *Game of Thrones* without the embellishment of gory entrails to follow it up.

The girl with plaits gave a scream of panic, looking at Abby as if she were a sea monster about to swallow them all up. Her instinct was to tell her to calm down, to say there was nothing to worry about if they just got out, but that tact hadn't worked before. Perhaps better to continue the way she was.

'*Exo!*' she growled, clapping her hands together, then slapping them to the water, making noise and effect, wading nearer to the children and directing them towards shore like a lollipop lady creating safe passage.

Abby was sodden, her bare feet going from soft sand to picking out rocks, shoulders relishing the cool water, the fabric of her dress not so much. It was only when the children began to stop their game, move towards the shore, that she realised she was breathless, had been scared. And then the roaring of the two boat engines started to grow louder …

Theo was beginning to sweat. He had had to use every ounce of powerboat training technique he'd had to keep Igor and his friends from endangering themselves, anyone else still out on the water and himself. The wind was strong on open water, as was usual on Corfu in the evening, and the waves had thrashed both boats about. As the Russians totally disregarded both speed and spatial awareness, Theo's attention had been on keeping them out of the harbour, but now they had turned. They were making for San Stefanos, faster and with more conviction than before – because he had raced them. He looked ahead, hoping against hope that the children were out of water.

'Slow your boat down!' he screamed into the air, moving parallel to the other vessel. He turned the wheel a little, brought the boats closer together for a second. They were almost back inside the horseshoe shape now, with two superyachts, sailing boats and other stationary sea traffic to avoid.

The sailors all sang louder, engine still at full throttle and Theo realised he had no other choice. He had to be the one to reach the shore first, be the barrier to the peril.

Twenty-eight

The blue-and-white boat with the lone occupant overtook the smaller hire boat filled to capacity, powering past it as Abby looked on. The furious wake was sending smaller boats nearer shore up in a dangerous sway, rocking them hard and causing a yanking of their tethers.

People from the village were moving to look now. Shop owners, taverna waiters, tourists, were all shifting in their seats to get a better view, or standing, hands shielding eyes from the sun. Abby's gaze went back to the sea, her chest was tight, her body solidifying, feet sinking down into the wet sand and staying there like it was thick clay. Theo's craft was thundering towards her and the children, and blind terror seemed to be stopping both fight and flight.

But then, the smell of fuel the incessant rumbling of the boat engine, worked in unison to kick-start her instincts.

'*Ela!*' she screamed at the children, attempting to run forward through the water. '*Tora! Tora!*'

Yelps and shouts and movement of people from the buildings closest to the water seemed to spur the boys and girls into action and they finally seemed to understand that this wasn't a game and that Abby wasn't a crazy person.

Taking a glance back at the boats Abby held her breath. Theo's vessel was just a few metres away now and there was no way she was going to be able to outrun it. There was only one thing she could do. Duck down under the water and pray. She closed her eyes, bringing her shoulders up to her ears, almost waiting for the pain to hit. Dying in Corfu had never been on her bucket list. She tried not to dwell on death since her father passed, had focused on filling her life with career ambition and as many trips out as she could afford and ... Darrell. No! She did not want Darrell to be the last person she had on her mind when she was taken by the angels. She swallowed, shivering, heart racing ... she was about to be mown down by a man who looked sooo good naked. How achingly unfair was that?

'Are you OK?'

Hands went down on her shoulders, hard and heavy. The voice rough, angry and terrified all at once. It took Abby a second to realise that the boat noises had stopped and that the voice belonged to Theo.

She turned around, faced him. 'How ... I ... you were ... on the boat and ...' She looked over his shoulder at the boat then. It was almost close enough to touch, but not the front of it, the length of the side. Igor's stolen one was a little further out, wedged between a huge yellow doughnut ring used to fling holidaymakers off and a flagpole flying the Greek flag at the end of one of the pontoons.

'Abby,' he repeated forcefully, eyes wild, gripping hold of her shoulders. 'You are OK, yes?'

'Yes,' she stuttered. 'Yes, I'm OK.' She panted. 'And the children are OK.'

He let her go then, all the energy seeming to disappear completely from every part of him as he slouched, core slackening, shoulders rolling forward, legs weakening.

'Theo,' she said softly, concerned. 'Are *you* OK?'

He didn't answer her, just stood, bent double in the water, hands at the top of his knees, his breathing uneven. She couldn't see the expression on his face, but she could see the utter exhaustion and relief in his body language. He didn't look OK at all. She could sense there was a whole lot of not OK right here.

'Theo,' she said softly. Slowly, she reached out her hand, not really knowing what to do with it, whether contact would help. She placed it gently on his shoulder and the reaction couldn't have been more forceful. He straightened immediately, rocking back a few steps in the sea, almost hitting his boat.

'*Ime kala*,' he stated quickly. 'I'm fine.'

He didn't look fine. She swallowed as she looked into his tear-filled eyes. 'Why don't we—'

'Theo!'

Leon came splashing into the water, grinning and proceeded to slap Theo hard on the back in congratulations. Abby watched Theo try to back away.

'What driving you do!' Leon continued. 'The way you spin the boat around to block their approach. Everyone is talking about it. They say it is the most incredible thing they have ever seen, well, since Stathis perform the headstand on the unicycle.'

'I have to get back to work,' Theo stated.

Abby watched him, desperate to leave, not wanting to talk about it, needing to be anywhere but in the sea with his over-enthusiastic friend. 'Leon ...' she tried to deflect.

'It was crazy! I think the Russians are going to kill the children and Abby, then I think they smash into *your* boat, then the pontoon ... but, no jest, *you* ... you just do everything completely right! You save everything and everybody! You are a hero, my friend!' Leon took hold of Theo's shoulders and shook him thoroughly.

Abby saw Theo's expression cloud even further, his eyes dimming like his mind was elsewhere. She took hold of Leon's arm, pulling him away. 'Leon, would you be able to get us some towels? My dress is wet and Theo is wet and … it would be so lovely if you could do that. Perhaps George has some?'

Leon gasped. 'Sure! I can do that! I will go now!' He turned around and began hurrying out of the sea towards the growing crowd around the group of saved children.

'I do not need a towel,' Theo said immediately, moving through the water to the back of his boat.

'I know you didn't want Leon making you out to be eligible for a Pride of Britain award.'

'What?'

'I saw what you were doing with the boat,' Abby stated. 'You knew they were all drunk and reckless and you saw the children.' She followed him around the stern, finding it hard to wade with her dress collating around her thighs. '*I* saw the children from George's Taverna. If you hadn't stopped them, they could have … well, it doesn't bear thinking about.'

'I don't want to talk about it,' Theo snapped. 'They are *malakas.*' He rephrased. 'Idiots.' He pulled down the small ladder. 'But you should not have come into the water. It was a stupid thing to do.'

Abby balked. 'What?'

'You put yourself in danger.'

'I saw the children. They needed to get out and they weren't listening to you.'

'So, you thought you would give them something more to aim at?' He scoffed. 'Great plan.'

'What's wrong with you?' Abby bit back. 'I was trying to help.'

'Yeah?! Well I do not need any help! Not from you. Not from anyone,' he snarled.

Theo put one foot up on the ladder, ready to haul himself back on board and set about returning the vessel to its original position. So many feelings were running through him right now. Dread. Panic. Overwhelming relief. Desperation. And all of a sudden, he couldn't move. He couldn't get back on board. He looked back to Abby, powerless, hating that he had snapped at her, knowing it was only for self-preservation.

'You should go,' he told her, foot still on the first rung of the ladder but unable to complete the action.

'Oh, I should go?' She stood her ground, hands on hips. 'Aren't you the one with the boat?'

'You're wet,' he reminded her. 'Your date for the *panegyri* is getting you a towel.' Why had he said that? Now he sounded jealous as well as looking pathetic, perched here, half up, half down, the water lapping around his hips.

'Why can't you get back on the boat, Theo?' Abby asked him.

He laughed then. It came out stilted, as nervous as he felt. He slicked a wet hand over his hair, touching the nub of the bun at the back of his neck. 'Why don't you go into shore? You can have the honorary heroine status. Have Spyridoula sign you up to speak at her next council meeting. Tell everybody about your rescue of the children.'

She was still looking at him. Those honest eyes, that beautiful, fresh face … her expression though was unyielding. 'Why aren't you getting back on the boat?'

'I am,' he stated quickly.

'When?'

'When I am ready,' he answered. But he could already feel it. The very thought of climbing back aboard, now all the adrenalin and desperate rush had subsided, was making nausea swirl.

'What happened, Theo?' Abby whispered.

He closed his eyes. He couldn't do this. He *didn't* do this. Talking about it was over the minute he'd left his father's business. He'd made an oath to himself. He might still have the nightmares, he might still think about it, but he never talked. Not after the counsellor. And Abby, she didn't even know who he really was …

'You! You are crazy!'

For once Theo was glad to hear the loud Russian-accented words. He regained control of his leg and stepped off the ladder completely.

'The boat has crack!' Igor carried on. 'Lots of crack!' The group were on the nearest dock, all looking a little wet, still drunk and now angry.

Theo waded towards the landing platform and hauled himself up onto it, standing tall. He wanted these men to realise just what their stupid behaviour had almost caused. He pointed a finger, jabbing it hard against Igor's chest. 'It is not your boat! And you will have to pay for the damage!'

'I will not pay! You do this!' Igor growled.

'*I* do this?!' Theo exploded. 'There were children in the water! You did not listen! You could have killed them!'

Abby hurried through the sea, rushing to get to a lower point on the dock where she could safely pull herself out. She reached up, palms flat against the sun-warmed, grey splintered wood, dragging her body out of the ocean.

'What the wanging hell are you doing?'

Melody grabbed hold of her arm, helping her out and up onto her feet.

'Come and help me,' Abby begged. 'Get Igor and his friends to go away.'

'The village isn't happy,' Melody responded like San Stefanos was a living, breathing hive mind. 'I'm not sure they'll be allowed to stay here.'

'Good,' Abby answered. 'Now come and stop them getting into a fight because I think there's been enough drama for one evening.'

'Yeah,' Melody agreed. 'And my bloody pork chops are getting cold!'

Abby hurried down the dock and rushed up to Theo, while Melody put herself in front of Igor.

'Igor!' Melody exclaimed. 'That was some excitement!'

Theo snorted, shaking his head.

'You make noise of pig at me?!' Igor yelled, stepped forward, body tone set to aggressive.

'No one's making any pig noises at anyone,' Melody insisted, running a hand up the Russian's forearm.

'You put your hands on anything that is not yours again and you will suffer!' Theo warned.

'Is that so?' Igor responded. 'How about her, huh?'

Abby's breath left her chest as Igor shifted Melody aside, then stepped forwards, swinging an arm around her neck, dragging her into his body. It took only a second for her to notice the colour rising in Theo's face, his jaw tightening, his hands clench up into fists. And then she was back in Romsey Sports Centre, mad and sad over Darrell, the eighteen-stone-plus bulk of self-defence instructor Henry Not-Quite-The-Rock Johnson squeezing the air from her lungs to simulate a nasty back alley assault. Channelling her inner Davina McCall, she snapped back her elbow, hitting Igor centre chest, then, once free, she turned, chopping him hard in the middle of his windpipe. He recoiled immediately, gasping for breath, hands at his neck like it had been severed.

She stood back, *her* hands now made into fists, poised to attack again should the first phase not have rendered him useless.

All at once, Theo and Melody collided in their attempt to get to Igor who was coughing and spluttering and being attended to by his cronies. It was Melody who pushed on through, thumping the Russian on the shoulder and sending him flailing into his comrades, a very angry expression on her face.

'No one does that to my sister!' Melody spat. 'You ever come near either of us again and I'll cut off your balls and make them into borscht!'

'Come on, Igor,' Andrei said, pulling at his brother's arm. 'Let us go.'

Igor growled something in Russian that sounded like a threat of the highest order, but Abby couldn't have cared less. They were beating a retreat and that was all that mattered.

'Yeah, go!' Melody yelled as the group made their way down the deck towards the beach. 'Piss off back to Russia, and take your tiny little dick with you!'

'Melody!' Abby exclaimed. 'Maybe a little too much?'

Melody sighed. 'I was always hopeful, but he never really delivered on the promise.'

'I *meant* too much information,' Abby said.

'You all right?' Melody asked, taking Abby's hands and looking deep into her eyes. 'First you almost get driven over, then you get in a Russian headlock and then – well, where did you learn those karate moves?!'

Abby smiled at her sister's enthusiasm until she realised there was someone else missing from the boardwalk. She turned, looking for Theo, only to see him, retreating over the sand towards The Blue Vine.

'Well?' Melody asked, expectantly.

'I'll tell you later,' Abby said. 'Let's go and see if the children are OK, and eat our dinner.'

Twenty-nine

The Dolan House

Abby sat on the edge of her bed, looking out the open window at the strip of sea and the frontline properties enjoying the first rays of morning sun. There was a hint of freshness to the air, the scent of earth and citrus before the heat enveloped everything. It was a new day after the high drama of the night before and somehow now, with the village so peaceful in the early light, none of it seemed real. Had crazy Russians been motoring around the small harbour? Had she performed her best self-defence moves on a wooden dock? Had she successfully stopped her sister from starting on tsipouro by reminding her she had important driving duties to undertake today? Had Theo been close to tears after the near disaster? Part of her had wanted to suggest one last drink at The Blue Vine after their delicious meal at George's to see how Theo was, but George had presented them with their easel, freshly painted in bright white, the blackboard clean and darkened too. He had offered to deliver it, but Jackie had refused and, despite Melody's protestation that even though Abby could perform 'kick-ass karate' she was the stronger of the two due to her foray into almost-erotic dance, it had taken four hands to get the signage back to Desperately Seeking.

'Abby! It's eight o'clock!' Jackie called out. It sounded like her mum was downstairs already and the tone was keen, even after the champagne, which thankfully hadn't been that expensive.

'Coming!' Abby replied, getting up and closing the mosquito screen on the window.

She hurried down the stairs and opened the door to the lounge/diner/kitchen. The sight that greeted her made her gasp a little. The wobbly old wooden table was full of food and her mum was pouring tea from a china pot.

'Mum, what's going on?' Abby asked.

'What d'you mean what's going on? It's breakfast.'

Jackie said the word 'breakfast' like she really meant 'banquet'. Abby took in the fresh bread her mum had obviously gone to the supermarket for, the slab of feta cheese, the chocolate granola Melody always raved about and there was pastry ... a pile of tightly folded parcels holding who-knew-what inside. There was a steaming cafetière filled with coffee she didn't even know they owned, a tea pot in her mum's hand, and a jug of what looked like apple juice. For someone who usually made hot drinks from the cold tap and microwaved them, this was *catering*.

It was then she noticed what Jackie was wearing. A lovely maroon knee-length dress in a chiffon fabric that floated naturally over her curves, on her feet a pair of contrasting oxblood coloured leather court shoes with at least a six-centimetre heel. She looked *lovely*. She looked smart and professional and much more like the person she had been when she'd started the estate agency business, full of plans and enthusiasm. Abby then realised she had been quietly assessing the scene for far too long than was natural.

'It looks ...' She mustn't make a fuss. She mustn't say words like *amazing* or *astonishing*. Gushing was definitely out. A definite change had occurred, be it from the excitement of having a prize property on the Desperately Seeking books or from George's Greek treats, but it had to go under the radar for now. Her mum didn't need a reminder of how bad things had got when she was at the beginning of turning things around.

'I'm so hungry,' Abby stammered, heading to the table and pulling up a wonky chair. It was a total lie. Her stomach was still full from the six baklava bites she had devoured after the large starters and her delectable fish with spinach and artichoke main. 'Where's Melody? Still in bed?'

'No,' Jackie answered, moving to pour Abby a cup of tea. 'She's gone to collect George's car then she's driving over to Peroulades to get the couple for the viewing.'

'She's in good time,' Abby commented.

'Well,' Jackie began, scanning the table as if looking for something amid the overkill of plates and bowls. 'We might have had a sticky few months, but we've always kept good time.' She sniffed. 'I can't find the milk. Why can't I find the milk?'

'Maybe the fridge, Mum?' Abby suggested.

'I wanted it in a jug!'

'Mum,' Abby said. 'Why don't you sit down and eat something with me?'

'I can't eat,' Jackie said, stepping towards the fridge, pulling open the door and taking out the milk carton. 'I'm full of butterflies and … nervous energy.'

'That's a good thing,' Abby said, smiling.

'Tell that to my stomach,' Jackie breathed. 'It feels like someone's treading grapes inside there.' A false laugh left her lips. 'And it didn't help that I bumped into Diana at the bakery. I thought I'd nip out before the sun was properly up and there she was, looking like a million euro … with Valentin.'

Abby opened her mouth to say that her mum shouldn't be getting jealous over anything to do with the rich Russian but Jackie continued.

'They'd just got back from a moonlit sail over to Erikousa Island.' Jackie sighed. 'Do you know, I've never been there and it's only eight miles from here. They'd had Swiss chocolates and champagne ...'

'We had champagne,' Abby reminded.

'We didn't have champagne,' Jackie said. 'In all the time I've known George he's only ever served sparkling wine.'

'Well,' Abby said. 'It was very nice sparkling wine.'

'Anyway, you need to eat,' Jackie said. She plucked a knife off the table digging into the hunk of feta and cutting off a piece the size of a large gravestone. Abby eyed it with fear, knowing if she ate all that in one go it might give her the type of indigestion that led to a premature plot in the cemetery.

'Mum,' Abby said, watching Jackie cut up the fresh bread in no smaller slices than the cheese. 'It's great about the viewing today and everything but—'

Jackie stopped slicing and dropped the knife. 'There's something you're not telling me, isn't there! I knew it! I said to Melody, you haven't been here for so long, there was always something keeping you in England and now you're here, without either of us having to beg.' Her mum's eyes turned all Chief of Police. 'What is it, Abby? You can tell me anything.'

This was the bit where she was supposed to confess everything. Here, in her mum and Melody's lovely rustic kitchen, in the beautiful, safe sanctuary they had made in Corfu. English time all but stopped here. Romsey could almost be another planet in a whole different solar system.

'I was just going to say that … it's the first viewing on a property that's not been on the market more than twenty-four hours.' She took a breath, heart thumping an out-of-time beat. 'The first couple to view it – they might not actually buy it.'

Jackie let out a sigh and then a smile spread across her face … her *foundation* covered face. Abby swallowed. There was definite eye-liner and mascara there too.

'Abby, I've been selling houses for a while now. I'm not naïve.'

'I know, I just …'

The gigantic plate of cheese and bread was plumped down in front of her.

'Tell me what you haven't told me or there'll be no pastry until you've eaten all of this.' Jackie picked up the tea pot again and began filling Abby's mug to the very brim.

Her mum's voice was soft but Abby knew she wasn't going to be able to put this off any longer. She had to tell her something.

'I …' Abby started. Once she got it out it would feel better. 'I lost my job.'

The tea pot slipped out of Jackie's hands and fell to the floorboards with a crack. Abby leapt up as hot tea splattered her legs.

'Oh! Oh, Abby!' Jackie exclaimed. 'Are you OK? Did it burn you? Oh, I'm such a klutz, I just wasn't expecting you to say that. I'm not sure what I was expecting you to say, but not that.' Jackie handed Abby a tea towel, then bent down, picking up the broken teapot.

'I'm fine,' Abby said, dabbing the brown liquid from her shins.

'What happened? I thought things were going so well at The Travellers' Rest.'

'They are,' Abby said, returning the tea towel to the table. 'I mean, they were ... I didn't do anything wrong. I wasn't sacked. I was just ... not needed any more.' As she said it, all the memories came flooding back. Her lovely cactus plant on the reception desk that bloomed pink in the winter, Chef's scones, the Beat the Winter Blues January Christmas parties ... then came the vision of Darrell and Amber and that kiss over the cakes. If it was coming out, it may as well all be out ...

'Mum ...'

'I always thought you were too good for that place anyway. You're so creative with your ideas. You were always going to be limited by what you could do in a chain.'

'Mum ...'

'What does Darrell say?' Jackie asked.

'I ... he ...'

'Isn't there something at his place you could get your teeth into? Even financial advisers must need an ideas team,' Jackie carried on. 'And I know how things are over in the UK with food prices and Toys 'R' Us closing down. We do hear all that in Greece, you know. And you don't want to lose your savings, if you're going to be saving for a wedding one day.'

Abby swallowed. It was enough for one session. She had feta cheese to eat and a multi-million-euro villa to house doctor.

'There's nothing to worry about, Mum, really,' she said, breaking a pinch of the white, creamy boulder of cheese off with her fingers.

'Is that why you came over here now?' Jackie asked, hand on Abby's shoulder. 'A bit of a break before you look through Situations Vacant?'

'Something like that,' Abby said with a nod.

'You'll be snapped up in no time,' Jackie stated confidently.

'I know,' she said. She hoped so. Because one person's wage was all it was going to be when she got back.

'Just … let's not let it slip to Diana while you're here,' Jackie said. 'She would make out you're on the employment scrapheap.' Jackie gasped. 'Can I say Darrell's applied for *The Apprentice*? Diana said her nephew was on it last year, but I don't believe her.'

The feta cheese stuck in Abby's throat as she forced a nod.

Thirty

Villa Pappas

'Theo!'

The voice echoed loudly, like someone was entombed deep in a cave and screaming for help. He rolled over in the bed, muffling his ears with a pillow.

'Theo! Wake up! They will be outside soon.'

His aunt? Again? Was it not enough that he was working until the early hours of the morning serving drinks to her and her friends? Did she have to come round in the mornings to make sure he hadn't drunk his father's entire drinks cabinet of aged spirits after his shift had finally ended? Shit, a memory was coming back ... Leon and him swigging back Metaxa Grande Fine. Then something else hit his brain ... the house viewing. Someone was coming to nose around his home ... *Abby*.

He bolted out of bed, naked, searching for his underwear.

'Man! I was going out for *loukanika* but how can I now?' Leon shielded his eyes.

'The estate agency people,' Theo said, pulling on his underwear then reaching for a T-shirt.

'I know,' Leon stated. 'You tell me last night and you do not need to worry. I have set everything up.'

'What? Set everything up?' He looked at a grinning Leon. 'What do you mean?'

'Come on, Theo, you planned it all last night,' Leon began. 'Used plates and glasses all over the kitchen, clothes and washing in every room, on every surface, grass cuttings and bushes from the garden all through the home. Aleko won't be selling this house today.'

He felt sick as all the words he'd said under the influence of alcohol and melancholy made a trickling return. What had he been thinking? And why did Leon think Aleko from Ionian Dreams was coming here?

'What have you done?' Theo asked, swallowing back a mixture of bile and brandy.

'I've done it all,' Leon stated proudly. 'Everything is ... sweet chaos.'

He closed his eyes, head beginning to thump and wished away all the units he'd consumed the night before.

'What's wrong?' Leon asked.

'Leon,' Theo breathed. 'It isn't Aleko selling the house. It's the shop that was pink. Abby ... her mother's business.'

He watched Leon pale.

'You jest,' his friend stated.

Theo shook his head. In the light of day, he no more wanted this viewing to be easy than he had last night but to actually create mayhem, a mess for Abby, who had done nothing but try to help last night ...

They both heard the key in the lock and the stand-by beeping of the security alarm.

'Oh my God!' Jackie exclaimed as her shoes hit branches and leaves. Abby stared around at the open-plan living space, trying to find any resemblance to the beautiful, tidy, light-filled haven she had valued only a day ago. Whole boughs of trees blocked their path and the state-of-the-art kitchen area was piled high with soiled crockery like it had hosted a party for fifty guests.

'Abby,' Jackie said, lifting her dress a little and attempting to climb over the heap of wood. 'Was this how it was when you saw it yesterday?'

'No!' Abby stated immediately. 'No, not at all. Nothing like this.' The alarm was still beeping. Had they been told the code?

'Because I know some people think "rustic" is en vogue right now and there's all this living, breathing, forest wall-paper ...'

'It wasn't like this,' Abby repeated. She pushed her hair back behind her ears, navigating her way around fronds of green and knocking olive fruit onto the tiles. 'It was minimalist and bright and ... clean.' She needed to get to that keypad and shut the noise up.

'Are these someone's pants?' Jackie held black fabric up in the air between the very ends of ... were they false French-polished nails her mum was sporting?

The alarm suddenly stopped beeping.

'*Kalimera.*'

Abby turned her head in the direction of the Greek greeting, knowing it was Theo, not knowing he was bare-chested. Why did he never have clothes on in this house? She wet her lips, mad at him, despite the delectable ab display.

'You do know that a gardener is supposed to get rid of cuttings not spread them around their employer's house!' she exclaimed.

'I can explain—' Theo started.

'We are here to dress the house ready for the first viewing. My sister tells me that means doing something arty with cushions, getting the scent just right and opening up all the windows.' She took a breath, watching Theo pull his T-shirt over his head. 'It smells like something died in here ... of alcohol poisoning.'

'It wasn't meant to be like this ... I just ...'

'I should call Mrs Pappas,' Abby carried on. 'Report you.'

She watched Theo's expression. There seemed to be a little remorse, a genuine look of regret. But that barely explained away the hideous near-Hazmat zone they were standing in.

'We don't have time for that,' Jackie stated, manhandling a large limb of tree. 'Melody is going to be here at nine with the potential purchasers and this place has got to look every euro of its asking price.'

'Leon,' Theo began. 'He is already making good the other rooms.'

'Leon is here?' Jackie said with a tut. 'Say no more.' She dragged branches towards the door.

Abby's eyes pricked with tears. 'You mean all the other rooms are as messed up as this one?!' She couldn't have this happening. Her mum had finally ditched her shapeless outfits and was back into professional garb with proper shoes and everything. This was Desperately Seeking's big break. And she wasn't about to let anyone spoil it.

'You,' she started, pointing at Theo. 'You will move all these cuttings out of here and make it tidy. Do not put them in the garden. Put them in black bags or hide them until the clients have gone. We will ...' Abby looked to Jackie who was coming back through the door.

'We will start washing up,' Jackie stated, clapping her hands together. 'Theo, be a lovely and open some windows.'

'*Endaksi*,' he replied, beating a retreat.

Abby hurried over to her mum who was opening cupboards in the kitchen area as if trying to find something. 'Mum, it really wasn't like this. I promise.'

'Boys will be boys,' Jackie answered, shutting one cupboard door and opening another. 'And you have *been* in Leon's taxi, haven't you?'

'Yes, it's terrible, but, I just want you to know that …' She had to spit it out. 'I might have been relieved of my duties at The Travellers' Rest, but my eye isn't off the ball.'

'I know that,' Jackie said softly, gently touching Abby's shoulder. 'Come on, I'm sure we said this villa has a dishwasher. Help me find it.'

Thirty-one

The couple who had come to view the villa didn't look rich enough to afford the price tag, in Theo's opinion. They were English – the man (Paul) dressed in neon yellow shorts and a vest; the woman (Lynn), the skin of her boyish frame pink from the sun, was sucking on her second cigarette of the visit so far. But what did he know about English wealth? Just because his father was never seen out of business attire didn't mean everyone with money was the same way. Take his current appearance, for example, who would think he was the son of a millionaire?

Leon had commented about Dinis' collection of vintage alcohol earlier, but before his friend could continue, spill that Theo was not in fact employed by the Pappases but a Pappas himself, the taxi mobile phone had rung and Leon had departed. However, his friend had still had time to make a show of cutting a sheaf of lavender from the garden and presenting it to Abby to display on the dining table. Theo had to admit it was a step up in fragrance terms from underwear and leftover *gyros*.

'Infinite views from here I'm sure you'll agree,' Melody said as she led Paul around the terrace.

'What's the Wi-Fi like?' Lynn asked, drawing on her cigarette like it was a stick of life itself.

'It's very good,' Jackie jumped in. 'And you'll find, what with being on a small island and being so close to that huge antenna at the top of the mountain, the 4G is excellent too, should there be a loss of connection for Wi-Fi, not that there should be.'

Melody breathed in deeply, closing her eyes and letting her hands rest on the pillared wall. 'Listen,' she whispered. Then she opened her eyes and looked to the clients. 'Paul, Lynn, come and both stand here. Close your eyes and just … listen.'

Theo snipped at the clematis bush he was pretending to prune and this injection into the quiet drew a look from Abby. She was standing a little behind the group, writing in a notepad every so often and saying very little. She was angry with him and he didn't blame her at all. Last night he had been nothing short of obnoxious and today he had made work for her. His father wanted to sell the property. It was going to happen no matter which estate agency he used. Fighting it was futile, unless he wanted to directly take on and talk to the man himself as Spyridoula had suggested.

'Hear that?' Melody asked, her voice gentle.

'All I can hear is bugs,' Lynn stated roughly, exhaling a plume of smoke into the warm air.

'Cicadas,' Jackie said.

'Lovely,' Lynn replied, stubbing her cigarette out on the wall. 'I do like a good Mexican and I haven't eaten breakfast.'

'Er … the cicadas are the insects you can hear,' Jackie stated. 'Here, you're in the midst of everything. The woods just behind and the sea right in front of you. It's a prime location and a property that isn't going to stay on the market for long.'

'I like it,' Paul said. 'The bedrooms aren't as big as the other one we saw but—'

'The other one we saw was next to that traditional coffee shop. It was all old men playing chess and speaking Greek.' Lynn sniffed. 'I don't know how anyone is supposed to relax with all that going on!'

'Can we see inside again?' Paul asked.

'Of course,' Jackie said quickly. 'Let me take you back through everything while Melody makes us some drinks.'

Theo watched Jackie mouth something at her blonde daughter before going back into the property. Abby made to move behind her mother and it was then he seized his opportunity.

'Abby.'

'I need to get back into the house,' she said hurriedly, about to brush past him.

He took hold of her arm, pulling her to a stop. 'Please, just for a moment.'

'I don't really see what there is to say.' She looked at him directly, those almond-coloured eyes vying for dominance with his. 'Your stupidity might have cost my mother a very important sale today.'

'I know, I wasn't really thinking.'

'And clearly you think it's OK to treat someone else's house like your own. I can only imagine what Spyridoula would think if she knew how you were living here.'

He need not imagine on that score, but he nodded his head anyway. 'I have taken liberties,' he admitted. 'With ... my position here.'

'It's very hard to sell houses,' Abby hissed in a whisper. 'It may be beautiful, but it needs to look *perfect* when people come to visit.'

'I can do perfect,' Theo told her. 'Let me show you.'

'What?'

'I ... Tonight. Let me dress the house. Let me cook for you, *vradino*, dinner.' What was he saying? Where had this come from? He seemed unable to stop the words from falling out of his lips.

She didn't answer and his fingers were still very much attached to the soft, milky skin of her arm. He could feel the heat channelling through him, raw yet deep and undeniable.

'I need to catch up with my mum,' Abby said. She moved and his fingers lost her. It was for the best. After all, Leon had an interest and Leon was worthier of good karma than he was. He watched her turn away and his insides thwacked at him.

'Eight,' he stated quickly, almost breathlessly. 'Be here at eight.'

She had stopped, briefly, but long enough to hear? He didn't know. And then she was moving again, stepping back into the villa.

Thirty-two

Sidari

'This is one of the prime spots for giving out leaflets,' Melody announced, thrusting a flyer into the hand of the dad of a passing family. 'I used to work a bit for one of the bars here. They had this tribute-act guy who could impersonate Bob Marley, some ancient act Mum likes – Billy Ocean, I think – *and* Craig David. Mum always had one too many ouzos and tried to get him to do Lionel Richie but he never did.' Melody smiled at an approaching couple, leaflet poised. 'Want to live the dream in Corfu? We're having a party this Saturday in San Stefanos, wine, cocktails and gorgeous Greek nibbles, free raffle ticket for anyone who signs up to our newsletter.'

Abby watched the woman take one of the flyers they had picked up from Acharavi an hour ago. Melody had decided their first stop to do handouts should be lively Sidari. Abby had only been to this resort once, last year, when she and Darrell had managed to fly over for a long weekend. He had moaned about missing football, but it was one of the few times she had insisted on a visit. And it hadn't felt long enough. Back then, Melody had taken them on a tour of the Sidari night scene. It had started innocently enough, eating outside at a lovely restaurant called The Hive then degenerated into karaoke and watching a drag act called Lady Jayne. But daytime Sidari was very different. Beautiful sand and shingle beaches and a cool, laid-back vibe to the town despite the high concentration of bars, restaurants and tourist shops. Abby took a breath, looking out over the sand to the cerulean sea and finally feeling a loosening in her shoulders. If Desperately Seeking got a boost with this large sale, this is what her mum and sister's lives would go back to being. Hard work to keep the business sustainable, but also relaxation in a place full of sunshine and none of the rat-race mentality that had taken over the UK. That's what she wanted for them. That's what she wanted for herself. She just wasn't sure quite how she was going to find it.

'What did Paul and Lynn really think about Villa Pappas?' Abby asked Melody.

Her sister sucked in a breath, tidying up the pile of flyers in her hands so they were all perfectly straight. 'I don't know.'

'That wasn't what you said to Mum,' Abby said.

'What did I say to Mum?'

'You said you thought they might go and see a few more houses but they'd be back to us by the end of the week.'

'They probably will.'

'Probably?'

'Well, Abs, did you see what Mum was wearing this morning?'

'The dress …'

'And the shoes.'

'I did,' Abby replied. She waved at an approaching lady and stepped forward into her orbit. 'Oh … would you like an invitation to our party? Wine, food and a chance to win a prize.'

The lady took the invite with a smile. 'Thank you.'

'I didn't even know she still had those shoes,' Melody said. 'She sold the rest.'

'You said,' Abby remembered.

'She's been really "up" since you got here and started helping,' Melody admitted. 'I mean, I tried my best to keep her enthusiasm going but it's been really hard.'

'I know. I can see that. And from what you've told me ...' She suddenly felt really guilty for having stayed away. She hadn't wanted to keep them both at arm's length but she had been so caught up in The Travellers' Rest and her life with Darrell ...

'She does need a man, though,' Melody blurted out. 'You shouldn't be widowed that young and have no one new to share your life with.'

'I did think about Aleko when I first saw him,' Abby said. 'He does have a look of Jeff Bridges.'

'And he owns the business that wants to see us bankrupt.'

'What about George?' Abby asked.

'George?! Taverna George?!'

'He's good-looking in an older-man way and he's kind. He let you borrow his car. He's painted Mum's easel ...' She didn't know why that sounded like a really bad euphemism.

'I think she should set her sights a little higher than that,' Melody said, as a group of twenty-something males approached them. 'Well, hello, look at you all bronzed and gorgeous. How do you fancy a party?'

Abby turned away as her sister went into full-on flirt mode. They had discussed the type of clientele they were supposed to be approaching – people who looked like they could afford to buy a holiday home, not people who were only here for the kebabs and killer tans.

Her phone buzzed and she drew it out of her small cross-body pleather bag, checking the notification. *Darrell.*

She'd previously amended her settings to display only the sender's name and the words 'text message' so as not to be distracted by the headline opening ... Did she really want to read it? It had been weeks now. Almost four weeks. What could he possibly have to say to her?

'Oh!' Melody exclaimed. 'You're here with your mums! Well, that's just fantastic because your mums are going to love my mum and, while they're talking about all the designer shopping available in Corfu Town, you and me are going to be drinking the bespoke cocktails I'm making.'

Abby sat down on the low wall just outside a shop selling everything from water squirters for the pool, Greek flag towels, beach bags of every size imaginable, to mini bars of olive soap and all manner of hats. She opened up the message and read.

I miss you. I'd give anything for another chance. D xx

What?! What was he doing sending her a message like that? How dare he! How did he have the nerve to send it?! That was not the sort of text you sent someone first thing in the morning ... because in the UK it was barely past 9am. She was furious! She leapt up off the wall, bursting with angry energy. She needed to move. She wanted to run into the middle of the beach and scream at the sky.

'Abs?' Melody's voice barely registered as she began to walk down the strip. 'Take a couple of invitations, guys and I'll see you on Saturday. Abby!'

Thirty-three

Abby needed a drink. A proper one. Like a pint glass full of Old Fashioned. She swept up into a bar, walking through the main area and heading towards where she could see light and beach and a man stood in front of almost every optic imaginable.

'*Bira, parakalo*. Fix.' Beer. She had ordered beer. Why had she ordered beer?

'Abby,' Melody said, catching up to her. 'What's going on? We still have loads of leaflets to give out. Ugh!' Her sister's exclamation was directed towards the bottle of beer. 'Beer? It's not even lunchtime.'

Abby sucked at the bottle as if it held long-life elixir. The cool, slightly bitter taste with the scent of banana and apple felt so refreshing on both her tongue and her mindset. She finished the slug, eyes going to the lure of the beach, other people relaxed on loungers, something she hadn't even done for a second since she'd arrived. 'Shall we go and sit down for a bit?'

'What's going on?' Melody quizzed. 'You're acting all weird.'

'Do you want a beer?' Abby asked.

'No … it's the middle of the morning,' Melody protested. 'And I'm not on holiday. That's the trap ex-pats fall into, you know. Making every day a holiday. Before you know it, you're splashing crème de menthe in your coffee.'

'That actually sounds nice,' Abby said.

'Wanging hell!' Melody turned to the barman who was studying them like they were rare specimens. 'I'll have a ... a ... really, really weak vodka and Coke.'

'Please,' the barman said. 'I will bring it to you.'

Abby needed no further encouragement and she stepped towards the open doors that led out to the outside seating and the beach. The sun hit her skin and, just like that, she felt revived, alive, ready to cope with this new life-blip. She chose a table on the very edge of the sand, dappled in sunlight, a sandstone candle holder at its centre and sat down. One more mouthful of beer and she was going to ... tell the truth.

'I lost my job,' Abby declared as Melody lowered herself to a seat.

'Fuck!' Melody missed the edge of the chair with her bum and slipped down onto the decking with a thump.

'Oh, Melody, are you all right!' Abby leapt up, reaching out for her sister's flapping arms.

'No!' Melody shrieked. 'I'm not all right. You're talking crap. I mean, you can't ... *you* can't have lost your job. That doesn't happen to you. That stuff happens to me and ...' Melody got up off the floor, dusting her short pink pantsuit off with her hands. 'If it's really happened to you, then I'm expecting that mad little man from North Korea to push his nuclear button at any second.'

'It's true,' Abby admitted. 'Just before I came here.' She breathed, strength coming with every nuance of this island – the sweet breeze, the smell of eucalyptus and mint, the sound of the gentle waves sweeping the shingle shore.

'God, Abs, why didn't you say anything?' Melody asked, looking across the table at her. 'And why didn't I ask for a really, really *strong* vodka and Coke?'

Abby smiled. 'I was going to say something as soon as I got here, but then I saw how Desperately Seeking was struggling, and my plight didn't seem quite as immediate.'

'I didn't ask,' Melody said, folding her arms across her chest. 'I was too caught up in trying to rip off Igor and ... bar-dancing.'

'And keeping Mum's business afloat,' Abby reminded her. 'Because that's what you've been doing for the past eighteen months. With no help from me.'

'Does Mum know?' Melody asked. 'About your job?'

Abby nodded. 'I told her this morning.' She breathed in the humidity, letting it scorch her lungs a little, burning in an invigorating way. 'She was all excited about the viewing and the table was full of food. I thought she could cope with the shock ... and she did.'

'Wow,' Melody said, looking over her shoulder. 'Where's that barman with my drink?'

'Mel,' Abby started tentatively. 'There's something else. Something I *haven't* told Mum.'

'God, Abs, seriously?!' Melody's hands went to her messy bun, fingers weaving into the nest of hair and poking it about. 'You're not pregnant, are you?!'

Abby shook her head. 'No.'

'Phew, because I want a few more years of mopping up my own drool before I have to deal with anyone else's.'

The barman arrived with the drink and put it down on the table in front of Melody with a '*parakalo*'. Abby waited for her sister to take a sip. She was going to say the words. No matter what she thought about Darrell's latest message, she needed to cite her relationship status out loud to someone.

'Right,' Melody said, putting her drink back down and adjusting herself in her seat. 'Now I can cope with anything ... well, anything apart from you telling me you've ditched Darrell, because that's about as likely as Ellen DeGeneres turning straight.'

No. Going. Back. Abby took a deep breath, her fingers curling around the beer bottle. She looked straight at Melody. 'Darrell and I ... we broke up.'

Melody's deep I-live-in-Corfu tan seemed to fade like cheap clothes on a hot wash and she turned quickly. 'Parakalo! Another vodka and Coke.' She had the barman's attention now and delivered the final word. 'Megalos.'

'I thought drinking in the morning was banned in case you turn into an alcoholic,' Abby stated in response to the request for 'big'.

'It isn't every day I get news like that! I mean, Abs, you and Darrell, you've been together since ... before ... longer than ...'

'Ant and Dec?' Abby offered.

'What happened?!' Melody was leaning forward now, her bodyweight on the table. 'I mean, I know I thought he was a bit irritating and you know I hated him talking about work all the time and, well, his fashion sense ... well, he didn't really have any, did he? But, even after saying all that, I know you loved him, so ...'

Abby took another sip of her beer, letting the bubbles fizz over her tongue, the malt coat her throat all the way down. 'He cheated on me.'

'Bastard!' Melody hissed. 'Sorry, but *fucking* bastard! Who the fuck does he think he is? *He* cheats on *you*?! Has he looked at you? He has looked at himself in the mirror? *He* was punching so far above his weight in every respect. I always thought that.'

Tears pricked Abby's eyes in an immediate response both to Melody's words of sisterly solidarity and to the hurt she still felt over the whole situation. But she had told someone. She had told her sister. That had to be a good thing. One more step towards acceptance ... if it hadn't been for this latest text.

'He just messaged me.' Abby took another sip of her beer. 'Said he wants another chance.'

'Yeah, I just bet he does. Arsehole.' Melody downed the dregs of her first drink. 'No,' she stated with fierce determination. 'No second chances for anyone who treated you like second best. He will do it again, as long as you let him.'

'I know, but ...' She had to think about it logically. The years they had spent together. Good years. Months and months of perfectly content memories ... why wasn't she thinking words like 'fantastic' or 'amazing'?

'No buts. He dissed, dismissed and disrespected you. There's no coming back from that, d'you hear me?'

Abby nodded but her heart was going to take a little more convincing. Perhaps she needed to ask her sister's opinion on something else ... like Theo's invitation to dinner.

'So ...'

'Mum's going to freak, you know that, right,' Melody carried on.

'I don't want to tell her,' Abby blurted out. 'Not yet.' She sighed. 'She fills every moment she's not worrying about the business or keeping up with Diana with talk about me getting married.'

'Yeah,' Melody said. 'I was kind of hoping you'd get me out of the whole nuptials thing completely and have some stonking great bash she could talk about for decades to come.'

'Sorry,' Abby answered.

'So, you're not going to tell her?' Melody said. 'At all?'

'Well …'

'Because she saw this awfully boring leather briefcase thing on our last trip to Corfu Town she was going to get Darrell for Christmas.'

'No, not at all,' Abby said with conviction. 'Just let's get the party done and the Pappas Villa sold and then … we'll see.'

'Shit,' Melody said as the barman returned with her stronger drink. 'And I thought my life sucked … well, you know, apart from the endless sunshine …'

'And the gorgeous Greek food,' Abby added.

'The beach barbecue trip!' Melody suddenly shouted out. 'You never came to a beach barbecue trip! We need to do that while you're here.' She downed some of her drink. 'Totally not Darrell's scene at all. Way too much fun.'

Abby smiled, taking a sip of her beer. Suddenly life was feeling a little bit more under her control again and, looking out at the gorgeous sea scene ahead of her, she was actually starting to relish the thought of new horizons.

Thirty-four

Desperately Seeking

'Good afternoon, Desperately Seeking.'

Jackie had only just put the phone down and already it was ringing again. Abby had made lemonade. A few over-hanging fruits from the garden of the next-door property, soda water, sugar and a squirt of lime juice, just like Chef's from The Travellers' Rest. She walked to the small table she had cleared of files and placed in the centre of the room, and put the jug down. The office was already looking so much more clean-lined, devoid of pink and ready to welcome in new and existing clients. They had the lovely rattan seat set outside in the sun, with a parasol, should it be required, and then table and chairs in the cooler inside environment. Melody was currently quiet, biting her lip and concentrating as she carefully and decoratively trailed swirling chalk lines on the new blackboard easel.

'Yes, we have a wide variety of two-bedroomed properties in that location. Have you been on our website?' Jackie tried to scribble onto a pad but then looked up, hooking the phone under her chin and waving frantic hands at Abby. Abby grabbed a biro from the centre table and hurried to give it to her mum. 'Oh … you saw a poster about our party on Saturday? Yes, that's right, it's from one o' clock … The Tom Hanks looka-like? Um … yes, that's right. Tom will be here.'

Abby widened her eyes in horror. They didn't have a Tom Hanks lookalike and she was certain there had been no mention of that on any of the invitations she'd had printed.

'Melody!' she hissed.

'Ssh! Please do not disturb me now or this "s" is going to look like a number five.'

'Melody, where are the leftover invitations?'

'Abs!'

'It's important!'

'In my bag!' Melody stuck a hand out, indicating a hessian and feather item Abby didn't remember seeing earlier. She rushed to it, opening the zip, parting the fluffy feathering and delving in until fingers met invitation-shaped paper. She pulled the small wad out and read:

Your new life in the sun starts right here ...

You are invited to the party of the summer and the relaunch of

Desperately Seeking
North Corfu's premier estate agency

Saturday 15 July
From 1pm
Desperately Seeking Offices, Harbourside, San Stefanos
Join us for cocktails and a light buffet plus your chance
to win a fantastic prize in our FREE draw!*

*terms and conditions apply

No Tom Hanks. Absolutely *no* Tom Hanks. She had definitely talked her mum down from that idea and triple-checked the invitations before she got them printed. So why did this caller think there was going to be a lookalike?

Jackie slammed down the phone and got to her feet. 'We need Tom Hanks.'

'No,' Abby said immediately. 'No, we don't. See!' She thrust an invitation at her mum. 'I took it off the invitations when we agreed it was over the top.'

Jackie took the paper, her eyes skimming over its contents. 'Well, that's all well and good, but that woman has seen scores of fluorescent orange posters advertising the party from here to Arillas.'

Abby was confused. She hadn't done any posters. And on fluorescent paper?! They were moving away from the bold and not-so-beautiful garish look. She swung around, looking at Melody, still almost statuesque with the chalk in her hands. 'Melody, did you make posters?'

'What?'

'Posters!' Abby exclaimed. 'Did you make orange posters for the party and stick them up everywhere?'

'Are you out of your mind?' Melody snapped back. 'Bugger!' The chalk in her hand snapped. 'Now look what you've done!' She stood up, glowering at Abby. 'When have I had time to make posters?'

'Well, we only have two options now,' Jackie stated, frantic. 'We either find these posters and take them down, or we find a Tom.'

'Good morning! *Kalimera!*'

All eyes went to the office door and standing there, a large sunhat as big as a sombrero on her head, vintage cream-framed sunglasses hiding her eyes, was Diana.

'Fuck's sake,' Melody muttered under her breath as she stepped back and crushed another piece of chalk.

'Hello, Diana,' Jackie greeted, voice attempting calm. 'Lovely, *lovely* day out there, isn't it?'

'Goodness,' Diana said, stepping in. 'Have you had time to actually leave your premises? I was under the impression it was all hands to the pump organising a party for Saturday.'

'It is,' Abby jumped in. 'But everything's organised.'

'And we've been doing a viewing this morning,' Jackie continued. 'A gorgeous villa. Belonging to Spyridoula Pappas's brother.'

'Really?' The tone sounded disbelieving.

'Really!' Abby found herself insisting.

'It must be very nice to *finally* have similar properties to Aleko.' Diana let out a sigh, whipped off her hat and began fanning her face with it. 'Perhaps the commission will lead to the installation of better air-conditioning.'

'Actually,' Melody said, rising up from her crouching position. 'Before you came in there was a lot less hot air in here.'

'Would you like a glass of lemonade?' Jackie offered quickly, coming out from behind her desk. 'It's one of the specialities from Abby's hotel.'

'Is it made with lemons?' Diana asked, putting one high-heeled sandal in front of the other and treading cautiously like she might be in the centre of a minefield.

'It's *lemon*ade,' Melody replied with an exaggerated eye roll.

'Are they ripe?'

'They were yellow,' Melody continued. 'You know, fruit ... slightly waxy skin ... grow on trees round here.'

'I'll pass,' Diana said, the moment Jackie picked up a glass and the jug. 'Save myself for the wonderful Greek fruit punch Aleko is serving on Saturday, at *his* party.'

Abby felt the humidity in the room rise tenfold and suddenly her lungs seemed incapable of providing her with oxygen. What had Diana just said? Aleko was having a party – on Saturday. Before she could even open her mouth, Melody had pounced.

'What did you say?'

'Oh, I thought you were bound to know. In fact, I thought it was deliberate on your part, having your little soirée at the same time as the one at Ionian Dreams. A bit of healthy competition, like, I suppose, a small-scale expo.'

Abby watched Jackie's expression. All their hard work with the quick rebranding, the invitations and culinary party planning and their arch-rival was trying to scupper their event. Perhaps the facts were correct, but she was not about to let this horrible woman come into their office and rub their noses in it.

'Of course we knew,' Abby interrupted, stepping towards Diana with as much confidence as her body could create. 'What better way to get more people to San Stefanos than for both of us to have an event on the same day? It gives people a choice and here at Desperately Seeking, we're all about choice.'

'That's why we have a wide range of properties on our books,' Melody continued. 'From ruins costing less than ten thousand euro to houses like the Pappas Villa. We don't exclude. We are *all inclusive*.'

'And that's why I'm still here,' Jackie joined in. 'Almost ready to celebrate the business's second anniversary. Because of the wonderful *Greek* community spirit.'

'Aleko has free pens,' Diane countered.

'We have cocktails that are going to knock everyone's sandals off,' Melody informed.

'And then there's the free spa days—'

'Well, we have … Tom Hanks.'

Right at that moment Abby wanted to gag her mum but she held on to her smile, Melody at her side, all three of them facing Diana like a vision of unity.

'Goodness!' Diana exclaimed. 'A Hollywood A-lister.' Her eyes roved around the interior of the office. 'In … here.'

'Take an invitation,' Abby said, holding the flyers out. 'And perhaps some for your Pow Wow and Pikilia group.'

'Delighted,' Diana said, accepting the invitations. 'See you on Saturday.'

'We will reserve the very best plastic cocktail glasses just for you and your … what's the word I'm looking for?' Melody asked. 'Ah, yes … *friends*.'

All three of them held their stance (and their nerve) until Diana had left the building and then …

'Mum! Why did you mention Tom bloody Hanks?!' Melody exclaimed.

'I don't know! I didn't want her trumping us with Aleko and his bloody spa days and his free pens.' Jackie took a frenzied breath. 'I can't believe that little weasel has planned a party the same day as our party. It's sabotage! And he knows, I'm sure he knows, how close to the wind we're sailing financially.'

'Trump!' Melody stated, eyes wide.

'What?' Abby asked.

'I might be able to get Donald Trump.'

'Melody, that man wants to build a wall around Mexico. He's not someone I want associated with our business. Tom Hanks, on the other hand, made a friend out of a football and played Sully. And everyone loves Sully.'

'Not the real one!' Melody exclaimed. 'There was a lookalike who worked in Sidari last season. He did photos and let people throw wet sponges at him and stuff. He really did look like him.'

'Even the hair?' Jackie asked.

'Especially the hair.'

'But he's not Tom,' Jackie stated with a sigh.

'Tom's a very busy man. He could send Donald in his place.' Melody grinned. 'Mum, come on, how much would everyone enjoy throwing stuff at Trump?'

Abby showed them both the screen of her phone. 'Life-size cardboard cut-out of Tom Hanks or ... celebrity face mask just £3.57 on Amazon. How quick can they get it to Corfu?'

'Next day,' both Jackie and Melody answered together.

Melody laughed. 'We know a hack.'

Abby smiled. 'Let's get a cardboard Tom and trump Aleko with Trump.'

'So wanging.'

Thirty-five

Pelekito

Before Theo's job at The Blue Vine, every day had been a day off here in Corfu. But back in the routine of work, with a whole day to fill, he had been at a loss as to what to do, until he had opened up his father's garage. The aroma had hit him straightaway, right in the heartstrings. Oil, dust, polish and leather, notes of these scents had all spiralled around him as he stepped inside the large space in the under-build of the villa. Here, in spring breaks when the weather wasn't too hot, he and his father had worked – tinkering, improving, fixing. These were about the only things Dinis did not pay someone else to take care of. Most of the time they had worked alone, together but not together. Side by side, but separate in their project and their thinking, until one needed the other for advice or a second opinion. Breathing in the nostalgia, Theo had surveyed the two vehicles sat in front of him, both immaculately presented, their gleaming chrome and paintwork showroom-ready. It had taken him mere seconds to decide between the speed and ostentatious appeal of the Porsche and the guttural grunt and freedom of the motorcycle.

The breeze from his speed on the bike flicked loose strands of his dark hair around his face. The helmet, as was the some-time Greek way, he wore strapped to his arm. It felt so good, to travel like this, liberated by the winding roads, a new, fresh, enchanting scene at every turn. He never got tired of Corfu. It had always meant a break from normality, a time-out from the stresses and strains of working life – or his *father's* working life when he had been a child. Days filled with sunshine, laughter, family ... but here he was, alone. And alone seemed to be sending him to Pelekito and that olive-wood workshop.

He turned off the main road, taking the natural curves in the road with as much speed as he could without slipping over to grass and earth in the olive groves. Within seconds he was pulling the bike to a stop outside the ramshackle building. It was hot today, even under the shade of these olive-laden trees and Theo pulled his T-shirt away from his body, trying to get some air under the fabric.

Suddenly the door to the workshop opened wide, a section of corrugated iron falling to the ground with the force. Two sheep trotted out at speed and Stamatis came afterwards, a large, heavy, banister of wood in his hands.

'*Ela! Exo!*'

Theo clapped his hands at the animals, forcing them away from his father's motorbike and off into the wood.

'What is this? I don't see you for months then two times in two days?'

Stamatis' tone was rich with sarcasm, but Theo didn't miss the slight upturn on his mouth that said something else entirely. The older man was pleased he was here.

'I can go,' Theo teased, 'if you are too busy for coffee and ...' He flipped up the lid of the box at the rear of the motorbike and pulled out a paper bag. 'Apple cake.'

'You have apple cake?' Stamatis asked, moving his lips as they appeared to moisten.

'Do you have time?' Theo asked.

Stamatis shook his head. 'What is life without time for apple cake?' He turned his back on Theo, retreating into his domain.

Within a few minutes, the man had made a pot of coffee and given over a rustic bowl with a misshapen edge to house the pie. And there they both sat, at Stamatis' favourite workbench, the coffee and pie set among shavings and off-cuts. Theo watched his friend tucking into the dessert like it was the first meal he had eaten in weeks. Perhaps it was. He well remembered the times Stamatis had worked late into the night, having forgotten to eat lunch and not seeming set for supper either.

'Your father is not here?' Stamatis broke the companionable silence that had been accompanied only by the sound of chewing.

'No,' Theo answered. He felt no need to say anything further.

'He is coming later?'

'No,' Theo responded again. Then, 'I do not think so.'

'He came here last July, for a week.'

Had he? Why didn't Theo know about this? He racked his brain, trying to remember last summer. What he had done. What the family had done. He had stayed on the mainland, looking after the business while ... his father had travelled to a boat exhibition. Was that what Dinis had done? Or had he flown over to Corfu?

'You saw my father?' Theo said.

Stamatis nodded, his mouth full. 'He did not come here, of course. He was at the petrol station in Acharavi. With the fancy car.' The man smiled then, humour filling his wrinkled features. 'I pulled up next to him in my van.'

Theo laughed then, imagining the scene. Stamatis' van was even more rundown than the workshop. It was held together only by the thick, red, metalwork paint he slathered over it every winter.

'Stupid little car,' Stamatis continued. 'He is almost six feet tall. He has to bend himself in half to get into the driving seat.'

'You are jealous,' Theo teased. 'Of the car and his height.'

Stamatis shook his head. 'No,' he said firmly. 'Jealousy, it is a wasteful emotion. There is no point to it. It does not make anybody feel good and it is a feeling mostly about dissatisfaction with your own choices.' He chewed up a mouthful of cake. 'We are all in control of our own destiny, Theo.'

Theo's mouth suddenly felt dry and he had a job to swallow his portion of cake. He was in control of his own destiny now. But it didn't feel liberating. It felt terrifying.

'Who is the girl?' Stamatis said suddenly, slurping at his coffee.

'The girl?'

Stamatis grunted. 'Pah! There is more than one? Shame on you, Theo.' He shook his head. 'I blame your crazy hair.' He slurped at the coffee again. 'The girl you bring here.'

'Abby,' Theo said. Her name on his lips always felt so good and he had no idea why that would be.

'You remember her name at least!'

'She's …' What was she? He had only known her a few days. She had been a customer at The Blue Vine but the destiny Stamatis talked about did seem to be putting them in each other's paths. 'She's … someone I would like to get to know better but …'

'You have not brought a girl here before.'

'No, well, she wanted to buy a sign.'

'I have not seen you look this way before.'

'I do not know what you mean.' He did know, because the old man's scrutiny was making his insides react as well as his cheeks.

'Theo, I have lived a long time.'

'And will continue to,' Theo said quickly.

'I have seen many things and I have let many things slip through my own fingers.' He sighed. 'And I do not mean trunks of trees.'

'I am not letting anything slip,' Theo sat back on his stool a little. 'There is nothing to slip.' He swallowed. 'Leon ... he likes Abby too.'

Stamatis nodded for the longest time and Theo could almost see the workings of his mind churning over the scenario that he had no intention of sharing when he had ridden over here.

'Let me share with you one thing I have learnt over all these years.' Stamatis picked up a stick of wood and held it out like a sword, swishing it back and forth over the bowl full of cake.

'That you wish to have been a knight?' Theo offered, smiling at his friend's display.

'That I wish I had not stepped away from what I truly wanted. That I had not let pride and stupidity and tradition stop me, and someone else, from being happy.'

Theo looked at the old man now, the stick shaking a little in his gnarled hand. This was a piece of a story he had never heard before.

'I know that what happened on the sea has changed you forever,' Stamatis carried on. 'But you have an opportunity to make those changes count. With everything negative there can be a positive. But you must let the positive in. Do not let the black clouds swallow everything, including you.'

Theo opened his mouth to protest, to brush off the man's claims, to say that he was fine, everything was fine, that the old fool did not know what he was talking about. But his voice didn't come out and instead he found his eyes moistening, his leg beginning its tell-tale twitch as he felt the need to jounce it up and down.

Suddenly, the door of the workshop opened, then just as quickly it closed again, as if a rogue wind (or sheep) had breached the mix of wood and steel. The moment was broken and Theo picked up the tin mug, putting it to his lips. Stamatis took another section of cake and said nothing more. Eventually the silence was too much to for Theo to bear.

'Stamatis …' Theo stated.

'Yes, Theo?'

'I have invited Abby to dinner and I have no idea how to cook.'

Stamatis let out the deepest roar of a laugh that shook both the wooden wind chimes and the spindles on the shelves waiting to be fashioned into chairs. 'You ask me! Someone who eats only from tins? A better person to ask would be your aunt.'

'Now you really do joke with me,' Theo said with a shake of his head. 'Spyridoula has never made anything in her life. She even buys tzatziki from the supermarket.'

'Now, perhaps,' Stamatis said. 'But only a few years ago there was every dish imaginable produced in her kitchen.' He nodded knowingly. 'Ask her.'

Thirty-six

The Dolan House

Abby had decided she wasn't going to go to Villa Pappas to meet with Theo. Being ready to feel slightly more settled about being single was one thing, dating was another matter entirely. And she hadn't accepted, so she wouldn't really be letting him down. He had just said eight o' clock and she had run into the house to help finish the viewing. She didn't even have his phone number to call or text, and anyway she was too busy finalising things for the relaunch party.

She was enjoying sitting on the edge of her bed writing a list of things to do, a cool evening breeze drifting through the open window. And then her door crashed open, banging against the wall, Melody barrelling in.

'Mum's made a right pig's ear of the canapes! They're supposed to be feta, chive and tzatziki mixed together and rolled into a tortilla then cut up into individual wraps – look pretty, taste nice and save money – but ...'

'What's happened?' Abby asked.

'She's dropped the sugar bowl into the mix! It's this new mother we've got! The one who wants to use every plate we have to serve us wholesome meals we haven't ever seen the like of before!'

'But we have to remember that this mum is full of confidence again. She's enthused about the changes, the opportunities selling the Pappas Villa has already brought to Desperately Seeking, with new interest and quoting opportunities.'

'I know,' Melody said. 'But we do need this party to be the best it can be and … let's face it, she's no Candice Brown.'

'What do you want me to do?' Abby asked.

'Speak to George.' Melody said it so quietly, Abby almost didn't hear the words.

'You want me to ask George to do the catering?'

'Well, you can't ask Maria from the World Café because, although her food is amazing, it's also pricey. And I don't remember you being an absolute whizz in the kitchen.'

'And your idea of nutrition is a multipack of Walkers crisps.'

'Lays,' Melody retorted. 'Here, their branding is "Lays".' She sniffed. 'And the paprika ones are so good.'

'What are you doing?! What is this?!'

It was Jackie's voice but it was coming through the open bedroom window and both women moved towards it, squeezing themselves into the gap to get a view of the street below.

'It's George and Mum,' Melody stated, as if she were providing commentary for someone who was partially sighted.

'I can see that,' Abby said. 'And, is he … holding an orange poster?'

'We should go down,' Melody said, easing herself out of the window. 'This could get ugly.' She rushed to the door and Abby followed.

'George, what is this?' Jackie exclaimed angrily.

Abby surveyed the scene when she and Melody arrived street-side. It appeared George had been planning to pin a fluorescent poster to the telegraph pole.

'It is a poster,' he answered. 'To advertise your party.'

'I can see that!' Jackie exclaimed. 'But why would you do that?!'

'To help you,' George said. 'Aleko, he is driving around a van right now, with a speaker system just like the one they use to call out the fruit and vegetables. I see your invitation and I know I have this very visible paper in my storeroom so I think I use this to help get more people to your office.'

'But no one asked you to do that!' Jackie continued to berate.

'Jackie,' George began. 'This is Greece. We do things for other people without the need to be asked.'

'Well, you shouldn't make assumptions that all help is needed.'

'Mum.' Abby felt sorry for George. He had been doing a good deed. He must have seen an early draft of the invitation before creating his poster – perhaps she left a piece of notepad in the restaurant – and not the final version.

'It's not a disaster,' Melody said quickly. 'George can tell us where he stuck the posters up and we can go to the places and just Sharpie out the Tom Hanks bit.'

'And just how professional is that going to look?' Jackie said, ripping the poster out of George's hands.

'Or we leave them,' Abby said, matter-of-factly.

'We can't leave them!' Jackie snapped back. 'It's a breach of the Trade Descriptions Act or something like that.'

'But nobody's paying anything,' Melody pointed out. 'I'm sure you can get away with pretty much anything if it's free.'

Abby reached out and touched her mum's arm, as if trying to her steady her angry energy. 'We are going to have Donald Trump and Tom in cardboard. That's going to be enough.'

'Is it?' Jackie asked, voice slightly calmer, eyes holding tears that looked close to escaping. 'Because I've dropped sugar in the entire mix I was making for the tortillas.'

'You were cooking for the party?' George inquired.

'I think the word "cooking" is slightly over the top,' Melody answered.

'You cannot cook,' George said.

'George! That is an extremely rude thing to say!'

'But true,' Melody said, daring to laugh.

'All the time you live here you only buy things in cans and packets that can be cooked in the microwave,' George continued.

'I was actually paid to cook for villas only a few months ago and ... how do you know the contents of my kitchen cupboards?!'

'I will make you food,' George said in a matter-of-fact manner.

'No!' Jackie said. 'We can't aff—' She stopped herself. 'We haven't budgeted for *outside* catering.'

George waved her protests away. 'I will make food for a hundred people. I will bring it in good time for the party. You let me know if you need more.' He bowed at Abby and Melody then began to make his way back down the street towards his restaurant.

'Wait! George ... stop!' Jackie said, beginning to trot along the road after him.

Melody let out a contented sigh. 'We didn't even have to ask.'

'He's such a lovely man,' Abby said, watching Jackie continuing to chew his ear off as he strolled. 'Do you think Mum likes him? I could see them getting along.'

'I think they've probably both been single too long,' Melody said, stretching her arms above her head in response to a shaft of light that lit up the street as the sun reappeared from behind a cloud. 'Don't let the grass settle under your gladiators, Abby, or you might end up in your fifties, chasing a Greek restauranteur down the street.'

'How long?' Abby asked, her thoughts suddenly filled with Theo.

'How long what?'

'How long should I leave it?'

'Leave what?! Abs! Come on! Spit it out!'

She swallowed. She deserved a bit of fun. She liked Theo in so many ways. He had shown her that beautiful olive-wood workshop she would definitely be going back to as soon as they had enough money for the new sign. He had helped her with the car. Fed apples to cows. Made her the best Old Fashioned cocktail she had ever tasted. *And* given her a Full Monty experience she definitely hadn't been prepared for. But there were other things about him that remained a mystery. His reaction to the boat incident. The fact he had trashed his employer's villa the night before her important viewing ...

'I've been asked to dinner,' Abby blurted out.

'What?! When?!' Melody exclaimed. 'Wanging hell.'

'Well, you just said there shouldn't be any grass growing under my feet.'

'Who by?! Leon again?' Melody shook her head. 'He's nice enough but he's never going to leave San Stef. I'm not sure he's even been to Athens. And he has a huge family – like fifty-eight brothers and sisters and twice as many aunts and uncles – and most of them live in that apartment above the bike hire shop.'

Abby swallowed. 'It isn't Leon. It's Theo.'

'Theo,' Melody stated.

Abby nodded, unable to stop those flashes of naked flesh pricking her recollection.

'Fucking hell, Abs, I know he's only a gardener and a barman and not a rich Russian, but he's hot!'

Her cheeks immediately went nuclear. She knew he was hot. Hotter than Darrell. She shouldn't think that. But what if he was out of her league in the hotness stakes? The balance wouldn't be right. It could be a case of Katy Perry and Russell Brand all over again.

'Too hot?' she queried with her sister.

'There's no such thing!' Melody insisted. 'And you're gorgeous, Abs, maybe a touch darker around the eyes than me, but totally smoking. Where's he taking you?'

'He invited me for dinner at Villa Pappas.'

'My God! He's going to cook!'

'Or get George to bring him food if, like Mum, he can't,' Abby suggested with a smile.

'Well, what are you wearing?'

'I … don't think I'm going to go,' Abby answered, eyes moving to the water and trying to draw in some stabilising common sense from the gently rocking ocean.

'What?! Why wouldn't you go?! Are you mad?!' Melody shrieked. 'If you don't go then I will!'

'I need to help you and Mum with everything for the party.'

'Abby! That's an excuse! The party's all organised apart from Trump and cardboard Tom. George is taking over the food. All I've got to do is stop Mum putting that horror of a mixture into plastic boxes and making us have it on bread for the next week. I can manage that on my own.'

'I don't know,' Abby said, taking a faltering breath.

'Stop overthinking things. This isn't some handwash salesman at the hotel. You don't need to check budgets or have a meeting to find out the cost effectiveness of changing supplier versus possible superior quality and loyalty. This is dinner. With a hot guy. And you're totally single.'

'Ssh,' Abby begged. She looked down the road, Jackie had finally left George alone and was walking back towards them.

'Go out and have fun, I'll pretend I'm not jealous.' Melody smiled. 'And let me spray your hair with this new stuff I had shipped in from China.'

'What is it?'

'No idea,' Melody replied. 'But it kicks Silvikrin's arse.'

Jackie arrived back with them, a little out of breath. Melody and Abby looked at her, as if waiting for some sort of missive. Finally, it came.

'George is doing the food.'

'That's a great decision, Mum,' Melody put an arm around her and led her back towards the house. 'I know I was a little down on George's food the other night but that was because it was so long since we'd been there. It's a little rustic ...'

'Traditional,' Abby chipped in.

'Traditional,' Melody repeated. 'But comforting. One slice of his home-made sweet bread and most of the customers aren't going to be able to eat anything else. And they're going to feel full and content and ready to sign up to our newsletter at the very least.'

'I hope so,' Jackie said with a sigh. 'Unless Aleko has The World Café catering for him.'

'Well ...' Melody began.

'He doesn't, does he?!'

'No, Mum,' Melody said. 'Not that I know of.' She pushed open the door.

'Perhaps I need to speak to Aleko, business owner to business owner, make sure the parties clashing a little isn't going to turn into some sort of turf war, that we're both on the same page in taking the view that more people looking for properties in the village is a good thing for us both.'

'Perhaps you should have a nice, cooling shower,' Melody shepherded her mum towards the stairs, bypassing the chaotic kitchen.

Abby smiled and picked her phone up from the worktop. On its screen was another message from Darrell. Was this because she hadn't acknowledged his one earlier. Did she want to read it? Now she had decided to go to dinner with Theo. But putting off looking at it wasn't going to change its content. She unlocked the phone and tapped.

> Bit embarrassing. Ignore the message I sent earlier. Meant to send it to Amber. D ☺

Abby shook her head, biting her lip as her eyes welled up with angry tears. He hadn't wanted her back at all. Instead, it seemed Amber had had enough of him too. Well, there was only one thing to do. Get ready for a night with someone who made her insides sizzle.

Thirty-seven

Villa Pappas

Theo's hair kept falling out of its tie and over his eyes as he rolled the pieces of chicken in a dry mixture Stamatis had suggested. Despite the woodworker saying he knew nothing of cuisine, the dusty shelves of his workshop contained vast numbers of his mother's leather-bound tomes, some of which held long-forgotten recipes from Greek families of yore. Stamatis had seemed to enjoy thumbing the crumbling pages, picking out complex dishes Theo wasn't sure even the best chef would be capable of creating. Finally, he had opted for one with a mere twenty steps rather than fifty, although he had altered 'stoke up the fire' to 'pre-heat the oven'. He hadn't dared mention anything about cooking to Spyridoula.

'Hello! Is it safe to come in? Or are there people still looking around the house.'

It was Leon. Suddenly Theo felt guilty. Here he was, preparing dinner for someone he knew Leon liked. She was even Leon's date for the *panegyri*. He should tell him. He should be open and honest and say he had spent a few, chance hours with Abby and he wanted to get to know her better. That she had accepted. Except she hadn't. He was making all this effort in the kitchen and he didn't really know if Abby was going to turn up.

'What is that smell?!' Leon exclaimed, entering the kitchen, a pack of Fix beers under his arm. 'Is that dinner?'

'No ... yes ... but it is for later.'

'You are cooking for someone?' Leon asked.

Here was his opportunity to be completely direct and he was going to take it. 'Yes. Leon ...'

'Spyridoula is coming over with more people looking? She wants to create a *yiayia's* kitchen and you are doing this?' Leon had a confused look on his face.

'She has some people coming for dinner here,' Theo blurted out. 'She asked me to do this.' He swallowed. 'She is paying me.'

'Well,' Leon began. 'I was hoping to watch Olympiacos but I can do that at home, my other home, the one with the screaming brothers and sisters who want to test their make-up on me.'

'I'm sorry, Leon,' Theo said, genuinely meaning it for so many reasons.

'No, it is OK. This place is not for ever, is it? Soon you will move on, or the villa will be sold, and I will have to move back or, maybe, find somewhere of my own.' Leon seemed to muse on that idea for a moment. 'Perhaps I will leave the island.'

'What?' Theo exclaimed. 'Leave Corfu?' He put the chicken he was rubbing back into the bowl and wiped his fingers on the apron he was wearing over his jeans and T-shirt.

Leon laughed. 'You just said that like this island is the centre of the universe. *You* left.'

'It was never really my home,' Theo reminded his friend. 'It was my father's home until he was eighteen and *he* left. To me it has always just been the place for holidays, but for you – your whole family is here.'

'And I will visit.' Leon sniffed. 'Perhaps I need to look outside of Corfu, for my own family.' He smiled. 'Maybe I will go to England.'

'England.' The word felt ugly on his lips as he repeated it. He was instantly tense about whatever Leon was going to say next.

'I have never been and everyone says it is a great place with history like we have in Greece, only a little greyer perhaps. And ...' Leon smiled. 'I will have a friend there. Abby.'

Theo needed to say something. Leon was his best friend. Even though they lived so many miles apart, when they got back together it was like no time had passed at all. Leon was telling him he might move to the UK, visit Abby, and here he was making a meal for her. Something he had never done for any woman before ...

Leon laughed out loud and slapped Theo on the back. 'Your face! What is wrong? You are worried you are going to be left behind with only Spinster Madalena for company?'

He shook his head. 'No, I just ... England.' He took a breath. 'It should be a choice you make for you, for the best reasons, not for ... a girl.'

Leon laughed again. 'You think I am blind, Theo?'

'Blind?' he queried.

'Abby,' Leon carried on.

'What?' Theo hardly dared to breathe.

'She is not interested in me.'

'She is not?'

Leon shook his head. 'It is not usual for me to have to work so hard.'

'But the *panegyri*?' Theo questioned.

'Is a nice idea. It will mean I will not be lacking a dance partner but ... I feel we will just be friends.'

'OK.' Theo exhaled hard without even realising it.

'And,' Leon continued. 'As this is the truth ... if you felt you might like to ...'

'Like to?'

'With Abby.' Leon laughed. 'Come on, Theo, I know that you like her.'

'I ...' He did like her, but it was so alien to him. To want to get to know someone better. To want to spend time just being with someone. He had never had a relationship like that. The longest time he had shared with someone was weeks, not months or years. The whole concept of the idea of it had always felt ridiculous until now ...

'What is holding you back?' Leon queried, punching his arm good-naturedly. 'The way is clear, my friend.'

'I ... do not know how to do it,' Theo admitted.

'Do what?' Leon asked.

'To ... be with someone for more than a night. To do more than take somebody's clothes off. To talk.'

'Oh, Theo,' Leon said with sympathy in his tone. 'But you do this so easily when we go out.'

'After six or seven beers,' he said, 'when what I say is just a script. Lines I know the woman will appreciate.' He wet his lips. 'None of it comes from a very deep place.'

'And these deep words ... they are what you want to say to Abby?' Leon put the beers down, paying Theo all his attention.

Theo shook his head. 'I do not know. Maybe.'

'You want my advice?' Leon asked him.

'I do not know that either,' he admitted with a smile.

'You need to open up to someone,' Leon said bluntly. 'You need to talk to someone. You need to just get out how you feel. About the accident, Theo. You *have* to talk about that.'

This was not news to him. He knew it. He didn't like it, but he knew it all the same. Yet, immediately his body and mind went into some sort of lockdown. He looked away from his friend, his hands finding their way back into the bowl of chicken pieces. He knew Leon knew about what had happened, but even his very good friend had not heard it from him.

'I think, until you can do that,' Leon continued. 'Everything else will always seem too hard.'

'Leon the Philosopher,' Theo said, his voice more jovial than he felt. Leon didn't even know that Abby thought he was nothing more than the gardener.

'Taxi drivers hear a lot of things. It means they learn a lot of things also,' Leon stated. He put a hand on Theo's shoulder. 'Perhaps you should take Abby to the 7th Heaven bar. That view always makes everything else seem so much smaller.'

As his emotions gained momentum like a Red Bull soapbox cart, all Theo could manage was a nod.

Thirty-eight

'You didn't have to drive me,' Abby said.

'I told you it was as much for the car's benefit as it was for yours. Leave this thing for longer than a day and its brakes stick.' Melody turned off the engine then span in her seat to face Abby. 'So, remember not to touch your hair *at all*.'

'What happens if I do?' Abby asked. She had already scrunched her hands up in her lap, as just thinking about not touching made her want to touch.

'I don't know what they put in the miracle lacquer, but I do know there are YouTube videos showing some awful after effects if you ingest it.'

'What?!' Abby exclaimed.

'Focus on the fact that you're *not* going to touch it, let alone ingest it and your hair is going to sit there, very still, looking impeccable for the whole night. And ...' Melody winked. 'I mean the *whole* night. Believe me, this stuff has more than coped with the most energetic mattress-dancing.'

'It won't need to stand up to that,' Abby said, the car suddenly getting a little greenhouse-like. She looked for an air-conditioning button she already knew wouldn't be there because of the age of this model. She settled for winding down the window completely, but in flowed more heat, along with the cicadas' song.

'Well, what are you expecting from the night?' Melody asked.

'I don't know what you mean,' Abby replied.

Her sister's mouth dropped open. 'Don't tell me you didn't run through your Date Expectations while you were getting ready?'

Date Expectations? It sounded like something you would note down in a life journal, if you had time for a life journal. She preferred To-Do Lists. They were productive and sounded just a little bit less bohemian.

'He's invited me for dinner,' Abby ventured. 'I'm expecting food.'

'What's he making?'

'I have no idea.'

'What? He didn't ask what you liked? Or didn't like?'

'No but I ...' She hadn't even properly accepted. What if he had taken that as a 'no' and he wasn't even really expecting her? She might be about to make a colossal fool of herself.

'What if you had allergies?!'

'Melody, I don't have any allergies.'

'*He* doesn't know that!' She folded her arms across her chest. 'Does he know you aren't that keen on sun-dried tomatoes?'

'I'm sure I'll cope.'

'Well, if it's barbecue food, you totally *do not* stay the night – unless he's bought you a gift.'

Abby smiled. Melody did seem to live her life based on a whole alternative code of practice to most people. 'I won't be staying the night.'

'Why not? You don't know that. You're single. You're a modern woman. You're on holiday.'

'I don't do casual.'

'Because you've just been with Darrell for a billion years.'

'It wasn't quite a billion.'

'It was not quite a billion too many.'

Abby put her hand to the door. She didn't need a Melody pep-talk on dating expectations. If Theo thought she wasn't coming, or maybe wasn't even in, she would hang out in the garden until she was sure Melody had gone and then take a slow walk back to the harbour. No loss. Probably for the best, although the anticipation of spending a pleasant evening with someone she wanted to know a little better who also looked like he'd stepped off the pages of *GQ* was a little bit thrilling. 'I should go.' She opened the door and stepped out into the steamy air.

'Well, I'd sleep with him!' Melody called as Abby pushed the car door closed.

She took a deep breath then turned back to her sister and the open car window. 'After I've sniffed at my plate of sun-dried tomatoes and ingested my hair products, I'll let him know.'

'Abs! That isn't funny! Abby! Wait!' Melody called as she headed to the gate. 'Please *don't* suck your hair! I mean it!'

Abby lifted the latch on the iron gate. What she really wanted to do was stand and wait, compose herself before going in, but not with Melody as a spectator. She was hoping, as soon as she was inside the grounds, she could take a moment, get used to the idea of being here about to spend an evening with a man who wasn't the man she had thought she would be living the rest of her life with. She closed her eyes as soon as feet met the plaka stone of the terrace. She could do this. This was not sky-diving or abseiling or holding on to a wee you'd been needing since lunchtime. This was a pleasant meal, with good company, in a gorgeous setting, no expectations at all – because she wasn't her sister – and he might not have even remembered he had invited her.

'Abby.'

The low lilt of Theo's voice had her snapping her eyes open. He was here and she felt suddenly vulnerable, knowing she had been standing just inside the gate, eyes shut, between the creeping, hot-pink bougainvillea and the low wall planters filled with lemon-scented miniature cypress, bright red anemones and geraniums.

He was standing just by the edge of the pool, a bottle of wine in his hands. All her senses were in battle as sight, sound and smell all ached to react first. He was wearing dark-blue linen trousers that fitted him beautifully, skimming over those lithe limbs to Havaianas on his feet. Stretching over his top half was a white linen shirt – not too tight, not too loose – achingly perfect and enhancing every inch of the shape of him. His hair was fixed back, that tight bun at the base of his neck and those dark eyes, shrouded by eyelashes it should be illegal for a man to own, were looking right back into hers. She should say something instead of gawping. And then she realised, apart from her handbag, she had brought nothing else. What idiot came to dinner without at least a bottle of wine or some chocolates for the host?!

'Hello,' she said, her voice sounding like a mouse stuck in the depths of a cave. 'I … haven't bought anything. I'm so sorry. I got caught up with …' She swallowed. The words 'Tom Hanks issues' thankfully didn't escape her lips.

Theo held up the bottle of wine. 'I have white or red or I can make you an Old Fashioned.'

Just the thought of that gorgeously sweet yet bitter whisky concoction had her taste buds leaping. But she shouldn't indulge in shorts too early.

'Wine would be lovely,' she answered, taking steps towards him. 'White, please.'

Theo put the wine down on the table then held his position, waiting for her to reach him. She looked exquisite in the light, cream dress she was wearing. It fitted close to her body, accentuating her soft curves, then flared a little from the waist, the bottom of it skirting her mid-thigh. On her feet were sandals, with a small heel that gave her a few more inches to her height. He noticed nothing more, beguiled by those beautiful eyes. He leaned forward, his lips touching first one cheek and then the other. He stopped on the second touch, his mouth close to her ear, her hair touching his cheek, the warmth of the night coiling around him. '*Kalispera*,' he whispered softly. '*Pinas?*'

As soon as he said the word in Greek he realised exactly how it had sounded. He stepped back, cheeks reddening, mad with himself.

'Abby ... I ... that was Greek ... I didn't mean ...' This was the very worst start to a date he really cared about.

And then she began to laugh, her whole face lighting up, shoulders relaxing. 'You're lucky I've done a little course in Greek. I know exactly what "pinas" means.'

'You do,' Theo responded, a nervous breath leaving his body. '*Fandastika*.'

'And yes,' Abby answered. '*Ne, pinau*. I am hungry.'

'*Poli kalo*,' he responded.

'Is it sun-dried tomatoes?' Abby asked.

'No,' he replied. 'It is chicken.' He took a breath. 'This is OK? You are not vegetarian? I did not ask.' He tutted. 'I did not think to ask.'

She shook her head. 'No,' she answered. 'I'm not vegetarian and … I didn't really give you time to ask, did I?'

He smiled. 'Shall we sit down? I will open the wine.'

Thirty-nine

The wine was sweet, fruity and wonderfully chilled. A bit like Abby herself after her second glass of it. Theo had led the way to a table set up at the rear of the terrace, the position commanding the best views of the harbour and the ocean beyond. There were candles all around, on the pillared wall, by the pool and on the table, ready to light when the sun started to go down. And at the edge of the old stone planters were glowing lanterns, their citronella fragrance warding off the evening bugs.

They had nibbled on fresh bread, fat, purple Kalamata olives, and griddled *saganaki*, accompanied by *tzatziki*, *tirokafteri* (a spicy feta cheese dip with pepper and oregano) and *skordalia* (a dip with potatoes, garlic and almonds). The latter Abby had never tasted before, but the combination had been a heavenly one. She had tried not to indulge too heavily, knowing there was chicken to come, but dips were a weakness akin to her pastry addiction.

Now there was a plate of the most fragrant-smelling chicken dish in front of her, sizzling peppers, onions and courgettes in a hot pan centre-stage, along with a platter of stuffed aubergines.

'Theo,' she began as he sank back into the seat next to her. 'I have to ask.'

'Anything,' he replied, looking at her.

'Did you really make all this food?'

He grinned then. 'You think that I have takeaway boxes in the kitchen?'

'No ... I wouldn't be so rude to even think that ... I just ...' She couldn't say that she was judging him on Darrell's standards. That his idea of cooking was opening a tin of Heinz Big Soup.

'I make this,' Theo admitted.

'All of it?' Abby queried, aghast.

'Not the bread,' Theo said. 'It said it would take hours to make the bread so ...'

'It's delicious,' Abby told him. 'Really delicious.'

'I have not made it before.'

'It's a new recipe?'

'No,' Theo said. 'Yes ... I mean, I have not really cooked before.'

She dropped her fork to her plate. 'Sorry,' she said, picking it back up. 'You haven't cooked before? And you made all this?!'

'Growing up I did not have a mother for very long a time and my *yiayia*, she was very old when I was very young.'

'Your mother died?' Abby queried.

He nodded. 'I was four. My brother and sister, they were two and newly born.'

'Oh, Theo ... I'm so sorry. That must have been terrible for you.'

He shrugged, his body almost hardening like a toughened exterior had just been welded to his skin. 'It was a long time ago. It was a condition of her heart that no one knew anything about. One of those unfortunate things that could happen at any time.'

Abby nodded, memories of her dad coming to the fore. His heart had been weak too, but at least he had known what was ahead, and savoured those few precious years.

'My father died,' she said aloud. 'When I was a teenager.'

'He did?' Theo said. He took her hand in his, squeezing it reassuringly. His fingers wrapped around hers, warm and comforting. Immediate physical connection without concern for hidden meaning or misunderstanding.

'His heart was weak too, but he had an operation they hoped would cure it, but ... it didn't.' She sniffed, eyes filling. 'Well, it did, I suppose, for a little while. We had a few more years with him.'

'And you miss him still I am sure,' Theo said, his thumb softly caressing her skin.

She nodded, trying to hold steady. It was harder to hold in your emotions when someone was being so nice. She let go of his hand and picked up her napkin. 'So, did your father do the cooking for your family?'

'Some of the time,' Theo answered. 'The other times my aunts would come and cook and the one that can't cook would pretend that she had cooked.'

What was he doing talking about Spyridoula? Abby didn't know who he really was. If he told her it would change things, make things more complex. Acting a simple barman and gardener was suiting him in so many ways. There were no expectations, there was no pressure, no assumption ... no having to tell her about his past. But Leon's words were filling his mind.

'What do you mean?' Abby asked, looking at him with interest. 'One of your aunts hates cooking? She sounds a bit like my mum.'

He needed to relax. She had come. Abby had come to enjoy a dinner with him. And it wasn't because he had charmed her with cheap flattery in a bar and she was too inebriated to know better, or because he was from a rich family and unmarried, she was here simply because she *wanted* to be here. At least that was what he really hoped this was.

He smiled. 'Most Greek women, they are excellent cooks. They enjoy spending all day in the kitchen making a hundred different dishes for one meal ... this aunt, she is the opposite of most Greek women. She would rather spend her time out of the kitchen, buying food from someone else's kitchen.' Although that was not what Stamatis had said to him earlier that day.

'It is very traditional to think of all women in a kitchen all day,' Abby said, taking a sip of wine.

'Oh!' Theo exclaimed. 'Please, do not mistake what I am saying. I do not have outdated views about women.'

'No?' Abby queried, tilting her head a little and looking unconvinced.

'No,' he said firmly. 'But I also do not think that women are equals.'

'What?!' Abby blasted. She jolted her wine glass as she returned it to the table, a little bit of the liquid spilling out onto the cloth. 'But, you aren't allowed to say that. That's *definitely* having outdated views and there's nothing men can do that women can't!'

'Hmm,' he mused, finger on his chin. 'Pushing a car when it has run out of fuel?'

'I don't think that's a very fair example.'

'Moving cows from San Stefanos harbour,' he continued.

'I moved some too! I just ran out of apples!'

He laughed then, watching her frustration, the way her cheeks pinked and her eyes danced as the sky grew darker and the candles burned more brightly. 'What I was going to say,' Theo began. 'Was that I do not think women are equals because ... I think that women are superior.'

Now her expression changed, as he knew it would, and this wasn't just talk. He really meant it.

'I told you about my mother and her weak heart, well that was the only part of her that *was* weak, from all the stories I have heard.' He smiled. 'She climbed mountains before she married my father and broke in difficult horses. She jumped into the sea from clifftops before it was a trend, ran for miles and, some of our family, they believe she *knew* about her heart, sensed it somehow, perhaps packing so much into her life because she knew she did not have long.' He wet his lips. 'My aunt, the one that does not cook, she had her own business too. One small boutique that became a chain of others in Greece. My sister too, she is strong. She has to put up with my brother-in-law.'

Abby laughed.

'So, you see, I am surrounded by beautiful, strong women who do not let anything get in the way of their ambition.' He tore a piece of bread in half and dipped it into the sauce of his chicken. 'Men, we can only do one thing at a time. You must know this!'

'That's not true in your case,' Abby answered. 'You work in a bar and you look after this villa. That's a little multitasking.'

'What do you do, Abby?' Theo asked, moving the conversation on. 'In England.'

'I ... I used to help manage a small hotel.'

Abby had thought about lying. Talking in the present tense and making her previous job at The Travellers' Rest sound how her mum would want it to sound if she was talking to Diana Le Carré. But what would be the point? There was no going back and, being here in Corfu, weeks down the line from that day in the café when her whole life had blown up, the grief was dying, and rebirth seemed suddenly possible.

'Wow,' Theo said, looking truly in awe. 'That was a difficult job, I imagine. All those customers wanting this and wanting that and wanting something you cannot possible provide to them.'

'It wasn't that bad,' she admitted. 'I liked the customers – apart from the guitar players. They always seemed to think being a "musician" was OK at any time of the night.'

'You do not like music?' Theo inquired.

'Oh no, I do like music. I like music a lot.'

'Who do you like best?'

'Gosh, I don't know really. I just like "happy" music. Songs that make me smile and feel good.' Was it wrong if she said Jess Glynne?

'OK,' Theo said, getting to his feet. 'Let me see if I can make the music happier.'

'Theo, but you haven't eaten your meal!'

He was already halfway around the table and heading inside to control the music they were listening to on the terrace. Abby took a moment to breathe. She had never had an evening like this before. She had known Theo mere days and yet everything about this situation felt so natural, so normal, so right.

Pinpricks of lights from the village below skirted the dark blue water, the tall trees and brush on the hills like shadowy sentries. She could smell the herbs and spices from their meal but also the fragrant perfume of clematis, jasmine and lemon. Warmth spread through her entire body. Was this the dream her mum and Melody had chased when they had moved here? The hard work but the gorgeous reward of this view, this peace, endless nights being wrapped up by these simple un-buyable pleasures?

The music changed then and Abby smiled as a drumbeat began, followed quickly by the thrum of guitar, cymbal and trumpet. The vocal was Greek and the tune was completely her definition of 'happy' music, a fusion of Euro-pop with a lick of folklore.

'Abby!' Theo called, reappearing. 'This is happy music, no?'

She laughed and nodded, her attention turning to him. And then he started to move, the way not many British straight men ever did. His hips were shifting, his arms coming up in time and his feet keeping the beat. Abby swallowed as she watched. Every inch of him was just sexy perfection and it was alerting parts of her that had been, for so long, settling for vanilla.

'Come!' Theo beckoned.

She probably would if she was given another few minutes of the shimmying on display. She swallowed again, trying to restore some sensibility, before getting to her feet.

Walking towards him, the Greek pop got a little louder. It was happy and rousing, giving off all the ultimate holiday feelings. She started to move as she walked, hips swaying a little, letting the rhythm guide her motion.

'Oh, Abby,' Theo said, grinning. 'You do not tell me you are a good dancer.'

'You didn't ask,' she answered, with a coquettish edge. She moved closer to him, her feet tapping to the beat, body twisting up and down to the intoxicating vibe.

Forty

Theo caught hold of her then, both his hands on her hips, guiding them along with the tempo. She was so beautiful and the way she was expertly tipping her body one way then the other, so fluidly, so sensually, was hitting every erogenous area he possessed.

She was smiling back at him as they moved together, him holding her hips, her arms moving upwards to clasp around his neck. He couldn't remember a time when he'd felt like this. It was so unscripted. Despite the veil over his true vocation, it was him being him, for the first time in a long time. He slid his face close to hers, drawing her nearer, as the song's pulse slowed to a sultry, passion-filled timbre.

'Tell me, Abby,' he whispered. 'What will your new job be?'

He felt her intake of breath, so long and slow, as if thinking hard. He said nothing, their bodies softly rolling back and forth together.

'I don't know,' she said finally. 'I never thought about *not* working there.'

An unexpected change of plans. That wasn't dissimilar to the position he was in. And he still didn't know what his future held.

'I came here to think,' Abby breathed. 'And to see my mum and my sister, but when I got here things … weren't quite how I thought they would be.'

'You think Corfu has changed?' Theo asked.

He felt her shake her head. 'No, not the island. It's the business … well … things, they could be a little better.'

He could read between the lines. Her mother's estate agency was no different to any other small business trying to survive in difficult times. There was so much more competition and no leeway in lean months. She was here to help her family. The sale of Villa Pappas was important to her. He closed his eyes, hating the current conflict.

'We're hoping the party will increase visibility and bring in some more customers – either buyers for properties already on our books, or sellers who want to make the most of the current upturn.'

'I am sure this will work,' he answered softly.

'I hope so.'

He felt another breath leave her, the warm exhale seeping through the thin fabric of his shirt. 'Can I do anything to help?'

'I … don't know.'

He raised his head then, moving to look directly at her. 'You have everything you need? Food? Now I know I can do something with this.'

Abby smiled. 'Thank you, but George is helping us with that.'

'Drinks maybe? I could … make cocktails for your guests.' He had never wanted to help with anything more and he watched her pondering on his question.

'Don't you have to work?'

'I have a shift at The Blue Vine but I can work around this.' He put his hand to her face, gently cupping her jaw. 'Let me help you, Abby.'

She was gazing up at him now, those warm, sexy hazel eyes looking back. Normally he would not hesitate. Dancing so close, someone in his arms, it was natural to dive right in, do what nature intended, but something was holding him back. He held very still, halting his motion with the music for a moment.

'OK,' she whispered.

'OK?' he asked.

'You can make cocktails,' she elaborated.

He swallowed. Right now, the only mixology he was interested in involved their tongues. Why was he holding off? What was he waiting for? Hadn't he had a telling off from Stamatis about not letting moments pass you by? 'Abby,' he whispered.

'Yes, Theo.'

His name on her lips was enough to tip the balance. Dropping his head to hers, he captured her mouth with his, pulling her closer.

What was happening? It felt like someone had set off fireworks and Abby was in the middle of the display, perhaps the biggest rocket of them all. Theo was kissing her. *She* was kissing Theo and it was a rush like no other she had experienced. His velour tongue was urging hers into an unknown, but very pleasant tempo and as each scintillating second passed she found herself wanting to get nearer to him, inside those linen trousers and what lay beneath. God, he tasted of all things nice! Lemon and … spice and … man flesh. Man flesh so moist and warm it was like feasting on a just-prepared peach flan … only sexier … with less pastry. This was one time where less pastry was definitely a good thing.

She broke away to breathe. 'Theo—'

He caught her mouth with his again, those full, gorgeous, ripe lips encouraging hers to part and let him in for more delicious making out. His hands were on her bare skin, fingers tracing her shoulders, slipping under the straps of her dress ... and she didn't feel the need to tell him to stop because ... she didn't *want* him to stop.

'Theo!'

Abby fell away from him, startled by the interjection of a third-party voice. Was that Spyridoula Pappas?

'Abby?!'

Her mouth dropped open then, as she looked to the owner of the *other* voice who had called her name. 'Mum?' She didn't know why she had felt the need to clarify Jackie's identity except that being caught with your tongue down the throat of the gardener of the property you were trying to sell in front of the client's sister, probably wasn't the most professional thing she had been involved in. And Jackie thought she was still in a relationship with Darrell ...

'We were just having some dinner,' Theo informed calmly. 'Would you like a glass of wine?'

'I have been calling your mobile phone,' Spyridoula stated, strutting towards the table, bracelets jingling together as she began to gather up their plates. 'The people who came to see the villa before. They want to see it again. Tonight. In thirty minutes. They are in Kassiopi right now. Leon is fetching them.' She paused before adding. 'After he has cleaned that skip of a taxi.'

'Abby, what's going on?' Her mum looked a little like she was in shock. The Greek 'happy' music was still playing but Jackie's expression was rather like a *Holby City* extra who'd been given bad news.

'Nothing's going on,' Abby said. 'I just ...' What was she going to say to this? What *was* going on? She'd kissed a rather gorgeous, sexy man and she enjoyed his company – and Greek dips – apart from that she didn't know. 'Shall I help you tidy up? Dress the house?'

'I asked you a question, Abby,' Jackie stated, a little angrily.

Abby closed her eyes momentarily, then took a breath and made a move for the table. 'I'll pick up these plates, shall I? And wash up.'

'Abby! I'm not blind. I saw what was going on,' Jackie stated a little too loudly. 'What about you and Darrell?!'

She stopped walking, not needing to look up to know that both Theo and Spyridoula would be looking at her. There was only one way out of this and it was long overdue. She raised her head and turned back to face her mum.

'There is no me and Darrell, Mum,' Abby said. 'Not any more.' She took a breath. 'Not for almost four weeks.'

'What?' Jackie couldn't have looked more crestfallen. Her stance was wavering. Abby wondered if she should guide her to a chair. Instead, she walked towards her and took hold of her hands.

'I'm sorry I didn't tell you when I first got here, like with my job, but you told me about the business and I went into prioritising mode. You and Melody and the business seemed to be more important than *anything* I had going on in my life, and it gave me something else to think about when I didn't want to think about Darrell.'

A chink of a bowl both distracted her and reminded her that they weren't alone. That the man who had seemed like he wanted to strip her was in fact listening to all this along with the woman who was employing them to sell the villa.

'What happened?' Jackie asked, eyes welling up with tears.

'Mum, please,' Abby begged. 'Can we do this later? At home? Not here when clients are due and there's tidying to do?'

'Please,' Spyridoula called with a hint of sarcasm. 'Do not mind us. What use is a nephew if he cannot clear up the great, big mess he has created?'

'What?!' Both Abby and Jackie had said the word together but it was Abby's heart that hit her chest wall like a gymnast landing heavily on a crash mat. Her *nephew*. Theo was Spyridoula's *nephew*.

Theo dropped the plates back to the table and moved towards Abby. This was not how he had wanted his identity to come out. He had just needed a little more time. A few more dates of being just Theo, not Theo *Pappas* and all the family responsibility that went with that. He hadn't really lied. He hadn't put on a persona. He had just stripped things back a bit.

'Abby,' he said as her neared her. 'Let me explain.'

He could see her dynamic had changed. Gone was the fluid, loosened-up, smiling Abby who had danced with him to the happy music. Barriers were in place.

'You told me you were the gardener,' she whispered.

'I know,' he said. 'I never intended to do that. It was stupid and—'

'You tell her you are the gardener?' Spyridoula laughed out loud. 'Theo does not know one end of an olive from the other. Unless he is making the Dirty Martini.'

'Abby, please, let me explain.' He took hold of her hands then, squeezing them tightly. 'I did not really lie. I only did not say … who I was related to.' He couldn't have sounded more pathetic.

For a second, he felt a little hope. She hadn't wrenched herself away, was holding on to him. But her eyes refused to meet his. She shook her head. 'I have to help my mum secure this sale.'

'A text from Leon,' Spyridoula announced. 'He is almost leaving to pick them up.' She clapped her hands. 'Everybody working together now, *parakalo*.'

Forty-one

Desperately Seeking

'But him being a Pappas means he's rich,' Melody stated. 'Did he look at your hair?'

It was the morning after the night before and Abby had a vicious headache that wasn't being calmed by anything containing aspirin, especially not the ancient, out-of-date-been-around-every-handbag-Jackie-ever-owned packet her mum had produced. They still hadn't got Paul and Lynn to commit to buy Villa Pappas, she had had to go into detail about breaking up with Darrell with her mum as soon as they had got home, and she had left a beaten-looking Theo being verbally horsewhipped by Spyridoula about hanging clothes to dry on the master bedroom's balcony. Last night she had been mentally exhausted; the best date she'd ever had cut short, blighted by the arrival of her mum; the fallout over Darrell and some quite important misinformation that had once again rocked her faith not only in the male population but in herself. Where was her good judgement and her Prior Preparation Prevents Poor Performance life hack when she needed it?

'Did he look at her hair?' Jackie queried, struggling with a guy rope on their supposedly easy-to-put-together-pop-up gazebo. 'Listen, I know with regard to Igor and Valentin the lines got a little blurry, but a man's attention to your tresses shouldn't be what you judge him on, Melody. Respect and good conversation are so much more important.'

'Not when you've spent a fortune on imported products and no one's noticed!'

'He made a beautiful dinner,' Abby said wistfully. Although, if she was honest, she could still taste more of Theo himself than the feast he had made.

'He's probably used to eating out in fine restaurants, being super-mega-loaded.'

'Melody,' Jackie said, using warning tones.

Abby stood up from her seat at the table where she was helping Melody with sorting raffle tickets and sign-up lists, moving to help her mum with the gazebo. It was another beautifully warm day, the harbour area already alive with tourists. Small boats for hire had been chugging around in the water for the past few hours, cool boxes and six packs of water bottles being loaded, hat-wearing holidaymakers slicked up with sun cream getting aboard. And everything seemed to be under control for the party, even Cardboard Tom had arrived. The lack of panicking was concerning. Nothing involving the Dolans usually ever happened without some degree of flapping and perspiration.

'Well,' Melody continued. 'Rich blokes don't go working at bars or pretending to be gardeners for no reason. Maybe he's on the run.' She nodded at her 'brilliant' suggestion. 'You know, one of those white-collar crimes—'

'You've been watching too much *Ozark*,' Jackie said. 'Although, I have to admit, Jason Bateman could launder anything of mine any day of the week.'

'I'm just saying, either he's on the run, or he's left the business under a cloud, or maybe … maybe his millionaire father hasn't really got a million any more. Yes!' Melody sucked in a confident breath. 'We know from experience how tight things have been for small businesses here in Greece. Perhaps it's the same for larger firms too.'

'Ssh!' Jackie shushed. 'You know the village has more ears than a cornfield. And remember that's Spyridoula's brother you're talking about – the woman who recommended us to him for selling the highest-priced villa we have on our books.'

'And why's he having to sell it, huh? Ask yourself that.' Melody pointed a finger into the air at nothing in particular. 'But this could have an upside. Maybe Theo has run off with a business bank account full of money, off-shored it to the Caymans or wherever it is tycoons hide money these days, and he's hiding out in the villa.'

'There's two issues with that scenario,' Jackie began. 'One, he isn't hiding, Spyridoula, his aunt, knows he's here. And he's working in a bar.'

'His father's business is going well. They've just won a big multi-million-euro contract,' Abby said, tugging on the rope, making sure it was secure enough to withstand gale force winds should Corfu turn into Hurricane Central.

'How do you know that?' Melody asked.

'I googled Dinis Pappas,' she admitted.

'Could you google "Dinis Pappas married?". And was there a photo?' Melody turned towards Jackie. 'If Abby marries the son, you could marry the dad and all our financial woes will be over. Hang on, wait. Abs, you'd have to marry Theo first otherwise he'd kind of be your step-brother – but that's allowed, right?'

'Dinis Pappas is widowed,' Abby said. 'At least, that's what Theo told me.' She still wasn't sure how much of what he had said was true. How could she trust someone who had pretended to be something he wasn't? Or was she being harsh? After all, hadn't she hidden her lack of employment and break-up from her family for as long as she could? Wasn't that, in effect, exactly the same thing?

'For how long?' Melody quizzed. 'Recently? Too recent for Mum to give it a go? We've got his email address, right? I'm thinking a little introductory electronic letter ... have you still got that lovely photo I took with Canal D'amour in the background and the flower in your hair? You could attach that as part of the email tail. Like a business Tinder. *Bin-der*!' Melody laughed. 'Or is that too *trashy*?'

'I thought, after the Russians, we'd decided to focus on fixing what we've got with hard work and determination, rather than degrading ourselves by going after questionable men,' said Jackie.

'I wouldn't call Dinis Pappas questionable,' Melody said.

'What would you call him then?' Jackie asked.

'I'm hoping "Daddy".'

Abby gave the last rope a hefty tug before her attention was drawn to the road, the noise of a large vehicle approaching breaking the near-tranquillity of the Greek radio playing from one of the tourist shops and the soft roll of the waves.

'What's that?' Melody asked, getting up from her seat and joining Abby on the edge of Desperately Seeking's terrace area. 'It sounds a lot bigger than a delivery truck.'

Abby shielded her eyes from the sun as she looked down the road. It was a coach. There was nothing unusual about coaches, bearing in mind convoys of them relayed tourists from the airport every season, except the road through San Stefanos harbour was small, too small for a vehicle like that.

'It's a coach,' Abby said.

'Don't be stupid,' Melody replied. 'You can't get a coach down here. They struggle with the delivery vans. Spiros has to do an eighty-five-point turn to get back round.'

'It's definitely a coach.'

'Going where, exactly?'

'*Kalimera*, ladies!'

Aleko waved a hand as he sauntered past Desperately Seeking. He was dressed in white trousers, a bright turquoise Hawaiian shirt festooned with white palm trees and a straw fedora on his head. He stopped, waving both hands as if beckoning the oncoming single decker towards him.

'What are you doing?' Melody left the terrace for the road. 'Is that coach something to do with you?'

'You know I have a party, yes?'

'Yes, we bloody know,' Melody snapped. 'You organised it the same day as ours in a deliberate, rather pathetic attempt at sabotage!'

Aleko laughed. 'This is not true, Melody.'

'I don't believe you.'

'Aleko,' Abby interrupted. 'Where is the coach going? Because we were going to set up a table just in front of the office here with speakers on, to play some music while we give out leaflets.'

'*Outside* the office,' Aleko stated, turning to look at Abby, his expression a little like she had just announced Kit-Kats were now only going to be made one finger.

'*Just* outside,' Abby added, the roar of the coach engine getting louder.

'You have a permit for this?' Aleko inquired.

'A permit?' Abby queried. 'For a table *just* outside the office?'

'And a licence to play music?'

Abby looked to Melody. 'He is joking, isn't he?'

'This is Greece, Abs,' her sister replied. 'You're meant to have a piece of paper for going to the toilet, but don't flush it down there because you're not allowed to do that either.'

Aleko began his arm swooping again as the coach slowed to a crawl, its wing mirrors appearing to get dangerously close to neighbouring buildings.

'Aleko, I really don't think that coach is going to fit down the road,' Abby said. The engine had slowed now, the vehicle's speed at the crawling rate of a very old tortoise as its driver attempted to manoeuvre its bulk onwards without causing damage.

'Everything has been measured.' He put a hand either side of his mouth. '*Ela!*' he called. Then he turned to Abby. 'Please move your easel.'

'No,' Melody stated, putting her hands on the chalkboard George had painted and re-blackened and she had adorned with swirly writing advertising the event. 'The easel is on the edge of our terrace, not on the road.'

'Please move the sign,' Aleko ordered.

'Didn't you hear me?' Melody asked. 'Should I say "no" in Greek?'

'Aleko,' Abby said, trying to keep her voice a lot more level than her sister's. 'I really don't think the coach is going to fit down the road.'

'You English with your closed ideas and your health and safety.' He tutted and moved to the middle of the street, looking to the left and right of the creeping bus, before making more come-hither motions with his hands.

'I know what's going to happen,' Melody said. 'That coach is going to try and come down here and it's going to get stuck right between our olive tree there ...' She pointed at the over-hanging branches. 'And Makis's flagpole there.' She indicated the slim metal pole from which a Greek flag was proudly displayed on the frontage of the small store. 'And the whole bloody giant thing on wheels is going to be outside our business, stuck, so no one can see it or get into it, for the whole wanging day!'

'It's going to ruin everything,' Abby whispered, suddenly struck with the seriousness of the situation.

'Not if I've got anything to do with it!' Melody stated. She strode up the road, towards the coach, making hand gestures opposing the guidance Aleko was handing out. 'Back it up! Right back up! Whoever's on there is just going to have to get out at the end of the road and walk.'

'They cannot walk,' Aleko exclaimed, moving alongside Melody.

'Who's on board?' Abby heard her sister ask. 'More of the grey pound you're going to try and con out of their retirement pot?'

'They have instruments!' Aleko shouted.

'What?'

'Yes, Miss Desperately Seeking, you may play your music without the correct licences, but nobody will hear this over my steel band!'

And right at the very moment, when the news of Ionian Dreams' Caribbean calling hit Abby's consciousness, a dreadful screeching noise, followed by the sound of crumpling metal filled the air.

'Aleko!' Melody shrieked. 'Get this coach out of here! It's just taken out Stathis's bicycle! Let's hope, for your sake, he wasn't on it!'

Forty-two

The Blue Vine

'So, let me get this straight,' Leon began, as he watched Theo arrange a selection of bottles containing multi-coloured liquids on the bar top. 'You told Abby you were a gardener.'

Theo was still cringing about it now. Why hadn't he been able to see that starting a friendship with someone on a lie was never going to work out well? 'Yes.'

'I do not know if I should laugh or cry,' Leon said.

'I am feeling exactly the same way,' Theo admitted.

'I may not be an expert with ladies, but I do know that lie-telling is right up there with not complimenting them enough and watching too much football ... actually, I think telling a lie is worse. That goes for mothers, grandmothers and sisters too, if you are Greek.'

Theo let go of a sigh and ran the flat of his hand over his hair, pushing a few stray strands into the band at the back. 'I just wanted to be me, Leon. Me without my ... heritage.' He straightened up, picking up bottles and loading them into a crate. 'The good parts of me I hardly remember, instead of the son of Dinis Pappas, the heir to a boat empire – if he hasn't cut me out of his will as well as stopping access to my trust fund.' He had discovered his more limited funds while he was in Lefkada. It had never been his intention to continue to use the family money when he'd left, but he also hadn't anticipated his father taking that back-up plan away so quickly. Once his wages started to deplete, it had been a case of living on a very slim budget and scraping together enough to get over to Corfu. And now he had The Blue Vine. Despite how he had first felt about the job, it *was* giving him enough to live on, especially when you had a luxury villa at your disposal … but for how long?

'Come on, Theo. You have never been like those Russians. Throwing money around like it is Greek pots at Easter.'

Not here on Corfu. But he had on the mainland. He had indulged in the high-life, using his status to get in the best clubs, wasting euros on champagne and food he did not even like, just because he could. Leon did not really know that side of him, and right now he was so very glad.

'I should not have lied to Abby. It was stupid.' He squeezed another bottle into the crate then scoured the bar top for something he was missing. 'Do you see the vermouth?'

'Theo,' Leon began. 'I drink only beer. You could be talking of a country.'

He turned around, eyes going along the mirrored back wall, searching the shelves of tightly packed bottles for the required alcohol. There it was. He snatched it up and put it into the crate with the other ingredients.

'What are you going to do?' Leon asked him. His friend was now primping his hair in the reflection from the stainless-steel beer pump.

'I thought about hiding,' Theo informed, selecting a batch of straws and putting those into the box.

'This is San Stefanos, remember. Nowhere to run. Nowhere to hide.'

'I thought about leaving the whole island,' Theo reminded.

'And going back to the business?'

'No,' he said firmly. 'And I'm not ready to leave Corfu yet.' It was a strange feeling. The fact he was starting to feel settled here. Here in this tiny village of a few tavernas and shops, rustic traditions and limited recreational offerings, when compared to the bustling city he was used to dwelling in.

'So,' Leon stated. 'No hiding. No running. What is your plan?'

'Facing up to things,' Theo said with a lot more confidence than he really felt. 'Apologising,' he added. 'And making cocktails for Desperately Seeking's party.' He picked up the crate and shook it at little, making the bottles chink together.

'That sounds like a good plan, although ...' He lowered his voice to a whisper. 'Hera does know you are taking the cocktail ingredients out of her bar, yes?'

Theo smiled. 'Yes, she does.' He moved from behind the bar, container in his arms. 'And I am paying for these from my wages, and working a double shift tomorrow.'

Leon smiled, shaking his head. 'Giving money away. Helping others. That is a sure way to make up for gardener impersonation.'

'That's what I am hoping,' Theo admitted. 'Are you coming?'

Leon hopped down from the bar stool. 'Lead the way, my friend.'

Theo got to the open doors of the bar just as the beeping of a large reversing vehicle pierced the air. Plumes of smoke infiltrated the sea air as the engine worked hard to back up accurately, each inch seeming to count.

'What is a coach doing down here?'

'If it is not careful it is going to fall down onto the beach. Hey!' Theo called. 'Stop!'

Forty-three

Desperately Seeking

'He's got a steel band,' Jackie whispered, fear in her voice.

'It doesn't matter, Mum,' Abby said. 'We have Donald Trump coming and George's Greek delights and … our raffle.' She swallowed. They didn't have a prize for the raffle. She needed to *think* of a prize. Something sensational but not budget-blowing … she could call it a 'mystery prize' while she was giving out the tickets. That would give her a good few hours before announcing the winner.

'Where did he get a steel band from?' Jackie asked.

'Mum, get with it!' Melody ordered. 'We don't need someone playing a beaten-up oil drum to get our party started.'

'Steel bands sound so *holiday*,' Jackie said. 'And people like that Caribbean vibe. That's the *only* reason anyone watches that awful *Death in Paradise*.'

'Listen to me.' Melody took hold of her mum's shoulders, forcing her to focus. 'We are in Greece! Not Guadeloupe! We are giving people the real, traditional experience, coupled with wet sponges at a moronic American president and … and …'

'A raffle!' Abby jumped in. 'Everyone loves a raffle.' At least they did at The Travellers' Rest. What were the prizes there? A few bottles of Merlot, some lily-of-the-valley-infused handkerchiefs and those hand-warmers that everyone thought were a great idea but, in reality, really didn't know what to do with them. She could think of something better than that.

'Besides,' Melody started again, whisking a mosquito out of her orbit. 'By the time the coach has found somewhere non-obstructive to park and they've got their very heavy instruments off the bus, they might be too sweaty and exhausted to play. And ...' She added, pressing at her iPhone. 'We can always out-reggae them if we have to. I've got old school Bob Marley or new school "Whine to Di Top".'

'That's how I usually like my chardonnay,' Jackie responded with a smile.

Abby smiled too, patting her mum's bare shoulder – it was off the collarbone cream chiffon today. 'That's better,' she said. 'Enthusiasm and positivity. The party is going to be brilliant. We just need to get the rest of the bunting into position, bring out the drinks ... Melody, did you mix up that cocktail recipe?'

'Done at seven this morning. It's in an old five-litre water bottle next to the fridge. I hope it's going to be enough.'

'It will have to be,' Abby stated. Because after last night's date disaster she couldn't see Theo turning up to help like he said he would. And that, she'd decided, was most definitely a good thing.

'*Kalimera.*'

Abby looked up to see a smartly dressed George and two equally well-dressed, rather dashing twenty-something Greek men standing at the entrance to their terrace, arms laden with platters of clingfilm-wrapped food.

'*Kalimera*, George.' Jackie's face flushed, her eyes not seeming to know where to look. Their mum never seemed to be able to do normal when George was around.

'Where would you like the food? Inside?' George asked. 'Until the time of the party.'

'Yes,' Jackie breathed. 'Yes, that would be lovely. I'll show you where.'

Melody straightened up, flicking her bouncing curls back, pulling her very short dress up a little higher and regarding George's two helpers. 'Shall I show *you* where?' she asked, listing a little towards the first assistant. 'Or perhaps both of you?' She looked the second man up and down.

'Melody,' Jackie called. 'Leave George's nephews alone, please.'

'Mmm,' Melody said, running her tongue along her top lip. 'I never knew George had nephews.'

Abby took hold of her sister's arm and dragged her over to the table. The sun was getting stronger by the minute and, although they now had the gazebo up and most things underneath it, come midday it was going to be extremely warm. If only she could think of something novel to cool guests down … she wasn't sure borrowing wet sponges destined for Mr Fake News was going to work.

'We need a raffle prize,' Abby said, picking up a line of Greek flag bunting.

'You haven't got one?!' Melody exclaimed.

'Ssh! Don't let Mum hear you. She's barely holding it together after the idiophones …'

'The what now?'

'The steel drums.'

Melody laughed. 'I thought it was a posh word for dickhead and you were talking about Darrell.'

'Don't forget that Mum's also mourning her chance to make *Mamma Mia 3* with me as a Greek bride.'

'Well … I think there's hope. As I said at breakfast, Theo is even more of a catch now he's super-rich as well as super-hot.'

Abby shook her head. 'He lied to me.'

'Pah!' Melody said, unwrapping a lemon-flavoured boiled sweet supposed to be for invitees and popping it into her mouth. 'Have you wondered why he didn't tell you the truth? I mean, if he *likes* you it stands to reason he wouldn't tell you his net worth. It's what celebrities do when they're trying to ward off gold-diggers.'

'So, you think he thought I was a gold-digger?' Abby asked, shocked.

'I don't know, I'm just suggesting, that perhaps there was a reason he wasn't fully honest.' She sucked on the sweet, moving it around in her mouth. 'I mean most guys would use their wealth and status to attract a girl, not try and lure them with their oh-so-interesting bar and gardening work.' Melody laughed and nudged Abby's arm. 'Although I know you're a little bit different to most girls.'

'What's that supposed to mean?' Abby asked, affronted.

'Well, for starters, you *had* to be dating Darrell for something other than his looks, and his personality, come to that. So what was it?'

Abby found herself unable to answer the question. Darrell had been interested. That was all. At the very beginning, he had been interested, when there had been nothing but work and the odd beer-and-balti night with her friend Lauren – who had got married and moved to Germany with her soldier husband. Deep analysis over the past few weeks since the break-up had only provided her with more and more evidence that they had had nothing in common apart from a mutual appreciation of *Orphan Black*. Their whole time together had been nothing more than a string of acceptable times. Where was the need, want and passion in that? She swallowed. Darrell had also poo-pooed her learning Greek. *Philistine*.

'Raffle prize. Think,' she blurted out at Melody.

'Just get some booze,' Melody suggested. 'Everyone appreciates that ... Oh, hello.'

Abby looked over in response to Melody's greeting and there, toned arms taut from the box he was carrying, was Theo. Her entire insides reacted to his appearance, popping and locking like Ashley Banjo as she perused the athletic physique covered only by a white, abdomen-skimming vest top above black jeans. But that was just chemical, she told herself. It was like dining out on Zac Efron in *Baywatch* and not paying attention to the actual film. It was superficial ... do not focus on the 'super' bit.

'Good morning,' Theo said. 'We are here to make cocktails for your guests.'

Melody poked Abby in the ribs with her elbow, jolting her into movement.

'Oh ... I ... we ...' she spluttered. Like. An. Idiophone.

'Desperately Seeking Ladies!' Leon bounded onto the terrace, one arm around a small box, the other waving what looked like something you would hit a steelpan with.

'Was that a greeting?' Melody asked, plucking the box right out of Leon's hands. 'Or a singles advertisement?'

'Just jesting! So feisty, Melody. It is going to be a party, no?' Leon said. 'Fun times, for everybody.' He used the stick in his hand like a conductor's baton.

Melody snatched it from him. 'Where did you get that from?'

'I found it on the road.'

'One down. How many to go?' Melody asked, then looked to Abby. 'How many players are in a steel band?'

'I don't know,' Abby answered. She was having trouble joining in with this conversation. There was this bubbling cocktail mix of tension as she remembered her and Theo's almost dirty dancing last night and their oh-so-sexy interrupted kiss ...

'Come on,' Melody said, grabbing Leon by the arm. 'I've got heavy lifting for you to do inside. We need another table brought out.'

Abby wanted to grab her sister's freshly serumed hair and stop her from leaving, but she was twenty-four, not thirteen. She was a strong, independent woman perfectly capable of conversation no matter how handsome the interactor.

'Cosmopolitan,' Abby blurted out.

'Your party?' Theo inquired. 'Or the village now there are people with metal drums?' At the mention of the band, a group of men and women in brightly coloured Hawaiian shirts wandered past the office heading towards Ionian Dreams' establishment.

'I meant the cocktail,' Abby replied. 'I just ... wondered if that might be the one cocktail you make to suit everyone best.' She swallowed. Cocktail talk might lead to a Between the Sheets or a Hanky Panky. She shook her head hoping the ridiculousness would fall out through her ears.

'I am here all day,' Theo told her. 'I can make a different cocktail for everybody. Whatever they want,' he said. 'Whatever *you* want.'

The only way he could have made that last sentence more suggestive would be to have delivered it naked, without the modesty lilo.

'You don't need to do that,' she stuttered. She had to remember she was mad at him. He had lied to her. She had started last night having dinner with a gardener-cum-barman and ended it dancing with the son of a Greek tycoon. 'Melody has mixed up some sort of alcoholic rocket fuel and, well, I'm not sure we could afford to pay you for your time, or the bespoke cocktails.'

'Please,' Theo said. 'You do not have to pay me. I said last night. I want to help. I want to ... apologise for not being honest with you.'

Theo held his breath, watching her react to his words, wanting so much for it to be in a positive way. Or had his twisting the truth turned her away for good? It was worrying him how much he didn't want to have upset her. He was caring. *Really* caring what she thought of him. That had never happened before. He wasn't even sure why it was happening now, right now, when his life was so far from together he barely knew which way was up.

'I just ...' Abby began tentatively.

'Yes?' Theo asked.

'Don't understand why you didn't tell me that Spyridoula is your aunt or that Dinis Pappas is your father.'

'I know,' he breathed quickly. Those two words didn't contain any of the answers she was looking for either.

'Do you think I'm a gold-digger?' Abby spouted.

'What?' Now he was confused.

'Did you think if you told me you were rich I would be trying to get you to buy me designer goods to sell for money to help recover my mum's business?'

He blinked, looking at her conflicted expression. It was still so beautiful, despite the clouds of war on one side and the utter uncertainty on the other. 'No,' he breathed. 'I did no thinking at all. That was the problem.' He swallowed.

'Well, I'm not a gold-digger,' Abby stated with a sniff. 'And I don't ordinarily go on dates with men I've only known half a week whether they're a gardener or an heir to a boat conglomerate.'

'OK,' Theo said. He was still holding the box of bottles and it was starting to make his forearms ache. But putting it down would perhaps signal he thought he was staying and that was no one's choice but Abby's.

'And, just for the record, Darrell is my *very* ex-boyfriend who kissed his assistant when it wasn't National Snog Your Secretary Day in my favourite bakery, over pink biscuits.'

He didn't know what to say. After last night, he would give anything to kiss *her* again, over any biscuits at all. He was thankful for this Darrell's screw up having sent her to Corfu ...

'He is an idiot.' His words were out of his mouth and into the air between them before he had realised he was going to speak his mind. He wanted to touch her hair, caress her cheek, run a finger over her bottom lip and draw her towards him ... why hadn't he put the box down?

'Yes,' Abby said. 'He is. And he no longer warrants any of my attention. Especially when I have a party to coordinate.'

He was aching to ask the question. Wondering how best to word it. Desperately wanting pardon, a second chance ... another date ...

'We've borrowed some glasses from George,' Abby told him. 'I'm not sure any of them will be proper cocktail glasses but we have plastic cups too, and they're free drinks so people can't complain too much.'

'I can stay?' he asked with a swallow.

'This is a huge day for the family business,' Abby stated. 'I can't afford to turn down any help.'

'Whatever you need, I can do it,' Theo answered with a confident nod.

'We'll see,' Abby replied, sounding a little undecided. 'Set the cocktail bar up there.' She pointed to one of the tables under the gazebo.

He nodded, moving in the direction she'd shown. She was letting him stay. It wasn't an immediate acceptance of his apology, but it was *something*. And, in fact, the very hint of a chance was much more than he really deserved.

Forty-four

'Can you hear the steel band?' Melody asked Abby.

Abby shook her head while she ripped up raffle tickets, depositing them into Stathis's bicycle basket which was, surprisingly, the only thing uncrushed from the coach incident of earlier. Thankfully, the old man had been pushing the bike, not riding it, and was unscathed but naturally miffed that the vehicle he'd been jockeying since the 1950s was no more. There had been lots of sighing and shaking of his bald head with cries of '*podilato mu*' until Theo had plied him with several Weep No More cocktails. 'I can only hear Donald Trump wailing "we are fighting fake news" every time someone thwacks him with a sponge and someone singing "I don't wanna wait in vain" on Spotify.'

Melody laughed, sipping from the straw of her pint glass of cocktail Abby knew Theo hadn't made. 'Irie! Shabba Ranks next. Or maybe Shaggy.'

'Melody,' Abby said, taking her sister's arm. 'We are supposed to be working. Achieving the party atmosphere is only half of the job. Don't forget we are aiming to give clients the real Greek experience. Selling the calm, relaxing, peaceful, holiday life so they can imagine what it would be like to own their own home on the island.'

'Mum has been signing people up to the newsletter left right and centre,' Melody said, nudging Abby and indicating

Jackie, under a parasol – held by George – talking to a well-dressed couple who seemed to be thoroughly enjoying the drinks Theo had made that were both purple and pink, layered up like a rainbow cake. 'The food's going down well and people are *lingering*. They aren't just taking dolmades and hot-footing it to Aleko's joint.' She grinned. 'And Donald is superb, isn't he?'

Abby glanced over at the lookalike, sat on a chair in a business suit combination the real DT would definitely wear, pouting, posing and fluffing up his very convincing hairpiece for the crowd as sodden sponges headed his way. 'He is very good.' Abby sighed. 'How much is he charging us?' She had tried to keep a handle on expenses, but despite everyone's goodwill, costs had mounted up.

'Don't worry about it,' Melody said, waving her hand dismissively.

'Melody! How much was he?' Now she was really worried.

'It's a party, Abs, chill out.'

'I'll pull your hair if you don't tell me,' Abby threatened, reaching for a strand.

'You're crazy, and not ten any more, and that's not fair.'

'Melody!'

Melody sighed. 'I said I'd dance before his next show next week.'

'Melody! We agreed the dancing was going to stop! That you and Mum were going to focus on the business and we would make do until that started to pay off.'

'I didn't agree,' Melody stated. 'And now the Russians have been driven out of the village … I can't live on bread and feta. I miss the chocolate granola.'

'No more dancing in those awful stripper shoes.'

'At least I don't actually strip.' She took a breath. 'Completely.'

'What?!' Abby exclaimed.

'Air. Hair, lair.'

Abby's attention was drawn away from her sister to the arrival of Diana, breathing her trademark greeting at her shoulder. The interjection was enough for Melody to skip off towards more new arrivals.

'Oh, hello, Diana,' Abby said. 'Welcome to our soirée. Please, come and let Theo make you a cocktail of your choice.' She led the way across the terrace, past a group of village children who were taking it in turns to try on the cardboard Tom mask.

'Aleko has the most wonderful band playing outside *his* shop. Traditional musicians, no aid from Bluetooth.' Diana smiled and Abby longed to channel her inner Amir Khan (when he was good).

'Well,' Abby said, trying to maintain professionalism. 'We are mostly going for the Greek theme here.' She indicated the harbour just a few metres ahead of them. It was like a beautiful painting, capturing everything that was special about Greece. Clear, turquoise water, clean sand-cum-shingle beach dappled with stones of every colour, the bright wellness-promoting sun making everything a little like a natural version of the Clarendon Instagram filter. She could smell fresh fish being griddled and all at once her mouth began to water. This place was seeping into her every pore whether she was allowing it or not.

'Playing reggae?' Diana queried, raising a way too-plucked eyebrow.

She did have a point. Abby should get Melody to stop competing with Aleko's theme on the musical front and get back to their own remit – selling the Greek dream. 'The food is traditional Greek and my mum has set up a slideshow of current properties on the screen at the back of the terrace, should you be looking for somewhere to purchase.'

Diana tittered. 'Darling girl, I already have a property here.'

'But don't you sometimes wish it had a little extra space, Diana? Is it one bedroom you have or two?'

Another voice had interjected and Abby turned to see Spyridoula, dressed in an eye-catching emerald-coloured dress, half a dozen of her friends around her. She had one of George's spicy lamb meatballs in between her fingers.

'I have two,' Diana snapped quickly. 'And a roof terrace.'

'Well,' Abby continued. 'We have a gorgeous three-bedroomed property on our books, at a great price with a garden, a roof terrace and a walk-in wardrobe in the master suite.'

'A walk-in wardrobe, Diana,' Spyridoula said. 'A whole room to put your beautiful, beautiful clothes.'

Diana sniffed. 'They do deserve to be preserved. Some of them belonged to the late Princess of Monaco.'

'Where are your friends?' Spyridoula questioned, eyeing up the Brit. 'Your Pikilia and Pow-Pow people.'

'It's Pow-*Wow* and Pikilia,' Diana corrected. 'It means a "gathering where people talk to one another".'

'And where are they gathering right now?' Spyridoula asked. 'Because they are missing out on this wonderful food.'

'They are at Ionian Dreams, taking lots of photos of the rather gorgeous musicians.'

'When there is the American president to make wet?! This is the funniest thing I have seen all of the year,' Spyridoula announced with a laugh. 'We will put this in the local magazine.'

'You will?' Abby said, breathing gratefully, if breathing gratefully was a thing.

'There is no real entertainment here. My ladies like to be entertained,' Diana said sniffily.

Spyridoula clapped her hands together. 'Daughter-of-Jackie, Abby has not told you about the dancing?'

'Dancing?' Diana and Abby said at the very same time.

'You have seen my nephew? Working at The Blue Vine? Here, with Leon, making the most divine cocktails?'

Abby looked to where Theo and Leon were serving drinks. Theo was smiling as he juddered two metal cocktail shakers, throwing one in the air, catching it, spinning the second, then deftly pouring the resulting liquid into glasses he had lined up. She could vouch for his skills in making divine cocktails. He was divine too, all swept back hair and square-jawed delicious-ness. Except she shouldn't really be thinking any of that …

'As much as I love a good cocktail,' Diana began. 'I wouldn't describe the art of mixology as dancing.'

'No,' Spyridoula stated. 'Theo and Leon, they have been dancing since they were three years old. In a short while, they will be teaching everybody traditional Greek dancing.'

Diana did a rather obvious eye-roll where her whole iris and pupil disappeared under her eyelids. It briefly turned her into something from *The Walking Dead*. 'We've all been to Kostas's in Kassiopi.'

'This is different,' Spyridoula continued.

'How so?' Diana asked, sounding intrigued.

'They will do this … Pappas style.'

Abby swallowed. What was going on? Dancing was not on her timetable. The only two things scheduled were her mum giving a speech about the Desperately Seeking ethos and the raffle draw.

'Does it entail balancing a stick on their nose? Or a small child on a small chair? Because we've seen that too.' Diana looked completely unimpressed, so much so she folded her arms across her chest.

'They do this like … strippers,' Spyridoula whispered.

Abby felt like she had been struck by a lightning bolt. What was it with this village and people taking off their clothes? And now all she could see was a slideshow of Theo *in flagrante* on the sun lounger at the villa, plus the memory of his hot, hard body tight against hers as they danced last night.

'They take off their clothes?' Diana asked. Now her eyes were bulging like a tarsier.

'Your friends will not want to miss this,' Spyridoula said confidently. 'And if you do not have interest in the three-bedroom house with the walking in wardrobe I will tell Cybele Karkaris. She has very many shoes.'

Diana readjusted the handbag on her shoulder and cleared her throat. 'I will be back.' She looked at Abby. 'Do not start the dancing without us.'

'I … won't,' Abby replied tentatively. She waited until Diana had disappeared off the terrace and onto the road before she looked to Spyridoula with concern. 'Greek stripper dancing?' she said. 'That wasn't part of my plan.' She sucked in more air. 'And I don't think I can allow it. It's my mum's business … I'm not sure it's the right image we're going for.' As much as she really wanted to see it.

Spyridoula laughed, slipping an arm around Abby's shoulders. 'Come,' she said. 'We will tell Theo and Leon what they will do together. Maybe just the shirts … unless the crowd insist on more.'

Forty-five

'You jest!' Leon exclaimed in horror. 'You joke with us, Mrs Pappas.' He inhaled. 'Please,' he begged. 'Tell me you joke with us.'

'It wasn't my idea,' Abby added.

'We realise that,' Theo answered. 'Because it sounds very much like something my aunt would organise.' He stood his ground and eyed Spyridoula, changing to speaking in Greek. 'What if we say no? It is complete exploitation after all.' He knew exactly what he was going to say next. 'What if I said you and your ladies were to dance in nothing more than your underwear?'

A worrying smile appeared on his aunt's face then. 'My ladies wait for this very moment half of their lives.' She put her fingers to her lips and whistled. 'Ladies! It is time!'

'Wait,' Abby said. 'What's going on—'

Theo bit his lip. He had been expertly played again. He knew Spyridoula had absolutely no intention of taking off her clothes and dancing, but if he really pushed the issue he also had no doubt that she would, and he couldn't do that to Abby.

'Stop this madness,' Theo said, taking hold of his aunt's arm.

Abby stepped forward, as if trying to get between them. 'Honestly, please, don't feel that anyone has to dance ...' She cleared her throat.' ... half-naked or otherwise, on my account. Diana will just have to be disappointed. I don't really know why my mum feels the need to please her anyway. I—'

'No,' Theo said. 'We will do this.' His eyes went to Leon, hoping for a show of solidarity he probably didn't deserve.

'Theo, come on, we are not three years old, running around in the garden with nothing to show,' his friend reminded him. 'I do not know about you, but I have plenty to show now.'

'But we have been dancing together, when we get together ...' He swallowed as long-ago memories crowded in upon him. 'For almost all of that time.'

'But not half-naked.' Leon raised his eyes. 'My mother wanted to open a Greek dancing bar once. She had plans for me and all my brothers to dance there, every night.' He shook his head. 'Why do you think I drive a taxi?'

Theo slipped an arm around Leon's shoulders. 'It is once,' he pointed out, then dropped his mouth closer to Leon's ear. 'To help Abby.' Theo owed it to her. For the half-truths. To remind her how sorry he was ...

'If my sisters come by and see me ...' Leon said through gritted teeth.

'They will be very proud,' Theo said, slapping him on the back.

'Come,' Spyridoula said, linking arms with Abby. 'My friend, Meredith, she has a house she is thinking of selling. Her husband passed away and I think she needs to downsize. Do you have a nice, low maintenance two-bedroom house to sell to her too?'

'Really?' Abby asked. 'Because we do have a beautiful one with a lovely garden and gorgeous views. Someone was interested but the garden wasn't big enough for her ... I'm pretty sure it's low maintenance. I can grab the details.'

'Then let me introduce you,' Spyridoula continued before throwing a glance back to Theo. 'While Theo is removing his clothing.'

Ten minutes later, Abby had left Jackie with Spyridoula's friend, Meredith, talking up the merits of downsizing and telling her how much money she should be able to get for her sizeable three-bedroom property with a parcel of land. It was the only moment that day she had had to take stock of everything that was going on around her. She stood in the doorway of the freshly whitewashed store front, admiring what she saw. How different the area looked now from when she had arrived, blinded by pinkness and plastic flamingos. Now the terrace and approach to the shop was sleek, charming and welcoming, professional yet approachable. The planters held no fake neon additions, just the natural blooming floral beauty of bougainvillea, and San Stefanos harbour needed no added enhancement either – the sparkling water, bobbing boats and gentle burr of activity around the beach captured the relaxed vibe perfectly. Shrubs of lavender provided the subtle, summery fragrance, just like Abby had wanted for The Travellers' Rest. But here, somehow, she knew it worked better than it ever would have done in Romsey, because everything here was just a little bit more charming, a shade brighter, positively sunnier all round. The past week had been so much hard work, but never had Abby felt more rewarded. She was helping her mum and her sister flourish. And she could never have envisaged how much more satisfying that would feel, even when compared to a job that had been her whole world. But where did she go from here? A sharp prod of a reminder came from her consciousness. She didn't have time to think that far ahead yet, she still didn't have a raffle prize and draw time was coming up ... Then Melody's music from the speakers ceased and the sound of a lone stringed instrument began to drift up from the roadside.

A hush seemed to descend over the party, but not in an awkward way, in more of an awe*struck* way. Abby stepped down onto the terrace just as everyone seemed to part to either side, in preparation of something happening. People stopped throwing wet sponges at Donald Trump and the general hubbub of conversation ceased, the only sound the beautiful, traditional tone of bouzouki. And then the musician arrived, revealing himself to the crowd, walking slowly forward into the centre of the naturally formed circle playing a pearly white and Greek blue six-string instrument. It was George.

Fingers plucking his instrument slowly at first, then gradually gaining momentum as he moved around the onlookers, involving them in the music with head nods and encouraging gestures. Guests were reaching for their phones to video and snap pictures and Diana, a gaggle of well-dressed women her age at her back, bustled into the gathering, elbows out, desperate to find a space. Jackie's jaw had slackened, her gaze fixed on the restaurateur.

'Have you any idea what the wanging hell is going on?' Melody was at Abby's shoulder, whispering loudly in her ear. 'I was going to switch the mood to a bit of George Ezra in a minute, not Taverna George.'

'Did you know George could play the bouzouki?' Abby asked her sister. 'He used to have that little man who played in his restaurant. Why didn't he ever play himself if he could?'

'No idea ... whoa! Hello!'

Melody's exclamation said everything Abby also felt the very second she saw Theo and Leon take to the floor. Dressed all in white, rather appealingly fitted white skinny jeans on their bottom halves, shirts with sleeves rolled up, tucked in and belted with red scarves tied as belts ... it was like the best holiday eye-candy in one perfect scene.

Melody sighed then. 'Leon scrubs up well. Where did they get those clothes from?'

Abby couldn't reply. She was lost in looking at Theo, an expression of pure focus on his face. If he really wasn't relishing the execution of this dance then no one would know it. He appeared poised and prepared ...

And then they began to move. A step left, a step right, arms around each other's shoulders, a sirtaki dance straight out of Zorba the Greek, light-footed and perfectly in time to the song coming from the bouzouki. People began to clap in time, providing a back-beat, others tapping their heels to the stone floor, some lightly drumming on the tables with their fingers. All Abby could do was delight in what was going on before her, her love of Greece beginning to flow through her, like someone had just turned on a long-forgotten-about tap.

Theo spun around as he and Leon broke away from each other and his fingers went to the buttons of his shirt, deftly, yet tantalisingly slowly, unfastening each one in turn ...

'Sweet God,' Melody breathed. 'Are they ... going to ... is he ... going to take off his shirt?'

Abby found herself nodding, the inside of her mouth drying up quicker than unwrapped cheese left in the sun, the inside of her everything else flooding like she was caught in a really, really soaking wet day in November.

This was so much more than just a routine Theo had been forced into. How long had it been since he had danced like this? He couldn't remember. His existence before here and now, in Corfu, had become all about work and money and nothing about what he loved about life so much. And right in this moment, he was lucky. Even after everything, he *was* blessed, by so many things. Why had he forgotten that? Why had he been so intent on looking inward? Analysing what had gone wrong instead of recalling what had gone right. What could *carry on* going right if only he would let it. *He* had a chance. Unlike others whose lives had changed irrevocably.

Jumping high in the air, he whipped open his shirt as he sprang, landing one-footed and slowly, shoulder by shoulder, shrugging off the material and inching the cotton fabric off his muscular form.

A few women at the very front of the circle began to fan their faces with their hands and he moved towards them, grazing his shoes over the stones in a legato dance of pure seduction. Whether it would charm anyone into buying or selling a property today he didn't know, but if this crazy idea of his aunt's was going to help Abby in some way then he was willing to try – and while he was trying, he was going to enjoy every back-to-his-and-Leon's-roots second of it.

And then he saw her. Abby. Standing at the back of the circle, near the building's entrance, watching him, tracking him, eyes not on Leon or George but on him and him alone. It made his every part ache with a longing he didn't recognise. He wanted her connection so much. Yearned for it. To be observed in a way as if he mattered to her somehow. He stepped towards her, moving with purpose …

As Theo edged towards her, moving his hips to George's tune, Abby almost felt like she was floating above herself. It was like watching the whole scene from somewhere up in the clouds, slightly detached, but very much wanting to be part of it. Except she was *Abby* Dolan, not Melody Dolan. This gorgeous, sexy, Greek fantasy that every woman's vacation dreams were made of was coming her way, Enrique Iglesias hot, and she was both quivering with need and shaking with fear, worried that whatever happened it was going to end up with her making a complete ninny of herself. If she was Melody she would be sashaying forth, her every step a killer catwalkesque swagger, her movements transforming into an alluring routine to rival Shakira. But she wasn't her sister. She never had a use for stripper shoes or even considered purchasing hair lacquer from China …

Abby's cheeks fired up to woodburner-full-of-coal-and-logs level as Theo slid towards her, provocatively winding around giggling women, then high-fiving children. She needed to control the situation. Just like she had many, many times at The Travellers' Rest. This was just the same as taking owner-ship of Stanley's body odour issues. 'Left unresolved', her self-doubting mind whispered to her. She swallowed, tuning out of that side of her brain and trying to hone in on the rather sensual strumming of George's playing. She took a breath. Now every single thing she was thinking was dirtier than … a channel she had stumbled across when she'd hit 'adult' instead of 'shopping' on Sky. She had to own this moment and that might have to involve surprising herself as well as everyone else. She stepped forwards, taking hold of Melody's hand.

'What are you doing?' Melody hissed. 'Abby!'

Forty-six

'I said what are you doing?' Melody talked out of the side of her mouth like she was doing a rather poor ventriloquism act.

'This is our party,' Abby told her quickly. 'Desperately Seeking, a fantastic estate agency, selling the Greek sunshine dream. It's all about us, Brits who have settled on Corfu, at one with the tradition.' She looked at her sister as they neared a revolving Theo. '*We* have to dance too.' She waited for her words to hit home then quickly added. 'Don't swear.'

'Abby, I don't know Greek dancing!' Melody exclaimed as all around them the invitees began to cheer and clap their hands harder at the presence of the two women in the dancing space. 'I came here for the nightclubs, the cheap kebabs and the perma-tan.'

'Leon can show you,' Abby urged quickly. 'Just think more *The Durrells* and less … *Love Island*.' Giving her sister a shove towards the taxi driver who was proudly stamping his feet then flicking up his heels in a show of masculinity, Abby focused on the stunning vision of maleness right in front of her. And right then she knew what she wanted, even if it only lasted as long as her visit here. She stepped up to him, ensuring their bodies were only a mere very, very cheap thread count away, and locked her eyes with his.

'I don't care if you're rich,' she breathily informed Theo. 'If you don't mind that I'm only a few weeks out of a long-term relationship.'

'You don't?' he answered, slipping even closer to her.

She shook her head, taking one of his hands in hers, her other hand, moving to the scarf belt of his jeans and beginning to tug. 'So just how Full Monty does this Pappas dancing get?'

'Abby ...'

He looked a little bashful and that only made her more self-assured. For someone who danced so confidently and downright erotically, it was endearing to see he wasn't without a degree of self-conciousness.

'Spyridoula promised my guests a *big* ... *hot* ... Greek show.' She had deliberately sounded out the word 'hot' for as long as she could possibly make three letters linger on her lips for.

'You have no idea what I am thinking right now,' he whispered. He pulled her tight towards him until her body was practically absorbing all the heat from his. 'But, you should know, the best, *very* big, *very* hot Greek shows always happen in private.'

Abby was losing control now. She could feel it drifting out of her, her libido shaking up like one of Theo's excellently made cocktails. No. *She* was going to be in charge. It was her life. Her destiny. Never again would she let someone make her decisions for her. She would definitely go back to learning Greek ...

'Is that so?' she replied in sultry tones.

'I want to show you,' he whispered, still keeping up the dance but bringing her along with his every move.

She smiled, all thoughts of ending up looking like a ninny evaporating. This was the new Abby. The confident Abby. The

Abby who currently wanted to strip this man out of his white ensemble and straddle him.

'No,' she said. 'I want to show *you*.' With one tug she pulled the red scarf out of the loopholes of his jeans and swung it around her head like she was the winner of a lassoing contest. The onlookers let out a cheer. Then she wrapped the scarf around his neck, drawing him towards her, hips working a rhythm somewhere between her mum's old-school Lionel Richie and one of Rihanna's backing dancers.

'I want this party to end,' Theo told her in no uncertain terms. 'So, I can take you ...'

'Take me where?' Abby smiled. She had deliberately interrupted the sentence to make him stop right with the 'taking' element. Just the thought of it was sending her biorhythm into meltdown.

'*Everywhere*,' he breathed, his face closing in on hers.

They were in public. She had to remember that. She was currently being scrutinised by half the village, including her mum, and everybody she was trying so hard to impress – and sell properties to. But his mouth was just millimetres away, those lust-filled eyes gazing into hers ... She deserved this moment, this break from reality. Thinking was overrated when you were on holiday ...

'Nothing will happen here,' Theo told her.

What did he say? Why was he still talking? Why wasn't he acting? In fact, in this New Abby moment, why wasn't she just taking the initiative? She held her breath, edged her mouth towards his.

'I will not,' he repeated, gently edging back, still rocking her to the sound of the bouzouki.

'What if I don't give you a choice?' She was damned if she was going to let him crush her libido right now!

'I will keep us moving,' he said, lifting up her hand and forcing her to spin a rotation in time to the song.

'And if I make us stop?' she countered, pulling him firmly back into her body.

'Abby,' he whispered. 'I do not want to share our moment with Stathis, with Leon, with my aunt.'

Damn it, he had a point. A good point. He was being professional and committed to this important, alluring dancing aspect of the party. She needed to remember the part where she wasn't officially on holiday, where she was a member of the Desperately Seeking team, rebuilding their brand and shovelling holiday home potential at everyone they could.

'If I get to kiss you again,' he continued, voice pure lust. 'If you *let me* kiss you again, It will be on a beach, the sun on our faces, wine on our lips, the scent of—'

'Pastry.' Why had she said that? Sun, sea, sand, sexy Greek and her favourite savouries would be sensory overload.

'I was going to say "you",' Theo stated. 'The scent of you, Abby.'

She so hoped he was referring to her light Calvin Klein Beauty and not the July heat's effect on her sweat glands.

Another cheer went up from the gathered crowd and they suddenly all began to clap their hands in time. Abby's attention was finally drawn away from Theo to Melody and Leon. Her sister was grinding and winding around a chair that had somehow made its way into the centre circle, Leon performing a solo piece around her, working at the buttons on his fly. A little temptation for the patrons wasn't harmful but full-on nudity might just tip the balance, especially as they weren't all that far away from the nearest church.

She looked back at Theo, eyes pleading. 'You are both wearing underwear, aren't you?'

He smiled at her. 'I am not sure which reply would disappoint you the most.'

Her sensible head was coming back. Perhaps she should have had a small Old Fashioned when it had been offered earlier.

'Dance with my mum,' Abby said, letting him go, spinning with a flourish to stay connected to the dancing. 'Then Diana and her friends.'

'Where are you going?' Theo asked.

'To stop Leon taking his trousers off and to see a man about a raffle prize.'

Forty-seven

Theo couldn't stop looking at Abby. With the sounds of the village, the village of all the summers of his childhood surrounding him, he was starting to feel content here. A resting point between island-hopping was turning into a feeling of belonging. And, really, the feeling that somehow he fitted in had nothing to do with being a Pappas. But it had everything to do with being Theo.

'She is a very beautiful girl.'

He hadn't noticed his aunt come up to the makeshift cocktail bar, such was his distraction, but immediately his guard rose up. 'Who?'

'Theo,' Spyridoula answered with a shake of her head. 'There is no playing of roles in Greek dancing. You know that.'

'I do not know what you mean.' Still keeping a lid on things. Old habits die hard.

'The daughter-of-Jackie, Abby. She is hard-working with a good heart.' Spyridoula sniffed. 'The other daughter-of-Jackie Melody ... She tries, sometimes a little too much, but with very good hair.'

'Do you just want to talk or do you want a drink?' he asked, picking up a bottle of rum in anticipation of her order.

'I need apparently three White Ladies. This is a cocktail, yes?'

'Yes,' Theo answered.

'Diana says this is ordered in a book written by the author who is not her but has the same name.' She shook her head. 'I have either got that conversation right or I am drunk.'

'I am not sure,' Theo admitted.

'So … another viewing for the villa tomorrow.'

'There is?' He feigned disinterest, hackles rising. He knew, no matter how settled he might be feeling, the Pappas holiday house was never going to be a permanent solution for his living arrangements, but he still didn't like the fact his father was ready to sell on their family memories. Or perhaps senti- mentality really did have no place in Dinis's life. Hadn't he shouted as much before Theo left?

He looked up at his aunt then, suddenly struck by the element of nostalgia. 'Why do you not cook, Spyri?'

His aunt's reaction spoke more than a thousand recipes. 'You have been drinking your own cocktails,' she spluttered. '*You* are drunk and high from your half-naked dancing with Daughter-of-Jackie, Abby.'

'Stamatis told me you used to cook, years ago.'

'You are seeing Stamatis while you are here now? That is news to me.' She put her fingers to her earrings, twirling one around in her lobe. 'That damp, dark, shed of his he hides in. Why would anyone want to spend time there?'

'I like it there,' Theo admitted. 'It's peaceful.'

'It is a dump,' Spyridoula countered. 'It is a paradise for a hoarder. All little bits of this and little pieces of that, none of it any good to anybody.'

'But why do you not cook?' Theo asked again.

'Why do I not cook?' She threw her arms in the air as if that were her answer, but then followed it up with, 'I do not make clothes any more either. Do you want me to talk about that also?'

'Spyri,' Theo began, 'I did not mean to upset you.'

'What good can come from your questions about cooking? I ask you that, huh! Cooking, it is just a waste of time. Eating someone else's cooking is much more full of pleasure and that is what I wish to spend my time and money on. Filling my stomach with food I have not had my hands in.'

'Oh, I agree,' Jackie interrupted. Theo had only just realised she was there. He wondered how long she had been listening in to their conversation. 'To some extent, that is.' She pushed her glasses up her nose. 'Melody was always out and I was always too busy to think about all that preparation before. Happy with some crisps and a dip or a ham sandwich. But, now Abby's here and we're all together again, sometimes I think it might be nice to make something and enjoy it as a family.'

'Take my advice,' Spyridoula began. 'Book a table at Eucalyptus Taverna and save yourself the disappointment when your bread does not rise or your meat overcooks.' She put her finger up in the air as if she had just had a light-bulb moment. 'All of the fine taste and none of the washing up.' She focused back on Theo. 'Are my White Ladies ready yet?'

'In one moment,' Theo said, shaking up his mixer.

'It's been a wonderful party,' Jackie mused, looking out over the guests still enjoying the sound of George on the bouzouki, his nephews now accompanying him with a mandolin and small drum. 'Everyone pulling together somehow.' A contented sigh left her lips. 'And thank you, Spyridoula for recommending us to Meredith. Melody is going to show her the little two-bedroom tomorrow morning while I'm valuing her property.'

'*Kanena provlima*, Jackie.' Spyridoula looked to Theo. 'And any time you would like to borrow my nephew to dance for your customers—'

'*Ochi*,' Theo spluttered. 'That was a once-in-a-lifetime event.'

'Tell this to Leon,' Spyridoula said, hitching her head back and indicating his friend, minus his shirt, still dancing with the eager ladies of the village.

'We do have the *panegyri* coming up though,' Jackie reminded him. 'With everything being so hard with the business I'd not thought much about it but it's always so lovely and with Abby here this year ...'

'She will stay?' Theo jumped into the conversation. 'For the *panegyri*, I mean.'

'I hope so,' Jackie answered. 'You never really realise how much you miss family until you're all back together again.' She sighed. 'Well, not quite all of us, but ...'

Spyridoula slipped an arm through the Englishwoman's. 'This is a time for celebrating, Jackie, not a time to reopen sad wounds.' She stared at Theo warningly. 'Or to talk about using ovens.'

'You're right,' Jackie agreed.

'New beginnings,' Spyridoula said. 'And a toast to your new white paint.' She drew in a contented sigh. 'The council, they will be very pleased.'

'Have you got the basket of raffle tickets?' Abby asked Melody. It was time for the draw and she was really excited. It was a little bit of an outlay but she was combining it with a treat someone special deserved. Everyone had enjoyed the hilarity of the Donald Trump lookalike and taking selfies wearing the Tom Hanks mask – Melody had even drawn a face on a football to make a 'Wilson' prop – as well as the Greek flavour George, Theo and Leon had brought to proceedings.

Melody's response was a loud hiccup and a heavy arm landing around Abby's shoulders, the party spirit having been liberally indulged in now the work element had subsided.

'Did you know that Leon had abs, Abs?' Melody burst into a fit of giggles then, one hand stifling her mouth. 'Did you get that? Abs, Abs!'

'I got it,' Abby answered. 'Where are the raffle tickets? You were going to rip the rest up and put them in the basket.'

'I did,' Melody replied. 'Ages ago. They're in the office. Next to the photocopier.'

Abby practically skipped inside. Having worried about the raffle prize all day – when she hadn't been worrying about her ovaries exploding every time she looked at Theo – she couldn't wait to pick a lucky prize-winner.

'Abby.'

She caught her breath, hand going to her chest as a figure appeared in her sightline. 'Gosh, George, you almost gave me a heart attack. I didn't think anyone was in here.'

'I am just collecting my trays from the food,' he answered, indicating the platters in his hands.

'Oh, the food, George, it was heavenly, everyone said so, well, not Diana, but I'm learning she rarely has a good word to say about anyone.' She smiled. 'Thank you so much for making it and at such short notice. You must let me know how much we owe you.' Hopefully it was going to be some-where in the region of not more than a hundred euros or she was going to have to make a bigger dent in her notice money. 'And the music! The wonderful Greek bouzouki. We must pay you for that too.' She swallowed. Hell, entertaining was costly.

'Money is no matter,' George said, waving his free hand.

'Oh, but it is,' Abby said. 'I know it is. The summer season doesn't last forever, does it?'

He smiled. 'For the winter, I make soup from the summer leftovers and freeze this. Sometimes this can last until March.'

Abby fanned her face. 'It's so hot I can't even think about soup right now.'

'Abby,' George said, his tone serious.

'Yes.'

'I would … like to take out your mother.'

It took a second for Abby to process the way the sentence was worded and realise that George was not Aleko wanting to scupper a business rival. 'Take out my mother,' she repeated. 'On a date?'

'I think of a picnic,' George stated. 'I think she would like. Maybe to Kaiser's Throne … there is a nice view.'

Abby's mind flooded with images. Her mum on a blanket, kicking off her high heels, George feeding her sweet lemon drizzle cake, drinking retsina under a cloudless sky … *Dad*. She swallowed. Her mum and dad had had a wonderful, perfect marriage, blighted by nothing but his illness. They had loved each other deeply for as long as they had been together. Jackie was still young, years of her life ahead of her, years to enjoy working at the business but also, relaxing, really, fully living again. It was something Abby couldn't see her mum had had the opportunity to do before. George wasn't a man with too many hats (that she knew of) and he wasn't a Russian millionaire. He was just Taverna George. But Taverna George was kind, good-hearted, and funny. She also noticed Jackie lit up – or rather acted like a nervous never-been-kissed schoolgirl – whenever he was around.

'*Signomi*,' George said, his hand shaking a little as he steadied the trays. 'I should not have asked.'

'No,' Abby breathed quickly. 'No, don't be silly.'

'It is still not right,' George continued. 'Even after all this time.'

'George, honestly, I really think my mum would love to go on a picnic with you.' Why hadn't she spoken up sooner? She was in Greece now, not Romsey. And when in Greece you spoke from your heart and you didn't hesitate. You ate the baklava and you drank the ouzo and you worried about the consequences later. Theo came to mind again. Of all the Dolan women only Melody seem to be acting fully Greek ...

'I am sorry,' George said, bowing like he was paying a penance, heading towards the door.

'George, wait!' Abby ordered. She was caught between chasing after him and grabbing the basket of raffle tickets and, as she moved, her elbow caught the container and hundreds of small oblongs of paper scattered all over the tiled floor.

Forty-eight

'Wasn't there going to be a raffle draw?' Diana bleated at full volume. 'Or is the *actual* draw as big of a mystery as the so-called mystery prize?'

'Coming!' Abby called, shaking the basket of quickly swept-up tickets. She was hot and bothered now, desperately scanning the petering out crowd for George. She needed to let him know that asking her mum out on a date was completely the right thing to do. Her mum needed this in her life. It would give her something more than Desperately Seeking, a social life of microwave meals and the re-boot of *Dynasty*. Abby coughed. Not that there was anything wrong with that when you were between periods of your life, or just enjoyed salty meals and over-the-top feel-good drama.

'Mum,' she said, approaching Jackie. 'You should pick out the winner.' She offered her Stathis's basket.

'What's the prize?' Jackie asked. Then her hands went to her mouth. 'We didn't get a prize!'

'There's no prize?' Diana queried, her ears as sensitive as a bat's.

'There is a *wonderful* prize,' Abby assured. 'Everyone is going to want to win it, I promise.'

'Aleko is giving away a flagon of tsipouro,' Diana stated.

'Well,' Abby said. 'Ladies and gentlemen, if you please all get out your raffle tickets ready to check, my mum is going to pull out the winning number.'

'We don't have any tickets,' Diana informed.

She smiled at Diana. 'They are white, just like our new branding. Melody should have given you all a ticket when you came in to the party.'

'No,' Diana stated loudly. 'She just told us our number.'

This could not be happening. Hyperventilation felt imminent as she searched the party for her sister. Melody was coiled around Leon, hands smoothing over his still-exposed chest. Striding over, she hissed. 'Melody, a word.' Then she grabbed her sister's hand, pulling her over to the shade and quiet of the olive tree.

'What's going on? Did you get a bottle from the supermarket for the prize?' Melody asked.

'What did you do with the raffle tickets?' Abby asked frantically. 'Why has no one got any?'

'Ugh, is that all? Leon was just telling me all about this great club in Corfu Town—'

'Melody!'

'I just told them their number,' Melody responded with a sigh. 'That way we didn't go through as many tickets. There's a list somewhere. I noted them down.' She smiled as if she were a genius. 'And, I used up the books we had from when we did the last prize draw before I started on the new ones.'

Abby felt the creeping sense of dread growing bigger and stronger as every second ticked by. She had to ask the question, but she felt fearful that she already knew the answer. 'So, what did you do with the matching strips?'

Melody giggled. 'Are you talking about my pole work again?'

Abby rushed to the table where a raffle book was laying open, grabbed it up and brought it over to her sister. 'Look! Two strips! Both with the same numbers on. One for the basket. One meant for the customer to keep. What did you do, Melody?'

The alcoholic bravado seemed to dissipate then as reality hit home and her sister's tan turned a shade of pearl. 'I put them all in the box.'

'My ladies want you to dance Pappas at the *panegyri*,' Spyridoula informed Theo. While everyone waited for the draw to take place, he was packing up the cocktail bar as proceedings started to come to an end. He had been busy all day, people complimenting him on the drinks. Despite everything being free, he had even earned some tips. Ordinarily, such was his need for cash now he wasn't tapping into his trust-fund account, he would have pocketed the euros and spent it on beer. But he was going to do something else with it and hope it hit the right note.

'What are *you* doing for the *panegyri*, Spyri?' Theo turned the question around.

'Not cooking,' she blurted out. 'Or spending any time with the Widow Alexakis. I know black is tradition and there should be time to mourn, but she has been mourning for more than a hundred years. And,' Spyridoula began again. 'The way she talked about her husband you would think he was the god of all husbands, when really he could not even catch a fish! Here! In San Stefanos! Where the fish almost jump into your lap!'

'We could catch fish,' Theo said suddenly.

'What?' his aunt inquired.

'For the *panegyri*,' he continued. 'We could catch some fish, like we used to, and Stathis could sell them on his grill.' He shrugged like it didn't matter. 'Perhaps it will buy him a new bicycle.'

Theo slipped another bottle into the box he was preparing, followed by some of the glasses he had gone back to borrow from Hera. When he looked up it was to see his aunt's eyes brimming with tears.

'Spyri ...' he began.

'Do not talk to me,' she ordered, opening her handbag and putting her whole face inside as if searching for something. 'Do not even think about talking to me.'

Classic Spyridoula – shouting and not wanting to show emotion. It was a Pappas trait. He could do one of two things. He could give her a moment, or he could brush off the sentiment he knew she had absorbed. Instead he passed her a serviette. 'Sometimes,' he began. 'The fumes from the tequila makes my eyes water.'

She snatched the offering and blew her nose loudly.

'Ladies and gentlemen,' Abby's voice rose above the happy chatter and background *laiko*. 'The prize is ... a trip to the beautiful island of Erikousa where you will be able to spend the day either soaking up the sun on Porto beach or visiting the clifftops and delighting in the panoramic views.'

There was an excited intake of breath.

'My latest novel involves a clifftop chase followed by romance on the sand. What fantastic research that would be,' Diana stated.

Erikousa. It was an island just eight miles off the coast of Corfu and he had never been there. Never really thought about it. Melody had told him a number when he'd arrived and suddenly, without any concrete reason, Theo found himself really wanting to win.

'Erikousa,' Spyridoula stated wistfully. 'I have not been there for more than forty years.'

'And the winning ticket is …' Abby began.

Be a high number. Be a high number. The higher the number the less chance Abby thought there was in the ticket being a duplicate. A quick sweep of the office had not produced Melody's list. She just had to hope the guests were going to play fair. There was always the chance they would all claim they had been given whatever number came out. She had to hope for a little good will. She couldn't have the whole raffle called into question with Diana already scrutinising everything.

Jackie dipped her hand into the basket. Abby could hear the swirling around as her mum swished the tickets from left to right, mixing. It seemed to go on an age until Jackie removed her hand, a white ticket in between her fingers. Abby held her breath as she watched her mum unfurl the paper until finally …

'And it's number … fourteen!'

It was a *low* number. This wasn't good, but how bad could it really be? Abby began to pray under her breath, well, not pray exactly, but force words of encouragement to the heavens. *Please! Please! Be nice! Remember how I never actually told Miranda how stupid she was for not knowing the difference between a paperclip and a staple …*

'That's my number!' Diana exclaimed excitedly.

Abby didn't know whether to cry or introduce manic laughter into the situation. The noise that left her lips was somehow a combo of both. 'Congratulations, Diana!' It was over. One winner. Just one extra boat fare to pay.

'I was given number fourteen also,' another voice spoke. 'Well, not me, my uncle George. See, he got me to write it on my hand.' George's tallest nephew proffered forth the knuckle of his thumb joint, a ballpoint number 14 clearly visible.

'Wanging hell,' Melody exclaimed loudly. 'Where's the list?'

'I am sorry, Daughter-of-Jackie, Abby, but I am sure I also have the number fourteen.' It was Spyridoula now. Abby wanted to hide, run off the terrace, down the street and find the nearest bottle of Fix again. Why had she left Melody in charge of the tickets? Why hadn't she written blow-by-blow instructions? The answer of course was because she thought a child of three could probably work out what you did with a simple book of perforated slips.

'We could draw it again,' Jackie suggested.

The loudest shriek of a 'no' came from Diana. 'You cannot draw it again. Drawing again would be against every rule of competition etiquette there is.'

'I've found the list!' Melody exclaimed, hair bouncing as she appeared to wipe a sticky purple substance off a rather scrunched-up piece of notebook. 'We'll get this sorted, find out exactly who has number fourteen and wins the prize.'

Abby watched her sister's eyes scanning the paper as everyone seemed to focus on her, waiting for the answer to the cliff-hanger like it was the season finale of *Riverdale*. But then Melody started putting her fingers out in turn, like she was counting. Abby then knew this was really bad and there was no way out.

'How many?' she asked, voice wobbling.

Melody looked up, eyes wide. 'Five.'

Forty-nine

The Blue Vine

'*Signomi*, Old Fashioned.'

Theo put the glass of orange-coloured liquid in front of Abby and slipped down into the chair opposite her. She had been sat at one of the tables closest to the water for the past hour. One of his colleagues had brought her a drink and complimentary crisps and she had broken each piece up into crumbs and thrown them into the water for the fish. Now her fingers were wrapped around the glass tealight holder on the table, smoothing over every ridge and bump in the pattern, her eyes appearing to be watching her trail of movement but not really paying full attention. She hadn't seemed to notice the arrival of another drink ... or him.

'Abby,' he said gently. 'The trip to Erikousa ...'

'Is a bloody disaster,' came the reply.

He swallowed, instantly knowing she was in a bad place. 'Please, have another drink.'

'Yes,' Abby agreed, swiping up the cocktail. 'Let me have another drink to drown away the fact that I've successfully screwed up my mother's business by getting Desperately Seeking into more debt because now I have to pay for five winners to go on the Erikousa trip!' She practically inhaled the alcohol. 'Not to mention my sister has to do a spot of lap-dancing to pay off Donald Trump and goodness knows how much George's catering fee will be!'

'I am sure Spyridoula will not want her prize,' Theo suggested. 'I will talk to her.'

'No!' Abby spoke quickly. 'That's the last thing I want. As Dolans, we pride ourselves on our integrity. We always have. If you promise something you see it through and deliver on that promise, no matter what.'

'OK,' Theo said. 'Then what are you going to do?'

She shook her head, tears welling up in her eyes. 'I have no idea. Pay, I guess, on my credit card if I have to. I really thought that a nice prize would be the perfect end to the perfect party but Melody was right.' She sighed. 'I should have just bought a bottle of something from the supermarket. Then I would only be looking at five bottles of plonk, not five expensive boat tickets.'

'This is not your fault, Abby,' Theo stated. 'Melody was in charge of the tickets.'

'But it's been me who has taken charge of everything since I got here.' She took a deep breath, as if emboldening herself. 'I said they had to rebrand. I said they had to paint and put on a show and ... what do I really know about anything? What have I ever, really been in charge of my whole entire life? *Lists!*' Abby blasted. 'Bloody, stupid, pointless lists! Itemising my world like I'm clicking things into an Amazon basket!'

'Abby.' Theo reached for her hands, swiftly removing the tealight holder and replacing it with his fingers, interlocking their digits as tightly as he could. For a second Abby seemed to still, her skin placidly comfortable next to his and then she shivered.

'You feel so nice,' she said, voice a lot softer.

'You feel nice too,' he replied, squeezing her hands.

She looked straight at him then, those beautiful, if slightly sad eyes, locking with his. 'I've never been in this situation before,' she whispered.

'This situation?' he queried.

'I have no axis.' She whispered the words even more quietly. 'I'm not anchored to anything.'

'This is a good thing,' Theo responded. 'It means you are as free as those birds out there.' He nodded towards the swallows, dipping and diving over the ocean then through the eucalyptus trees that surrounded the cove.

'No,' Abby said, shaking her head. 'It means I'm scared of what comes next because I don't know what comes next, and I've always, *always*, known what comes next.'

He squeezed her hands again. 'I know what comes next.' He injected every confidence into his tone.

'Another Old Fashioned?' She nodded to the glass.

'Perhaps,' he replied. 'But not here.' He checked his watch. 'We have a few hours until the sun goes down. Let's go to Logas Beach.'

'I can't,' Abby answered straightaway. 'I have to … my mum is appraising Meredith's house and Melody is … she's showing Meredith the two-bedroomed property and I have to—'

'Every moment you have been in San Stefanos you have been working,' Theo reminded her. 'Painting, pushing cars, searching for signs, walking with cows …'

'I stopped to do some dancing to happy music,' she reminded him. 'And I've eaten quite a lot of pastry.'

Theo put her hands to his lips as he leaned across the table, kissing the skin. 'Go and get your bikini and meet me here in twenty minutes.'

'Theo, as lovely as it sounds—'

'You are not anchored to anything, remember?' he said, getting to his feet. 'Let me show you that sometimes this can be a good thing.'

Fifty

Logas Beach, Peroulades

Theo could have chosen the motorbike or the Porsche but neither had felt right and he knew that the kind of person that Abby was meant she would not have been impressed by either. Instead, he had left a note for Spyridoula and taken her seen-better-days but still functional Namco Pony. He had always thought the car was both ugly and beautiful, a cross between a small flat-bed truck and a Jeep, but some of the best memories of his childhood were wrapped up in its no-nonsense rustic interior, and probably some of the cake crumbs were still there too. He hadn't remembered it rattling quite so much the last time he had driven it, but then that was some years ago.

'Do you have a car, Abby?' Theo called over the roar of the engine and the hot air rushing through the windows as they wound up the mountain roads.

'No,' she answered. 'I live a short walk from where I work. It seemed silly to have one parked up most days.' She stopped talking for a moment. 'But, I suppose that's going to change, seeing as I don't work there any more. How about you?'

Was she asking about his job? Straightaway he felt the urge to move his leg – a little awkward when you were in charge of a car – but he controlled it. He knew, if he was going to begin something with Abby, whatever guise the *something* took, he would have to open up. He didn't feel wholly comfortable that he was ready but …

'I expect you have more than one car, being rich and everything,' Abby continued, her tone teasing.

He couldn't stop the slight surge of relief at her addition to her question.

'Three of them,' he answered honestly. 'In Halkidiki.'

She nodded. 'I can imagine.'

'No,' he said quickly. 'They are my father's cars and I always have to stop for petrol because they drink so much. You are too worried to eat gyros inside them because of the light-coloured seats. Many, many problems.'

She laughed then and it made him feel good. She seemed lighter, her worries a few miles away, almost relaxed as they bumped along. He completed the final turn and pulled the car into the car park where there were many vehicles already. In his eyes, all of Corfu was spectacular, but this spot was well known for its magnificent scenery and sunset views.

'Oh, my goodness,' Abby exclaimed, her hands clamouring for the handle of the door.

Theo watched her looking, out of the windscreen, out of the passenger door, seeking as much scenery as her eyes could grasp. She opened the door and stepped out onto the sandy ground, shielding her eyes from the intense sun.

Abby held her breath as she took in the view ahead of her. Despite having been on the island numerous times she had never been here and she had never seen anything quite like this. Travelling upwards and around in the car should have prepared her for this cliff-top vantage point, but somehow it hadn't. None of the fields, the blossoming brush or the houses of cream, terracotta and stone had hinted at the surprise of what lay here.

Stretched out in front of her, as far as the eye could see, was a rich blanket of sea, the purest of blues. It rippled with the light breeze, the sun changing the shade from aqua to peacock and back again. There was nothing spoiling the ocean, no boats, no swimmers to be seen, nothing but the vastness and power of the water surrounded by almost white sandstone cliffs.

'It is amazing, right?'

Theo's voice was close, so close that if she decided to lean back a little his body would be right there. That thought gave her a thrill but, instead of leaning back, she turned and faced him. 'It's breath-taking. Just the most ... beautiful view I've ever seen.'

'Come,' he said, holding out his hand. 'There is a path then there are steps down to the beach.'

She took his hand and let him lead the way.

'So, is this where you take all your women?' Abby asked, when they carefully began to navigate the steep stone steps down to the shore.

'All the gold-diggers?' Theo queried.

'Sorry, I didn't mean ...' She didn't know what she had meant. She was finding it hard to fully embrace how much she enjoyed his company while she was busy being axis-less. Perhaps she had said it to remind herself she was here temporarily.

'I have not been here for many years,' he answered. 'Since I was a teenager, maybe. With Leon and his family.'

'You didn't come here with your mum?' she asked softly.

'I do not know,' he breathed hard. 'Maybe.' He smiled then. 'Going down these steps would not have been enough for her, I know that.' He pointed to the craggy rocks either side of them. 'She would have wanted to hang from the cliff by a rope or come down on a parachute.'

'She sounds like such an adventurous woman,' Abby stated. 'I haven't done anything like that.' She swallowed as the fact of her words settled awkwardly on her conscience. She hadn't done much of anything. Because everything different or new she had suggested to Darrell, even if it was only the minutest bit out of his comfort zone, led to moaning or, sometimes, laughter. Had she really let him govern her choices so hard? She could feel her entire soul getting mad with itself.

'You speak like your life is over already,' he said. 'How old are you, Abby?'

She smiled, taking another precarious step, the breeze blowing her hair around her face. 'It's not the done thing to ask a lady her age.'

'The done thing?' Theo asked, sounding bemused.

'I'm twenty-four,' she answered. 'The slightly older Dolan sister with the lot less blonde hair.'

'You want to have blonde hair?' Theo asked.

She thought about it for a moment then smiled. 'Actually, no. It suits Melody. I'm not sure it would suit me.'

'I think your hair is beautiful,' Theo told her. 'Just how it is.'

His compliment distracted her and she almost slipped, her sandal grazing the sand-coloured steps, body unbalanced. He reached out, catching her, holding on to her, his arms strong and stabling.

'You are OK,' he breathed. It wasn't a question, more of a statement, telling her she was safe. Locked in his embrace, she looked up at his handsome face, those black olive-coloured eyes under soft lashes gazing back at her, protective as well as sexy ...

'I don't know the rules, Theo.' Abby allowed herself to stay in his arms, thoroughly enjoying every second of being held.

'The rules?' he queried.

'I've had one relationship. One full-on relationship I thought was going to be the relationship of my whole life. I haven't done dating or ...' She didn't really know what to say next. Where was all this leading? 'Or, being held by a gorgeous, lovely, slightly mysterious man.'

'Mysterious,' Theo said, a smile on those luscious lips that thrilled her to the bone.

'I want to know more about you, Theo but I'm scared to know more about you.'

'Scared?' She saw his expression change just a little, like the sun altering the colour of the water below them. 'Because I told you I was a gardener?'

'No,' she said. 'Because I can't get attached to you.'

He brought her body towards his, making their forms connect while still holding her a little suspended in his arms. 'I can't *wait* to get attached to you.'

Abby shivered. It was a deliberately cheesy double entendre yet completely erotic – the perfect mix – and it had elicited the strongest of reactions within her.

'I don't live here,' she said simply.

'I do not live here also,' he whispered.

'Then we shouldn't, should we?' Was she asking herself or asking him? And what *was* she asking him? She was already almost into something. Except nothing was completely clear when you were being held halfway down a cliff face, the most beautiful seascape laid out before you, the gloriously hot Corfu sun sizzling your skin, staring up into the delectable eyes of a Greek god.

'Life is short, Abby,' Theo whispered on the wind. 'We both know this. I am starting to understand that hiding from the things that scare us the most is not the answer.'

'What is the answer?' she asked, a little breathless with anticipation.

'I do not know,' he replied, his lips now just millimetres from hers. 'But I want to not be too scared to find out.'

His mouth seized hers then and she yielded to their lips coming together as completely as she ever had, winding her body into his, her arms around his neck, fingers slipping into the tight knot of hair at the back of his head. It was a mind-spinning kiss, filled with desire, their mouths keen to taste, to explore, to love freely without the need for promises. It was raw, it was beautiful, it was a list-free, in-the-moment moment.

He dropped a gentle touch to her lips and she palmed the slight roughness of his jaw, smiling, giddy, and feeling like an Abby Dolan she never knew existed. She liked this Abby. Apparently, this Abby gave good tongue over a Greek beach ...

'I love to see you smile,' Theo said as she finally stood, carefully making sure her sandals hit the flat of the step.

'Don't think I've forgotten,' Abby said, slipping her hand back into his.

'Forgotten?' he queried.

'You distracted me with your lips.'

'I am hoping this was not a one-time event.' He moved to kiss her again, but she stopped him, laughing, squirming away from his advances and dropping her feet down another step.

'How old are you, Theo?' she called.

He waved a hand. 'Age, it is just a number.'

'Now I'm worried.'

'Why do you worry?' he asked, joining her on the next step down. 'You think I am too old for you?' He winked. 'Or too young?'

'It doesn't matter,' she spoke finally. If he said he was forty – although she didn't think he was for a moment – what would it matter? If he said he was eighteen she might feel a little Demi Moore but … actually, she really did want him to be older than eighteen.

He smiled. 'I am twenty-six.'

A breath of relief left her although she didn't really know why. Ashton Kutcher had come to no real harm …

'Young,' he continued. 'Strong.' He flexed his muscles. 'Experienced …'

'I'm not sure I want to know about that.' She raised an eyebrow. He'd probably had scores of women and she had just told him she was almost as green as Jane the Virgin.

'I was going to say experienced in Greek dancing.'

'Oh.' Now she felt a little stupid.

'Abby,' he said, taking her face in his hands. 'You have had this relationship, one for a long time.' He looked at her, deeply, his expression suddenly serious. 'I have never had this … with anyone.'

He looked as if he had exposed his deepest, darkest secret. As if what he had told her was wrong in so many ways. It only made her want to know what made him tick even more. She smiled. 'We are total opposites. How does that work?'

He smiled back. 'I think a little like yin and yang … or Zeus and his wife, Hera.'

'I don't know much about Greek mythology,' Abby admitted.

Theo waved a hand. 'At the end of every conflict they all sat down together and ate souvlaki.' He squeezed her hand. 'Are you hungry, my opposite?'

The odd endearment warmed her, as did the thought of succulent chicken on a skewer with fat chunks of ripe, juicy peppers, and red onion, drizzled with a little lemon.

'There's somewhere down there on the beach?' She queried, gazing over at the very slim stretch of golden sand.

'No,' he answered. 'But when we have walked down all the steps, along the beach and back up again, there is a great restaurant overlooking the view.'

She playfully thumped his shoulder, sending him down onto the next step. 'That might call for pastry as well as souvlaki.'

Fifty-one

7th Heaven Bar, Peroulades

Abby took a sip of the divine cocktail that had been presented to her by the barman. It was called a Paloma, and featured tequila and grapefruit juice with a large wedge of fresh pink grapefruit hanging on the side of the glass. It looked almost too pretty to drink but, having walked up and down a cliff, chased Theo up the sand until her lungs were begging for mercy, she was both thirsty and extremely hungry for the kolokithopita and souvlaki they had ordered.

'Good?' Theo asked her.

'It's very good,' Abby breathed. 'This whole place is almost unbelievable. The views are just breath-taking. I can't believe I didn't even know it was here.'

'You have been to Corfu many times?' Theo inquired, sipping at his bottle of beer.

'My mum and dad brought us here for the first time when I was six. We stayed in at Agios Georgios in the south of the island. I don't remember much about it. I was into ice cream and building sandcastles at that age. Then we came again when my dad was recovering from his operation. That was the first time I came to San Stefanos.' She smiled. 'Then I've been back a few times to visit my mum and Melody. But not as often as I should have.'

'The villa,' Theo began. 'The Pappas villa, it is where we would spend our family holidays.'

'It's so beautiful. I thought that the moment I stood on the terrace.'

'And was greeted by the impressive Greek view,' Theo teased.

She flushed immediately, knowing he knew she would. That day, with Theo naked on the terrace, felt so long ago. 'It was very unexpected. But I'm glad it was me surveying the villa and not my mum.'

'Me too,' he answered.

'So why is your father selling the property?' Abby asked, taking another sip of her drink. 'Does he not holiday here? Does he need to release some funds?'

She watched him shake his head. 'He is … a complex man,' Theo answered.

Theo didn't know what else to say. He didn't want to be dishonest with Abby in any respect, but talking about his father was hard. It would involve laying everything on the table. He wanted to do that, but it wasn't going to be easy. Little by little. And the truth was, he didn't really know why his father was selling the villa. His first thought had been out of spite, to make Theo go back home, or to make his staying on Corfu more difficult, but would Dinis really do that? There had to be more to it.

'Like you,' Abby said.

'I am not complex.'

'So, it's normal to deny who you are and pretend you are a gardener?' There was humour in her voice. She was no longer angry, but she was curious.

He took a breath. 'There *is* something you should know about me, Abby.'

'I know there is,' she answered. 'I see it written on your face. And it's coming from somewhere deep inside you. I saw it that night after you stopped Igor on the boat.'

He took another breath. 'Abby, I am not rich.'

'You're not?'

'No,' he said, shaking his head. 'And that is why saying I was a gardener was not that far from the truth. It is why I am working at The Blue Vine. It is why I have been clearing tables in restaurants and cleaning pools and working my way across islands from Halkidiki.'

'I don't understand.'

'I know,' he answered, but said no more.

'You are angry with your father for something?' she guessed.

'A little.'

'He is angry with you?'

'A lot more.'

'Are you on the run?' Abby asked. 'Have you done something illegal with gold bullion?'

'No,' he said. 'Nothing like that.'

'Then what is it?' Abby inquired.

From inside the pocket of his trousers he felt his mobile phone vibrate. Who would be calling him? Hera? To check he really had got Panos to cover his shift? Spyridoula? Having got his note and needing her car?

'Is that your phone?' Abby asked. 'I can hear something buzzing.'

'I should turn it off,' Theo stated, making no attempt to retrieve it.

'No,' Abby said. 'It's OK. You should answer it. It might be important.'

He couldn't imagine there was anything more important than being here with Abby and slowly, somehow, trying to release everything he had held inside his troubled mind for months …

'Honestly,' she said. 'Answer it. Please.'

Theo took the phone from his pocket then and checked the display. It said the one name he hadn't even considered. *Pateras*. Father. Seeing the name and photo on the screen threw him. Dinis hadn't called him, not once, since he'd left. A number of times, in particularly low moments, maudlin from too much beer, haunted by the sounds of the sea, he had thought about calling his father. He'd never known quite what he would say, whether there would be more fiery accusations or something else. But each time, although he'd punched in the number, he'd stopped himself from making the connection. Sometimes he had wondered if his father was sat back in Halkidiki going through the exact same scenario and now ... this call.

'Theo?' Abby said. 'Is everything OK?'

He realised then he had been looking at the phone for a long time. He pressed to ignore the call, returning the phone to his pocket. 'Just a friend,' he told her. 'I will call him back later.' He reached across the table, taking her hands in his as a waiter arrived with their food.

Fifty-two

En route to San Stefanos

Abby's stomach was as content as it had ever been. Filled with courgette pie, chicken souvlaki and three Paloma cocktails, she was finally starting to feel in the holiday mood.

Leaving the stunning vistas over Logas Beach behind, they were bumping back up and down the hills in Spyridoula's unique vehicle. Somehow, over the delicious food, she and Theo had talked about anything and everything – music, films, Brexit, and how terrible it was that croissants seemed to be getting smaller (more on her part than his, if she was honest) – but he still hadn't revisited the remark about him not being rich. She looked across at him, watching him expertly steer the car around tight, winding bends and the odd rogue goat. She liked him. She really liked him. No matter how soon it was after Darrell. She hadn't been looking – she had hardly ever looked in her life – and she didn't care how much money he had or didn't have. What she did care about, however, was his story. And there had to be one. There was more to him being here working a bar and needing to forget he was a Pappas, she could sense it.

'How about a detour?' he asked suddenly. 'Do you have time?'

'Well,' Abby said. 'I haven't had any frantic calls from my mum or texts containing numbers instead of letters from Melody.' She smiled. 'I have time.'

They travelled on until the road became a little less crater-filled and more familiar to Abby. The tree-covered hills and olive grove copses that lined the road toward San Stefanos looked glorious as the sun began to set. Instinctively, Abby knew Theo was going to turn towards Pelekito and Stamatis's workshop in the woods. She had loved the cavern of hand-crafted treasures but she didn't have the cash to spare for a sign. She and Melody had done their best using the most appropriate font Microsoft Word could offer and laminated it before sticking it to a piece of wood crate. It was cheap but effective ... and the main thing was it wasn't pink.

'Theo, I love Stamatis's work, but I still can't afford one of his signs.'

'It is OK,' Theo said, smiling at her. 'I have not brought you here to spend your money.'

He pulled the car to a stop in his usual spot and killed the engine. 'Come on,' he said. 'Let us go and see what he is up to today. My guess is eating something disgusting from a tin.'

Theo opened the door of the car and breathed in the scent of woodland, olives, dust – all fragrances that brought back fond memories. Running through the trees with Leon and other friends on Corfu for the holidays, making bows and arrows, getting all kinds of muddy ...

The door of the workshop opened and Theo prepared for Stamatis to greet him with the usual mix of annoyance wrapped up with genuine affection, but it wasn't Stamatis he saw first, it was his aunt.

She was smiling, with her eyes, as well as her lips, her skin glowing, her cheeks a little flushed as she turned to look back at her companion. Theo felt a little like he was intruding and he had the sudden urge to jump back into the car.

The sound of a breaking twig had Spyridoula turning, and catching sight of him and Abby.

'Sorry.' Abby pulled a piece of stick out of her sandals.

'Ah! Here is my car! Not stolen but joyridden by my nephew!'

His aunt was back in her usual firm form, marching away from the workshop, gesticulating at him. Theo's eyes went to Stamatis. Quiet, assessing.

'Did I not teach you to ask before you take something? Do I have to again bring up the rizogalo situation when you were seven?' Spyridoula was now stood right in front of him.

'I left you a note.'

'I did not see a note.'

'Is that why you came here?' Theo queried. 'To see if I was here ... with your car?'

'Yes,' Spyridoula stated. 'Of course that is why. Why else would I come to this awful, insect-ridden, hole of filth?'

'To see Stamatis?' Theo offered.

'Why would I want to see that ... dust-covered, annoying, grumpy old man?' She sniffed. 'Where have you been, Daughter-of-Jackie, Abby? Has my nephew taken you somewhere nicer than this weed-covered shack?'

'Oh, yes,' Abby answered. 'We have been to Logas Beach.'

'Logas Beach,' Spyridoula said, sucking in a breath. 'Very nice views. Very nice cocktails too, I remember. Now, what is to happen with my raffle prize?'

'Oh,' Abby began. 'It's all going to be sorted out very soon. The trip is in a few days. I will let you have the details.'

'Very good,' Spyridoula stated with a nod. 'I am looking forward to it.' She began to walk towards her car.

'You are taking your car?' Theo asked. 'Now? Abby and I need to—'

'I am not taking the car,' she replied. 'I am taking Stamatis's moped.' She pointed at the vehicle parked nearby. 'The seat is torn and there is more rust than there are olives in these woods. If it gets me back to San Stefanos it will be a miracle, but do not worry.'

'If you wait for a little while I can take you home,' Theo offered.

'Why would I want to wait?' Spyridoula asked with a tut. 'I have already spent too much time here. If I stay any longer I will turn into a piece of wood and the crazy man will hang me from his ceiling with all the other old, warped bits of things.' She hoisted up her skirt then deftly mounted the moped, picking up the helmet and strapping it to her arm. 'Do not stay here too long either,' she called. 'He might make you into a coffee table.'

With that said, his aunt set the moped engine roaring and took off up the track, a plume of dust circling in her wake.

'Gosh,' Abby said. 'She's ever so good on the moped.'

'That is my aunt,' Theo stated. 'Always full of surprises.' He wondered what mode of transport Spyridoula used to get here from San Stefanos. While he was debating this with himself, a voice called from inside.

'Are you coming in? Or are you going to stand out there until it is too dark to see?'

'Come on,' Theo said, holding his hand out to Abby. 'I want to show you something.'

Fifty-three

The Olive Way Workshop, Near Pelekito

'You would like some bougatsa?' Stamatis offered.

'Is that food?' Abby asked. 'Because we just ate the most wonderful and rather huge meal in Peroulades. I couldn't fit in another thing.'

'I did not know they sold bougatsa in tins,' Theo remarked as they walked into the main area of the workshop. It was brighter today, like someone had opened up the back doors and let the outside flood in.

He then saw the custard and filo pastry pie on one of the work benches, in a rather familiar bowl.

'Why are you here today?' Stamatis asked. 'Why come here after a dinner of romance on the west coast?'

Theo saw Abby blush, and in the time it had taken for him to look away and back again, Stamatis had covered the pie with a piece of fabric.

'Do you still have some of my work?' Theo asked the man. 'Or did you sell each piece for hundreds of euros the second I was done?' A part of him secretly hoped it was the latter. It would be good to think that the old man had made some profit from some of his summers of carving.

'You want to show off your wood-making skills to your girlfriend?'

Was it just him or was Stamatis being a little inflammatory today? A bit more mad with the world than usual.

'Theo told me more about the summers he spent here over our dinner,' Abby said. 'I'd love to see something he made.'

Theo eyed his friend. Then Stamatis nodded and began walking towards where the light was coming in.

'It is too hot for him today,' Theo said as he and Abby followed Stamatis through the granular atmosphere. 'He should rest more. Get some fresher air.'

'You care about him a great deal, don't you?' Abby whispered.

'He's not getting any younger. He moves a little slower.' He sighed. 'Maybe he put my things in his shed of rubbish.' He shrugged then, as if it didn't matter. 'Maybe they are not as good as I remember them.'

'The only thing I ever made was an awful coaster that wasn't even flat,' Abby admitted. 'My dad still put it on his desk at work and let his coffee rock up and down on it.'

Theo then realised Stamatis *was* heading outside of the main workshop and they followed him through the open doors – the last rays of sun lighting a path – into his patch of garden to the rear of the shop. Compared to the inside of his building, this was a virtual oasis of calm and was – almost – tidy. Part grass, part forest floor, it housed a small wooden table and matching chairs, a bench in the shade and a few planter boxes containing what looked like vegetables. It seemed like another section was behind a low row of bush and this is where the owner seemed to be heading.

'This is so pretty,' Abby remarked.

'The vegetables were never here before.' Perhaps Stamatis had started looking after himself a little better.

'*Ela!*' Stamatis called, beckoning them further into the garden.

Theo and Abby stepped behind the hedgerow into a section Theo had never seen before. There was a wooden slide and climbing frame, a sand pit and in the corner, enjoying both sun and shade, was a rockery garden, fragrant herbs of green and colour sprouting forth as water trickled gently over the traditional rocks that surrounded them.

Stamatis plucked a wooden figure from the rockery and held it out to Abby. Theo recognised it immediately, despite it being weathered. Abby took it in her hands.

'Meet Theo's father,' Stamatis said, his lungs producing a heavy, crusty laugh. 'Little Dinis. It is a good likeness.'

Theo shook his head, a little ashamed. He hadn't always been at war with his father, but they always had the kind of relationship that had mountainous highs and earth's-core-deep lows.

'It's so detailed,' Abby remarked. 'How old were you when you made this?'

Theo shrugged. He had been hoping Stamatis had kept some of the more refined pieces.

'He was twelve,' Stamatis said. 'It was his second piece. The first Little Dinis he made, the head fell off.'

'His neck was too thin,' Theo explained. 'And I had not got proper control of my tools.'

'This train could have been sold many times but I decided to keep it,' Stamatis said, picking a beautifully carved locomotive with three carriages out of the sandpit and lifting it for Abby to see.

'Stamatis, what is this place?' Theo asked, taking in the sunflower carvings on the back fence and drawings of happy, smiley faces.

'Are you stupid?' Stamatis asked him. 'It is for the children. You make the children happy, the parents stay longer to look at expensive olive wood.'

'But how long has it been here?' Theo queried. 'Did you make it all?'

'They have crazy golf at Pyramid and a rotating gorilla ride at Finikas Bar. I was advised to ... think of the children.'

'Advised,' Theo repeated.

'And it has been successful,' Stamatis stated. 'Only this morning, three children run around throwing sand in each other's eyes while their parents ordered a large dining table.'

'It's lovely,' Abby told him. 'Isn't it, Theo?'

'You still have no other staff?' Theo queried. 'No one else to help you?'

'You are my manager now?' Stamatis questioned gruffly.

'Well, what does your *adviser* think of you working this place on your own?'

Stamatis focused on Abby, almost dismissing Theo with the shift in his glance. 'This is one of my favourite pieces that Theo made. A wind chime.'

Stamatis pointed to the olive-wood circle hanging from the tree outside the garden, whose branches extended over the rockery. Suspended from the circle were delicate, slender wooden tubes – shaped like long pieces of macaroni – gently swaying together to produce a gentle, almost ethereal sound. He had worked so hard to get the balance just right. Each tube he had engraved with tiny woodland creatures. He watched Abby creep closer, admiring the lizard, the owl and the cicada.

'He was sixteen when he made this.' Stamatis came up behind Abby and gently pushed the wind chime to make it sound again. 'It is as good as anything I have made.'

'That is not true,' Theo said straightaway.

'Take what I say, Theo, after all, you bring your girlfriend here to show off your talent, no?' He grinned at Abby. 'To show her there is a side to you that does not involve making millions of euro. You would like to see Theo's puppet now?'

Abby nodded. 'Very much so.'

Stamatis put a hand on her shoulder as he moved forward. 'I will go and find it. I am sure the little devil gets up in the night and walks the floor.'

'I will help you,' Theo said, following the man. He looked at Abby. 'I will be a moment.'

'I'll sit down,' she answered. 'It's so peaceful here.'

He followed his friend back into the workshop, eager to get him on his own and follow up on the real reason for this visit.

'Stamatis,' he called as the man turned left into one of the twisting trails of wooden shapes. 'There is something I want to ask you.'

'I am sure there is, but it really is not for me to answer.'

'What isn't?' Theo said.

'What do you want to ask?' Stamatis turned right then quickly left again, the space seeming to narrow.

'I made some money today. I worked, helping Abby at her mother's party, making cocktails for her guests, cocktails I will pay back Hera for. I made almost a hundred euros in tips.'

Stamatis pulled a ladder out and proceeded to lean it against one of his unstable-looking racks then started to climb. 'Very good. Do not spend the money on Mythos.'

'I know what I want to spend the money on,' Theo swallowed before continuing. 'Would you make a sign, for Abby's mother's business?'

'Ah, here it is.' Stamatis stood on tip-toes, reaching up for a large leather-clad box. Theo reached out, steadying the ladder as the old man climbed down.

'Did you hear what I said, Stamatis?' Theo asked him. 'I know the sign will cost more than what I have, but I will pay in instalments or I will help here when I can.'

The woodworker popped open the lid of the box and took out the Pinocchio-like puppet. It wasn't a boy though, it was a cat, roughly scoured to create the illusion of fur. Its eyes weren't straight and one of its legs had had to be repaired. 'He can still dance,' Stamatis said, moving the cross-shaped controls to make the strings shift. 'Do you remember his name?'

'*Tycherós.* Lucky.'

'*Ne, Tycherós.*' Stamatis made the wooden cat gallop in the air.

'Stamatis,' Theo said. 'Please, will you make Abby a sign?'

Stamatis answered. 'No.'

'But—'

'*You* are a woodworker too, Theo,' Stamatis reminded him. 'And you should know that something from the heart cannot be made by anyone else.' Stamatis put a hand on Theo's shoulder. 'You come here. You take your pick of the wood and *you* make the sign. But there is one condition.'

'What?' Theo asked.

'I want you to ask Spyridoula about the bougatsa.'

Theo took a breath, looking at the old man and trying to decide if he was serious. Nothing but the depth of his sincerity was reflected in his eyes.

'We have a deal,' Theo agreed, putting out his hand.

'Good,' Stamatis answered, dumping the puppet cat in Theo's palm. 'Now let us show your Abby your fine feline creation.'

Fifty-four

Desperately Seeking

'Oh, here she is, Mum. Abby, the Dolan daughter moving from man to man in the blink of an eye. And you thought *I* was fickle!'

Melody was stood on the terrace guzzling from a bottle of fizzy wine. How her sister could handle more alcohol after all the cocktails she had drunk throughout the day was anyone's guess. It took Abby a second to really take on board the slight.

'That's not fair,' she began.

'I'm only joking,' Melody stated with a laugh. 'So, how is he in bed?'

'Melody!' Abby exclaimed.

'Ssh,' Melody said, putting her finger to her lips. 'Sorry, you probably don't want to talk about that in front of Mum.'

'I do know how these things work, you know,' Jackie commented. Abby watched her mum snatch the bottle of fizz from Melody and begin to pour some liquid into two glasses. 'Come on, Abby, come and have a glass of this. It's the best the supermarket had.'

'Are we celebrating the success of the party?' Abby queried, moving onto the terrace and stopping at the table. Everything was almost back to normal apart from the bunting that Melody wanted to stay (plus she hadn't been able to get it down). Stripped bare of the gazebo, the extra tables, Donald Trump's wet sponges, it was almost like the party hadn't happened. Apart from a rather full list of names on sheets of paper, signing up for the Desperately Seeking newsletter.

'Not just that,' Melody said. 'We sold two houses.'

'Two!' Abby exclaimed, taking the offered wine flute.

'Meredith liked the two-bedroomed property. The owners wanted to see her three-bedroom property. They liked that. Two for the price of one,' Jackie stated joyously. 'Easiest sales I've ever made.'

'That's fantastic! Well done!' Abby felt a rush of love and pride run all the way through her as she looked at her mum and her sister. It felt like success. Well-deserved success for all their hard work.

'You've been out with Theo Pappas?' Jackie asked.

Abby nodded as she took a seat that faced the setting sun, the very last rays of light warming her skin. 'We went to Logas Beach.'

'I wanging love it there! Did you walk across the glass platform and stare down?' Melody asked. 'It's like the Spinnaker Tower but with beach on the ground not concrete and fag butts.'

'We did,' Abby answered. 'We had a nice meal and we talked and—'

A blast of a horn had all three of them jumping in their seats. It was Leon's taxi, screeching to a halt, almost careering into someone carrying a steel drum. The drum hit the front bumper of the car.

'Those musicians,' Melody exclaimed. 'I don't know how good they are at playing but they seem to be bloody useless at walking in a straight line.' She got to her feet. 'Wait! I saw everything!' She waved to Leon and went bounding down onto the road.

Left alone, Abby looked at her mum. There was definitely an ease about her features that hadn't been there when she'd first landed on Corfu. Lines had been lifted, her skin was slightly less wan and her professional businesswoman clothes were back where they belonged.

'Mum,' Abby began. 'I'm sorry about the raffle.'

'Don't be daft! It wasn't your fault. It was Melody's. You know what she's like after a few too many spirits.'

'I know but I should have kept a check on it.'

'People have to be allowed to make mistakes sometimes. That's how we learn.' Jackie took a sip of her drink. 'Melody will never make a mistake in a raffle again.'

'I'll sort it out,' Abby said. 'Somehow.'

'What made you think of a trip to Erikousa?' Jackie asked.

'You said you really wanted to go there,' Abby replied. 'And I saw a sign for the trip in town. It looks lovely.' She smiled. 'And it sounded a lot better than one of Aleko's spa days.'

'Thank you, Abby,' Jackie said.

Abby watched her mum take a sip of the fizzy wine, settling back into her seat, appearing more relaxed than she had seen her.

'What for?'

'Coming to Corfu, getting the business back on track, helping Melody and I see what's really important.'

'I wanted to come,' Abby said. 'For so many reasons.'

'But mainly because Darrell hurt you.'

'And I lost my job … and Poldark.'

'What?!' Jackie exclaimed. 'Poldark died?! Oh, Abby, why didn't you tell me that!'

'He hasn't died,' Abby breathed. 'He's been catnapped by my neighbour, but it's OK.'

'It's OK?!'

'Well, I know Mr Clements is lonely and he's there all the time and he can afford to buy Poldark the good stuff, although I'm not quite sure just how good corned beef is for a cat long term. And just as his furry butt was disappearing through the next-door window I was thinking about packing my case to come here.'

'And now there's Theo Pappas,' Jackie said.

'Mmm,' Abby replied. She had meant to sound non-committal but instead she had nailed a just-biting-into-a-Magnum-ice-cream moan.

'Abby, Greek men can be ever so charming but—'

'But what?' Abby asked, intrigued.

'Well, it's the holiday feel, isn't it? It's hot. *He's* hot. You're feeling a bit kicked in the teeth by Darrell – and rightly so, I might add. I've a good mind to ring him up and give him what for.'

'Don't, Mum,' Abby sighed. 'He isn't worth it.' And he really wasn't. She had nipped onto Facebook earlier while she had been sitting at The Blue Vine contemplating just how close she was on her credit-card limit and there was Darrell's status update. *In a relationship with Amber Stevens*. Obviously, he had managed to send the right person the crawling apology text after all. But, as she'd read the words there had been no deep, heart-numbing pain. All she had felt was disappointment. The feeling that she had wasted all that time on someone who could do that to her.

'I like Theo,' she admitted. 'But I'm not starry-eyed or intoxicated by spanakopita enough to think it's a forever feeling.' She sighed. 'Plus, I have to go home at some point.'

Jackie paused, putting her finger to the middle of her glasses and pushing them up her nose. 'Do you?'

'Mum ... I ... of course I do. I have the flat and—'

'And what?' Jackie asked.

'And ... things.'

'Like?'

'Well, my life didn't completely revolve around Darrell and my job.' She was struggling with what she was saying because even though she hated the fact, none of the lines she was delivering were ringing true.

'You could stay,' Jackie said. 'You could live here, with us. We could run the business together, all of us, just like I dreamed about.'

Her mum had dreamed about her being involved with the estate agency from the beginning? She had always thought the offer to join them, when it had come, was more a case of not wanting to leave her out, knowing she would never leave England because she was all set with Darrell.

'Did you never want to come?' Jackie asked. 'Really?'

'I ... didn't really think about it. It just never seemed real, until you went and then it was too late to think about it,' Abby admitted.

'Oh, Abby!'

'I know! I am the absolute opposite of every female character in *Hidden Figures* and I hate myself for it.'

'Why didn't you say something?' Jackie asked. 'I just presumed you were happy in England with Darrell.'

'I thought I was,' Abby said with a sigh. 'No ... I *was*, but I think, if I look back, perhaps I just wanted to stay because it was safe. I think I was too scared to leave something I knew for something I didn't.'

And she was the only one still there to tend her dad's grave ...

Jackie nodded. 'You've been that way since your dad died.'

'Well, no, I wouldn't say that exactly.' Her mum had turned mind-reader.

'I would,' Jackie said. 'And I should have helped you more.' She took a long, slow breath in. 'I was so grief-ridden I couldn't think about anyone but myself. I let you get caught up with Darrell. I was happy for you to lean on someone else. This whole situation is my fault.'

'Mum, that isn't true. You did everything for us after Dad died. Everything and more.' Abby reached for her mum's hands, enveloping them in hers, emotion bubbling in her stomach.

'Then I started to run away to Greece every summer, hoping to reconnect with someone I shouldn't want to reconnect with when I was newly widowed.'

'What?' Abby asked, not really understanding. And then the realisation seemed to hit her. The 'moments' she had witnessed, the painting, the whispered remembrance of the model and make of car, the deliberate avoiding of the taverna until recently …

'George,' Abby said.

Jackie nodded. Her eyes immediately filling with tears.

'Mum, George is so nice. Why are you crying?'

'Because I was you, Abby. I fell for a Greek man when I was on holiday and he broke my heart.'

Fifty-five

Villa Pappas

Theo had dropped Spyridoula's car off at her house and was now walking back to the villa. Under a darkening sky, the air still felt like it held more humidity than a steam room. The day had been both fun-filled and exhausting, but his overriding feeling was that he was finally beginning to reconnect with life again. And Abby. He was connecting with Abby on a level he had never connected with anyone before ...

He stopped walking at the approach, noticing the garage door was slightly open. But there was no light on. Was Leon in? Was he putting the taxi in the garage? His friend had never done that before. Something about it wasn't right. He stepped forwards cautiously, heading to the left of the property where the drive dipped down. As he neared he could hear movement, then the crash of equipment, followed by Greek curse words. Someone was definitely in there, and it sounded like they were raiding the tools.

Theo grabbed hold of the garage door and wrenched it up and open, ready to take on whatever would-be thief was behind the corrugated metal. A shadowy figure was lurking by the Porsche. Theo grabbed at the nearest thing which happened to be a foot pump.

'This is private property! Get out before I call the police!'

Theo threw the switch and the figure was suddenly bathed in light. The person seemed to shrink from it like he was a vampire.

'Turn it off, Theo! I am trying to look at something with the torch!'

'Dad?'

It was Dinis. Dressed in overalls, a cap on his head, looking every inch the mechanic he used to be when they had toiled together on the car and the motorbike.

'Everything has changed in this garage! Nothing is where it should be. Did you do that?'

'No ... I don't know ... Dad, what are you doing here?' Theo said.

'What does it look like I'm doing?' Dinis barked back. 'I am trying to find something in the engine of this car that is making a hideous noise when it is started. It needs the torch in a specific spot, not this floodlight above my head.'

'But—'

Dinis lifted his head out of the bonnet for a second, looking him up and down. 'I called you earlier. When I got here. You didn't answer.'

'I was ...' What did he say now? That he had ignored the call? That he had been busy? Would either of those wash? Why was he still worried about what his father thought? He had severed ties.

'You were not having a haircut, it seems,' Dinis stated. 'You need to fix that before you come back to the business.'

And there it was, already: the reminder that his father was still very much of the opinion he was going to come back to the business someday.

'Why are you here?' Theo asked for the second time. 'To help with selling the house?'

'I have a client I'm meeting here, and I came to see you.' Dinis came out from under the bonnet again to look at Theo once more. 'To stop this difficulty between us.'

'This difficulty?' Theo repeated.

'A lot was said on both sides,' Dinis continued, wiping his hands on an oily rag. 'Things we did not mean.'

'I meant the things I said,' Theo responded immediately.

Dinis sighed, a little as if Theo was still a small child needing to be seen and not heard. 'I know the accident hit us hard. Hit *you* hard and—'

'Stop!' Theo ordered. He wanted to press the flat of his hands to his ears to block out the words, but he knew that would only highlight his vulnerability, something his father would latch on to in a second.

'Theo, the accident was not your fault. No one, not even Christopher Columbus, could have foreseen that swell or done anything else about it. The investigation said so.'

The tremor in his leg was starting, he could feel it building up and he tried his best to stand firm, channel strength. This was one of the problems. His father had never blamed him. Not once. Theo had blamed himself. What his father had done was have no understanding as to why Theo needed to do something about it. And that's why he had had to leave.

'The girl lost an arm, Theo! She did not die!'

Theo put a hand over his mouth then, tears of hurt, anger and frustration bursting forth. He had no control now. In his mind, he could hear the furious water, the echoes of screaming and see the blood …

'Listen, I did not come here to go through it all again. I came here to say let's put the past behind us. Let's work together to move the business forward. I have a fantastic new contract coming up.'

'She lost an arm,' Theo repeated. 'You think that is something you can just move past?' Bile was in his throat now, making speech difficult.

'She is fine,' Dinis insisted. 'She is adjusting.'

'Adjusting? Dad! Don't you hear how you sound?' He headed back towards the garage door, needing the air, no matter how humid. There was nothing in the garage except everything he had tried to run away from.

'Theo, this tragedy did not happen to you,' Dinis said, following him. '*You* did not lose an arm.'

He shook his head, not wanting to hear anything else.

'Without your quick thinking with the tourniquet she might have lost her life.'

Where was he going to go? Into the house? Dinis would just follow him in. The Blue Vine? Offer to work the last part of his shift? Clear up for free? Or drink? Just be a customer, drown how he was feeling in beer?

'Spyridoula said you went on the boat.'

Theo stopped walking then, faced his father.

'I did not believe her.' Dinis shook his head. 'Theo, I am not stupid enough to think you can ever drive a boat again.'

'What?' His throat was dry.

'If you come back to the business I can find you another role. You can be Head of New Ideas or something. You can make the role your own.'

A deep anger threatened to reveal itself. Theo had always known that working for the family business might be perceived as just being because of birthright, not talent, but he also knew he was good at his job. And now his father was offering him a position that sounded meaningless and made-up.

'I drove the boat,' Theo said. 'Spyridoula was telling you the truth.'

'Your counsellor said he did not think that was possible.'

'My counsellor told you that?! So much for patient confidentiality!'

The fear and adrenalin he had experienced chasing Igor and his friends around the harbour was swelling around him again now. He had hated it. It had frightened him. But he had done it. He had done it.

'Well, I would be happier if you took a desk role. Like I said,' Dinis continued. 'The head of a department.'

'You want me *not* to sail again?' Confusion formed on his brow. 'But I thought the counsellor was all about making me well enough to sail again.'

'The counsellor was to make sure you did not kill yourself,' Dinis said bluntly.

'Dad,' Theo said, shocked.

'Don't look at me that way.'

'I don't want to have this conversation.'

'You never want to have this conversation.'

'Well,' Theo said. 'Here I am.' He held his arms out wide. 'No noose around my neck. On Corfu. Working, and about to captain a boat trip to Erikousa.'

'What?' Dinis queried.

Suddenly the chirruping of the cicadas became the only sound as Theo realised just what he had said. Had he already thought of it earlier? As soon as the raffle prize was announced? Or later, when he was kissing Abby on Logas Beach? There was no going back now. As much as he thought he did not want to return to his father's business, he also didn't want to be thought of as a failure, an oddity, the man from a boating family who was scared of the sea.

'I am taking the Pappas boat to Erikousa on a trip for one of the local businesses,' Theo continued. 'It seems that some people on this island still have a little faith in recovery.' Now he knew exactly where he was going to go.

'Theo!' Dinis called. 'Theo, come back!'

Fifty-six

Desperately Seeking

While Melody had gone to Kassiopi with Leon, Abby had listened to how her mum had been in love with George since she was a teenager. Jackie Malone had been holidaying in Corfu every year since she was ten and Abby had never known. Nanna and Grandad Malone had apparently adored the Greek island too and saved every spare penny they had to escape for a fortnight each summer. And one summer they had ended up in San Stefanos and a teenage Jackie had met George. Two weeks of falling in love under a cerulean sky and the pair vowed to meet up each year, no matter what resort the Malones picked to stay in. Except one year, five years after their tentative beginnings, George told her he was getting married. His parents had paired him with someone from a good Greek family. It would help their restaurant business, there was an opportunity to open a second taverna, perhaps a third.

'I tried to forget him,' Jackie spoke, tears running down her face, her make-up destroyed. 'I *did* forget him. I met your dad. Your lovely, lovely dad.'

'Mum,' Abby said, her voice choked with emotion too. 'You haven't done anything wrong.'

'Haven't I?'

'No,' Abby insisted. 'It's like that ... that bit in *Titanic*, you know, at the end, when Old Rose is telling everyone about

Jack, her first love. No one doubts that she loved the man she married and had children with, but love runs deep ...' Abby swallowed. 'So I've read.'

'When I decided to move here it wasn't *because* of George. I thought he was still married right up until your dad wanted to come back after his operation. But then there George was, the same dark-eyed handsome George I'd gone on picnics with, danced with on the sand.' She sniffed. 'And I felt so guilty because when I saw him, even with your lovely dad sat right there, getting over the horrendous ordeal of the hospital, I felt something. It was like a school of lobsters were doing jazz-claws over my heart.'

'Oh, Mum,' Abby said, squeezing her hand. 'You have to put an end to this.'

'I know,' Jackie breathed. 'I just have to tell him that too much time has passed. That we both need to leave memories as memories and—'

'No!' Abby exclaimed. 'That's the very last thing you should do! Mum, you have to stop feeling guilty and grab life, grab George.' She took a deep breath. 'He wants to take you on a picnic.'

'He does?' Jackie asked, wide-eyed like a love-struck prom attendee.

'He tried to ask my permission and my answer didn't come out right because I was stressing over the raffle, but Mum, you need to have a date. Make it a proper new start, no regrets kind of date.' Abby smiled. 'As he's one of the winners of the trip to Erikousa why don't you make sure he knows to bring a picnic blanket?'

'Oh, Abby, I don't know how Melody's going to feel. I've been so stupid. One minute George was painting our house, the next we were boycotting his restaurant. I've been up and down more in the past two years than Ant McPartlin.'

'Melody's Melody, Mum. Whatever she says what she's really going to mean is she's happy for you.' Abby smiled again. 'And *I'm* happy for you. George is lovely, and he makes the best food.'

'Oi,' Jackie exclaimed. 'I put on quite the spread the other morning.'

Abby laughed, but then her attention was directed to the terrace. She had sensed him, then smelt him – that heavenly combination of olive wood, citrus fruits and Adonis – before she caught sight of him. *Theo*.

'Mrs Dolan ... *kalispera*,' he greeted Jackie.

'It's Jackie, Theo, and *kalispera* to you too.' She smiled. I take it you want my daughter and not me.'

'I—' he began.

'Don't be stupid. Let me go inside and start shutting the office down. It's time we went home. After today, I'm absolutely exhausted.' Jackie headed into the office while Theo came closer to the table.

'What's wrong?' Abby asked. 'You look like you've seen a ghost or something.'

'Not a ghost,' Theo said, shifting uneasily. 'My father.'

'He's here?' Abby asked, getting to her feet.

Theo nodded. 'He was at the villa when I got back.'

'So, he's going to want some action on the house, isn't he?' Abby stated, whipping herself up into organisation mode. 'That's why he's here. I should tell Mum.'

'Abby, wait,' Theo said, reaching for her hand. 'I want to do something for you.' He swallowed. 'I want to ...' The breath seemed to be catching in his throat. 'Erikousa ... let me take everyone to Erikousa. On the Pappas boat.'

Abby looked at him, unsure of what response to give.

'You need to get five people to the island, you don't have the money ...'

'Actually, it's eight, with me, Mum and Melody.'

'It seats ten, Abby. We can get to the island faster. It will make more time for sightseeing, no?'

His expression was such a contradiction. There was excitement and enthusiasm but there was also something else, urgency, trepidation ...

'Theo, as much as I need a way out of this dilemma ...' Abby wasn't quite sure what to say.

'Let me help,' he begged. 'I really want to help.' He seemed to need her to agree. Why couldn't she? What should hold her back? Especially after her talk with her mum about wasted opportunities and missed connections? But what of their unfinished conversation about money and what she thought he was holding in ...

'Are you totally sure?' Abby asked. 'We must pay you something.., for your time and the fuel and—'

'I do not want anything,' Theo said, taking her in his arms. 'Just give me the chance to go somewhere beautiful with you.'

Abby lay her head on his chest and felt his hot, hard body against her. Corfu was providing her with no end of never-before-tasted stimuli but, a little like her mum back in the seventies, she wasn't quite sure what came next.

Fifty-seven

San Stefanos Harbour

'You do have the proper licences, don't you?' Diana asked, looking Theo up and down a few days later as he helped the Desperately Seeking raffle winners board the Pappas boat.

'I do,' Theo answered, taking her hand and assisting her.

'I mean for boat craft,' Diana continued. 'Not cocktail-making.'

It was the kind of July day made for postcards. No clouds were interfering with the clear blue sky, the sea was a flat calm, not a hint of white caps and it was deliciously hot. Abby couldn't wait to get to Erikousa, strip off her sundress and dive into the tempting ocean again. She had been reliving that first tip-toe into the water at Logas Beach for the past few days while things had gone crazy with the business, and there hadn't been any time for finding that holiday vibe she had only touched upon. After the party, people had made contact. She had done viewing after viewing on a three-bedroomed villa in Kalami – borrowing George's car to get there when Jackie's had appeared to stroke out – and there had been plenty of interest in the Pappas Villa. She had even met Dinis Pappas – in a purely official capacity, what other capacity was there really? He had been tinkering with a motorbike when she had brought a family round for a viewing and she had found him quite pleasant, businesslike, but not without being personable.

He had let the child of the family sit on the bike and pretend to ride it.

But the one thing she hadn't had enough time for was Theo. He had been working at The Blue Vine, making up for the shifts he missed to help her out, earning more time off for today, and she really *did* want to spend time with him, especially as she had a decision to make. An email had reminded her the lease on her flat was up soon. She either needed to sign for another six months or … not. The likelihood was she still wasn't quite brave enough to start living in Greece, so every extra moment she could get with Theo was going to be precious. This break was turning into the summer adventure she'd never had. It was hard work, but so rewarding, and all the moments spent with her mum, her sister and this captivating man more than made up for the feet- and brainache at the end of the day.

'I have all the licences needed for boat craft,' Theo reassured Diana, helping her down and on to the boat.

'Is everyone here?' Abby asked, looking from the dock to the occupants inside.

'I am here!' Spyridoula raised her hand.

'I am also here,' Mrs Karakis said. 'Still wishing that Roberto was here.' She sighed heavily.

'We have Theo,' Spyridoula reminded. 'If Erikousa isn't enough for us he can do some more Pappas dancing.'

'That will not be happening,' Theo said firmly but politely.

'Mum,' Abby said, turning to Jackie. 'Where's George?'

'He won't be long. He wanted to bring some extra water, it's going to be hot today.'

Her mum looked completely radiant today in a bright, custard-yellow dress that lightly curved over her figure and stopped at her knee. Her tanned legs were enhanced with gold wedges that elongated her frame. Jackie was getting ready to live again, not just as a mum and a business owner, but as a woman in the prime of her life, looking for romance with a man she had loved for a very long time. Abby couldn't have been happier for her.

'Did someone say water?' Melody remarked, appearing on the dock, each arm laden with a carrier bag. 'I've got ouzo, retsina and … Metaxa was on special offer.' She shook her mane of hair and smiled at everyone on the boat. Large sunglasses covered most of her face, but her body was barely covered in mini denim shorts and a red polka dot bikini top. Abby had one of Melody's more substantial bikinis under her sundress but she had no intention of stripping it off until her party were happily disembarked on the nearby island.

'Abby,' Theo called. 'How many do we wait for?'

He was stood on the helm of the boat looking particularly gorgeous in linen shorts, Havaianas on his feet, wearing another vest top – this time dark grey – that looked like it had been slashed up the sides in order to reveal his hot, tanned obliques.

'There's George,' Abby said. 'And someone called Mastik.'

'Oh no!' It was her mum's voice sounding panicked and Abby's attention went back to Jackie.

'What's the matter?' Abby asked. 'Have we forgotten something?' They were only going eight nautical miles, Erikousa was quiet but there was life there … and a hotel.

'What's Aleko doing here?' Jackie gritted her teeth together. 'Why is he carrying a parasol and why does he look like he's heading to our boat?'

Abby looked to the shore, the part where harbourside met dock, and there was Aleko, carrying a large straw basket in one hand, a bright pink parasol underneath his arm. As he manoeuvred along, the end of the protruding umbrella almost took the hat off a woman sat on the beach reading a book.

'He didn't wanging win!' Melody remarked. 'He didn't even come to the party. He spent the whole time trying to disrupt our party with his stupid fake, non-Greek Caribbean band.' She sniffed. 'Where's Mastik from the launderette in Acharavi?'

'You know Mastik?' Abby asked.

'Who do you think does our washing? Mum doesn't have a machine and you know she's never going to go old school and wash her pants in the sea.'

'*Kalimera*, everybody!' Aleko waved a hand and the parasol fell from his grip and landed on the dock.

'Have you come to see us off, Aleko? Wish our prize-winners well on their day trip to beautiful, tranquil, picturesque Erikousa?' Jackie asked him.

'No,' Aleko answered, all smiles. 'I have come to join you.'

'No way,' Melody stated immediately. 'This is a *private* excursion. For raffle prize-winners only.'

'I realise this,' Aleko said, still continuing to grin. 'It is unfortunate but Mastik could not make the trip today. One of his tumble driers, it does not tumble, or dry, so he offered me his place.'

'No,' Melody said at once. 'No, no, no, no, no!'

'Melody,' Jackie interrupted.

'What? He's coming to spy,' Melody said loudly, narrowly her eyes at Aleko.

Abby watched their mum take her by the arm, pulling her to one side as Aleko approached the vessel. Abby shifted closer as Jackie dropped her voice to those low tones she'd used when admonishing them 'privately' in public when they were children. She remembered one particular hissy fit Melody had had over Uncle Ben's Boil in the Bag in the middle of Tesco.

'What is he going to spy on, Melody?' Jackie asked.

'We're going to give out our new special August offers and drop some at the hotel on Erikousa.'

'Aleko is going to see those anyway when we take them all over town. Just like we saw all the promo about his spa days.'

'But—' Melody began.

'Mel, let's just show him how Desperately Seeking entertain their clients. We can talk endlessly about all the deals we've done this week, let him know that the Dolans are a force to be reckoned with,' Abby suggested brightly.

'We are, aren't we?' Melody said. 'Now we have you on our team, Abs, things are going to go next level for us.'

'Well … I don't know how much I've really had to do with it,' Abby said.

'It's *all* down to you,' Melody said. 'Before you came we were down to our last thousand euros and I was dribbling all over a greasy Russian.' She pulled a face. 'What was I thinking?'

'Well …'

'Melody, why don't you go and get on the boat and hand out those Erikousa information sheets and the picture quiz?' Jackie suggested.

'Did you add that picture of Clare Balding mixed with a horse?' Melody asked with a snigger.

'Just be nice to Aleko,' Jackie ordered, as Melody sashayed towards the helm.

Jackie let out a sigh then and looked at Abby. 'Don't listen to her, Abby.'

'What?'

'And don't listen to me either.'

'I—'

'I know what I said the other day, but as much as I would love to have you here in Corfu with us it isn't my decision to make. Nor is it Melody's.'

'Oh,' Abby said, realising the purpose of this conversation.

'And although George and I are having … *tentative beginnings* … it doesn't mean that every Greek romance is going to last beyond summer, not that I don't like Theo or can't see his attraction.'

Abby watched her mum's eyes go to Theo who was looking particularly resplendent against the backdrop of cobalt sky and shimmering sea, strands of hair from his loose man bun fluttering against his face.

'He's very lovely,' Jackie said softly.

'I have thought about staying.' Abby carried on quickly before her mum got her hopes up. 'But I haven't decided yet.'

Jackie did well to mask her crestfallen look and instantly Abby sensed all those conflicted feelings doing battle like they were warring factions in *Britannia*.

'But, Mum,' she said, her voice almost a whisper. 'If I do decide to stay it won't be for any man, no matter how lovely.'

'Mum!' Melody bawled. 'George is coming now. Get on the boat!'

'Shall I put up my parasol for you, Diana?' Aleko called. 'Look! Look how pink it is. Jackie, does it not perhaps remind you of something?'

'Er,' Melody jumped in. 'The colour of your embarrassed face when we win the Estate Agent of the Year award?'

'All aboard then everyone,' Jackie said, waving to George.

Fifty-eight

En route to Erikousa

Theo took a long, slow breath inwards, filling his chest cavity to the max. He had distracted himself making small talk with the guests as they readied themselves for the trip, trying his best to ignore the fact that every bit of him was wanting to scream to a stop. Not start the engine, drop the anchor, re-tie the rope to the dock and run away. No one could know this was a do-or-die moment for him, that every receptor in his body was shaking so strongly, quaking at him to give in. Although he suspected Spyridoula had her suspicions. Each time he turned a little from the sea to check the passengers, her eyes were on him. And, when this happened, he pretended his feet were glued to the deck so his leg didn't wince.

'Beautiful, isn't it?' It was his aunt, at the wheel next to him, her carefully pinned hair whipped out of its gripped security. 'Nothing like Athens.'

'Or Halkidiki,' Theo added.

'Corfu, it is special,' Spyridoula agreed. 'And your mother, she thought so too.'

Theo held onto the steel wheel a little tighter, his thoughts jarring, his mind drifting back to his childhood, so little of it containing memories of his mother. No one talked about her much unless they were drunk on ouzo and in the mood to reminisce. And that was where most of his knowledge came from – old photographs and other people's stories.

'She hated the villa though,' Spyridoula continued. 'She told Dinis it was like parading his ego up and down the street in front of everyone.'

'She hated it?'

'Too showy. Too big. That was not your mother at all.'

'No,' Theo agreed.

'She lived life for the experience, the joy, not all the things that money can buy.'

'What are you trying to tell me, Spyri?'

'That perhaps your father sells the villa because he wants to remember your mother, not because he wants to forget her.'

Theo gazed out onto the water, the island coming into sight as, behind him, the party of travellers broke into a raucous rendition of a song he did not recognise.

'I know you have been leaving early and working late into the morning to avoid talking to him,' Spyridoula said.

'It has been very busy at The Blue Vine.'

'You cannot avoid each other forever.'

'It will not be forever,' Theo said. 'Soon he will have to return to the mainland and the villa will be sold. I do not know which will come first but the result is the same.'

'And is that the right way forward? To have unrest in the family? Is that what you think your mother would have wanted?'

'Of course not.'

'Then talk to him.'

'And have him tell me he has a fake job waiting for me?'

'Theo … he is just worried about you.'

Spyridoula held onto the stanchion by the wheel as the boat steamed along. 'He called me this morning, said he was worried about you taking the boat out today.'

He shook his head and focused. He had been worried too, petrified, in fact. A row of sleepless nights invaded by nightmares of that day on the sea and the capsizing. His nose flooded with salt water, his lungs and eyes burning, breath taken from him, feeling panicked and desperate ... But he couldn't give in. He couldn't let the fear win and he could not, *would* not lose a point of principle to his father. And, Abby needed him to captain this trip and look after everyone on board and that was what he intended to do. For her and for his own sanity and to prove to everyone he was still capable.

'Are you worried about me, Spyri?' Theo asked, looking at her.

'About you driving the boat?' She shook her head. 'No.' Then she took a breath. 'But about the future, about you and my brother ... yes.'

Theo took a moment, checking the boat's course, watching for traffic, then he said, 'Stamatis told me to ask you about bougatsa.'

He watched the colour drain from his aunt's cheeks as if she had suddenly developed sea sickness. Immediately he knew it was the wrong moment. He had thrown it out spitefully, in retaliation, even though he had no idea what it was all about.

'Excuse me, Captain, but I think I will rejoin the party now.' Spyridoula turned slowly, making her way to the back of the boat.

'Spyri, listen, I ...' he began. It was too late. His aunt was already repositioning herself next to Mrs Karakis.

Fifty-nine

Erikousa Island

Melody had screamed hysterically every time Theo had picked up a little speed and then she had laughed, full-bodied, with all her soul. A lot less vocally, Abby had felt that same impassioned surge of excitement. The salt spray from the ocean licked her face, and the hot sun and scent of aniseed aperitif became a glorious summer mix that invigorated every sense.

They had docked in Porto, the main settlement of the island, tying up to the concrete pontoon already rich with boats, some like the Pappas boat, others larger and looking like they could contain scores of day trippers. All the passengers had disembarked safely and had been told they would be leaving no later than 4pm to ensure they were back on Corfu before the afternoon wind picked up.

And now Abby was standing on golden sand, pressing her feet into the warm grains, letting the feel of it soak through her. Could there be any better feeling? Being here on a beautiful paradise island, the sun on her skin, the sea so inviting, all worries suspended. She closed her eyes, relishing the way the sunshine uplifted her spirits. Could she stay in Greece? What would she do here? Fall into the business with her mum and Melody or strike out on her own? Do something else …

Next, before she even realised, the warm feeling had suddenly got more intense, a strong pair of arms were around her waist and she felt that lithe, athletic frame at her back. *Theo*.

Hot lips grazed her neck and she shivered, wriggling to turn to face him, putting her hand to his face and halting his advance.

'We can't do this here,' Abby whispered. 'I'm one of the faces of Desperately Seeking. I have to maintain a certain degree of professionalism.'

'Hmm,' Theo said, brown eyes darkening almost wickedly. 'How about we make degrees of our own ... right angles together on the sand.'

'Theo ...'

'I know you want to,' he breathed, catching her lips with his.

'*I* know I want to,' she replied. 'But we can't. Not here. Not yet.' She swallowed, the thought of breaking out of her comfort zone as well as her clothes was thrilling her. Then she smiled. 'What was it you said when we were dancing? About not wanting to share our moment with your aunt and ... Stathis.'

He brushed a stand of her hair back from her face. 'Stathis is not here.'

'But Spyridoula is.' Abby pointed to where Theo's aunt and Mrs Karakis were kicking off their shoes and skipping across the sand like they were children. Behind them were her mum and George, carrying a picnic basket and blanket between them.

'That is one of the troubles of Greek families,' Theo responded with a sigh. 'They are always everywhere.'

'And I can't leave my sister,' Abby told him. 'Everyone is paired up except Melody. I even thought Aleko and Diana were going to start holding hands on the trip over here.'

Theo kissed her again. 'I do not think you have to worry too much about Melody.'

'No?'

'She was introducing herself to the waiter at the restaurant.' He spun Abby around, directing her gaze to where her sister was peeling off her denim shorts and being admired by one local in particular. Her lovely, uninhibited sister, using summer just the way it should be used.

Abby looked back at Theo, drinking him in in all his deliciousness, before removing her sun dress, perhaps a shade provocatively, until her size twelve curves were revealed, clad only in a bikini.

'Wow,' Theo uttered, his voice rapt.

'You are wearing far too much,' Abby said, her hands going to the flimsy vest, fingers skidding through the side splits until they met skin.

'I was thinking this same thing.'

He wasted no time in removing his vest, revealing that honed abdomen she admired so much. Then he unfastened his shorts, dropping them to the sand to reveal Daniel Craig-style trunks. She swallowed, her mouth suddenly dry, then reached for his hand. 'Let's get wet.'

The sea was the kind of turquoise transparent you never really believe exists until you see it for yourself. And now Abby was chest-deep, indulging in its coolness, swimming, splashing, feeling so light and free. It was an almost indescribable sensation, and opened her eyes about what was important in life and what wasn't.

'I'm here! I'm present!' she shrieked at the top of her voice.

'You are crazy!' Theo called, swimming around her, splashing her.

'I'm not,' Abby insisted. 'I'm serious.'

'Very seriously English,' Theo teased. 'Would you like a cup of tea?'

'How rude!' She sniffed. 'You know I'm a sucker for a cocktail.'

'I think this is why you like me,' Theo teased. 'Only for the way I make your cocktails.'

'It's true,' Abby answered. 'When you told me you weren't a professional mixologist I felt nothing but deep disappointment.'

'Hey,' Theo said, splashing her again. 'Do not think I am not professional at this. My uncle has a bar. I have been learning to make cocktails since I was very small.'

'A man of many talents,' she answered.

'And some of them you have not yet discovered,' he said, his voice pure seduction.

She clasped her arms around his neck, nestling close as the water swilled around them. 'I am in the moment,' she told him. 'Deeply, absolutely, in this moment with you.' She looked up at him, seeing him and only him, quietly, softly, with a different outlook. Just because forever wasn't on offer it didn't mean this time couldn't count. She wanted it to count.

'I am in this moment too, Abby,' he whispered.

She kissed him then, their mouths wrapping together, their bodies gently rocking with the movement of the water. With the warming sun on her shoulders, and this gorgeous, engaging man suddenly part of her summer, Abby realised exactly what she had been missing. Independence. Spontaneity. A combination of loss and fear and lists had made her rigid and unvarying. Well, no more. She was the mistress of her own destiny and nothing needed to be anally predetermined like it had been.

She pulled away from him, touching her finger to the lush pad of his beautiful bottom lip, her thumb grazing the slight roughness of his jawline, the sea lapping her back and shoulders. Then she pointed, to the shoreline, but higher, to the flat-topped hill that towered over the sand. 'I want to climb that hill.'

Theo spun around, holding her in his arms, to look where she had pointed, the water splashing them both. 'To climb we must have equipment. It is very steep and dangerous.'

Disappointment shrouded her new-found bravado and she knew it was written all over her face.

'Hey, do not look so sad, my opposite,' Theo said, tickling her neck and making her squeal. 'We cannot climb today but we can hike.' He pressed his lips to hers again. '*Ela.*'

Sixty

Katergo Hill, Erikousa Island

Theo sunk his teeth into the rich, ripe fig he had plucked from the tree. It was so good, fresh like this, the flesh sweet and yet heavy with its special syrupy liqueur.

A groan of pleasure came from Abby, just a few metres behind him and it served to prick his desire.

'Oh, Theo,' she continued. 'This is so good!'

He swallowed, his mind delivering all manner of visuals involving her bikini. He took a moment, before turning to look at her as he continued to walk the dusty trail upwards. Her lips were wet with fruit, fingers sticky with fig juice.

'It's like the sweetest honey,' Abby said. 'It's wonderful.'

'Better than figs in England?' he queried.

'We don't really eat many figs in England,' she replied. 'And when we do, we tend to put them in puddings and ruin them.'

'Look,' Theo said, pointing ahead of them. 'Look at the dragonfly!'

He held still as Abby came slowly, quietly alongside him, keenly seeking what he could see.

'You see?' Theo whispered. It was a particularly good specimen. A slender, bright teal body with wings of the same colour, a shining, swirling pattern on them, the tone of an abalone shell.

'It's beautiful,' Abby declared.

It was beautiful, as was this whole day. He couldn't remember the last time he had absorbed the natural wonder around him. Even in his days of island-hopping he hadn't really stopped and looked, he had just stopped and drank beer, stopped and switched off, disconnected. Here with Abby it felt like he was learning to fully re-engage again.

The dragonfly took to the skies and Theo reached for Abby's hand. 'Come, we are nearly at the top where there is no vegetation.'

'No vegetation?'

'But there is a great view,' Theo reassured.

'This island is full of views,' Abby answered with a contented sigh.

A few more metres brought them to the summit and Abby let out a laugh, her feet finding not earth or greenery but tarmac. 'What is this?' she asked. 'Don't tell me this is a car park.'

Theo smiled, shaking his head. 'No.'

'It seems odd,' Abby said. 'To have all this beauty then to have concrete up here.'

'There is a good reason for it,' Theo responded, as they walked to the centre of the space.

'Did someone build something pink?' Abby asked, a wry expression on her face.

'It is a letter,' Theo said. He scuffed his sandal on the ground. 'See?'

Abby looked, then took a few steps back and surveyed the area in its entirety.

'It's an "H",' she said.

'*Ne*,' Theo answered. 'A helipad.'

'Wow,' Abby replied. 'So, this is where Bruce Willis and Jude Law land their helicopters when they want to escape stalkers like my sister in Corfu.'

'No.' He smiled. 'It is a little more serious than that.'

'Oh?'

'It is for the fire department,' Theo explained. 'There are very many fires on Corfu in the summer when it is so dry. It only takes one moment of carelessness with a cigarette or a bottle thrown into the grass that the sun catches and it can cause devastation.' He sighed. 'One summer there was a fire on the headland at San Stefanos. All the villagers, they work together with buckets of water to try to stop the spread until the helicopters arrive.' Walking over to the edge, he pointed to the wide, wavy blue of the sea below them. 'We have all the water we need to put out the fire but the helicopters must have somewhere to rest and refuel.'

'And this is the place,' Abby breathed.

'This is the place.' He turned his head to look at her. 'Not as romantic as you thought, maybe?'

'I don't know,' Abby replied, matching his gaze. 'You can see for miles up here.' She took a breath. 'And there's no one else around.' She moved herself a little closer to him, desire igniting. 'And I'm pretty sure I don't know anyone else who's ever had sex on a helipad before.'

'Abby,' he breathed, his fingers gently touching her face. 'You talking that way ...'

'What way?' she half-whispered.

'Of sex,' Theo answered.

Him saying the word only made her G-spot quiver all the more. She wanted his lips on hers again, then she needed to rip off her sundress, drop them both onto Black Hawk Down and ... rotate.

Suddenly an alarm sounded and all thoughts of propellers were whirled away.

'*Signomi*,' Theo said, reaching into the pocket of his shorts.

'What is it?' Abby asked, heart still thumping, her lady bits cursing the mobile phone interruption.

'I set an alert,' Theo pressed the screen of his phone and tried to shield it from the sun.

'Lunchtime?' Abby asked with a sigh of frustration.

'No,' he said, screwing up his eyes as if to focus. 'It is a weather app. For boats. For sea conditions.'

There was no way he was going to take any chances. Despite what his father and, apparently, his counsellor thought, he knew his craft and he hadn't been about to voyage off in charge of a group of people without proper care and due diligence.

'It sounded like someone was announcing *The Ten o'Clock News*,' Abby said.

This did not look good. There were several warnings in place from the Hellenic Meteorological Service. A storm was on its way, in a little over an hour. This was the last thing he needed.

'What's wrong?' Abby asked.

'*Tipota*,' he answered quickly.

'Your expression says more than nothing.'

He didn't know why he had said 'nothing'. Keeping up appearances? That was what his father did. And lying about the severity of matters only made things better for a very short period of time. Then, either the truth revealed itself or you had no choice but to say what you should have said at the very beginning.

'There is a storm on its way,' Theo stated. 'High winds.'

'A thunderstorm?' Abby asked.

'*Ne.*' But it wasn't just a thunderstorm. Thunderstorms were common on Corfu, usually brewing up in the afternoon after a particularly hot day, but this, this was predicted to be a wind he had never encountered before. He needed to make a decision. They should either cut short their day trip and leave Erikousa now or ... or what? Face battling the storm later? It was insane to even think of risking it. Even the most experienced of sailors wouldn't be stupid enough to attempt it. But this was Abby's big prize, a special day, a culmination of so much work since she had landed on this Greek island ...

'Theo,' she said. 'Please, tell me what's wrong.' She looked worried as well as beautiful right now. He reached out, touching the edges of her hair.

'We need to make a decision,' he told her. 'A bad storm is coming, a very bad storm.' He took a breath, looking at her as he delivered the news. 'We need to leave Erikousa in the next thirty minutes or we will be, how you say, stranded.'

'Stranded!' She clapped her hands to her face, eyes wide. 'What do you mean stranded?'

Theo took her hands down from her cheeks and squeezed them in his. 'Come, we must tell the others.'

Sixty-one

Porto, Erikousa Island

Abby's chest was tightening as the beachfront came into view. The descent from Katergo had been done at pace, with no time to pick any more figs or take in the scent of the floral beauty that lined the undulating tracks that made up this island. This was a tour organiser's worst nightmare. Her lucky winners were not going to be happy whatever course of action was taken. Their day would be cut short, the event ruined, Aleko gleeful he had seen it all ... but safety had to be paramount.

The first recognisable shape that came into view was Melody's bouncing hair as she jiggled herself out of her short shorts, one bare foot on a sunbed.

'I will go and prepare the boat,' Theo said to Abby.

'Yes,' she answered. 'And I will deliver the bad news.' She took a deep breath and approached her sister.

'Melody,' she began. 'We have to get back to Corfu.'

'Abs, honestly, relax. You've hardly had a day of holiday since you've been here and now you're panicking about getting everyone back on time.'

'Not back on time,' Abby stated. 'Back now, alive.'

'What?'

'Theo says there's a big storm coming. High winds and rough seas. We need to leave now or we might not be able to leave at all today.'

'Is this a joke?' Melody put her hand over her eyes to shield them from the sun. 'The only thing I can see is a very blue sky and my afternoon with Milo over there, stretching out gloriously in front of me.' She sent a non-coy wave over to the waiter.

'I'm not joking,' Abby said. 'I'm deadly serious. Theo has a boating app and he's looked at all these charts online and it's not looking good for later.' She had to make Melody understand. 'We need to leave now. Help me get everyone together.'

'You're serious, aren't you?'

'Yes! Come on!'

'We can't,' Melody's eyes turning horrified. 'Mum and George went off to the other side of the island on a tour.'

'Well, we have to get them back.'

'And how do you propose we do that? It's a hike away with no car and I've only got flip-flops on!'

Theo re-checked the weather warnings on his phone. The front was moving quickly. If they didn't get going soon they would be chancing meeting the predicted high winds and dangerous tides.

'What is going on?' Spyridoula called out from the dock. 'You are taking the boat around the harbour?'

'No,' Theo answered. 'We have to leave very soon. Abby is getting everyone together now.'

'There is bad weather?'

'Yes.'

'How quickly does it come?' His aunt's sense of urgency started to prick his already heightened concern.

'Soon,' he replied. 'We need to leave within the next thirty minutes, to be safe.'

'You are OK with this? Spyridoula asked.

'Of course.'

'Then why do you check the life jackets three times already?'

'We haven't been here very long at all. I've not even had *petit fours*,' Diana complained when Abby had explained the situation to her and Aleko at the restaurant.

'We have time for coffee, Diana, I am sure.' Aleko raised his hand in the air. '*Dhio kafedes, parakalo*.'

'No,' Abby said. 'We don't have time for coffee. We don't have time for anything! I'm serious! The weather might look beautiful now but—'

'I can smell a storm,' Aleko informed. 'All I can smell right now is good Greek coffee.' He stuck his hand in the air again. '*Signomi*.'

'Are you listening to me?!' Abby practically barked. 'We need to leave and we need to leave now!' As the words hit the air the bright sunlight suddenly diminished and Abby looked out over the sea that had been so still and calm just a few moments ago. The colour of the water had changed. No longer a deep, rich blue but a bright, dazzling, somehow foreboding turquoise. The hairs on the back of her neck stood to attention as the sky darkened.

'Get your things, pay for your meal and get down to the boat straightaway.' Abby's phone began to ring and she pulled it out of her bag. *Melody*.

'Melody?' she answered.

'Mum's not picking up and neither is the guy from the hotel who took them off.'

She closed her eyes, willing her body not to panic. But they couldn't go anywhere without Jackie and George.

'Just keep trying them both,' Abby said. 'And let me know as soon as they're on their way back.'

Sixty-two

'Where are they?' Theo looked at his watch again, only a mere minute since his last time check.

'The sky is becoming black,' Spyridoula commented. 'Maybe we should just wait out the storm.'

'But if we do that,' Theo began. 'It will mean everybody has to stay at the hotel. And everyone will expect Abby and her family to pay and they do not have the money.'

'And they will not have the money to pay if you take this boat out in bad conditions and someone gets hurt, or worse.'

Theo swallowed. He needed no further explanation. He pulled at the rope tethering them to the dock. He didn't know why, he just needed to feel the firm connection.

'Theo, you need to know that your father paid the family money. The family of the girl who was hurt. Just like you wanted him to.'

Theo's whole body swayed and it had nothing to do with the rhythm of the ocean.

'No,' he said, shaking his head. 'I do not believe you. He said to pay money was to accept liability. That was everything we fought about. He said it would ruin his business. He said it would send a message that we were weak, as a company. As Greeks.'

'Yes,' Spyridoula said, scuffing her feet on the concrete landing platform. 'There is so much Pappas bullishness and, not just with the men.' She sighed. 'Too much pride. Too much concern about what people think. So much wasted time.' She shook her head, tongue clicking in annoyance. 'He went to see her too, the girl with only one arm.'

'Limoni,' Theo said. 'Her name is Limoni.'

'Your father made sure she is having the very best rehabilitation. Not to avoid a lawsuit like you might think but because underneath that hard, proud, uncompromising outside is a good, genuine person.'

'Why did he not tell me, Spyri?' Theo asked. 'Why did he simply not say "Theo, you were right, helping Limoni was what we should do"?'

'Because you know why. Because he is stupid and stubborn, just like you.' Spyridoula swallowed before continuing. 'Just like me.'

Theo's eyes went from his aunt to the darkening sky that was signalling that nothing good was coming their way.

'You ask me about the bougatsa,' Spyridoula said softly. She held her hands together, her fingers trembling a little. 'When I was much younger, bougatsa was something I made all the time for the man I loved.' She paused, seeming to fight with her emotions. 'And I made gigantes plaki and froutalia and kokkinisto ... so much cooking and eating and being in love ...'

'I do not understand,' Theo said, now studying his aunt intently.

Spyridoula sighed again, heavier this time. 'That wizened old man in his house of sticks in the woods.' She raised her eyes to the heavens. 'He has always had my heart and I let my parents keep me from him.' Her lips curled a little. '"You are a Pappas, Spyridoula, you will go to college and you will learn your fashion and you will open a design house, be successful, be powerful."' She tutted. 'I should have stood up to them, stood up for what *I* wanted – the love of a man who does beautiful things with wood.'

'Stamatis,' Theo breathed. 'You are the one who advised him on the garden area. You are cooking for him again.'

'We are both proud, stupid, egotistical people, but we are also too old to waste any more time or care too much about what the village thinks. I do not want to be the princess to his frog. I want to be frogs together, old, warty toads hopping about in the sun and eating until our stomachs weep.'

'All those years not being happy.' Theo shook his head.

'Because that is how things were with us, but that does not have to be how they continue. Do you hear me, Theo?'

'I hear you,' he answered.

'Then believe me when I say I have not been spying on you. I have not been doing your father's bidding. I hoped to give you a little time, some space, a chance for a different viewpoint. I do not want you to become like your father or like me, Theo. Life is a song. You must sing it.'

Spyridoula's words touched him hard and he had to quickly swallow, then take an edifying breath.

'So, you need to make sure you take Daughter-of-Jackie, Abby to the *panegyri* and maybe also take along your old auntie and her man from the trees.' Spyridoula sniffed. 'There will be those who whisper about us.' She smiled. 'By the time the festival is over I will be three times pregnant with kittens and joining the gypsies, you know how village gossip is.' She shrugged. 'But it is time for change, no?'

'Yes,' Theo replied. 'I agree.'

'So, now you know about the bougatsa ... about everything.'

'And we need to get out of here,' Theo stated. He jumped off the boat, landing next to Spyridoula. 'Let's go and get everybody. Right now, and then—'

His last words were drowned out by a big bang of thunder, and then the sky opened up and fat, hard raindrops began pelting the earth.

Sixty-three

Hotel Erikousa

'This is nice, Diana. Isn't this nice?' Spyridoula commented a little later as the party sat inside the hotel restaurant watching the storm outside. Abby had had no choice but to try to get rooms for everyone at the hotel the moment Theo declared it unsafe to sail. But it was July and the hotel was the only one on the island. Diana had been given the best room they had available, Aleko was in a single with George on a sofa bed, Spyridoula and Mrs Karakis had a comfortable double and Jackie, Melody and Abby were sharing a king-size bedroom. Theo had opted for the only remaining option, the wooden shell of a shack on the beach that was being renovated.

'It's an adventure,' Jackie said. 'Let's think of it that way. We like an adventure at Desperately Seeking, don't we?' She wafted her arms around in a bid to get someone to agree. 'New horizons, new lives in the sun ...'

'New newsletter coming soon,' Melody chipped in, winking at Milo.

'Can I get anyone a hot chocolate?' Abby asked, the rain still hammering on the roof, the atmosphere humid and oppressive, the sky seeming to blacken further every few minutes.

'I think this whole disaster calls for something a little stronger than zesti sokolata,' Diana said, folding her arms across her chest.

'Red wine?' Aleko suggested. 'Or perhaps a little Metaxa? I notice they have a twelve star on the drinks menu.'

Abby swallowed. She had no idea how they were going to afford to pay for the rooms, let alone enough food and drink to keep everyone happy. She wished, not for the first time, that she had opted for something simple and sparkling from the supermarket as the raffle prize. But, it was meant to be a treat for her mum and Jackie looked radiant despite the weather/travel/staying over chaos. She and George had finally arrived harbourside, albeit too late, glowing with a hue only two people falling in love could radiate.

'I will buy some drinks,' Spyridoula said, getting to her feet. 'What would everybody like?'

'Oh, that's very nice of you, Spyridoula, but—' Abby began.

'How about a little Muscadet?' Diana suggested.

'House white?' Spyridoula overrode. 'I hear it is very good here.' She made off towards the bar and Abby looked over to Theo. He was sat at a table on his own, a beer bottle in one hand, eyes on the raging ocean outside the window. She crossed the room to join him.

Slipping into the seat opposite him she put her glass of lemonade down on the table. 'We did the right thing staying,' Abby said. '*You* made the right decision.'

He didn't turn his head from the sea scene. 'I did not do anything. We ran out of time that is all.'

'I know, but perhaps my mum and George going off and not getting back soon enough was meant to be. It stopped us having a choice.' Abby shivered a little. 'I wouldn't want to be caught up in those waves.'

'The sea is powerful,' Theo agreed. 'It must be respected at all times.'

'Will the boat be OK?' Abby asked, looking through the driving rain to the dock where everything tethered was being tossed around by the force of the storm.

'I do not know,' Theo answered. 'I have to hope. But there is nothing we can do about it. Nowhere else for it to go.'

'Are you OK, Theo?' Abby queried.

'I do not like storms,' he admitted. 'They are unpredictable and violent and—'

'You're sleeping on the beach tonight,' Abby said.

He shrugged. 'It does not matter to me where I sleep. It matters only that your prize-winners are looked after. I feel I have let you down.'

'That's silly,' Abby insisted. 'You haven't let me down at all. If it wasn't for you bringing us here we would have been bankrupted paying for everyone to come by a tour.'

'But now they are expecting food and drinks and there is a night at a hotel,' Theo reminded.

'I know,' Abby said. 'But that's Dolan Law. We never seem to get things easy and straightforward.'

Suddenly Theo's phone erupted into life and Leon's photo flashed up on screen. He picked it up, answering.

'*Ne ... yassou, Leon ... ochi.*'

Abby watched Theo's expression turn from being a little disheartened about the storm situation to something like absolute fear. He ended the call, jumping up from his seat and slipping his phone into the pocket of his shorts.

'I have to go.'

'Go?' Abby exclaimed. 'Go where?!'

'I have to take the boat out.'

'Theo, what are you talking about?! Take the boat out where?!' Abby jumped out of her seat as Theo began to make a move towards the door to outside. 'Theo, stop! This is mad – what's happened?!'

'My father, he heard about the storm. He thought we were going to try and sail back. He left Corfu two hours ago and he isn't here yet. He's out there, somewhere, in this weather, looking for us.'

'Oh my God!' Abby exclaimed, hands going to her mouth.

'I have to go and find him,' Theo said, one hand on the door knob.

'Wait! Please!' Abby said, frantic. 'Wouldn't it be better to call the coastguard or something? They're professionals. They would send a helicopter. They would know what to do and— Theo, if you go out there you're going to be risking your life too!'

'It is my father,' he said firmly.

Theo's chest was burning and fizzing with panic. His dad had forced a boat company to give him the keys to a boat and had headed out into the storm to rescue him. Except he hadn't needed rescuing. He had done the sensible thing, the right thing, listened to his gut, looked at the warnings and known, once time had run out, that staying put was all they could do. Now Dinis was probably fighting the vicious waves, or had already succumbed to the sea, been capsized … or worse.

'Theo, please! Please don't do this!' Abby said, taking hold of his arm.

'Abby, I have to.' He pushed at the door with his free hand, battling to open it against the force of the wind.

'But you're in shorts, you've no coat …'

He stopped his retreat for a brief moment and looked at her wide, frightened eyes. She cared for him. He could see that so clearly. And he cared for her too, more than he had cared for any woman.

'Abby,' he whispered. 'You lost your father. I lost my mother. You know I have to try.'

She looked like she might burst into tears and he felt his own torn emotions twisting and turning as they battled to take control.

'What is going on?' Spyridoula appeared next to them, a large jug of wine in her hand.

'Nothing,' Theo said calmly, trying to rid his expression of the concern that was zipping through his body. 'I am going to check on the boat that is all.'

'Check on the boat?' Spyridoula looked at him with a large degree of suspicion. 'I can see the boat from here. It is going up and down like it is a ride at a carnival. What is there to check?'

'I just ...' Theo started. 'Thought I should make sure it is tied up tightly enough.'

He saw Abby look away from Spyridoula, unable to join in with his lies. He hated himself. He should tell his aunt, but he knew she would, quite possibly, barricade the door to the outside if she knew what he was planning to do.

'You check,' Spyridoula said. 'And then you come back and help make a quiz.' She sniffed. 'Everyone wants another quiz.'

He nodded stiffly and waited for her back to be turned before he pushed at the door again. Abby grabbed hold of his arm and held on tight. Looking back at her, all he saw written on her face was not desperation now but sheer determination.

'If you're going to do this,' Abby said. 'I'm coming with you.'

Sixty-four

Theo had burst out of the door without reply and Abby immediately followed. The full force of the storm hit her the moment her feet touched the terrace, the flowering vines entwined over the pergola that shielded the outside seating were being ripped and whipped, just like Abby's hair. The wind was warm but wild and her dress felt like it was being torn from her. This was like a hurricane. A big, scary, damaging hurricane.

'Theo!' she screamed into the wind. 'Wait for me!' She rushed down onto the sand.

'Go back!' Theo yelled as she caught up to him and he strode onwards towards the dock.

'No! I'm not letting you do this on your own,' Abby said. 'If I really can't stop you then I need to help you.'

'You are crazy!' Theo yelled, finally looking at her. 'The weather is—'

'Life-threatening?' Abby shouted back. 'I can see that! But you won't stop so—'

'I won't let you on the boat,' Theo told her.

'You're not going to be able to stop me!'

Adrenalin was flooding her. She didn't want him to go. *She* didn't want to go but it seemed neither of them were about to give in.

'Abby, please, go back into the bar!' Theo's hair had all but escaped from its bun, dark jaw-length swathes blowing up around his face. He swept it back, staring at her but Abby stood her ground.

'No,' she said with every amount of determination she owned. 'I'm not going to stand here and watch you risk your life.'

'Instead you are going to risk yours too?'

The sky roared with thunder and Abby tried not to flinch, swallowing the urge to scream with terror. Out to sea, the waves were like large, gnarly monsters, ready to swallow up anything that dared cross their path. As the wind billowed around her, almost blowing her off her feet, Theo raced onto the pontoon, heading for the Pappas boat.

'Theo! Don't you dare!' Abby screamed. 'Theo!'

She started running, desperately, frantically, fighting the ferocious wind to get to the boat before he could start the engine. She watched him jump on board then begin to untether the rope.

'Theo!' she yelled. She had to move faster. She had to get there. Then the engine roared into life ...

There was absolutely no way she was going to let him go without her now. At least, with two of them, they had a better chance of being able to deal with whatever crisis came their way, and being in the midst of this weather, that was a given.

She reached the boat and, uncaring for the widening gap between bow and dock, launched herself off the solidity of the pontoon, praying her sandals planted on the craft. Foot slipping on the wet surface she fell, first down onto the seats then further to the floor, the boat listing with the current. It hurt. Her chin, her ribs, her shins ... but she was on board.

'Abby, what are you doing?' Theo demanded.

She could only see his feet from her near prostrate position. She took a breath and then he was gathering her up, lifting her off the floor, holding her in his arms. It felt so good but also so wasteful. There wasn't a lot of time. Anything could be happening to his father at sea.

'Please, Abby, please get off the boat,' he begged.

She shook her head, holding on to him so tight as he set her back onto her feet. 'I'm not getting off. I'm going with you. But please, Theo, please let's call the coastguard, get them looking too … in case we can't find him.'

He nodded, bracing himself against the boat as he got his mobile phone out of his pocket to make the call. As he spoke against the sound of the raging wind, Abby surveyed the ocean ahead of them. This was a suicide mission, wasn't it? What was she doing? Risking everything for someone she hadn't known very long? But it felt like the right thing to do, the only thing to do. And then, something appeared, right at the edge of her line of vision, just coming into sight.

'Theo!' she called, trying to stand still on the reeling boat. 'Theo! There's a boat!'

Turning his head to the open water Theo spoke quickly into the phone before ending the call. He could just see the vessel. It wasn't faring well with the waves, being so small and a lot less powerful than the Pappas boat, and it looked like it could be engulfed at any moment. It had to be his father, but he couldn't see anyone on board.

'Can we make it over there?' Abby called, swaying as the boat was rocked even more violently by the swell.

Theo got behind the wheel. It was just five hundred metres away, maybe a little less. They could get to the boat, tie it to them and get it into shore.

'Sit down, Abby,' Theo urged. 'And hold on.'

He needed every skill he possessed to do this but at least the vessel was in sight. They weren't going to be scouring the ocean with no idea where to find it, if it was Dinis. But then who else would be crazy enough to be out on the water and heading to Erikousa?

He had to get this right. Slow and steady, working with the water as much as he could. Going too fast, not showing the sea enough reverence, meant he would be putting himself and Abby in more danger. He throttled up a little, heading across the ocean rather than straight ahead, each metre seeming like a struggle as the water sprayed the boat, soaking everything, including him.

'Abby, are you OK?' he shouted back.

'Yes!' she called.

It was so tempting to go faster, to reach the boat quicker, but if they capsized there was no chance of saving Dinis and maybe not even themselves.

And then the rain started again. It felt like hailstones. Fat, hard rivulets began to hammer down from the sky pinching his skin. It was making the visibility even worse. He edged the power on a little more ...

The small boat was being tossed around like it was made of paper and he hoped that Dinis was somehow still on board, perhaps hunkered down on the floor, holding on, hoping to wait out the storm. What other choice was there?

They were creeping nearer, the boat finding it difficult to navigate the almost mountainous waves, but managing, somehow, under his guidance.

'Can you see Dinis?' Abby called. 'Can you see your father?'

He swallowed, eyes tracking the vessel for any sign of someone on board. There was no one at the helm, it was no longer being driven, it was just drifting, rolling up and down under the sea's power. And then ... was that something? Was there someone? An outline? A figure, sat low? Or was it just debris? Lifejackets? Things that somehow hadn't been blown out of the ship already.

There was movement, a hand, appearing on the side of the boat. An arm and then, a body, a head ...

'I see him!' Theo called to Abby. 'He is on the boat!'

'Hurry!'

Theo's hand went to push the throttle on to engage the power of the engine, but it still was not the way to handle it. He had to be so careful. This was a matter of life or death.

'Theo, the storm ... it's getting worse,' Abby shouted above the howling of the gale.

The rain was pelting down so hard the drops were hurting Abby's face. Her dress was soaked through and every exposed inch of skin was burning from the dual assault of furious ocean spray and driving deluge. Her fingers were numb from holding onto the rail at the side of the boat. They were being banged and thumped with each forward motion, the sea seeming to spit them along before throwing them down on its surface like a heavy aeroplane landing.

But what happened next chilled Abby to the bone. One enormous wave hit the little boat ahead of them and it turned over like it was a child's bathtub toy. For a second she couldn't believe it had happened when they were so close, but then, very quickly she knew exactly what she had to do. Letting go of the rail, she grabbed at the cupboard that held the life jackets, ripped two from the store and put one over her head. Then she called to Theo.

'I'll bring him to the boat.' She didn't wait to listen to any reply, because she knew what it would be. *Don't go! Come back! Let me!* But they needed the Pappas boat in one piece. She couldn't captain, but she *could* swim. Taking a deep breath, Abby jumped into the tumultuous water.

Sixty-five

Theo felt like his heart had stopped beating. He had just seen his father's boat be tossed up in the air like it was a feather and now, Abby had jumped off into the water – and he couldn't see her. Anywhere. He didn't know what to do. Did he stay with the boat in the hope that she surfaced, that they *both* somehow surfaced? Or did he jump too? Try and find them? He was torn between acting with all his experience and thinking logically, or thinking with his heart.

'Abby!' he screamed into the dark turbulent air. 'Abby!'

Seconds felt like hours and his eyes were burning from the salt spray and the violent rain. Looking into the black ocean was like searching for two needles in a haystack. It was impossible and he felt sick. That this was happening again. That he was going to be unable to prevent another tragedy.

'Theo!'

Had he heard Abby? Was that really her voice calling on the wind? Or was it a trick of the storm, playing games with his mind? But then a flash of yellow bobbed up near the stricken vessel, now only a couple of metres ahead. It was her! It was Abby. And she was holding onto the second life jacket, his father clinging to the other side of it.

*

Abby had thought she'd been cold to the bone before. Once when it had snowed in Romsey for three whole days and The Travellers' Rest boiler had broken down, another time when it had ice-rained at the New Forest show and she'd had to take shelter with a man who whittled walking sticks. But now, being literally sucked into a savage whirlpool where the breath was taken from her and water inhaled with each passing moment, she really *really* knew what cold to the bone was. Now she just hoped, having by fluke or by God's grace, found Dinis, that she could hold him and herself above water until Theo could make it to them.

She drew in a breath before the water covered her face again and tried to think of hot, warming things. A piping sausage roll, pastry moist and flaky, meat well-seasoned. The sand beneath her bare feet and the Corfiot sun on her back. Theo's body pressed against hers, his mouth caressing—

'Give me your hand!'

It was Theo's voice. Just when she thought she might not have enough energy to keep awake, she forced her eyes open, her hand still gripping the spare life-jacket and shook her head. 'Take your dad first,' she said. 'I think he's hurt.'

'Abby! Give me your fucking hand!'

She hadn't heard him swear like that before. And he was looking every inch moody and very Greek, leaning out of his boat over the sea. Another wave washed over her and she tried not to breathe in the salt water.

'Abby!' he called again.

'Get your dad!' she roared back. And then her fingers gave up. She just couldn't hold onto the life jacket any longer.

Sixty-six

'I want you to know that you are the craziest, most stupid, mad, *insane* person I have ever met.'

Abby's throat felt like it had been scrubbed with rock salt by someone taking no care and using an extra wide brush. She was exhausted, but she could hear Theo's voice, his beautiful, if annoyed, voice shouting at her over the howling storm. She was being carried through water from what her blurry eyes and other senses were telling her. She tried to move but his arms held her firm.

'No! You do not move! You do as you are told for once! You keep still and you keep your eyes open and you listen to me shouting at you!'

'You sound … like Spyridoula,' Abby breathed.

'You are OK!' Theo sounded a little surprised by this. She was OK, as far as she could tell, numb with cold and not really being able to feel her body parts. But at least they didn't hurt … but where was Dinis? Did she save Dinis?

'Where's your dad?' she gasped, again trying to move. Next a bout of coughing ensued and salt water crept its way up her throat. She wanted to spit but not really in front of Theo.

'Spit it out!' Theo ordered.

OK then. She turned her head, half-spitting, half-vomiting then clearing her throat before saying again, 'Theo, your dad ... Dinis.'

'He is fine,' Theo said. 'Spyridoula and Mrs Karakis have him. They will call the doctor if they need to, or make potions from the trees.'

The ground felt different. Were they out of the sea at last?

'Wanging hell! Abs! Is she all right? Has she hit her head? Has she swallowed a load of water? Because I saw this programme about secondary drowning!'

Melody's voice was like music to Abby's ears. There had been a moment when she thought she might not hear anything but the tinnitus of the sea ever again.

'She needs to be warm,' Theo stated. 'I will take her inside.'

'How could you let her get on the boat with you? Are you out of your mind?! This is my sister! My only sister! I could kill you!'

Abby's heart surged with love for her sibling but she quickly answered, 'It wasn't Theo's fault.' She coughed. 'I made him.'

'Well, I'm sorry, Abby, but he's near-on six foot and well built and you're ... not. He should have forced you to stay put! Stay safe! Oh, I could wanging kill you!'

Abby suddenly got a mouthful of her sister's wet, candy-floss hair and it felt like one of the nicest experiences she had ever had. Melody rubbed their faces together like she had when they were children then retreated and looked to Theo.

'Bring her up to our room. She can have a shower and get some dry clothes on.'

'Abby! Abby!' It was Jackie. Her drawing of breath sounding like a puffing and panting London Marathon runner.

'Mum, she's all right. She's talking and she's being obstinate and she says it isn't *his* fault but I'm not so sure. Anyone who goes out on a boat in this sea has to be a little bit mental.'

'Oh my, Abby, you've never been that great at swimming. What possessed you to go into the water?' Jackie was holding her hands now, as Theo, still powering up the beach, headed towards the sanctuary of the hotel.

'I'm very good at problem-solving though and ... finding things ... then I just had to hold on,' Abby breathed.

'Let's get you out of this storm before you freeze,' Jackie said. 'Can't you move any faster, Theo?'

'What plants are good for someone who has been knocked unconscious?' Spyridoula asked Mrs Karakis.

'We need tea with St John's Wort and cayenne pepper and oats and, I think, Chinese skullcap.'

'What is Chinese skullcap?' Spyridoula asked. She was on her knees, beside her brother, wiping Dinis's forehead with a towel as he lay across one of the bar area sofas. His soaking wet form was dripping water on the floor despite the towels and blankets that were being used to raise his temperature and dry him off.

'It sounds like a hat I do not want to wear,' Dinis moaned, coughing and trying to sit up.

'Stay still!' Spyridoula ordered. 'I am so angry with you. What do you think of coming here in these conditions?!'

'Turmeric,' Mrs Karakis concluded. 'I will see if they have turmeric to make a tea. It is anti-inflammatory and helps with concussion.' She headed off towards the bar area and the staff, bypassing Theo who was biting his nails, observing his dad but keeping a little distance. The truth was he didn't know what to do with himself. He felt exhausted but also so full of adrenalin he was unable to be still.

'I have not hit my head,' Dinis protested as his sister put another cushion behind him. 'And that is not comfortable.'

'Good, you are trying to fight me,' Spyridoula stated. 'You will not win, of course, but this means you are not going to die today.'

'Where is Theo?' Dinis asked, eyes suddenly widening as if panicked. 'Is he OK?'

'He is OK,' Spyridoula replied.

'Where is he?' Dinis asked again. 'And the girl—'

'I am here,' Theo answered, shifting on his feet, wondering whether to step forwards or not.

'I think I will see if they have more towels and help with the turmeric tea. She does not make good tea at the best of times.' Spyridoula got up, wiping her hands with the towel before discarding it on a chair and leaving the room.

Theo looked at his father. Dinis seemed older than the last time he had seen him, the glimpses around the villa as he attempted to avoid him. Why had he done that? Why hadn't he just talked, minus the anger and regrets? If what Spyridoula had told him earlier was true then everything had changed.

'Were you trying to get back to Corfu on that boat, in that sea?' Dinis questioned, looking straight at him.

Theo shook his head. 'No.' He stood tall, put his hands into the pockets of his dripping wet shorts. He had refused all offers of towels and fuss, wanting to make sure his father and Abby were taken care of. His hair was down, a shaggy, bedraggled mess, a little like the rest of him. 'I decided we had to stay here the night. The reports were too bad to risk going back.'

'So why were you out in the bay?' Dinis asked, looking a little bewildered.

'Why was I out in the bay?! Why do you think I was out in the bay? Leon called me. He told me you were coming here. The weather was ... like it was ... I knew you would be in trouble.' He took a breath. 'I was coming to look for you!'

'Knew I would be in trouble?' Dinis shook his head. 'You have no faith in my experience.'

'Still you want to fight?' Theo said. 'Still you want to be the big Greek man? Well, here is the truth, whether you agree with it or not. That tourist boat you tried to sail in a storm force eleven is not fit to travel from San Stefanos to Barbati in fair weather. What you did went against everything you as a sailor should know. You put yourself in danger. You put me in danger. And you put someone I care very much about in danger too.'

For a moment Dinis didn't say anything and the only sound was the wind still rattling the battened-down shutters. Theo swallowed, then moved closer to his father, taking a seat in the chair next to the sofa he was laying on.

'Spyridoula told me you have been to see Limoni.'

Dinis dropped his eyes. 'Spyridoula says too many things. She was like this even as a child. Never knowing when to say nothing.'

'Why did you not tell me?' Theo asked. 'That you gave her family money? That you were making sure she had the best rehabilitation?'

'I was going to tell you,' Dinis answered. 'It was one of the reasons I came to Corfu but ...' He stopped talking.

'But what?'

'I wanted to know that you were OK before I told you.'

'That I was OK?'

'I have been worried about you, Theo. I told you that.'

'You told me you did not think I would sail a boat again,' Theo retorted. 'And that seemed to be the most important thing to you.'

'It was not the most important thing. The most important thing is that I do not lose you the way I lost your mother. Quickly. Suddenly. When I was too wrapped up in work.'

Theo put his hands together, suddenly feeling the cold. His whole body began to react to his body temperature and the frightening ordeal they had just been through.

'As a father I have been …' Dinis stopped again, as if fighting to find the most appropriate word. 'Challenging, and all the other things you probably thought of me. You and your brother and sister have had so little of me and so little of your mother because she passed. It must have been like being orphans. And I regret this. I truly regret this. Your mother, she would be abseiling down from a cloud if she could see the mess I have created.'

'Dad …' Theo started.

'There is no excuse. I lost sight of what mattered. I buried my own grief and threw everything into the company and I ignored being a father when you three needed me most. But, Theo, you are the one I let down the most.' His voice thickened. 'I tried to make you like me … but the bad version of me, the ruthless entrepreneur, the money-orientated businessman … and when the accident happened I felt like it had to be controlled or the only thing I thought I had – the business – would be taken away from me too.'

'You should have told us how you were feeling,' Theo interrupted softly.

'Theo, I am Greek, just like you are Greek. The only feelings we let out are joy and anger in equal measure. We do not tell people, not even family, if we cannot cope.' He sighed, his breathing still a little crackly. 'But we should. Because then you might have understood why I did not want to pay the family of Limoni at first, why I took things out on you, why I have been the worst father …'

'Not the worst father.' Theo reached across the space, the seat moving with him, sliding closer to the sofa, bringing him nearer to Dinis. He took hold of his father's cold, water-wrinkled hand.

'You are too forgiving,' Dinis had tears in his voice as well as in his eyes. 'I do not deserve it.'

'We all make mistakes,' Theo continued. 'I should not have run away.'

'You did nothing wrong, Theo,' Dinis told him firmly. 'Not on the boat on that day. Not anything since … apart from tonight.' He squeezed Theo's hand. 'You should never put yourself in danger for me.'

'You are my father,' Theo said, emotion flooding his senses. 'I would do the very same again.'

'But the girl from the estate agency – you took her with you.'

Theo sighed. 'I think she would have murdered me and driven the boat herself if I had stopped her from coming on board.'

'She jumped into that water to save me.' Dinis shook his head. 'She is as crazy as you.'

'Yes,' Theo answered. 'Yes, she is.'

Sixty-seven

The Beach House, Porto

The shack on the beach was just a shell but it had all the essentials. It wasn't centrally heated, but in the main room there was a small electric heater, one now made-up double bed, a rocking chair with a blanket and an electric kettle. A window ran the length of one wood-panelled wall, usually displaying the beautiful, star-filled beach and sea scene, but tonight showing the raw power of the ocean and the storm in its full force. And Theo could now vouch for the shower. He had stood in it for over twenty minutes until it turned cold, trying to get some warmth into every extremity and mull over everything that had happened. Now, a towel wrapped around his waist he stood, waiting for the kettle to boil to make black tea with sugar – good for shock, according Mrs Karakis.

Suddenly there was a knock at the door. His heart beat quickly in his chest and he stepped towards it, wondering what else could possibly happen to them on this island. He unlatched the door and the wind almost took it from him as he opened it. Standing there was Abby, wearing a hotel dressing gown, her hair plastered against her face, looking just as soaking as she had been when he'd pulled her up out of the sea.

'What are you doing here?' Theo dragged her inside and shut the wild weather out, making sure the door was firmly fastened.

'It's warm in here,' Abby said, moving across the room towards where the little heater was working hard. He watched her put her fingers to it, splaying them out and trying to soak up every little modicum.

'Abby,' Theo said. 'You should be inside.'

'I am now,' she answered.

'The real inside,' he countered. 'The hotel. Where I know there are powerful heating units and thicker blankets and more to drink than black tea and sugar.'

'You're making black tea and sugar?' Abby asked, heading for the rocking chair. 'Yum. Do you have enough for two? Or can we share?'

He shook his head. 'There is something wrong with you. You have been hit on the head by a rock in the sea, or the boat, or something. Why will you not do the right thing?'

Abby smiled. 'I've spent many years doing the right thing. I've even written lists about doing the right thing. Did you know, though, that in one of the popular lists of *things you need to make you happy* is "an adventure". Not tame little trips to see Benedict Cumberbatch performing a hammy script ... "an adventure", Theo.'

'An adventure should not include jumping into the sea in an almost hurricane force storm.'

'This whole time in Corfu has been an adventure for me. In so many ways.' Abby rocked in the chair, sticking out her feet and trying to reach the heat from the portable radiator.

'You have been through a trauma. For a few days you will feel you have suddenly worked out the meaning of life. It will pass.' He knew because he had been through it too. For a while he had clung to the fact that everyone had survived the accident, but then the reality that, despite survival, everything had changed that day sunk in.

'I don't think I know the meaning of life,' Abby said, getting up. 'But I do know that I am not leaving this island until I've taken off your towel, and taken off this dressing gown, and we've ... got naked together.'

As she moved towards him he closed his eyes as all his hormones seemed to go on a pillage, rifling through every piece of him, inciting action. 'Abby,' he breathed.

'Listen,' she whispered. 'I know I'm not long out of a relationship I thought was everything, and I'm guessing, because you told me you've never had a proper relationship, that you've probably had quite a number of not-proper relationships, but what it all comes down to really is ... I'm ready to move on and I would like to move on with you.'

She was close to him now, the V of the flimsy, damp dressing gown a little loose, the tie at her waist almost undone.

'And when I say "move on with you", I'm actually meaning "move on top of you" and "move under you" and most definitely "move in front of you". She turned around then, slowly, seductively, her cotton-covered bottom rubbing against his towel-wrapped groin. It was too much. Tonight had been too much. He had nearly lost his father, lost himself, lost her. And that had hit him harder than he could ever have imagined.

'You,' he said, his tone lust-filled, 'should not have got on my boat. It was the stupidest of all things to do.' His fingers went to the dressing gown belt, slackening at the tie.

'I've been a bad, bad girl,' Abby replied, pressing her bottom harder against him. 'You told me earlier.'

'But it was also the bravest, most daring thing I have ever seen.' He pushed his heat against her, the towel beginning to detach around his waist.

'It was?' she breathed.

'And now,' he continued, his hands, slipping the dressing gown from her shoulders. 'Now everyone is safe, I can say it was also very, very sexy.' He turned her around, wanting to see her expression as the dressing gown fell to the floor.

Abby gasped. Even though this was exactly what she wanted, it was still a slight surprise to find her gown pooled at her feet and to be standing opposite this gorgeous man, completely naked. But she didn't feel embarrassed or anxious, she simply felt empowered.

'I like boats,' she said, her hands going to his waistline and the covering of towel that was preventing him from being as nude as she was. 'The first boat I remember being on was a pedalo. They have them on a lake in Southsea and they're shaped like swans.'

'There are no swan pedalos in Corfu,' Theo replied.

'I know,' Abby whispered. 'But I've moved up a gear now. Nothing less than a hundred horse power.'

'Is that so?'

Her heart was hammering, she had goose bumps on her skin, not from the cold but because she was aching with longing. She ripped Theo's towel off and threw it away. And there he was. The perfect, honed, olive-skinned form she had shied away from when she'd first walked onto the terrace of Villa Pappas. There was no bashfulness now. She wanted him up close and personal and she wanted that right now.

She clasped her arms around his neck, drawing his whole body to hers as her mouth sought his. His skin tasted exquisite, of orange and soap and sea and she dived her fingers into his jaw-length damp, clean hair. Her lips moved over his, teasing, inviting him to join in and then his mouth claimed hers, hard, with intention as deep as the kiss he returned.

Running fingers across his chest, she kissed over his pecs and abs, and then turned around, her bum teasing his hardness as she looked at him over her shoulder.

It would be so easy, so good, to edge her over towards the bed, watch her brace for him and take her like he had taken women in the past. But he did not want that with Abby. As much as her dance of seduction was driving him wild, he needed this to be something different, something meaningful, for however long the relationship between them lasted.

He put a hand to her bottom, the flat of his hand smoothing over its roundness. But then he shifted, walked around her until he was facing her.

'I want to see you,' he breathed. 'I want you to see me.'

'Theo,' she gasped, shivering.

'Sit in the chair,' he told her.

He watched her make her way across the bare boards to the rocking chair. Slowly she sank down onto it, the throw dropping onto the floor. She was so beautiful, so natural, so full of heart as well as surprises. He stood over her, just looking, drinking in every little perfection as she stared back, eyes full of want.

And then he moved, closing the gap between them, kissing her mouth, and fitting his body into the space on the seat, holding off from connecting their bodies too soon. He wanted to take his time, as long as he could. He wanted this union to be something neither of them would ever forget, no matter what happened next.

Abby's hands found his penis and she felt him quake the moment she made contact, caressing him, tempting and deliberate. She urged him downwards, hands moving upwards, onto his shoulders.

'I want you, Theo,' she breathed. 'I want us.'

She gasped as he moved as close as he could get, sliding into her with no more prelude. The chair rocked in time to their motion and Abby held onto him, legs open, the rest of her falling apart to the rhythm of the song they were making. *This* was true abandon. *This* was deep passion. And she knew then, as Theo whispered her name, she had never experienced anything even close ever before.

'Theo,' she breathed, clawing at his skin as her body came alive with his.

'My opposite,' he replied. 'Look what you do to me.'

His eyes were dark and intense but the way he was looking at her was a mix of every emotion – sexy but also containing depth, a true fondness ... love?

She cried out then, the feeling too intense to control and suddenly it felt as if she were back in between the waves, being tossed up into the air and crashing back down again, the surf fizzing on her skin.

'Abby,' Theo grunted. 'Oh, Abby.'

'Hold me,' she begged, 'hold me closer.'

Sixty-eight

The sound of the sea woke Abby the next morning, but it was in complete contrast to the fierce cacophony of the night before. This morning it sounded as if calm had been restored and the waves were back to shushing up to the beach, just strong enough to tickle toes before retreating.

'Black tea with sugar.'

Theo placed the steaming cup on the floor next to the bed, then sat down on it, close to her, reaching to run his fingers through her hair.

After the rocking chair, they had made love on the floor and finally the bed, crumbling into each other in the early hours, falling asleep, sated and content. It had been the most dramatic twenty-four hours since the loss of her job, her boyfriend and her cat.

'Thank you,' she whispered, sitting up, drawing the blanket around her nudity and leaning forward to kiss his mouth. He was wearing his shorts, just about wearable after being dried out by the one heater.

'I do not like the blanket,' Theo said, his hands pulling it to one side. 'The fibres itch my skin.'

She discarded the covering completely and moved forward, enveloping his mouth with hers, wanting to deepen the kiss and possibly never let it end …

It was Theo who pulled away first, dropping the lightest of touches on her lips before sitting back and taking hold of her hands. He looked suddenly contemplative.

'What's wrong?' Abby asked, brushing his loose hair away from his face. 'Are you worried about your dad?'

He shook his head. 'No,' he breathed. 'He will have ingested half a cupboard full of herbs by now.'

'Then what is it?' Abby questioned. 'Tell me.'

'I have wanted to tell you, since the night you saved the children from Igor and his crazy friends on their boat.'

'I'm listening,' Abby said, taking his hands back in hers.

He swallowed, as if preparing himself physically and mentally. The tension in him was palpable, the air between them stirring like the beginnings of yesterday's weather.

'The reason I am here in Corfu is because … back in Halkidiki there was an accident, on a boat.' He took a breath that seemed to shake his whole body. 'My father and I, we were taking out some of the workers of one of the big businesses we deal with, for a treat and to show them how well the boat performs, so they can experience the thrill of what they are trying to sell on our behalf to their clients.' He paused, squeezing her hands, then looking directly at her. 'There was a child with us, a girl, she was the daughter of one of the salesmen. She …'

As he told the story, all the images that had haunted him flooded back. The completely unexpected swell, his inability to control the boat's reaction to it, the vessel flipping over, trying to locate everyone, panic, confusion, Limoni's screams …

'Theo …' Abby said softly.

He braced himself, straightening his core, trying to toughen up. 'She lost an arm.'

'Oh no!' Abby exclaimed. 'Oh God, that's terrible.'

He nodded. It was terrible. It was unthinkable. For an eleven-year-old girl to have to live the rest of her life without an arm. 'And I did that,' Theo stated. 'I made that happen.'

'But, Theo, you couldn't have known that was going to happen. Was there something wrong with the boat?'

'No.'

'Then was it just the sea? Some freak weather like we had last night? I mean, I have never seen the sea behave like that before, even on documentaries.'

She hadn't even considered it was something he had done ...

'I don't know,' he replied. 'Not for sure.'

'Have they investigated?'

'There was nothing found wrong with the boat.'

'Well, that's good.'

'They say ... they think ... it was nothing I had done.'

'Of course it wasn't,' Abby said straightaway.

'Why do you say that?' Theo asked her.

'Because you're so conscientious.' She squeezed his hands. 'That night when you chased after Igor, when you steered him away from the children, that was someone who was thinking three steps ahead to the tragedy it could have been. Someone who thinks like that doesn't make mistakes.'

'But what if I did?' Theo needed to tell Abby his greatest fears. 'What if it *was* my fault? And Limoni is living her life without an arm because of something I did?'

'Theo,' Abby said. 'Why do you want to punish yourself? If the investigation says it wasn't the boat and it wasn't anything you did, then it was simply an accident.'

He shook his head. 'But things like that should not happen. Not to someone so innocent.'

He could feel the raw sensation taking hold again now. He wanted to shout and cry and rage at the unfairness of life. He knew this wasn't just about Limoni. This was also about losing his mother. Another innocent taken too soon, leaving her family without its anchor.

'Unfortunately,' Abby said quietly. 'It's the nature of life. Like with my dad. His death was the reason I jumped into a relationship with Darrell. I needed someone to need me. I needed something I could get on with, be in charge of, fasten myself to.'

He looked at her, eyes glazing over, just like his. He wanted to put his arms around her, tell her everything was going to be OK, but he couldn't make that promise.

'It's not something I acknowledged until I had a conversation with my mum, and it made me realise that Darrell wasn't the love of my life I thought he was.'

'Abby …' He should be saying more. He should be telling her she had made him feel like he had never felt before. That despite everything in his life being the wrong way up she had been a beacon of light through it all.

'You are such a wonderful person, Theo. I am so glad I got to meet you and spend these weeks with you.'

His heart felt like it had been scorched. 'It sounds like you are saying goodbye.' He blinked, watching her expression. 'Are you?'

'No,' Abby said quickly. 'Not yet.'

'But …'

'I think we both need to understand our own feelings about life and the world before we think about any feelings we have for each other.'

She was right. She was always right. But somehow it hurt him absolutely. To think about being without her. To think about what? Going back to Halkidiki? Staying in Corfu? Moving on again? Things might have reached truce territory with his dad but there was still a lot to be worked out.

'Right now,' he whispered. 'I do not want to think of life or the world. I only want to think about the chair over there.'

'Is that so?' Abby asked, smiling as he reached for her.

'That is so,' he replied. In one quick move he lifted her into his arms and carried her across the room as she screamed with delight. 'Where is your phone? We need to play music.'

'Happy music?' Abby breathed.

'No,' Theo replied. 'Dramatic, dark … very sexy music.'

'Well,' she whispered in his ear. 'That's a playlist I definitely want to follow.'

Sixty-nine

Desperately Seeking

'Can I just say, again, that if I see another boat it will be too soon.'

Abby laughed at her sister. 'Mel, you live in San Stefanos. There are scores of boats just down there. You see them every day.' She pointed off the terrace to where the still-calm waters were swaying the hire boats back and forth waiting for tourists to take them out for a jaunt. It was three days since they had made it back from Erikousa and the office had never been busier. Abby hadn't been sure about using 'Desperately Seeking employee saves Greek millionaire in worst storm in a decade' as a PR campaign, but once all their feet were back on dry land and everyone was declared healthy and not at risk from secondary drowning, Dinis himself had insisted on it, and she hadn't been able to hold back on the idea. It had made the Greek national papers and Melody had been tweeting influencers for retweets since the story broke, all of which had led to more properties for them to value, and more people choosing Desperately Seeking to meet their holiday home viewing requirements. Although the cash-flow problem wasn't anywhere near solved, raffle prize-winners had, in the end, paid for their own accommodation in Erikousa, and with a sale going through imminently, a commission cheque was heading their way within days.

'I'm never getting on one again though,' Melody said, blowing out a breath.

'And I thought I was the one who went out in the gale and jumped into the sea.'

'You might well have been, but I was the one who threw up all the way home the next day.'

'On a flat calm,' Abby reminded. 'Meaning it had far more to do with the amount of ouzo you drank with Milo seeing out the storm than it did with Theo's sailing skills.'

Melody grinned. 'And you would know all about Theo's skills now, wouldn't you? *I* almost know … our house might have thick walls on the outside but on the inside, not so much.'

Abby couldn't help but blush. Theo had spent two nights at the house with her and last night she had stayed at Villa Pappas. They were on borrowed time. Theo was leaving with his father later that day, going back to Halkidiki, seeing his brother and sister and trying to work out where things went for him. There was a gnawing in her gut about him departing Corfu but, in reality, it was too soon to move on to something permanent. This surprise summer had been all about finding out about her own capabilities and skills, as well as being part of a *family* team. And Theo, he had been a beautiful, hot distraction that she would never forget.

'Well,' Abby said. 'I hear you're going to the *panegyri* with Leon. You do know he was supposed to be *my* date.'

'Shit, you don't mind, do you?' Melody exclaimed. 'I thought, with you being with Theo, it would be OK. Because having two men would be a bit greedy … when you're not me.'

Abby laughed. 'Of course I don't mind.' Then she quietened. 'Theo's leaving today.'

'Leaving? What d'you mean leaving?'

'He's going back to Halkidiki with Dinis.' She sniffed, dropping her eyes to her paperwork. 'It was always going to happen. He doesn't live here.'

'Yeah, I know, but … I thought … and Mum thought …'

'Thought what?' Abby asked. 'That she was going to get her big, fat, Greek wedding after all?' She was looking at the wrong column now.

'We thought that, you know, if Theo was here and you were, you know, getting it on with him, then you would, maybe, stay on Corfu.'

There was so much expectation, hope and affection in Melody's voice it cut Abby to the core. She knew that her family had loved having her here, that it had helped heal grief that had long been undealt with, and got them working as a force of Dolans once again, but she still hadn't decided how long her Corfu episode was going to last. She had a couple more days to make a decision on her flat and she knew she ought to make that decision once Theo had gone. She needed to see how Corfu felt without him. Not because she had relied on him for anything, but perhaps, without the olive-skinned honed body pressed up against hers, without his deep, infectious laugh and his happy Greek music, it all might feel different. Not necessarily different-bad, just different. And it needed to be different-right for her to make any sort of commitment.

'I haven't said I won't,' Abby said.

'Yay! You're staying! I knew you would!' Melody erupted.

'I haven't I said I will either!' She didn't want to give her sister false hope.

'God, just make your mind up already!'

'It's the rest of my life. It should be given quite a lot of consideration.'

'Pah!' Melody replied, waving a hand then slamming it down onto the table and flattening a mosquito. 'You don't have to think of it as dramatically as that. That's typical you. It doesn't have to be a big-picture-my-whole-life-decided-by-one-single-pro-con-list kind of thing. You could just stay for the summer and see how it goes.'

Could she? Could she give up the flat? Stay for the summer and if things weren't how she expected, fly back to the UK and ... find somewhere else to live. She guessed she didn't need to be in Romsey now The Travellers' Rest had disposed of her.

'Girls!' Jackie burst out from the office, face reddened despite the air-conditioning she'd been sitting in, but a vision in lilac. 'Can you two get up to Villa Pappas? I've got a family who want to view it and they're sitting right outside. I'd go but I've got someone coming here in ten minutes and I'm just putting a portfolio together.'

'I'll start the car,' Abby said, jumping up.

'Don't bother,' Melody stated, picking up her phone. 'I tried it earlier, it's totally wanged. I'll call Leon.'

Theo stood on the terrace, looking out over San Stefanos in all its glory. He did love the village and all the eccentric people who lived in it. Yesterday he had gone fishing with Spyridoula. They had talked about his mother and then managed to nab a haul big enough to sell to the Galini restaurant. Leon had taken the money and done a deal on a new bicycle for Stathis, complete with a horn the man was taking every opportunity to honk. Earlier, the noise had scared Madalena into barrelling into a whole basket of discounted watermelons, knocking them into the road. Some children had helped to pick them up, then taken one to use as a football on the beach.

It was a beautiful day today, a breath of wind to keep the temperature below forty and a few white clouds to enhance the skyline. A good day to fly, if you wanted to fly. He still wasn't sure he wanted to, but he knew that he needed to.

'You are packed, Theo?'

It was his father's voice behind him and, before he had a chance to look around, Dinis had joined him at the wall, looking over the village, beach and sea view.

'I did not bring much,' he answered.

'Leon will take us to the airport,' Dinis responded.

'He will?' Theo asked, regarding his father with a raised eyebrow. 'I thought you hated Leon's taxi.'

'I am still not sure it will get us to the airport on time, but I think he should have the money for the fare. He works hard. His family works hard.'

'They do,' Theo agreed. Inside his jeans pocket his phone bleeped and he pulled it out.

'Is it Hera?' Dinis asked him. 'Wanting to retain the best cocktail maker she has ever employed?'

Theo shook his head. 'Although she did tell me if I ever want to work here again she would gladly have me.' He sighed, trailing his finger over the name on the screen. 'It is Abby. She is coming here. Someone is coming to view the villa.'

'You are OK with that?' Dinis asked, looking to Theo.

He nodded. They had talked over the past few days, after getting back from Erikousa, about everything, his mum, his siblings, Villa Pappas. Nothing was completely clear, but it was all out in the open, being discussed honestly for the first time.

'Your mother never liked this house,' Dinis repeated what he had said a night ago. 'She said this house and my cars were like medals I needed to hang around my neck.'

Theo couldn't help but smile. He only wished he had heard her say it, got to know her a little better.

'Maybe she was right,' Dinis answered.

'It is a great house,' Theo stated.

'But not a home.' Dinis sighed. 'She was right. Women, especially Greek women, they are always right, whether we like it or not.'

'Abby is the same,' Theo said, almost proudly. Then he turned away from the view and faced his father. 'Do you think it could *be* a home?'

'What?'

'Villa Pappas,' he said. 'I know you say that Mum did not like it but, maybe if it could be different ...'

'I do not know,' Dinis answered. 'Perhaps. All I know is it is expensive to have it sat here, not being rented, not earning its way. I am a businessman, Theo, it makes no sense to keep it.' He patted Theo's shoulder. 'It does not mean that we will not come back to Corfu. Of course we will. I have to stop that sister of mine from marrying a woodcutter.'

Theo smiled. 'She told you.'

'She is crazy. She is old enough to know better.'

'But she is happy with Stamatis. That should be all that matters.'

Dinis sighed, then nodded with a smile. 'I know this. I am glad she is happy. I just ... do not really want to be related to someone whose home and place of work are the same, all coated in six inches of dust and bacteria.'

Theo heard the sound of the gate being opened and there was Abby, Melody at her heel, together with two other adults and two children, both eating dripping ice creams.

'My God,' Dinis said, turning around too. 'Please tell her to keep those children away from the sheepskin rug in the lounge.'

Seventy

'I do not know what I am going to do without you,' Theo said, his voice soft in Abby's ear, his mouth kissing the skin behind it as they cooled off in the pool. 'We have made love every day for the past four days. I cannot imagine a day without you in it.' He breathed hard. 'A day without me in you.'

'You managed perfectly well before I arrived, *very* well, if Leon's stories are to be believed.'

He put his arms around her neck, drawing her into him, the water at waist level.

'I'm not sure I've ever been wanted for just my body before.'

'You think that is all I want?' Theo asked, sounding a little put out. He held her away from him, looking right into her eyes.

'I ... no ... I just ... I don't know,' she admitted. Perhaps she should have worked on her phrasing.

'Abby ... I have had nothing this way before,' Theo said, his tone serious and deep. 'Nothing like this.'

It felt nice for him to say that and she really believed him. Their connection *had* been a great one. It didn't need to be thought about any further than that. This was the new Abby. Doing what she wanted without regret. Learning to live without lists – not too many of them, at least.

'For me too,' she whispered. And it was true. It was nothing like what she had had with Darrell. How could that be?

'What time do you have to go?' she asked with a swallow.

'Now you wish me to go already?' he joked. 'You have your eye on Stathis, I know it. Now he has that new bicycle and a very, big horn ...'

Abby laughed and thumped his shoulder playfully.

'In a few hours,' Theo answered. 'Leon will take us to the airport.'

She nodded, just letting it sink in.

'And what about you, Abby? Have you decided what you want to do?'

She sighed and slipped from his embrace to lie a little in the water, letting it soak her whole body, seep over her arms, wet her hair. It was gloriously cooling, but wasn't providing her with any answers. 'No,' she said.

'You think you might stay? On Corfu?'

'I don't know. I know Melody and my mum would like me to but ... Desperately Seeking is their creation, their dream. I don't know if it's mine. And I don't know yet if I want it to be.'

She watched him nod his head, the man bun back in place, those abs slick with water, looking the very same as he had that first day at the villa, but perhaps his expression was just a little lighter. And he said she had helped with that, without even really knowing it.

'We both have everything in the world out there waiting for us,' Theo agreed.

'Yes, we do,' she said, coming up out of the water and standing in front of him, adjusting her bikini a little.

He smiled at her, brushing his fingers down her arm, finding her hand and interlocking them. 'I spoke to Limoni this morning. She is such a great kid.' He shook his head as his eyes filled with tears. 'Do you know she is playing tennis for her school? Chosen, still good enough to be one of the best.'

'That's incredible.'

'I am going to see her, Abby, when I get back to Halkidiki. I want to ... I don't know ... not put things right because I cannot do that but ... just see her, let her know I think of her every day and ...'

She squeezed his hand tight, knowing he couldn't continue, everything was still so raw that even thinking about it was too much. 'You are a beautiful man, Theo. Inside and out.' She sighed and said it in Greek. '*Omorfos*.'

Taking his face in her hands, she pressed her mouth to his, wanting their every moment to make a million memories.

Theo closed his eyes and kissed her desperately. Part of him wanted to hold on and never let go, but that wasn't fair on either of them. Neither of them could make decisions on anything between them without coming to a decision about their own personal futures – what they wanted from their lives and where they wanted to be. And they had only spent a few weeks with each other. Nothing could have a real foundation in that short space of time, could it?

She pressed her body to his, swinging her legs around his waist and holding tight, her face close to his. It was a sweet agony to embrace her like this, knowing these were their last hours together.

'I don't want to say goodbye,' Abby said, her voice choking a little.

'I know,' Theo replied.

'No, Theo, I mean, when we get out of the pool, I'm going to go back to the office and I'm going to throw myself into work and I'm going to try really, really hard to forget that you're leaving.'

'Abby ...'

'I know it's silly, I know we said that it was just the best summer and that we're both not in the right place at the moment but ... I can't be there when you get into Leon's taxi and drive away.' She sniffed and he felt the tremble in her shoulders. He didn't know how to reply. She was now saying the hours he thought they had left were going to be mere minutes.

'I would be a complete cliché of all those rom-com films. I'd cry intensely, and I might run after the car a little bit or I might hold onto you so long that your dad would have to prise me off, or I would get in the taxi with you, stuck to you, embarrassingly and ...'

He pulled her form a little away from his, to look at her.

'Don't look at me,' she begged, closing her eyes as if that would hide her. 'I'm crying already.'

'None of that sounded so bad,' Theo whispered. 'Open your eyes.'

She shook her head. 'No ... I've got a lovely mental image of you I snapshotted just before I started crying and I want to hold on to that.'

'I could call you,' Theo said softly. 'As soon as I get to Halkidiki.'

She opened her eyes then, gazed at him for a moment and then shook her head. 'Theo ... we said we shouldn't.'

'I know,' he answered. 'And I agreed, but ... I'm not sure why.'

'Because you're not ready, and neither am I.'

'Ready for what?' His heart was jumping up and down at the thought of continuing something with this wonderful woman, despite what they had both said. Long distance didn't have to be long distance forever …

'We need solitude,' Abby said firmly.

'You're going to get that in San Stefanos?' he joked. 'Good luck.'

'I might not be here,' she reminded.

'No,' he said, sighing. He needed to rid himself of all the images he had in his mind, plus the ones on his phone. Abby sipping at an Old Fashioned cocktail, her face kissed by the sun before her lips were kissed by him, a selfie at the 7th Heaven bar at Logas Beach, that dramatic clifftop background just visible behind their glowing faces … She might not be in Corfu. She might be back in England, or somewhere else. She had so many choices. And she deserved every one of them.

'*Signomi*,' he said, holding her close again.

'Don't be sorry,' Abby said, a hand gently toying with the hair at the back of his head. 'Just let's … have another swim and then maybe you can remind me how good the waterfall shower in the master en-suite is.' She drew away, a teasing smile on her lips. 'For estate agency purposes, obviously. So I can get a full, hands-on user experience to share with potential purchasers.'

'Hands-on?' Theo repeated, his fingers moving to the straps of her bikini top.

'Hands … lips … I think I need to research every … single … position.'

Now her expression was pure wolfish and it was driving him wild.

'Let us not swim,' he said. 'I think I am more than ready for the shower.'

Seventy-one

Eucalyptus Taverna, San Stefanos

Who was Abby trying to kid? There was no way she was going to be able to 'throw herself into work' when the man she adored was about to leave the island. It had got to thirty minutes before the time Theo and Dinis were due to head to the airport and she had fled Desperately Seeking, jogging along the front, past Damianos, The Blue Vine and George's Taverna, searching for somewhere in the village that wasn't full of memories of Theo. Finally, she had found herself at the end of the beach, at a table for one at the lovely Eucalytus Taverna she hadn't even had time to eat at yet.

Avoiding cocktails and Fix beer she had ordered a half litre of white wine, some olives and bread and was sitting, watching people swim and splash happily in the azure water, their holidays carefree, her heart feeling heavier than it really should.

'Not even a proper member of staff yet and you're already pulling a fake sickie.'

Abby jumped at Melody's greeting, not having noticed her sister's presence behind her. She smiled weakly as Melody grabbed a glass from the adjacent table, filled it with wine then plumped down into the seat next to her.

'I've just come back from seeing a hideous little flat in Acharavi. I swear the owner is a hoarder, it's stashed with newspapers and bottles – empty bottles, I mean why? – books, carrier bags – again, why? – *but* once that crap is all cleared out, and it's painted it's got a sea view and it's a two-minute walk to the beach and everything else. I reckon I can market it now for one hundred thousand euro.'

'That's great,' Abby answered. It was great but the words had died on her lips. She tried again. 'That's really great, Mel.'

'Except you can't think of anything else apart from the fact your millionaire is leaving town in … fifteen minutes or so.'

'He isn't a millionaire,' Abby said, sighing. 'His dad is.'

'He's going to inherit that business one day, unless they fall out again.'

'I'm fine,' Abby said, lifting her wine glass to her mouth and taking a sip. It was light and refreshing and she was drinking it in an idyllic location overlooking one of the most amazing, tranquil, beach vistas there was. It was a haven of peace, a place to soothe your soul and perfect for smoothing over a slightly bent-out-of-shape heart.

'Because you look fine,' Melody stated brutally. 'You really don't, by the way.'

'Thanks,' Abby replied. 'Maybe I could borrow the Chinese hair stuff again later. I thought we could eat here. We haven't eaten here since I got back.'

'Are you really not going to say goodbye to Theo before Leon whisks him off to the airport?'

'I said goodbye earlier,' Abby answered with a sniff. 'In the infinity pool, and in the waterfall shower.'

'God! Are we going to have to get it disinfected before we show anyone else around?!'

Abby missed him. She missed him already. How could that be when he hadn't even left! Her chest was heaving with angst. What was she doing sitting here, drinking wine and eating olives when he was … leaving. But, it was better this way.

Cleaner. They had had their fun – more than fun, a lovely coming together in every which way – and both of them had come out of it more confident, fixed-up, better from the experience. Now it was time to move on.

'Abby, I know you're the sensible, level-headed one of the family, and I'm the complete opposite, but don't you think you might, you know, whether it's a bit soon or a bit weird, don't you think you might ... love Theo a bit?'

Abby swallowed. Her immediate reaction was to say what nonsense her sister was talking. *Love*. After a couple of weeks. After sex in numerous positions she'd only previously read about. Intertwined with saving children from Russians, saving her family's business from bankruptcy, a Jamaica versus Greece estate-agency party-off, pushing a car, herding cows with the aid of apples ... talking of loss and life and family, stealing kisses halfway down a mountain and in Stamatis' olive groves.

'I ...' Abby went to reply.

Her words were overridden by the blast of an air horn and the screech of brakes coming from the roadside. Leon's car came to a halt at the edge of the beach, spraying sandy stones across the concrete, fumes belting from the exhaust, seeping through the air and coating diners in Eucalyptus with the heavy gas.

Abby coughed, eyes adjusting to the new smog as the back door of the taxi opened and someone burst out. Wearing jeans and one of his trademark vests that covered nothing much. Theo.

She felt so many things in that moment. Bewilderment. Annoyance. Hope. But the feeling that rose above all others was one of pure delight. She scrabbled out of her seat, racing around the table, jumping down onto the road and heading towards him. Breath coming fast, tears falling from her eyes their bodies clashed together hard as they met in the middle of the street, a desperate tangle of arms and hands and lips and tears.

'I told you I didn't want to do this,' Abby sobbed as Theo's mouth caressed her cheeks. 'I said I was going to be weepy and pathetic and not strong and determined like I want to be.'

'I do not care,' Theo answered. 'I could not leave without seeing you one more time. Without holding you and telling you just how I feel.'

'Don't,' Abby begged. 'It's making it harder.'

'Abby,' he said seriously. 'I do not want to say *sagapo* without truly meaning it. But I feel it. I feel it, Abby.' He sniffed back emotion. 'No matter what I tell myself. I cannot change how I feel or what I feel … for you.'

'You have to go,' she said, swallowing hard as the tears just flowed faster.

'Look at me,' he ordered, raising her head with his finger. 'Abby, please, look at me.'

Those beautiful, black pools like the deepest, darkest Lavazza coffee were gazing back at her and it made her realise exactly what she was losing.

'I want to call you,' Theo stated. 'Every day.' He smoothed her hair with his hand. 'I want to tell you everything that is going on in my life. And I want to hear everything that is going on in your life. I do not know if this can work. I do not know if you even want the same but—'

'I am going to miss you so much,' she managed to get out.

'I am going to miss you too, my opposite. But, please, do not make this the end.' He held her face, looking at her as if she was his whole world. 'Let us make this only the beginning.'

And all at once she knew what her heart had been daring her to believe. She *did* care about him and she wanted to discover what might be possible if they stayed in contact. Perhaps it would be nothing, but perhaps it might just be everything. Only time would tell.

'You are so stupid,' she cried through her tears. 'You are the most stupid man I have ever met. I told you not to say goodbye and you ...'

'Come to say hello?' Theo answered with a hopeful smile.

She kissed his lips then, delighting in the way they matched hers so perfectly. Then she broke away, touching her hand to his cheek. 'Call me,' she told him. 'The second you land. Just to let me know you get there safely.'

'And then?' he queried, eyebrow raised in hope.

'Then,' she breathed. 'Call me every day after that. Tell me about Halkidiki. Tell me you got on another boat when the weather was nice this time. And tell me about Limoni ... and your brother and your sister and the house you grew up in ...'

He pulled her into his embrace, wrapping his arms around her and shielding her with his body like he needed to protect her from this separation.

'No goodbyes,' Theo whispered to her.

'Like *yassas*,' Abby said. 'You Greeks say that for "hello" and "goodbye".' She smiled, pulling away, taking his hands and just drinking him in.

'Theo!' Leon called from the taxi. 'We have to go, my friend. Or you will miss that aeroplane.'

Theo looked to Leon then back to Abby with a sigh full of regret.

'It's OK,' Abby said, voice still wavering a little. 'You have to go.'

'I will come back,' he promised. 'Back to you. Wherever you are.'

Abby cleared her throat, then stood tall with every ounce of strength she had left, ready for him to depart. Knowing that, despite what she had said earlier, she wasn't going to run after the taxi or glue herself to him. '*Yassas*, Theo.'

He wiped his eyes with the back of his hand, then grazed her cheek with his fingers. '*Yassas*, Abby.'

He moved forward, possessing her lips one last time, hard, firm and deeply loving, then broke away, turning and jogging to the waiting car.

'Now don't you dare fold,' Melody ordered, appearing at Abby's side, both of them watching Theo get in the back of Leon's taxi. 'You stand there, looking gorgeous and sun-kissed with your perfect straight hair and give him a memory to come running back to.'

Leon's engine started up with a clunk and a splutter, the fumes again rising from the back pipe.

'Oh, wanging forget that!' Melody yelled. 'Run! Let's run! And wave! Wave!'

Laughing and crying, the two sisters set off at a sprint, stumbling over the potholes, slipping on stones and sand, waving their arms like they were desperate concert attendees. The air horn played its tune and the Pappases drove out of San Stefanos.

Seventy-two

San Stefanos Harbour

Two weeks later

The village had been buzzing with activity all day in preparation for the annual village festival. Abby, Melody and Jackie had helped turn the beachfront into a carnival as the road was closed to traffic, chairs and tables were set up in every available space and stalls were made ready for the many food sellers who were right now beginning to provide the visitors with all manner of Greek delicacies. Whole lambs turned on mobile spits, stacks of warm pitta bread were being filled with sticks of succulent chicken souvlaki and every honey-coated pastry item was here for the taking. The air smelt of meat, pepper and spice with a soupçon of citrus and candy and a sliver of sun, sea and George's home-made fig wine they had all been first introduced to at a new family dinner last Sunday.

'Wanging love *panegyri* night,' Melody nudged Abby, her mouth full of lamb. 'Apart from the dodgy singing.' They were sitting on plastic chairs at a plastic table on the beach, just in front of the large dancing square that had been placed on the sand and shingle.

'There's not karaoke?' Abby asked.

'Almost,' Melody answered. 'This bloke called Adonis – and believe me, he is *not* one – gets up and does a kind of Greek

Pavarotti-style thing. It's pretty terrible.' Melody laughed. 'Last year was the best. He sang one song and said he was only going to do one more because a storm was forecast and before he could launch into it, the sky fell in and everyone had to evacuate for The Blue Vine. We were all getting soaked, the inside was packed and there were hundreds of us sheltering under their flimsy, non-waterproof canopy. And that was the end of Adonis's set.'

'I like the sound of Adonis,' Abby said with a smile. 'I think I'm going to enjoy him.'

'Here,' Melody said. 'Have my greasy napkin. You might want to stick it in your ears once he starts.' She stood up. 'Going to get another drink.'

Abby smiled, sitting back in her seat and soaking up the warmth of the end-of-July sun and the start of her new life in Corfu. She was *staying*. So much had happened in the last two weeks it was almost like Fate had been her guide. Desperately Seeking's sales were going well and while donning rubber gloves to help Melody clear out the hoarder's apartment in Acharavi, Abby had had an idea. Rentals. It wasn't a part of the market that Desperately Seeking or Ionian Dreams was covering and Abby thought it was something that should be exploited. And while she researched and planned and made lists she realised that Corfu was feeling suddenly *normal*, almost like *home*. So, she was staying, for the moment still living with her mum and Melody, but thinking of maybe renting some-where herself as soon as she found the right place. Having her own arm of the business made it feel less like walking into someone else's dream and more like finding her own feet while still maintaining close contact to her mum and sister.

Suddenly the buzzy vibe seemed to fade and Abby looked to the village rather than the sea. Like a biblical parting of the waves, throngs of people seemed to stand to one side and, almost marching through the centre of them, was Spyridoula, dressed in a bright turquoise-green shift dress, matching bracelets hanging from both wrists. Her mouth was set in a close-to euphoric beam, arm in arm with a non-aproned Stamatis. Around them there were whispers and sideways glances. Abby got to her feet, waving her hand. 'Spyridoula! Stamatis! Come and sit with us!'

The couple arrived at the table and Stamatis put a picnic basket in its centre before pulling out a chair for his lady.

'Take the basket off the table, Stamatis,' Spyridoula ordered. 'I know it has had contact with that thick with dust workbench of yours.'

'My workbench is no less thick with dust than your recipe books.'

'Humph! And only today I make you dolmades!'

'You did not make dolmades,' Stamatis answered. 'I know you bought them from the supermarket.'

Spyridoula sniffed as if annoyed. 'I tried to make them. The grape leaves would not stick together. It is not my fault. The fruit is to blame.'

'Would you like some wine?' Abby asked, pushing the large flagon towards them both. 'It's George's home-made fig wine. There's some plastic cups in the bag there.'

'No wine for me until later,' Spyridoula answered, dropping down into the seat next to Abby. 'I am going to get at least one dance with Stamatis while I am not under alcohol.'

'It will be a long, long drought,' the woodman answered, opening a can of Alfa beer.

Lines of coloured lights illuminated the street once the sun had gone down and the singing and dancing began. Balloon sellers found eager children, gypsies tried to sell roses to happy couples and dumplings smothered in chocolate were the most popular treat.

Now Abby was watching George and her mum. They were the very essence of a couple in love. Moving together on the dancing square they performed a very good rendition of one of the island's popular traditional dances, almost step for step. Their relationship was blossoming and so too was Jackie. Abby had witnessed an almost rebirth of her mum over the past fortnight. Gone were the drab, shapeless kaftans and worn-out Havaianas that she had been wearing when Abby first arrived. It was now closet-to-closet middle-market chic. Body-skimming work dresses and tailored trousers and smart tops, all accented with new high shoes. Finally, Jackie was back to being comfortable and confident and Abby couldn't be prouder.

Above the playing of the bouzouki and the hand-clapping, Abby's phone rang and she eagerly plucked it from the table, Theo's face filling the screen. She set it to speaker and answered.

'*Yassou*,' she greeted. 'Theo! I'm at the *panegyri*. Look! I'll let you see it!' She pressed to flip the screen around, determined to give him a view of everything that was going on in the village from the children playing in the sand, to the packed-to-the-brim tavernas and the villagers getting on boats to dance on board.

'Abby,' he called. 'Don't! Turn the screen back around. Let me see you.'

'Hang on,' she laughed. 'Just let me show you my mum and George.' She aimed the camera at the square of dance floor and then her heart stopped beating altogether. The screen hadn't just picked up her mum and George's side-stepping in time together, it had picked up someone else. She couldn't quite believe what she was seeing. And why was she still looking at the screen? She dropped her phone to the table and looked at the scene in front of her. It mirrored what was on her phone. *Theo*.

'Oh my God!' She got to her feet. 'Oh my God!' She hurried then, squeezing past her neighbours, two people in a cow costume and Stathis, sitting on his bicycle, desperate to get to the square.

Theo smiled, watching her awkward run, bowling into plastic chairs, kicking up dust and sand. He had wanted to surprise her but, Abby being Abby, she had wanted him not to miss out on anything that was happening here in the village, just like with their daily phone calls. His heart surged as she rushed towards him and he was ready, as she didn't slow for a second, to catch her in his arms, swinging her around as she gripped hold of him, body sinking into his so solidly. She let go, for a second, to kiss him, over and over, seemingly uncaring for being in the middle of the dance arena, uncaring who was watching, just determined to reunite them completely.

'Oh my God!' she said, tears falling from her eyes. 'You're here! You're actually here! I can't believe it!' She hit him hard on the arm. 'Why didn't you tell me you were coming?' Then she gasped again. 'Theo! You've cut your hair!'

'Ow!' he moaned, rubbing where she had thumped him. 'You have been spending too much time with my aunt!' He put his fingers to his new short crop. 'Do you like it?' he asked. 'When I grew it, I was unhappy. And ... I am not unhappy any more.'

'I love it,' she told him, then swallowed. 'But, Theo, you're here. How? Why?'

'How?' he asked, holding her hands in his. 'By aeroplane. You can get here by boat but it takes a very long time.'

'*Ilithios!*' She thumped him again.

'Why?' he sucked in a breath. 'Because I don't want to live my life without you. I could. But I don't want to.'

'Theo ...'

'I've got a job,' he stated. 'Two, if I need them.'

'What?'

'I have a job taking people out on boats. Tourists who want a guide for the day. And, Hera says I can have my job back at The Blue Vine. She says she has a new Italian but the only cocktail he can make is a Bloody Mary.'

'He is truly terrible,' Abby replied. 'But what about your dad's business, Theo? Here it's a simple life, it doesn't pay so much and—'

'Abby,' he whispered, squeezing her hands. 'I have never been about money. But, I do have a plan.'

'You do?'

'I want my *own* business one day. When I have enough money, *my* money, not my father's. I thought maybe, adventures ... hiking, quad-biking, abseiling, things my mother would approve of.'

'Oh, Theo! That sounds just perfect.' She went to hug him again, but he stopped her.

'Wait, just for a moment.' He reached to the nearby table for the package he had parcelled up only a half hour ago. He handed it to her. 'I didn't arrive a few moments ago,' he admitted. 'I arrived this morning, early, to finish something I started before I left Corfu.'

Abby looked at the parcel then back to him. 'What is it?'

'Open it,' he urged, a smile on his face.

With the Greek music continuing, revellers moving back and forth next to them, the beachside lit with hundreds of tiny lights, Abby unfastened the tape on the plain brown paper parcel.

'Are you like this at Christmas?' Theo said with a grin.

'Like what?' Abby asked, looking to him.

'*Ela!*' he begged. 'Come on!'

She slipped her fingers underneath the paper and gasped as the gift was revealed. It was the most beautiful thing she had ever seen. In her hands was an olive-wood sign, oblong-shaped and sanded with small carvings etched into it – a fish, a boat, olives, the sun, waves – everything that summed up Corfu and the sunshine dream. And in its centre, in a hand-carved yet contemporary font, were the words … *Desperately Seeking*.

'Oh, Theo, it's … I don't know what to say.'

'I paid for the wood with the tips I made at your party then I started it when I think I knew how I was starting to feel about you, and I did a little bit each day before I left. But I did not have time to finish it until now.' He took a breath. 'Do you like it?'

'Oh, Theo, I love it.' She swallowed, her body swimming with warmth and excitement and … love. 'And … I love you,' she whispered. 'I love you, Theo.'

She watched his reaction to her words, his whole body seeming to release, like it was completely unexpected, but so welcome.

'And I love you, Abby,' he said softly. '*Sagapo.*'

Greek Glossary

anglika (an-glee-ka) – English

apotheke (apo-theek-ee) – shed or outhouse

avgolemono (avgo-lem-ono) – lemon chicken soup

baklava (back-lava) – sweet pastry dessert with layers of filo, chopped nuts and honey

bira (beer-a) – beer

bougatsa (boo-gat-sa) – custard pie

bouzouki (b-zoo-ki) – Greek stringed instrument

dhio kafedes (thee-o kath-aid-es) two coffees

dolmades (doll-mar-des) stuffed vine leaves

efxharisto (ef-ha-risto) – thank you

ela! (ell-a) – come! hey!

endaksi (en-dak-see) – OK

exo (air-ho) – out

fandastika (fan-das-ti-ka) – fantastic

Fix (Fix) – brand of Greek beer

froutalia (fru-ta-lee-a) – omelette with sausages and potatoes

galaktoboureko (gal-lak-toh-boar-reko) – custard pie with syrup

gigantes plaki (gee-gant-es plaki) – baked giant beans

ilithios (ee-leef-ee-os) – stupid

ime kala (e-meh ka-la) – I'm fine

kalimera (kali-mare-a) – good morning

kalispera (kalis-pair-a) – good evening/afternoon

kanena provlima (ka-nay-na prov-lim-a) – no problem

ke (keh) – and

ki ego (key e-though) – reply to nice to meet you

kokkinisto (cock-ee-nis-to) – reddened beef stew

kolokithopita (ko-lo-kith-o-pita) – courgette/pumpkin/squash and cheese pie

koritsi (kor-rit-see) – girl

laiko (lay-ko) – type of Greek music

loukanika (loo-ka-nee-ka) – Greek sausage

loukoumades (loo-ko-mar-des) – honey-soaked doughnuts

malaka (ma-laka) – wanker

megalos (me-galos) – big

Metaxa (meh-taxa) – Greek brand of brandy

mia xara fenese (mee-a hara fin-essay) – you look great

milo (mill-o) – apple

mu (moo) – my

Mythos (Mith-os) – brand of Greek beer

ne (neh) – yes

ochi (Och-kee) – no

Olympiacos (olympi-arcos) – Greek football team

omorfi (o-morph-ee) – beautiful

ouzo (oo-zo) – Greek alcoholic drink, tastes of aniseed

panegyri (pane-yri) – gathering or festival

parakalo (pa-ra-kar-lo) – please/you're welcome

pikilia (pee-kee-lee-ah) – a variety of appetizers

pinas? (pee-nas) – are you hungry?

pinau (pee-now) – I'm hungry

podilato (po-thee-lato) – bicycle

poli (pol-ee) – good

poli kalo (pol-ee kar-lo) – very good

psonmi (ps-son-mee) – bread

retsina (ret-seena) – Greek wine

rizogalo (rizo-gar-lo) – rice pudding

sagapo – i love you

signomi (sig-no-mee) – sorry/excuse me

sirtaki (sir-taki) – traditional Greek dance

souvlaki (soo-vla-ki) – meat or vegetables on skewers

spanakopita (spana-ko-pita) – spinach, feta cheese, onions, garlic and herbs wrapped in filo pastry

tapenade (tap-en-ard) – olive paste

taramasalata (ta-ra-ma-sa-la-ta) – pink, creamy, cod-roe dip

thalassa (thal-la-sa) – sea

tipota (tee-pot-a) – nothing

ti protinete? (ti pro-tee-ne-tay) – what do you recommend?

tora (tour-ra) – now

tsipouro (sip-pour-roe) – Greek alcoholic drink – highly intoxicating

tycheros (tee-hair-os) – lucky

vradino (vrath-e-no) – dinner

yammas (yam-mas) – cheers

ya sena (ya-sena) – for you (informal)

yassas (yas-sas) – hello (formal)/goodbye

yassou (yass-oo) – hello (informal)

yiayia (ya-ya) – grandmother

xero poli (hero pol-ee) – nice to meet you

zesti sokolata (zes-tee sock-o-la-ta) – hot chocolate

Letter from Mandy

Thank you so much for reading *Desperately Seeking Summer!* I really hope it put a smile on your face, gave you a little taste of Greece and warmed your heart too!

For me this was a book about many couples ... Abby and Theo obviously, but also Jackie and George, Spyridoula and Stamatis and maybe ... Melody and Leon? What do you think? I would love you to talk about the book and let me (and the world!) know, who was your favourite character? Or, which part made you laugh the most?

I love connecting with my readers so please do tweet or Facebook me, or maybe share some photos of you and *Desperately Seeking Summer* on Instagram wherever you read it – be it home or away!

Twitter: @mandybaggot
Facebook: @mandybaggotauthor
Instagram: @mandybaggot

Reviews also mean the world to authors so, if you enjoyed the story, please leave a review where you usually hang out – Amazon, Kobo, iTunes, Goodreads etc.

And, if you want to find more of my romantic reads, why not pop over to my website. You can even sign up to my monthly newsletter for exclusive prizes!

www.mandybaggot.com

Thank you again for choosing my book this summer and … here's to lots more happy-ever-afters!

Mandy xx

Acknowledgements

Thank you to Kate Nash for your guidance and friendship over the years. You helped shaped my writing career so much and I will always appreciate that!

A huge thank you to my lovely new agent, Tanera Simons. Your enthusiasm, passion and support for my work has already been second to none. Here's to many more crazy books together!

To my absolute best friends in the whole wide world – Rachel Lyndhurst, Susie Heath, Sue Fortin and Linn B Halton. Without you this past year I don't know what I would have done. Your friendship means the world to me. Love you ladies!

To my Bagg Ladies! I have THE best street team and we've had a rollercoaster year of highs and not-so-highs this time. Your constant support, thoughts and help are the best thing an author could wish for. You are all shining stars! I'm looking forward to our summer party! Let's make the next one in Corfu!

To Gillian Green, Katie Seaman, Tess Henderson and Steph Naulls and all the team at Ebury Publishing. Thank you all for your amazing work and your support of my books. Here's to lots more reads together!

To EasyJet, yes you are my airline of choice and I have to thank you for always transporting me – hassle free – to Corfu throughout the year so I can continue the Greek research (and ouzo drinking!).

To all my friends on Corfu who always provide me with endless inspiration. You thought those nights out were all just about the gyros and retsina ... wrong! LOL!

And last, but not least, thank you to my gorgeous family. How lucky are we to have each other and be on this Baggot journey together? So many smiles, so many laughs, maybe a few tears too, but what we have I wouldn't swap for anything. Thank you for all your love and support!